P9-CMT-302

SUSPICION OF RAGE

ALSO BY BARBARA PARKER

Suspicion of Madness
Suspicion of Vengeance
Suspicion of Malice
Suspicion of Betrayal
Suspicion of Deceit
Criminal Justice
Blood Relations
Suspicion of Guilt
Suspicion of Innocence

DUTTON

SUSPICION OF RAGE

BARBARA PARKER

WITHDRAWN
Jefferson-Madison
Regional Library
Charlottesville, Virginia

30234 7023

DUTTON
Published by Penguin Group (USA) Inc.
375 Hudson Street, New York, New York 10014, U.S.A.
Penguin Group (Canada), 10 Alcorn Avenue, Toronto, Ontario, Canada M4V 3B2
(a division of Pearson Penguin Canada Inc.)
Penguin Books Ltd, 80 Strand, London WC2R 0RL, England
Penguin Ireland, 25 St Stephen's Green, Dublin 2, Ireland (a division of Penguin Books Ltd)
Penguin Group (Australia), 250 Camberwell Road, Camberwell, Victoria 3124, Australia
(a division of Pearson Australia Group Pty Ltd)
Penguin Books India Pvt Ltd, 11 Community Centre,
Panchsheel Park, New Delhi – 110 017, India
Penguin Group (NZ), Cnr Airborne and Rosedale Roads, Albany, Auckland, New Zealand
(a division of Pearson New Zealand Ltd)
Penguin Books (South Africa) (Pty) Ltd, 24 Sturdee Avenue,
Rosebank, Johannesburg 2196, South Africa

Penguin Books Ltd, Registered Offices: 80 Strand, London WC2R 0RL, England

Published by Dutton, a member of Penguin Group (USA) Inc.

First printing, February 2005

1   3   5   7   9   10   8   6   4   2

Copyright © 2005 by Barbara Parker
All rights reserved

REGISTERED TRADEMARK—MARCA REGISTRADA

LIBRARY OF CONGRESS CATALOGING-IN-PUBLICATION DATA

Parker, Barbara (Barbara J.)
Suspicion of rage / Barbara Parker.
p.   cm.
ISBN 0-525-94805-8 (hardcover : alk. paper)
1. Connor, Gail (Fictitious character)—Fiction. 2. Quintana, Anthony (Fictitious
character)—Fiction. 3. Americans—Cuba—Fiction. 4. Cuban Americans—Fiction.
5. Married people—Fiction. 6. Women lawyers—Fiction. 7. Miami (Fla.)—Fiction.
8. Cuba—Fiction. I. Title.
PS3566.A67475S877 2005
813'.54—dc22   2004021572

Printed in the United States of America
Designed by Nancy Resnick

PUBLISHER'S NOTE: This book is a work of fiction. Names, characters, places, and incidents either are the product of the author's imagination or are used fictitiously, and any resemblance to actual persons, living or dead, business establishments, events, or locales is entirely coincidental.

Without limiting the rights under copyright reserved above, no part of this publication may be reproduced, stored in or introduced into a retrieval system, or transmitted, in any form, or by any means (electronic, mechanical, photocopying, recording, or otherwise), without the prior written permission of both the copyright owner and the above publisher of this book.

The scanning, uploading, and distribution of this book via the Internet or via any other means without the permission of the publisher is illegal and punishable by law. Please purchase only authorized electronic editions, and do not participate in or encourage electronic piracy of copyrighted materials. Your support of the author's rights is appreciated.

This book is printed on acid-free paper. ∞

For Hector Palacios and Gisela Delgado

SUSPICION OF RAGE

1

A wind from the north brought a damp, bone-biting chill to Havana. The sun was a pale disk behind high, thin clouds. Waves crashed into the seawall and exploded upward, then over, engulfing the cars and flooding the street. When night closed in, the temperature dropped. Fingers of cold air slid through the buildings fronting the sea, sent paper flying, and shook the tree-tops even a mile inland, where Mario Cabrera hurried along Tulipán Street.

At the corner of Estancia he paused and pretended to adjust the strap of his flute case. The handle was gone; he had tied a woven cord to the metal rings. He looked around and saw the people one usually saw on a street like this: workers heading home, some girls going out for the evening, a woman with grocery sacks weighing her hands. A car went by, a decrepit Volvo with one headlight and a smoking exhaust. The apartment building was farther on, an eight-story gray box of poured concrete. Lights shone through glass louvers. From the patio railings, white plastic shopping bags, rinsed and hung up to dry, fluttered like ghosts.

Walking up the hill among others going in the same direction, Mario reached the front steps of the building. In a patch of street light, a group of boys in jackets too big or too small for them squatted on the ground shooting marbles. The fat blond woman from the neighborhood watch sat in a folding chair with her knees pressed together and her arms crossed, holding onto the warmth in her sweater.

Mario stopped when she called out, "Young man! We've had some complaints about the noise! Tell Tomasito. You boys have to stop playing the music by eleven o'clock."

He turned his smile on her. "Sure, I'll tell him. We're sorry to bother anyone. Hey, are you busy later, beautiful? We could go dancing."

She laughed and waved him on. "Be careful, the lights in the stairs are out again."

Mario went up the steps cursing silently. Only his third time coming here, and this woman knew him: a friend of Tomás, who lived on the top floor. Next time she might ask his name, want to see his papers. He wondered if she knew the others too. It would be better, he thought, not to come back.

In the lobby, fluorescent tubes buzzed in the low ceiling. He moved around a group of middle-aged women whose laughter echoed against the tiles, then took the steps two at a time. The elevator was still broken. Luckily the stairs went along the side of the building, and light from the city filtered into the stairwell. He held his flute case steady as he bounded upward. The wind rushed through the aluminum grid on the landings, whirled his hair across his face, and fluttered his jacket. He had left the zipper open; his fast walk from the apartment in Centro had made him sweat.

Crossing the landings he could see into the halls, hear the televisions through open doors, the same news on all channels. Tourism improving. A new resort with major investment from the government of Spain. Mario caught the smell of roast pork, and his stomach reminded him that he had eaten nothing all day but a pizza slice and a soda from a sidewalk lunch counter.

He swung around the turn in the stairs and bumped into a white-beard hanging onto the railing, pulling himself along slowly, painfully, one step at a time.

"Oh, I'm sorry, sir." This earned him only a hard stare from the old man.

On the next landing Mario heard the clatter of high heels. He saw bare brown legs, a tight yellow skirt, then a short coat made to look like fur. The woman came into view, a morena with orange lipstick. Her teeth flashed white when she spoke to the man just behind her. Mario moved aside. The man had light hair, could be German. He stank of old sweat. Why had she brought him *here*?

Couldn't he afford a hotel? Mario murmured to the woman to go out the back; there were eyes on the front steps. She glanced at him and nodded. "Thanks, love."

On the sixth-floor landing three young guys were drinking beer and listening to American hip-hop. A cord ran from their CD player through the door of an apartment down the hall. They held up their fists as Mario went by, and he tapped them with his own. They didn't know him, but he was dressed as they were: ripped jeans, earrings, T-shirts from somewhere else. Mario's had a map of the Paris Métro.

Finally reaching the top floor, he stopped to catch his breath. He faced the city and held his jacket open to cool off. He saw the uneven pattern of dim streetlamps, red taillights, the blue letters of the Habana Libre hotel. Spreading his arms, he curled his fingers through the aluminum grid of the security screen. He could see cars moving along the Malecón, the white dome of the Capitol, ships docked in the harbor. Across the harbor, the statue of Christ. The lights of El Morro, the stone fortress on the point. Past that, only darkness. No stars, no boats. Nothing.

He entered the corridor and knocked at the third door. Tomás's voice asked who it was.

"State Security."

The lock was pulled back and the door swung open. Tomás was a small man with neatly combed brown hair and wire-framed glasses. If he ever laughed, Mario had never heard it. He lifted the strap of his flute case over his head. "Where is everyone?"

"Nico and Chachi are in the back. Raúl's on his way."

They maneuvered around a black vinyl lounge chair with lace on its arms. That and the matching sofa took up most of the space in the small living area. A plastic Christmas tree sat on top of the television, its blue lights blinking on and off, reflected in a mirror over some shelves that sagged with the weight of Tomás's books. Tomás was fond of pulling quotations out of his memory: *The blood of martyrs is the fuel of freedom.*

The apartment belonged to Tomás's girlfriend, Lisette, who lived here with her twin daughters. The girls' father had gone to Miami five years ago on the visa lottery, and Lisette hadn't heard from him since then. On nights of the meetings, she would take the kids over to her mother's house and come back around midnight.

Mario tossed his jacket to the sofa. "Do you have anything to eat? I'm starving."

"Fish and potatoes. It's good. I'll fix you some. Go see what the guys are doing."

At twenty-nine, Tomás was the oldest among them. Mario had brought him into the movement two years ago. They had met at a dance club in Varadero, where Tomás had played trumpet.

In Lisette's room, Chachi and Nicolás sat cross-legged on the bed with an old towel spread between them to protect the sheets. They had brought tools, metal pipe, a box of powder, a roll of wire. They nodded at Mario when he came in. Chachi and Nico were students at the university, classmates of Mario's before he'd been kicked out. The Movement had been Nico's idea in their first year at the University of Havana. He had brought in Chachi, then Mario, then more people they trusted. Some stayed, others left. Now there were five at the top level and a dozen others who could be counted on.

They had named themselves the Twenty-eighth of January Movement, for the birth date of José Martí, and at first they had been boys with paintbrushes or chalk, attacking the system with words. The police had arrived quickly to paint over the slogans. *Liberty for the people* or *Socialism = death*, followed by the signature, *M28E*. It had all been juvenile and useless. Then Raúl had taught them how to make bombs. Nico had casually slipped one under a parked police car. The gasoline tank exploded, and the car had burned beautifully with a lot of black smoke. Three other bombs had been set off in trash bins in the last month. The Party newspaper, *Granma,* called the perpetrators terrorists, traitors, delinquents, the criminal element. The targets had been inconsequential, more noise than effect. The Movement was about to change its tactics.

Mario propped a pillow against the headboard. He watched Chachi's pale, slender hands roll paper into a funnel and fill the pipe with powder. Tomás came in with food and a beer, and Mario ate with the plate balanced on his knees. The air conditioner fan was on for the noise. No one was likely to hear them, but they were careful.

A little while later Raúl arrived, a muscular man, very dark, age twenty-six. Raúl had a bad knee, thanks to the police. They'd shoved him down some stairs during an arrest for selling lobster on the black market. He held up a shopping bag from the Carlos III mall and said he'd brought them a little present. He lifted out some clothing—a cheap pair of men's pants and a knit shirt. He laid the clothes on the bed and unfolded them, revealing a small black pistol.

"Beautiful!" Nico pounded him on the back. "You did it, man."

"Trust Uncle Raúl, my boy." Raúl extended his arm and aimed at himself in the dresser mirror. "What a beautiful little bitch she is. You barely have to touch her, and she goes off."

Mario asked, "What kind of gun is that?"

"It's a pistol. Makarov. The magazine holds eight rounds. Small, light, easily concealed, reliable as your grandmother's cooking. I used one just like this in the army." Raúl held the pistol on the flat of his palm, showing it off. "Sexy, don't you think? You want to kiss it?"

Chachi said, "This won't work. To get rid of one man . . . it won't do any good. We can't get away with it. We'll die for nothing."

"You are wrong," Tomás said. "This act represents the beginning of freedom for Cuba. Such a small thing, but believe what I tell you: It will start another revolution—or better to say, to finish the revolution they have abandoned. They get fat while we starve. They grind their boots into our backs and keep us in chains. They're worse than the Americans they pretend to hate, much worse. They have betrayed the revolution, betrayed the people—"

Nico said, "Shut up, will you? If I want to hear a speech, I can turn on the television. What do we do next?"

"You and the others will set the trap." Raúl aimed the pistol at the lamp on the nightstand. "I'm going to take care of Vega."

Nico laughed. "You? With that leg of yours?"

"I'm the only one with military experience. You boys are amateurs."

"Let me do it," Chachi said. "I could dress like a woman and get right up to his window. They'd never suspect."

Raúl whooped. "Ha! Show him your ass, sweetheart. Vega will pull you into his car. Oooooh, what is this little *thing* you have here?" Raúl held Chachi down and pretended to lift the hem of a skirt.

"Stop it," Tomás ordered. "This is serious. First we decide how to get to Vega, and then we'll talk about which of us is best suited to carry out the operation."

Nico said, "I am. I was on the track team in high school. I can kill him and get away before he hits the ground."

The target was General Ramiro Vega. He was moving up fast, a hard-liner. His sort would take power when the older ones died off. If the Movement could eliminate a man like Vega, the moderates would lose their fear. Still better, the entire structure could collapse.

Raúl set the pistol on the nightstand, and they talked about the best way to do it. As usual, Tomás led the discussion. Mario didn't think of him as a friend, but he would follow him. Tomás was right: The nonviolence of the dissidents had accomplished nothing. The state allowed the dissidents to exist because it served their interests: See how lenient we are, how we are changing. But there would be no change without blood. It would not happen in Cuba. It had never happened in Cuba.

Mario imagined Vega's face, which he had seen on television. His bald, shiny brown head, his clean white shark's teeth behind smiling lips. His green uniform fit smoothly across his chest. His campaign ribbons were over his heart. Mario reached over and picked up the gun.

"Put that down, it's loaded," Raúl said.

They talked some more, trying to decide where precisely to do it. Not at his office, too much security. On the street near his house in Miramar. They would have to stop the car somehow, perhaps stage an accident. Otherwise, they couldn't get close enough to fire directly through the window. How would they determine when Vega left his house? Was his routine the same every morning? Vega had no bodyguards, only a driver who took him back and forth to the Ministry. Nico suggested the intersection at Fifth Avenue, where the driver would turn. After that, the car would pick up speed. Tomás said no, they should wait for Vega as his car came out of his driveway.

"It's hopeless," Chachi said. "We don't have automatic weapons, we have *one damned pistol.*"

Raúl acknowledged this with a shrug. "It's a challenge."

Still leaning against the pillow with one knee raised, Mario spoke. "What we have to do," he said, "is to get close enough to put the barrel against his head."

"Oh! Yes, yes, of course, perfect." Raúl laughed.

"There's a way."

Raúl motioned for him to go on. "Well?"

"I know his wife. Her name is Marta Quintana. I can use her to get inside the house; then I'll kill him."

"Inside the house? Well, you're pretty enough. Are you going to seduce her?"

"Listen—"

Chachi said, "Mario, have you ever fired a gun?"

Nico pushed Chachi's shoulder. "Do we keep blowing up trash cans?"

"Be quiet, all of you, and listen." Mario rolled off the bed and stood up. "My mother works at a veterans' home in Vedado. There's an old man who lives there, Luis Quintana. I've met him. He's Vega's father-in-law—and he's blind. Several times a week Vega's wife comes to take her father to her house for dinner. She's a busy woman, and it must be a bother. I could help her. I could offer to drive Señor Quintana, and naturally I'd take him inside. I would do it once or twice to establish some trust, and then I bring the gun and kill Vega. All I need is a car."

A gust of wind rattled the air conditioner fan, and a draft of cold air slid through the glass louvers.

"We can find you a car," Tomás said.

Raúl nodded. "The idea has some juice."

"It wouldn't matter," Chachi said. "They would know who he was. They would find all of us."

"He'd be trapped," Nico said.

"Not if he was fast enough."

"But they would know who he was."

"And?"

"They would track him down. They would make him talk."

"Not if we got him out of Cuba."

"Could it be done?"

"Yes," said Tomás. "Yes. It could be done."

Nico said, "Mario, what do you think?"

Mario touched the dark, gleaming barrel of the pistol, moving his fingers over the hammer and down the black plastic grip. "No. I won't leave. I will kill him, and then I will stay here and continue the fight."

"Exactly!" Tomás cast a fierce glance at the others. "We will not fail. Even if we pay with our blood, we will not fail." He made a fist. "When the people awaken, the *nomenclatura* will run for their lives. A new revolution, my friends."

"We go underground," Raúl said. "There are people who would hide us. What about you, Nico, Chachi? No more parties."

They nodded. Nico said, "We're with you."

Mario picked up the pistol. Makarov. Tiny letters were stamped into the metal. His hand fit nicely around the grip, and his thumb lay along a ridge on the left side. He moved a lever and saw a red painted dot.

"That's the safety, you idiot. Give me that." Raúl took it away.

"When do we do it?" Mario said.

"Be patient," Tomás said. "We need to plan for every contingency. Raúl, how long do we need?"

"We could be ready within a month." Raúl rolled the pistol into the clothing. "Mario, take a ride with me out to the country tomorrow. I'll let you shoot at my brother's chickens."

"First Vega, next Fidel." Chachi swooped imaginary letters across the bedroom wall. "I want to see that on the monument to Martí."

Mario's mind went to the view from the top of the stairs. The lights of the city below him, the movement and color, the empty black ocean beyond. He could be dead in ten days, probably would be dead. How strange, then, to feel so content.

2

A widening rectangle of light fell onto the terra-cotta tiles as Gail Connor opened the door and came outside. She looked along the portico with its turned Moorish columns and drapery of red bougainvillea. No one was there, only a row of empty cane-backed rocking chairs and champagne flutes left behind on a table. Crossing her bare arms against the cold, Gail walked down the steps to the front lawn. Landscaping lights shone on royal palm trees, beds of winter flowers, and the coral rock fountain splashing into its wide bowl. The brick driveway was jammed with cars. It was two days after New Year's, and strands of twinkling lights wove through the ironwork that topped the wall. The only person in sight was the parking attendant, tipped back on the legs of his chair.

Coming back, Gail glanced through the windows into a swirl of color. Two of her friends had cornered a good-looking guy by the piano. Somebody was bravely attempting to play "Livin' La Vida Loca," and a middle-aged woman pulled her husband out of a chair to dance. A waiter slid around them with a tray over his head.

Gail murmured, "Anthony, where are you?"

She had thought that he and his friends might have come out to smoke a cigar and get away from the women, the older ones mostly, like Aunt Fermina, who wanted to know if they planned to have a baby, now that they were married. Or Aunt Zoraida, deaf in one ear, who had offered to do a Tarot-card reading for them. Anthony's grandmother, Digna Pedrosa, had clung to his arm all evening. This party had been her idea, making up for the fact that her grandson and his new wife had invited literally no one to their wedding last month; no friends, no family, not even Gail's twelve-year-old daughter, who had said it was about time they got it over with.

Señora Quintana.

The name sounded strange, probably because of the way it had happened, a sort of spur-of-the-moment idea, going to the Florida Keys for the weekend, coming back as a couple. Of course Gail had *wanted* her daughter to be there, but then Anthony's children would have had to come too, and so would Gail's mother. If Irene were there, Anthony's grandparents couldn't be left out, or his sister Alicia and her kids, or his brother, or the rest of the tribe, which seemed to Gail at times to consist of half the Cubans living in Miami.

She glanced at her watch. It was almost ten o'clock, and they hadn't finished packing. *She* hadn't finished. Anthony had done this so many times that he could pack in five minutes with his eyes closed. His suitcase waited by the door of their apartment. Hers and Karen's were still lying open on the living room rug surrounded by stacks of clothes. Not only clothes. Shampoo and soap, towels, hand lotion, sunscreen, a money belt, a first-aid kit, even a compass, every last thing that she'd heard you had to take to Cuba or do without. Anthony had stood over the pile shaking his head.

They would be staying at his sister Marta's house in Havana. She was married to Ramiro Vega, a general in the army, and Anthony had said they lived very well by Cuban standards, whatever that meant. Next weekend the younger Vega daughter, Janelle, was having her *quinceañera,* her fifteenth birthday party. Gail had bought her a dress at a boutique in Coconut Grove, wanting to please Marta as much as the girl. Buying something for Janelle had been the last thing on Gail's list to be checked off.

On only ten days' notice she had somehow managed to clear her schedule at her law office. Her secretary would forward messages via e-mail to Marta's house. An attorney friend in the same building would handle emergencies. As for Karen's father, Gail had expected a fight, but he hadn't objected. She guessed that he was happy to spend the extra time on his boat with his new girlfriend. But he had asked why. Why in God's name do you want to go to Cuba?

Because Anthony's sister invited us. Because it would be educational for Karen. Because I don't like the U.S. government telling me what I can and can't do.

None of these was the real reason. Gail wanted to see Cuba through Anthony's eyes. She wanted to know what he did there. Would he be different somehow in the place of his birth? And who were the people he called *los Quintana*, his other family, those who had not gone into exile? In addition to Anthony's sister, there was his father, who lived in a home for disabled veterans. Luis Quintana had been awarded a medal for heroism by Fidel Castro himself. Marta spoke four languages. She had a job in protocol at the Ministry of the Exterior. But their names were never mentioned here in this house. To Ernesto Pedrosa, who thought Castro a step below Satan, *los Quintana* didn't exist.

But they did exist, and they wanted to meet the new wife. At first, when Anthony had mentioned this to Gail, she couldn't imagine actually going there. Cuba wasn't a real place, it was myth; it was farther than China. Anthony would bring his two children. They were teenagers and had never met their Havana cousins. And of course Karen couldn't be left out. When Gail had told her mother, Irene had jumped up and down like a girl. *Oh, how exciting for you!* And then the long, guilt-inducing sigh. What was she going to do here in Miami all alone for New Year's? Couldn't she be of some help to Gail, keeping an eye on Karen?

So there would be six of them breaking the law. Six on the flight from Miami to Cancún, then Cancún to Havana. No begging the State Department for permission to take one of those miserable charter flights. Anthony had bought their tickets online through a travel agent in Canada. Gail found the subterfuge thrilling. It was theoretically possible they could be prosecuted. Gail wasn't worried. Anthony knew how to get in and out. They weren't going to set off alarms by smuggling boxes of cigars and a few too many bottles of Havana Club. They would say, if questioned, that they'd been lying on a beach in Mexico for ten days.

Gail turned to open the door just as a group of people came through it on a wave of bubbling conversation. A clerk from Anthony's law firm, a client, their wives. There were kisses on the cheek, more congratulations. Sorry we have to leave so soon, a great party, *buenas noches.*

One of the men leaned closer and whispered, "When you get to Havana? Here's some advice. Watch out for those potholes in the sidewalks. And take along some toilet paper, you'll need it." He winked. "Tell Tony we want a postcard."

She waved as they crossed the yard. "Thank you for coming."

Inside, she closed the heavy wooden door and leaned against it. No one was supposed to know about this trip. Anthony had said not to tell anyone until they got back. U.S. travel restrictions didn't bother him, but his grandfather did. If Ernesto found out, he'd have a seizure. If sufficiently pissed off, he might phone one of his friends in Washington and demand to have them stopped at the airport.

The foyer was softly illuminated by a chandelier. A young couple sat on the stairs embracing, oblivious to people walking through. Still no sight of Anthony. Gail could see into the formal dining room. The invitations had said NO GIFTS, but the long mahogany table was stacked high with expensively wrapped boxes. She expected to take home a lot of crystal and porcelain, very upscale Cuban, not exactly her style.

She spotted some curly auburn hair among the crowd in the living room and went closer to make sure it was her mother. "Mom!"

Irene Connor detached herself from the man she'd been talking to. Her eyes were bright, and she held a *mojito* with mint leaves swirling among the ice cubes. "Well, there you are, darling." She was a petite woman, shorter by several inches than Gail, and sequins twinkled on her peacock-blue cocktail dress when she swung her hips. "*Vamos a bailar.* That means 'Let's dance.' See that man over there? He's been teaching me things to say at the clubs in Havana."

"Oh, Mother, please, you haven't been talking about it."

"He's cute, isn't he? And he's not married. *No es casado.*"

Gail pulled her mother into the hall. "Have you seen Anthony? I've lost him, and we've really got to start making an exit."

"Already?"

"You know how Cuban parties are. It's going to take an hour just to say good night to everyone. I haven't finished packing, and we have to be at the airport at eight in the morning."

"Fine. We'll go." Her eyes went back to her friend. "Oh, you asked me about Anthony. He was here a minute ago wanting to know where *you* were." She pointed across the foyer. "He went down that hall, he and that little black man who works for Mr. Pedrosa—well, not really black. They say *mulato*, don't they? I've forgotten his name."

"Hector Mesa."

Irene went on, "*Mulato. Negrito.* My friend over there said they use those words all the time in Cuba, and nobody cares."

Gail gazed along the empty corridor on the opposite side. It led to Ernesto Pedrosa's study. Anthony had been summoned there. For what? Not so the old man could slip him some traveling money. He would be demanding explanations and making threats. Anthony would stand there calmly, letting out a breath through his teeth. He would offer no apologies. He would slam the door on the way out and swear on his mother's grave not to enter this house again. That would last for as long as it lasted, or until everyone else was worn out and begged them to reconcile.

"Mom, could you find Karen for me? I think she's playing pool in the game room. I'll be right back."

The corridor ran past a vacant sitting room, then turned. Wall sconces lit her way, and her high heels tapped softly on the tiles. She shifted her weight to her toes. As she neared the door, she could see it was closed, no surprise. She tilted her head to listen. No one was yelling, which was odd. Male voices came from inside, but they were too muffled for her to make out the speakers, not that she doubted who was in there.

She lifted her hand to knock.

"Señora?"

Startled, she turned to find a small, gray-haired man in a somber suit and black-framed glasses. He might have dropped silently down from the ceiling on a web, for all the notice he gave.

"Hello, Hector. I'm looking for Anthony."

"He is with *el viejo*."

"Yes, I thought he might be. It's late and we need to go."

Hector Mesa shrugged. "They have a meeting, and some friends of Señor Ernesto will be here in a minute. I'll tell Señor Anthony that you looked for him." Hector extended a hand toward the way she had come, an invitation to leave.

"A meeting at this hour? With whom?"

Another shrug. "I think some people from out of town."

There was a separate entrance around a turn in the hall, and if guests came and went, they could do so unnoticed. Gail said, "And you don't know who they could be, or where they're from. How long is this meeting supposed to last? Should Karen and I catch a ride home with my mother?"

"If you wish, but I think it will be not so long." The creases in his forehead deepened as if it pained him to lie to her. Gail had learned things about Hector Mesa: He had worked in black ops for the CIA. He carried a folding knife in his belt and a .22 Beretta on his ankle; he had used them both. She doubted there was much that pained him. If Hector Mesa was posted outside the door, it meant something was going on. Or not. She could never quite be sure.

"All right. When you see Anthony, could you please tell him we need to go home?"

"Of course, señora." The little man made a slight bow, and the sconces in the corridor flashed their dim light on his glasses.

A faded Cuban flag, with its blue-and-white bars and red triangle, had been hung like an Old Master behind the desk. The brass picture light picked up spatters of mud and several bullet holes in the fabric. In June 1960, a Cuban army squadron had kicked in the door of an apartment near the Capitol in Havana, finding several *anti-castristas* and a supply of bomb-making equipment. Leonardo Pedrosa had grabbed the flag and dived out a window screaming *"¡Abajo, Fidel!"* He staggered through thunderstorms for two miles with a bullet in his back to a safe house in Vedado. He died just as dawn broke, but not before obtaining his brother's promise to fly the flag one day over a free Cuba.

This according to Ernesto Pedrosa.

Anthony sat across the desk from his grandfather, waiting for him to finish lighting his cigar. An excellent cigar, but not Cuban. Ernesto would not support the dictatorship by smoking Cuban tobacco. He laboriously clipped off the end of his *puro* with large, veined hands weakened by a stroke three years ago. He was eighty-five years old and refused to admit it. His folded wheelchair was pushed out of sight. It formed a slight bulge behind brocade curtains framing the windows on the east side of his study. The windows themselves were covered by wooden louvers, exactly as in Havana. Except that here, the louvers were not falling out of their frames.

A ceiling fan revolved slowly overhead. The air smelled of leather and smoke. A signed first edition of the poems of José Martí was enshrined in a glass case. A landscape of thatched-roof *bohíos* and royal palm trees filled the space behind the sofa. There were black-and-white photographs of deceased relatives, of Havana street scenes from the early 1900s, of anti-Castro commando groups, of Ernesto Pedrosa with every Republican president since 1964. He had removed the Democrats, including John F. Kennedy, who had betrayed them at the Bay of Pigs, and Bill Clinton, under whose administration the raft boy, Elián González, had been sent back to Fidel.

Ernesto held his silver desk lighter to the end of the cigar and studied Anthony over the flame, his time-faded blue eyes magnified by thick lenses.

He had found out. It would have been impossible to keep him in the dark; Anthony could see that now. Everyone knew. His relatives had pulled him aside to beg for this or that small favor. Would you give this cash to cousin Rosario? Would you see if my house on Avenida 98 is still there, and if it doesn't look too bad, could you take a picture? Could you bring me some *Agua de Violetas*? A rock from the Colón Cemetery? Some of that asthma spray I can't find in the pharmacies here?

The old man knew, but he didn't seem to care. Anthony was puzzled by this. Shoving the lighter aside, Ernesto sank back into his wide leather chair and began to rock slowly. "I'll tell you what bothers me," he said. "You lied. You hid it from me."

His Spanish was slow and perfectly pronounced. He had been a banker in a family at the top of society, and he maintained the image: custom-made suits, a neatly trimmed white mustache, a splash of cologne.

"I did not lie to you," Anthony said.

"You used your silence as a lie."

"Why would I want to give you another heart attack? Every time we talk about Cuba, you go crazy."

"I saved you from hell, yet you go back. You have hurt me deeply."

"Do we have to discuss this? I've been there several times, as you are well aware."

"Not 'several' times. Many times. Many. And tomorrow you will go once again and take your wife with you. I think it's wrong, but she is your wife, and a woman of strong will, and if that's what you and she want to do, there is nothing I can say about it. Your children will also travel with you. That is definitely wrong, but I leave Daniel and Angela to see the wreck that Cuba has become and decide for themselves."

"Grandfather, it's late. Gail and I have to get up very early."

The old man tapped the cigar over a crystal ashtray. Gold cuff links twinkled against spotless white cuffs. "You tell me, 'I want them to meet my father,' or 'I want to attend my niece's birthday party.' As for myself, I believe this. Others might not."

"Forgive me, but what are you getting at?"

"You have ties with Cuba. There are some who say you're an agent of Castro."

Anthony had learned not to laugh out loud at this sort of thing.

Ernesto continued, "I tell them no. My grandson has wrong ideas, but he is not working for the tyrant. Now. I have a question, and I want the truth."

"All right. Ask. What do you want to know?"

"Has Marta talked to you about leaving Cuba?"

"What do you mean, leaving?"

"Does she want to leave Cuba?" His grandfather's voice rose. "To get her family out. Are you going there to arrange it?"

Anthony wondered if the old man's mind was stumbling again. "No, Grandfather. I'm going for a visit. That's all."

"This is the truth?"

"Of course it is. Marta wouldn't leave Cuba. What gave you that idea? You haven't spoken to her in more than twenty years, and now you ask if she wants to come to Miami."

"She's my granddaughter."

"The last time I mentioned my sister, you called her a piece of communist trash."

His grandfather's expression darkened. "She is a communist, but she is also my blood. They brainwash people in the dictatorship, you can't deny it. Her children are my blood, and they belong here."

"I assure you, if Marta wanted to get out, I would know. We don't talk about politics, otherwise we would strangle each other, but she's happy—happy enough. Her children are there, her husband. She doesn't want to leave." Anthony spread his hands. "She doesn't. Grandfather, I'm sorry, but it's ten o'clock, and Gail will be looking for me."

"Let her wait." He batted away some smoke. "We have guests coming. A friend of mine, Bill Navarro. He wants to talk to you."

This change of topic stopped Anthony halfway out of his chair.

Guillermo "Bill" Navarro had been elected to the U.S. House of Representatives five years ago, thanks to money pumped into his campaign from big donors in the exile community. Navarro had been sent to Washington because he had the right attitude: Starve Cuba into economic collapse. He and his compatriots in Congress had forced successive administrations to go along with them or risk the loss of the Cuban-American vote, pivotal to winning Florida.

"Why does he want to talk to me?"

"He will explain it."

"You may be a friend of this man, but I am not. He's a pompous fake who has done nothing but make us look like a bunch of raving lunatics to the rest of the world." A thought ran through Anthony's mind. "What is this about? My sister?"

"Yes, and her husband. We have information that Ramiro Vega wants to defect."

This was stunning. That Ramiro would defect to the United States was beyond the bounds of imagination. Anthony asked, "Where did Bill Navarro get this information?"

"Bill can tell you."

"Ramiro has never said anything of the sort to me, not the least hint of it."

"How can he? Everyone is watched. He is afraid." Ernesto jabbed the air with his cigar. "Listen to me. I want you to talk to Marta. Tell her . . . say she is forgiven. This is her family. We will help her, whatever she needs for herself or the children. It has always been that way. But you must persuade her to leave. If she doesn't come, Vega might stay there, and that would be bad. She must escape. They must all escape."

His lips trembled. Ernesto Pedrosa hid his eyes and cleared his throat. "Our family. You understand."

Anthony softly replied, "Yes. Of course, if I can help her . . . if she asks for help, I will do it. Grandfather, what did Navarro say to you? When did he—"

He was stopped by a knock at the door.

"One moment!" Ernesto laid his cigar in the ashtray. "Bill is bringing someone with him, an aide on his staff, I believe. They will tell you they want Ramiro Vega. The man is a filthy communist son of a black whore, but if he is the price of getting the children out, so be it." Ernesto positioned his cane and stood up. "Come in!"

The door swung open. Hector Mesa stood aside to admit two men. Navarro entered first, a man in his late thirties with incipient jowls, a broad smile, and eyes that darted about in search of the person who might want to put a knife in his ribs. He had not been born in Cuba; he compensated with a severe, almost religious patriotism. There were two pins in the lapel of his navy blue sport coat: the flag of the United States and the insignia of a Cuban-American lobbying group that had bullied Congress for decades.

Anthony didn't recognize the other man. He was in his mid-forties, with a medium build, short graying hair, and an angular face one could easily miss in a crowd. His eyes went quickly around the room before he acknowledged Anthony's presence with a slight nod.

The congressman went over to the desk to embrace Ernesto, to thank him for seeing them on such short notice. He swung around and extended a hand to Anthony, who had risen from his chair. "*Mi amigo, ¿qué tal?* Good to see you again." He switched to English for the benefit of the American in the room. "Congratulations on your marriage. I apologize for interrupting the party, but we have a matter of highest importance to discuss with you. This is Everett Bookhouser. Everett is a policy advisor on my committee."

Leaving Anthony to fill in the blank: the House Intelligence Committee.

He shook the other man's hand as Navarro was saying, "We just flew down from Washington, and you're leaving in the morning, so there was really no other time—"

Anthony broke in. "My grandfather told me you believe that my brother-in-law wants to defect. May I ask where you heard this?"

Bill Navarro's smile vanished; he didn't like being thrown off his rhythm.

"*Siéntense*. Sit down, please, everyone." Ernesto lifted a decanter. "Bill, Mr. Bookhouser, may I offer you some brandy?"

Bookhouser declined. Navarro accepted and settled into a chair. "So. You're going to Cuba tomorrow."

Anthony glanced at his grandfather, who murmured with a shrug, "*Se lo dije.*" It was he who had told Navarro.

"You and I hold different views," Navarro said, "but let's put them aside for now. What we want, what I hope you will give us, is assurance. I believe that you're a man who, given the opportunity, would want to help his country."

"I assume you mean the United States."

"Of course." Navarro hid his annoyance by taking the glass of brandy passed across the desk. "Last month, early December, there was a meeting in Brazil, a conference on energy policy, which Major Omar Céspedes Ruiz attended. Céspedes was on the staff of General Abdel García. Do you know the name?"

"I don't think so."

"He's your brother-in-law's commanding officer."

"Ah. Is he?"

Navarro paused as if deciding whether this ignorance was genuine, then went on.

"Céspedes was assigned to the Ministry of Basic Industries, which García oversees. Céspedes basically knocked on the door of the American embassy in São Paulo and asked to be let in. We sent someone down to talk to him. In one of his interviews Céspedes said he'd received information that Vega wanted to defect to the United States. We had no way of confirming this, so I contacted your esteemed grandfather and said to him, 'Mr. Pedrosa, have you heard anything from your granddaughter or her husband?' He told me that he hadn't. But early this morning he called me to say he had just learned of your trip. He said you planned to fly to Cuba, and perhaps it had something to do with Vega."

"And so here we are," Anthony said. "Where did Céspedes get his information?"

"From someone we believe is reliable."

"Does this person have a name?"

"I said, a reliable source." Navarro sipped his brandy. "We need confirmation before taking further action."

Anthony looked past Navarro to the man on the end of the sofa, who so far had said nothing. "Mr. Bookhouser, who do you work for? The CIA?"

The man's deeply set blue eyes did not flicker. He said, "I'm an advisor to Congress, Mr. Quintana. We'd like to get your brother-in-law out of Cuba."

"Why?"

"Why? Ramiro is a brigadier general. What he knows could be helpful to us."

"No doubt, but I don't involve myself in politics, American or Cuban. If Ramiro wants out, he knows how to do it. He could do what Céspedes did—fly out of the country and not come back. Ramiro could get his entire family out if he wanted to."

"Have you heard from him?"

"No."

"Would you consider yourself a friend of his?"

"He's married to my sister. That's about the extent of it."

Everett Bookhouser looked at Anthony for a while as if deciding what to say next. Bill Navarro, too excited to sit, got up and paced.

"*Óyeme,* Quintana. Listen. We want to get Ramiro Vega to freedom. A general in *las Fuerzas Armadas Revolucionarias.* Don't you see what it would do? The blow it would strike at the regime?"

"They've managed to survive many such blows."

The congressman laughed. "Castro is on his last legs. He needs one more push."

"Good luck. How do you know Céspedes wasn't sent to spread disinformation?"

"We believe him. You're in a position to find out if it's true. We're asking for your help."

"You have spies all over Cuba. Ask one of them to talk to Ramiro."

By now Navarro was standing red-faced over Anthony's chair. "I don't want to say this in your grandfather's house, but I am appalled by your attitude." His nostrils flared. "What are you loyal to? To anything? You who have reaped the benefits of a democratic society? Don't you give a damn about this country? Or the freedom of Cuba?"

Anthony smiled up at Navarro. *"Qué gran mojón tú eres."*

Navarro leaned closer. "You could be arrested and prosecuted for violating the embargo. You and your wife."

The blood rushed into Anthony's cheeks; he could feel the heat of it.

Everett Bookhouser said, "Bill. Let me."

Navarro fell silent. Hands on his hips, his mouth in a tight line, he swerved away. Anthony could see who was in charge here, and it wasn't the congressman.

"Nobody's going to prosecute anyone." Bookhouser's words were unhurried. He leaned forward, hands clasped loosely, elbows on his knees. "This is what we've got. When this regime goes belly up, people are going to start scrambling for power. They're already getting in line. Ramiro is rising fast in the regime. For some people, he's a threat. He's also vulnerable because he's taking bribes from the foreign companies he deals with. That's not so unusual, a lot of high officials do it, but Ramiro is being watched, and they'll use it to get him. My bet is, it's going to be sooner rather than later. They'll make an example. Prison for life, possibly execution for treason. If they think Ramiro might bring them down with him, they won't bother with an arrest. Do you understand?"

"Yes." A chill passed along Anthony's spine. "Omar Céspedes told you this?"

"Most of it. According to him, your brother-in-law wants out. We can help him." Bookhouser reached into his breast pocket and withdrew a small notebook and pen. "You don't have to try and persuade him. Just tell him we talked to Céspedes. Tell him what I told you. See if he's interested." Bookhouser's pen moved rapidly across the paper. "If so, I want you to call this number."

He tore the sheet off and held it in Anthony's direction. "It's a cell phone in Havana. It won't be traced."

Anthony remained in his chair. "My wife will be with me. My children."

"We don't believe anyone's going to move against him right now. There's time," Bookhouser said. "It's completely up to you."

Anthony held out his hand, and Bookhouser leaned over to give him the piece of paper.

Anthony asked, "Who's going to answer the phone?"

"Probably me."

"Ramiro won't trust you."

"He trusts you."

"I don't know if he does or not." Anthony stood and found that the chill had worked into his gut. "I can't promise you anything. It depends on the situation."

"Fair enough."

He slid the piece of paper into his trousers pocket. "Forgive me, but it's late, and my wife is probably wondering where I am." Ignoring the congressman, he turned toward the desk, where Ernesto Pedrosa leaned on crossed arms.

The old man was tired; his skin sagged into shadows and lines. "Tell your sister for me that she's welcome in this house."

Anthony said, *"Buenas noches, abuelo."*

"Ten cuidado, m'ijo."

He walked into the hall with his grandfather's words in his ear: Be careful, my son.

ail said it would take only an hour or so to finish packing, and no, she didn't need any help, but thank you anyway. Anthony headed for the shower, and Gail went to her daughter's room to say good night.

Karen, in an oversized Miami Hurricanes T-shirt, sat at her computer. The desk lamp outlined her profile and made a nimbus of light around her long hair.

"Hey, sweetie pie. Shouldn't you be in bed?" She came in and shut the door.

"In a minute, okay?" Karen clicked the mouse as the cursor moved down the screen. "I'm downloading some games."

Gail saw the cable running from the computer to Karen's PDA. "Oh, Karen. You're not taking that with you."

"In case I get bored."

"Bored?" Gail sat on the end of the bed. "Be serious. We're going to Havana tomorrow. *Havana.* Don't tell me you plan to stay indoors playing Tetris."

The monitor light flickered on Karen's face. "Who am I supposed to hang out with? They're all older than me. Plus, does anybody speak English?"

"Well, if they don't, you can practice your Spanish."

Large blue eyes rolled upward for an instant, then fixed once more on the screen.

"Come on, Karen, turn it off. You're going to be exhausted tomorrow."

"Wait, wait, just let me get this one. That's all, I swear."

"You've got sixty seconds." Gail picked up two large pillows in their bright shams and stacked them on a chair, leaving the old, thin pillow that Karen had slept with since she was four. The Little Mermaid pillowcase was threadbare and faded, but Karen refused to give it up. Gail let her do her room the way she wanted, though it hardly matched the upscale decor of this top-floor, fully furnished, four-grand-a-month Coconut Grove apartment. Anthony was paying for it; he liked the view.

To turn down the comforter, Gail had to move Karen's backpack out of the way. The strap slipped from her fingers. "What've you got in here, bricks?"

Karen glanced over. "Nothing. Just stuff I'm taking with me."

"Mind if I see?"

"It's just magazines and stuff."

Gail unzipped the backpack and looked inside, finding Karen's iPod, headphones, and several DVDs in their plastic cases. And wrapped in an old T-shirt, a portable DVD player, which had been her father's overly extravagant Christmas present. "No way. You're not taking this." Over Karen's protests, Gail said, "It's too expensive, and I don't want it confiscated."

"Is that like stolen?"

"No, it's like when the customs agents take it away when you come into the country. Or they make you pay a huge tax on it. We're leaving it here. Sorry."

Sighing, Karen crossed her arms on the back of the chair and let her chin sink onto them.

Rummaging further into the backpack, Gail took out two dozen granola bars, boxes of fruit juice, some trail mix, a jar of peanut butter. "Karen . . . why are you taking food?"

"We might get hungry. People are starving in Cuba, but the police keep them out of sight so the tourists don't see."

"Where did you hear that?"

"Danny told me."

She called him what Anthony's son preferred: his middle name, Daniel. Luis Daniel Quintana had grown up in suburban New Jersey, and he barely spoke Spanish. Gail said, "That is absolutely not true, and we're not going to insult Marta's family by bringing our own food. They have more than enough."

"Are they rich?"

"I don't think so. Cuba doesn't have rich people anymore. But I guess some people have more than others, like anywhere else."

"Can I keep it for snacks?"

"Snacks only. At dinner you'll eat what everyone else does." Gail lifted out a blue nylon bag. "What's in here?"

Karen sat up straight. "My emergency supplies. I am definitely taking that."

"May I?" When Karen only stared back at her, Gail unzipped the bag and removed a compass, a first-aid kit, a mirror, some rope, a small flashlight with extra batteries, a rain poncho, an empty plastic bottle, and a pack of water purification tablets. Gail noticed a glint of aluminum foil at the bottom and took out an object about four inches long. She peeled back the foil and found the Swiss Army knife that Karen's father had given her. Holding it up between thumb and forefinger, she said, "Do you want to explain this?"

"That's so the X-rays at the airport can't see it."

"No, I mean how did you think you could get away with carrying a *knife* on an airplane? Are you trying to get us all arrested?"

"I just thought we might have to cut the rope or something."

Gail slid the knife into the pocket of her shorts, then reached out and tugged on Karen's hand. "Come sit here with me. What's going on?"

"We might need it. You just never know, Mom."

"Are you afraid something will happen to us?" Gail drew her closer and kissed her forehead. "Silly. Havana is perfectly safe. Maybe more so than here," she added.

Karen's sun-blond brows pulled together. "They say that if you go out after dark you can get robbed. Tourists are attacked there all the time, especially American tourists, and most especially women."

"Danny again?"

"He *knows*, Mom. He's Cuban."

"He's about as Cuban as you are. Anthony wouldn't let us go if it wasn't safe."

Karen gave a little snort. "What a jerk. I hate him."

"He was just teasing you."

"Because he's a jerk. Plus he's only sixteen and he drinks. A *lot*."

"When? Tonight?"

"Molly and me saw him in the backyard with some, like, older guys, and they were drinking and smoking."

"What were *you* doing out there? Spying on the boys?"

"I was showing Molly the house! We have a right to take a walk. Mom, don't tell Anthony what I said. I do *not* want Danny to think I was ratting him out."

"I won't say anything." She didn't have to; Anthony already knew about his son's misbehavior. A good reason for taking him to Cuba, Anthony had told her. Make the boy appreciate what he had. What Danny really thought about this trip, Gail didn't know. He had chosen to stay at the Pedrosa house pending departure. He and his older sister, Angela, would be in the limo when it arrived downstairs in the morning. They would pick up Gail's mother next, then head for the airport.

Gail told Karen it was late, to turn off her computer.

When the screen was dark, and the backpack refilled with everything but contraband items, Gail pulled down the comforter, and Karen got into bed. With the lamp on the nightstand sending a soft glow into the room, Gail scooted her over a little and lay down beside her. She smoothed Karen's hair. The honey-brown color had been brightened by long days in the sun playing soccer for her team at Biscayne Academy and sailing with her father. Karen had Dave's square jaw and strong nose. She would not be a beautiful woman, but she was loyal and good, and people would see that. Karen fought her own battles at school; she was protective of her friends. And her family. It had taken her a while to warm up to Anthony Quintana. She had measured him against her father, and though he'd come out second best, he was, in Karen's view, not so bad that he was bound to make her mother miserable. She liked him well enough, but he was still on probation.

"I love you, sweetie," Gail said.

Karen was already asleep, her breath coming softly through parted lips.

Gail turned off the lamp and quietly closed the door.

The master suite was at the opposite end of the apartment, past the living room with its floor-to-ceiling windows looking out over a marina, some small mangrove islands, and the bay curving toward the horizon. A gorgeous place, but leased for only a year. Soon they would look for a house, something to please all three of them, at a comfortable midpoint, if possible, between her office and his, yet close enough to Karen's friends so she wouldn't feel completely uprooted.

A few times, coming home from her office and riding up in an elevator full of strangers, Gail had the sense that she had stumbled into the wrong building. The feeling was not always dispelled when she opened the door to an apartment filled with sleek modern furniture and rugs she would never have chosen for herself. More than once she had heard a key in a lock and had seen a tall, dark-haired man coming in, and for just an instant wondered what he was doing there. But he would smile at her and drop his briefcase onto the sofa, and pull her into his arms. That moment promised all she could want of *home*.

They had met four years ago and battled their way through a relationship that neither could have predicted. But here they were. Gail trusted that it would last. What she wanted now more than anything was to feel the days gradually settle into a solid and predictable routine.

On her way into the bedroom she heard Anthony talking on the phone. He wasn't shouting, but he was getting close. Gail paused, unsure whether to interrupt.

"Go put a note on his door." Anthony pointed as if the other person were standing in front of him. *"Dile que me llame.* I don't give a damn what time he gets in, he must call. Otherwise, I will have him on a plane back to his mother." He paced beside the bed in his silk bathrobe, the phone to his ear. "No, *mi niña,* I'm not angry with you, I promise. We'll see you in the morning. Sleep well. *Duérmete bien."* He hung up and let out a breath.

Gail said, "Who was that, Angela? Is everything all right?"

Anthony made a dismissive wave. "Her brother went out with his cousins after the party. She thinks he went to South Beach. He isn't answering his cell phone. If he oversleeps in the morning, he can stay here. I don't give a shit what he does."

"Oh, come on. He's only sixteen."

"What kind of excuse is that? He's irresponsible and inconsiderate. I can see it now, chasing him down all over Havana."

"What's the matter with you tonight? Would you please stop yelling at me?"

Anthony lightly touched his temples before dropping his hands and fixing his dark eyes on her. "Forgive me." He leaned over and kissed her cheek, then patted it. "*Perdóname, mi amor.* I'm tired. Come to bed. Did you finish packing?"

"Not yet. I was saying good night to Karen."

"Honey, I told you, in Havana they dress like we do here. Casual clothes, but be a little conservative. Take a couple of dresses, if we go out at night. Not your best ones. How hard is that?"

"I don't want people to stare at me and say, 'Oh, look, a tourist.'"

"There are blondes in Cuba. There is every color in the world."

"There's no way I can pass for a Cuban."

"I didn't say you should. No, I like what you are, an American."

"It's funny when you call me that, 'an American,' as if I'm from another country."

He smiled. "In Miami, you are."

"Is that why you married me? Because I'm exotic?"

"Sexy and exotic. My friends are jealous."

"I'll bet. Skinny me. Your . . . *girafa linda?* You're the only one I'd let call me that, a pretty giraffe." She slid her hands up the satin lapels of his robe.

He took her hand and kissed it, then focused on her rings. "Leave your engagement ring here. And wear a plain watch."

"I know, you told me already. Anthony, why did your grandfather want to talk to you tonight? Hector was stationed outside his office like a palace guard and wouldn't let me in."

"Yes, he said you were looking for me." As Anthony walked away he removed his link bracelet. His gold watch was already lying on his dresser next to a leather jewelry case. He slid off his rings. Black jade ring into the case. Platinum and diamond next to it. Leaving the wedding band on. Tapping his fingers on top of the dresser.

Gail wondered how long it would take before he thought of an answer.

"You know how Ernesto is," he said. "Somebody spilled the beans to him about the trip. We talked about it. He made his point, and I made mine. It's no problem."

She waited. "Is that all you talked about?"

Turning around, Anthony must have seen the knowledge in her face. He said, "What did Hector tell you?"

"That you and Ernesto were expecting visitors. He wouldn't say who."

"Ah. Well, *I* wasn't expecting anyone. My grandfather set this up. Bill Navarro flew in from Washington. He brought an aide with him. I think his name was Bookhouser." Anthony closed the jewelry case, put it into the drawer, and slid the drawer shut.

Gail waited.

He said, "They asked me to talk to Ramiro, to invite him to defect to the United States."

"No way."

"Oh, yes. They said Marta can come with him, the kids too. You see what Navarro is after. If he can snag a Cuban general, he'll score some points for himself in Miami. I might talk to Ramiro, but I don't expect him to say yes, oh, thank you, I have been wanting so very much to resign from *las Fuerzas Armadas* and buy a little duplex in Hialeah."

Gail didn't smile. "You weren't going to tell me about this, were you?"

"I probably shouldn't have told you this much."

"I'm your wife."

"I know you are. I know. But some things . . ." He put his hands on her shoulders. "Sweetheart, this is not a matter that we can discuss openly. If Ramiro decided to leave, and people got wind of it, there could be . . . serious political complications. You understand."

"Of course."

"It won't affect our visit, I promise, but don't speak to anyone about this. Not your mother, not Marta. You know nothing about it. All right?"

"I understand."

"Good." Anthony kissed her lips. "Go pack your suitcase. You have half an hour, no more. Then I'm going to come and get you."

Gail had Karen's suitcase packed in ten minutes. Zipped it closed, rolled it across the living room. Then went back to hers. Yes to a jacket, no to the extra sweater. These two dresses, not that one. Folded them around some tops to keep them from wrinkling. Tossed two pairs of shorts onto the sofa, put the other three pairs in the bag. She checked her list: toiletries, cosmetics, lingerie. Hair dryer, in case Marta didn't have one.

How strange, she was thinking, that Congressman Navarro had come to Ernesto Pedrosa's house so late at night. Very strange that he hadn't come out to work the party and shake some hands, because the guests included quite a few of the people who ran things in Miami. And who was the other man, the aide? They had come all the way from Washington. The more Gail considered what Anthony had told her, the more certain she became that he had not told her everything. That was not unusual: Anthony Quintana could be infuriatingly secretive. This time, he might have a good reason. He could have simply said, *I'm sorry, I can't discuss it, national security.* Or whatever. He could have said that. But he had tap-danced around the truth, assuming she was too credulous to know the difference.

Gail put a knee on her suitcase to close it, wrestling with the zipper. When she rolled the suitcase to the front door, she saw a pair of high-heeled sandals on the sofa, the black ones that matched her dress for Janelle's *quinceañera.* Gail doubted that her suitcase would hold so much as a nail file. She took the shoes over to the big duffel bag on wheels that Anthony had filled with gifts for family and friends. He had said that his sister always told him not to bring anything because she didn't want to admit that shortages existed in her socialist paradise. But Anthony would come loaded, and Marta would accept the gifts and pretend she did it to be polite.

Under a package of new bed sheets Gail found a stack of books and some shirts still in their wrappers. Anthony said he was never searched at the airport in Havana, not he, the brother-in-law of General Ramiro Vega. The books were for his friends, Yolanda and José. Yolanda was a nurse, Gail remembered, who worked at the old-age home where Anthony's father lived. José was a journalist, a political activist who had been in prison. Together they ran a library out of their house. Gail had only a few details because this was another topic that Anthony avoided.

She sat on her heels, laughing softly at herself. "You knew what you were getting into, so shut up." Anthony didn't consciously intend to keep her in the dark. Privacy was a habit ingrained into criminal defense lawyers. Or was it more personal? A carryover from years of not discussing Cuba with his grandfather. Easier that way, keeping the two parts of his life separate. Miami here, Cuba there. Anthony dancing on the narrow wall between them, managing somehow not to fall off. Any woman who didn't get it shouldn't have married him.

Gail tried to wedge her shoes into the duffel bag but there wasn't room. She noticed Anthony's carry-on and knelt on the floor to unzip it. She saw a paperback novel, bottled water, airline tickets, passports, his Palm Pilot. There was a brown envelope full of letters to be delivered in Cuba. Anthony had shown her. They contained photographs; most contained cash as well. Someone's brother or cousin or friend writing to those left behind.

To get her shoes to the bottom of the bag she had to move the envelopes aside. She noticed that one of them had a name on it in Anthony's tilted handwriting. *Mario.*

Mario who?

It wasn't sealed. She lifted the flap and saw a stack of twenty-dollar bills. She counted ten of them. And a folded sheet of cream-colored paper, the kind Anthony used in his office. She could just make out the raised imprint of a ballpoint pen. Black ink.

The living room was empty and quiet. Gail took out the letter, then noticed her own reflection in the dark glass of the windows, a woman on her knees going through her husband's things, about to read his correspondence.

She put the letter back into the envelope, folded down the flap, and zipped the bag shut.

4

Over the western Caribbean a sheen of sunlight flickered on the water. Shadows of clouds made patches of indigo on deep turquoise blue. A delicate V of foam marked the passage of a ship. Gail leaned over her mother, who had put away her Spanish phrase book to look out. Irene said she could have sworn she'd seen a line of green out there. Gail didn't think so; they were still too far away to see Cuba. Haze obscured the horizon.

For a few moments longer she gazed at the empty ocean, then settled back into her seat. She felt that the jet was flying past the edge of the known world. Her stomach had that floating sensation one gets from losing altitude too fast, though the flight had been smooth.

At the airport in Cancún, through her sunglasses, Gail had looked around to see who might be taking notes on the passengers lining up at the Cubana de Aviación counter. She saw no one. The agent handed over their airline tickets and visas as though it were completely normal, a group of six Americans flying from Miami to Havana. The visas would be stamped at José Martí airport. The visas, but not their American passports. The Cubans knew how things worked.

Gail had dressed plainly—khaki pants and a long-sleeved white pullover—not wanting to draw any attention. Her mother didn't care what anyone thought. She wore gold hoop earrings, a yellow dress printed with red flowers, and brown leather sandals on her size-five feet. Her toenail polish matched the flowers. She had bought a new digital camera to document every moment of their trip. Her straw hat rested in the overhead bin. She would be as inconspicuous as a beach umbrella.

They weren't the only Americans sneaking in. Gail had chatted with her fellow passengers in the waiting area. Four guys from Ohio had bought a Canadian package tour to go deep-sea fishing. A couple from Atlanta would spend their honeymoon on Varadero Beach. There were Cubans as well: Cubans from Miami visiting relatives, and Cubans from Cuba, coming home from wherever they'd been. Gail was surprised by this, then told herself that of course they could travel, just not to the United States, not without hacking through miles of red tape on both sides of the water.

Across the aisle, Anthony's novel was open on his tray table, next to his Scotch and soda, but he wasn't reading. He had propped his cheek on extended fingers, sending his unfocused gaze down the aisle. Gail wondered what he was thinking about. His brother-in-law? What to say to him? Whether to talk to him at all?

She put a hand on Anthony's arm. It took him a couple of seconds to realize she was there. She leaned closer. "I miss you." He sent a smile her way and followed that with a kiss in the air. "If you let me change seats with Danny, we can make out."

"*Qué mala eres.*" Telling her she was naughty.

"Do we have our own room tonight?" Gail asked. "Or are they putting us in the barracks?"

"Barracks?"

"You know . . . General Vega, barracks. Never mind. Just making a little joke, Anthony."

He pulled her close enough to say into her ear, "What did we discuss last night? You don't know who could be listening. It's a small plane, and your voice carries."

She whispered back, "Sorry. I didn't think spies would pay to sit in first class."

"*Jesucristo.* Gail, please." He said, "To answer your question— Marta is giving us Paula's room. Paula and the baby will stay at a friend's house."

The older Vega girl was twenty-three and divorced, with a toddler. "We can't take Paula's room. That's not fair."

"It's the way we do it."

"We?"

"All right, *they.* My family."

"Fine. I just meant . . . we shouldn't make it hard for them."

"Look, sweetheart. They're excited, very pleased that we're coming. We can't stay at a hotel. Marta would feel bad."

"Who said anything about staying at a hotel?" But she had thought about it. Definitely had thought of it. Toast and juice on a tray. A bathroom to themselves.

He said, "Don't worry, you'll fit in. Within a week, you'll be as *cubana* as anyone." He squeezed her hand before going back to his Scotch and Tom Clancy. He read a paragraph or two, then closed the book on a plastic stir stick.

His usual drink, his usual taste in novels, but they weren't keeping his mind occupied. Gail saw him stretch, arms over his head, then speak to his son. No response. He nudged Danny's shoulder to get his attention. Danny thumbed the controls on his Discman and mumbled a reply. Anthony looked at him for a moment longer, then picked up his drink.

He had invited his son along so they could share the experience, but it wasn't happening. Gail studied Danny out of the corner of her eye. Except for the dark, wavy hair, there wasn't much of Anthony in him. Not his fire, not his humor or intelligence. Danny was more clever than intelligent, more sarcastic than funny. She had tried to like him for Anthony's sake, but her efforts at friendly conversation had fallen flat. Danny didn't like her—not that she'd ever done anything to him ... except for marrying his father. He wasn't openly rude; he just treated her as if she were irrelevant. It didn't matter. Danny would be on his way home to New Jersey as soon as they got back.

His sister, older by two years, was nothing like Danny. Gail adored her. Angela was thoughtful and kind, with gentle brown eyes and the delicate features of a porcelain figurine. She wanted to dance professionally, but she had been turned down by the Miami City Ballet. Gail suspected that things weren't going so well with her boyfriend either. Her father thought the trip to Cuba might lift her spirits.

Angela and Karen were in the seat just ahead. Gail heard the crinkle of paper, saw the edge of a map before it settled down on their laps. Angela's goal in Havana was to find the house in Vedado where her family had once lived. Gail had seen the pictures: a beautiful house with columns across the front, double doors, potted palms on the terrace, and balconies on the second floor. Her father had told her not to bother. The house had been cut into several apartments that were crammed with people who hung their wash on the old ironwork railings. Angela wanted to see it anyway.

Every family has its stories, invariably made more romantic in the retelling. Angela had heard the one about her grandmother, Caridad Pedrosa, a beautiful, blue-eyed girl of sixteen who had met a handsome young army lieutenant at a dance at the yacht club, she in a strapless satin gown, he in his dress uniform. This was before. Everything in Cuba could be divided into before and after the Revolution. The girl and the young lieutenant locked eyes, had one dance, and that was that. Love gave Caridad the courage to escape her chaperones. She got out somehow, went out the back way or—better still—climbed down off her bedroom balcony and into his arms. The inevitable happened, and they had to get married.

Did Angela know the rest of the story? The marriage was a horrible mismatch. Caridad's parents, the rich banker and his socialite wife, took them in, but by then Luis Quintana had joined the *fidelistas*. He wore a beard and carried a rifle. On principle he refused to live in a mansion and so moved his family to his birthplace in Camagüey province, a flat land of sugarcane and cattle. Caridad couldn't stand it, of course, all those chickens in the yard, the dirt, the illiterate *mulato* mother-in-law who practiced santería, and Luis sleeping around. When Ernesto Pedrosa told Caridad the family was leaving Cuba, she decided that she and her four children would go with them. But when the car came, her two older ones were off playing. Caridad called and called; she begged her father to wait. It was impossible; her husband would be home any moment. Ernesto had to unhook his daughter's fingers from the doorjamb and carry her, sobbing, across the muddy yard.

Marta and Anthony remained in Cuba. Their father told them their mother had abandoned them. They joined the Young Communist Pioneers. They practiced marching with wooden rifles and shooting at the imperialists. When Anthony was thirteen, his grandfather, through bribes and lies, managed to fly him to Miami for a visit with his mother. Anthony went so he could confront her, to demand that she return home. Of course the Pedrosas never let him go back. He grew up in Miami with his heart torn in two.

Gradually Gail grew aware of a murmur, a shifting in the aircraft. People were standing up, trying to see past the heads pressed

to the windows on the starboard side. There was an announce-
ment in two languages to remain seated. No one paid attention.

Irene was rummaging in her bag, whipping the lens cap off her
camera. "Gail, look! Over there, look. It's Cuba." She aimed the
lens out the window.

From the haze a long stripe of green appeared, paler at the
edge, a rim of lacy white—a shoreline. Then red soil, some houses,
roads with sparse traffic. Royal palm trees soared from the fields.
In the distance a brown haze. Blocks of buildings—the city. Anthony braced a hand on his daughter's seat back and said it looked
as though they would circle and come in from the south. He
turned to his son and asked if he could see the Malecón, the long
curving wall that kept the ocean from flooding the city.

"Danny, *mira el Malecón, ¿tú ves?* We'll go there when the wind
is blowing. The waves are so high they go right into the street."
His son lifted the shade on his window, some glimmer of interest
at last.

Gail reached up to touch Anthony's back. "Honey? You really
should sit down."

He leaned over and kissed her. His eyes shone. "We're here."

Coming out of the passenger walkway, Gail kept a firm grip on
Karen's hand. The terminal, larger and newer than she had expected, bustled with tourists. At customs, a young woman in an
olive-green uniform smiled, stamped their visas, and slid them
back under the glass. *"Bienvenida a Cuba."*

As Anthony had predicted, their bags weren't searched. He
tipped a porter to take everything outside. The pickup area was
mobbed, and their little group was caught in a wave of sun-baked
Germans heading for a tour bus at the curb. Then someone
shouted Anthony's name. Gail turned to see a woman with bronze-
streaked hair pushing through the crowd.

Anthony waved. "Marta!"

His sister was broad-shouldered and round in the hips, wearing a
plain blue shirt over dark pants. She embraced Anthony and kissed
him. She saw her niece and nephew and her arms opened wide.
"Angela, Luisito! *¡Ay, Dios mío, qué grandes son! Dale un besito a*

tu tía!" She was crying and laughing at the same time, pressing her wet face against theirs.

She pulled them toward their cousins. Introductions, more embraces. Giovany was eighteen, his sister Janelle three years younger. Their father's Afro-Cuban blood showed in their curly black hair, their smooth *café con leche* skin. Their clothes were perfectly clean and neat—the only thing that might have pegged them as foreigners, if they'd been in Miami.

Marta hugged Gail next. "Anthony, she's so tall, like a model. Welcome to Cuba, Gail. My new sister, eh? And your mother! Irene, how are you? I want you to know my children. Janelle, Giovany, greet your uncle's new wife. Paula has to work, I am sorry she isn't here. You'll see her tonight. And the baby! You won't believe how big he is!"

Somewhere in the avalanche of words, Marta's children embraced their uncle and kissed him and said how happy they were to see him again. Then more hugs and kisses for their American visitors.

Marta held Karen by the shoulders. "You are twelve years old only? No! You are very grown-up."

Gail's head was spinning. More people came out of the terminal, crushing them closer together.

"Let's get out of here." Marta looked around and spotted a man in a tan windbreaker standing nearby. She pointed at the suitcases. "Cobo, *el equipaje.*"

The man tossed his cigarette to the concrete and stepped on it. With big, square hands, he easily heaved the bags into the back of a Toyota minivan. There were two vehicles, and from luck or privilege Marta had found spaces at the curb. The other was a faded little blue car with rust around the wheel wells, some make that Gail hadn't seen before.

"Gio, *los primos contigo.*" Marta told her son that his cousins would go with him.

Before Gail could speak, all five got into the blue car, with Karen squeezed in back between the older girls. Spanish rap music blasted through the open windows as they pulled away.

Gail stared after them. The car swerved around a bus and vanished. Anthony turned her toward his sister's van. "Come on. They'll be there before us."

Marta took the front passenger seat. Behind them, Anthony sat in the middle so that Gail and Irene could look out the windows. The driver, Cobo, leaned on the horn to force a car out of the way. Marta opened her shoulder bag—brown imitation leather—and took out a pack of cigarettes: Hollywood. Gail wondered where they were made. Marta lit one and slid her window down halfway. She asked about their flight from Cancún. Was it all right? Were they hungry? Everyone wanted to meet the cousins and Gail and her family. Ramiro would be home later. Papi would be with them for dinner. She laughed and reached over to give Irene's knee a nudge. "You will meet our father. He doesn't speak English so good, but he likes to flirt with pretty women. Be careful!"

The billboards along the airport exit road weren't advertisements; they were political messages, such a cliché of what Gail had heard about Cuba that she wanted to grab her mother's arm and tell her to look, but Anthony was between them, leaning forward to talk to his sister.

En marcha hacia el futuro. On the march . . . something . . . the future. *Celebramos el Triunfo de la Revolución*. We celebrate the triumph of the Revolution. Fidel Castro in his green uniform. Che Guevara on a billboard announcing *Socialismo ahora y siempre*. Socialism, now and forever. The paper was peeling, and rust ran down the signs where they'd been nailed to the posts.

Neither Marta nor Anthony seemed to notice, as if these fading relics were only part of the background, like the electrical wires drooping overhead or the weeds along the road. Marta tapped her cigarette ashes out the window. Her nail polish was chipped. When she turned to speak to them, her profile revealed a resemblance to Anthony in the straight nose and full lips. She was older, forty-five, and a frown of concentration had drawn deep lines between her brows. Where her hair parted, gray showed through. She wore no wedding ring. Her jewelry consisted of a watch with a stainless steel band and a narrow gold chain around her neck. She was clearly a woman with more important things to do than look in a mirror.

"Irene, you will see *La Habana Vieja* tomorrow," Marta announced. "I'll be your tour guide, eh? I took some days off from work so I can be with you." Marta listed what they would see. The Capitol, the Malecón, the *Plaza de las Armas*, the cathedral—

The stream of words was exhausting. Gail's attention shifted to the scenes passing by the window. Run-down factories. Small stores with glass fronts. So many buildings trimmed in bright blue, as if no other color could be found. She saw people sitting under a mildewed bus shelter, others walking a path along the side of the road. A young woman in jeans and a Florida Marlins sweatshirt pushed an elaborate baby stroller. Gail supposed she had relatives in Miami.

Closer to the city, they followed a truck laying down a fog of blue smoke through a quivering exhaust pipe. The back of the truck had wooden sides, and people were holding on, not workers but ordinary people, nicely dressed, women mostly, and some children. Why were they in the back of a truck? "Anthony—"

"Look at that old car!" Irene pointed. "It's a 1953 Dodge, I swear it is. My dad owned a car just like that." Metal pipes formed the front bumper of the ancient machine, and brake lights had been welded on top of the rear fenders.

Anthony told her that it probably had a truck engine. "They put it together with wires and chewing gum, believe me."

Marta laughed. "Yes, we are geniuses with our old cars!"

Irene said, "You've got a very nice van, though."

"Anyone who works hard can have a car, but it takes time." Marta sent some ashes out the window. "We have shortages of everything because of the blockade."

Gail shot a glance at Anthony. The corner of his mouth turned up, and his hand, resting on her knee, gave it a little squeeze. *I told you*. He put his arm across the back of her seat. "When we cross the river, look down. There's a park. It's pretty this time of year. We should take a walk there. Would you like that?"

She understood: This was his city, if not in reality, then in his heart; he wanted to share it with her. She smiled back at him. "Yes, I'd love to see it."

Feeling a little overheated, she shifted to catch the cool breeze from the driver's open window. Images swept past her. A house with purple bougainvillea spilling across the roof. Small, boxy cars crammed with people. A collarless dog limping along the sidewalk. Gray concrete apartment buildings. Shade trees. Men at a card table playing dominos. A red-and-yellow awning, a sign announcing "Burgui"—a hamburger joint. The word *Venceremos*—we will conquer—stretching in faded blue and red across a long, low wall. The paint was peeling off. Everything needed painting.

The van swerved around a pothole.

Gail held on, staring mutely, Havana pouring into her mind.

The Vegas lived in a sprawling, flat-roofed tri-level built around 1950 for someone with a great deal of money. The house showed its age: The decorative aluminum railing on the porch had pits in it, and several of the glass louvers in the huge windows across the front had been replaced with wooden slats. But still, an impressive house. The palm trees, climbing philodendron, red-and-green crotons, and an overhanging poinciana tree led Gail's mother to say it looked just like home. Cobo carried their bags up while Marta showed them around.

Gail asked where the kids could be, and Marta replied, as she hurried across the wide living room with its polished terrazzo floor, that Giovany might have taken them for a drive through the city.

Dining room here, reception room there—heavy furniture, chairs with cane bottoms, gilded mirrors. Bedrooms upstairs, garage farther on. Then up a curve of free-floating black granite steps, down which, Marta explained, Janelle would walk in her gown the night of the party. On the second floor, Marta pointed out who would stay where.

A quick look at the master bedroom, darkened by heavy curtains. A big television in the corner. Liquor bottles on the glass-topped dresser. Then back downstairs.

Into the kitchen with its dated appliances and tile floor, scrupulously clean. Marta insisted they have something to drink, a soda, coffee, a beer, whatever. Anthony said no, they would unpack and be down later. He motioned for Gail to follow him. Irene said she would stay behind; she wanted to have some *café cubano, por favor*. Marta laughed. "*¡Qué chistoso!* All the coffee we have, *mi amor*, is *cubano*."

They returned to the last room on the second floor and closed the door. The voices from downstairs could barely be heard. Anthony grabbed Gail's hand, pulled her close, and gave her a kiss so deep they went backward onto the bed, bouncing and knocking the headboard into the wall. Gail started laughing when he went for the button on her pants. "What are you doing?"

"What do you think?"

"Oh, my God, we can't, not now."

Pinning her hands, he kissed his way down her neck. "Why not?"

"I feel like a trespasser, like somebody is watching us. What if Karen comes back?"

He rolled off. "Maybe we should have a hotel."

"Oh, shut up," she said, elbowing his ribs. "Later. I'll make you beg for mercy."

Paula's room could hardly have been more feminine. Pink pillow shams, lace curtains, a fuzzy pink area rug on the terrazzo floor. A baby crib full of stuffed toys took up one corner. Over it, cartoon characters had been taped to the wall, but Gail didn't recognize any of them. Getting up, she looked at Anthony lying across the frayed pink bedspread. The room was awful, but strangely enough, he seemed completely at home. Usually so fastidious with his clothes, he had pulled from the depths of his closet well-worn slacks and knit shirt for the flight to Havana. Even his white sneakers were old; in Miami he'd worn them only to hike on the beach.

Gail asked, "What happened to Paula's husband?"

"They got a divorce."

"I know that," she said.

"It's hard to be married in Cuba." Anthony sat up. "There's no place for young couples to live. They move in with their in-laws. I don't think he and Marta got along." The driver had left their bags in a neat pile just inside the door. Anthony went over and knelt to unzip his suitcase.

"Who is that man who brought us here? Cobo. Who is he?"

"You're full of questions." Anthony scooped up a stack of his clothes. "Cobo works for the family. He's been with them . . . I don't know, ten years or more. Ramiro gets a car and he gets a driver. Cobo does whatever they need him to do. He has a room in the garage."

"Does he have a first name?" Gail unfolded her shorts and tops.

Anthony paused, then said, "I've never heard him called anything but 'Cobo.'"

"He's their house slave." Gail laughed. "Yes, he is, don't deny it."

"You think so? I'll tell you this." Anthony slid back the door on the closet, a wooden affair built out from the wall. His niece had pushed her clothes to one side to make room. "Cobo makes a good living, and if you ask him, he would say he's part of the family. So don't prejudge things you don't know about." Anthony shook out his shirts and trousers and hung them up.

Making a little face in his direction, Gail wandered to the window to look out. She turned the crank, and a breeze drifted through the glass louvers. The window gave a view of the front yard and the driveway. A hedge with small, glossy leaves had grown through the chain-link fence. Beyond the gate and the hedge, the street curved, then intersected with another one. She wanted to see a small blue car with five kids in it. The only traffic was a man on a bicycle with flowers in a plastic crate over the rear wheel. He called out the same phrase over and over. Gail thought he might be selling the flowers, but she didn't understand his words. His voice faded away.

"Does Giovany have a cell phone?"

"I don't know," Anthony replied.

She turned from the window. "Could we ask? I'd love to know where Karen is."

"Nothing will happen to Karen."

"Your kids are missing too."

"They aren't *missing*. When they come back, I'll speak to Gio. All right?"

Gail sat on the end of the bed and dug some Advil out of her purse. She had noticed the door that led directly to a bathroom. She went in and shut the door behind her.

The bathroom reminded her of her grandmother's house— yellow tile, yellow bathtub, yellow sink in a peeling Formica cabinet. She took the pills with water in her cupped hand. Her cloudy image looked back at her in the discolored mirror over the sink. She picked up a silver tube from the vanity and unscrewed the top. Toothpaste. She dabbed some on her finger. It tasted of baking soda. She spit it out and rinsed her mouth.

A door on the opposite side led to another bedroom. Gail looked in. This was the room Karen and Angela would share with Janelle, an abundance of lace here as well. Stuffed animals covered the bed, odd for a girl of fifteen. A cot had been set up in the corner. Gail pulled the door closed.

She unzipped her pants, then stopped, staring down at the toilet. A cord came up through a hole in the lid, tied to a pencil so it wouldn't slip back in. Gail assumed this was how one flushed, by pulling the cord. And where was the toilet seat? A plastic bucket was placed by the toilet. Why? Before carefully positioning herself, she looked around for toilet paper and spotted a roll on the vanity. "Thank you, God."

At the sink she turned on the hot water faucet and waited, waited. She tried the other faucet. More cold water. She used that and some liquid soap, then dried her hands on the only thing available, a pink bath towel hanging on a rod by the tub.

Coming back to the bedroom she said, "There's no toilet seat."

Anthony turned around from the closet. "What?"

"They don't have a toilet seat."

"A lot of people don't in Cuba."

"Why not?"

A bottom drawer came open with a screech. "Because they can't find them in the stores. It's a luxury item in short supply. If you need a toilet seat, use Marta's bathroom."

"I'm not going to use her bathroom."

"Then don't." He put away his underwear in neat stacks.

Gail leaned on the closet to talk to him. "There's no hot water either. Okay, I can deal with the toilet, but how are we supposed to take a bath?"

Dropping his socks into the drawer, he said, "You have to turn on the gas first. There's a heater in the corner above the sink, didn't you see it? I'm sure you noticed everything else."

She crossed her arms. "At least they have toilet paper."

"Let me tell you something." He gave the drawer a hard shove with one knee to get it to shut. "This isn't Miami. It's not what you're used to. In Cuba, you have to accept things as they are."

"If you're going to tell me how to react, then maybe I shouldn't have come."

With a sigh he pulled her close. "Yes, you should. I'm glad you're here, Gail."

"Are you?"

He made an X over his heart. "Yes. And forgive my bad mood. I didn't get much sleep last night."

"Neither did I," she said. "And you've got Ramiro on your mind. When are you going to have your talk?"

"I don't know. Before we leave. There's no hurry." He patted her rear end. "Come on, let's finish this. They're expecting us downstairs." He sat on the end of the bed with his carry-on bag and pulled out his novel, their passports, an empty water bottle. A pair of high-heeled sandals.

"Sorry," Gail said. "I didn't have room in mine." She took the shoes from him. "Anthony, I wasn't prying, really, but I happened to see the envelopes, you know, the ones you showed me, and there was one to somebody named Mario. I was wondering. Who is that?"

Anthony lifted his eyes to hers. "Mario Cabrera. I've mentioned him, no?"

"I don't think so."

"I must have. He's Yolanda and José's son."

"The dissidents, right?" Gail said. "I'm sure you didn't tell me about Mario."

Anthony's eyes had not moved from her face. "Did you read the letter?"

"No."

He took the envelope out of his bag.

"You don't have to do that."

"Why not? There should be no secrets between us." He unfolded the letter, which she saw was written in Spanish. "I tell him hello, it's been a long time since we've seen each other—"

"Anthony—"

"And I hope that he is doing well. 'Your mother says you don't see her enough. You are an honorable young man, I hope you will think of her, she is a tremendous person, your father also. Here is some money, which you can put to good use. I hope that you will contact me when you can.' "

Gail sat beside him. "I didn't read your letter, but . . . yes, I saw the money. That's a generous thing for you to do."

He returned the letter to the envelope. "It's not that much. Two hundred dollars."

"You're fond of him."

"Well, I'm fond of his parents, whom I have known for a long time. Mario is nineteen . . . or twenty. A musician. He has a band, or had one. I don't know what he's doing now. He was getting his degree in music at the University of Havana, but he was invited to leave. Politically unreliable, that's the reason they gave. He moved out of the house, and where he's living now, who knows? Yolanda says the last time she saw him, he was starving. That is probably not true, but he can use the money. I haven't seen him since he was Danny's age. He's a handsome boy, very intelligent, very affectionate with his parents, but they rarely see him anymore. It could be that Mario thinks his connection to José puts him at a disadvantage, so he's staying away."

"That's cowardly of him," Gail said, then regretted her words. "Maybe it isn't. What do I know?"

"You're right. Cowardly . . . if it's true. But he's young, and maybe he thinks he has to do this to survive. I would like to talk to him face-to-face, but chances are, we won't see him. José and Yolanda want to have dinner for us tomorrow. You'll like them. They're extraordinary people."

"I don't know. It looks like Marta has tomorrow completely mapped out for us."

"It doesn't matter to Marta. Let her play tour guide to your mother."

"I'm surprised that you're helping José Leiva."

"Why are you surprised?"

"Because he's against the regime. You keep away from anything remotely political."

"It isn't politics. They're my friends. Listen." Anthony took her hand. "I must ask you a favor, *mi cielo*. Don't mention their names to Marta or Ramiro. You understand how it is."

"Of course. You don't want anyone to know you're a friend of the dissidents."

Anthony made a slight smile. "They know, but it's something we don't talk about. Like my grandfather. I don't talk about Marta and Ramiro with my grandfather, but he knows. Everyone knows everything. Marta sees Yolanda quite often. Yolanda works at the retirement home where our father lives. The job pays her the equivalent of about ten dollars a month, so I send her money for taking care of him."

"You never told me that," Gail said.

"No? Well, her family lived near mine in Camagüey, and Papi has known her all his life. To him, Yolanda's politics don't matter. If Marta had her way, the wife of José Leiva wouldn't be taking care of our father. She thinks it's bad for Ramiro's career. So. We don't bring it up."

"I'll add that to my list of things not to bring up," Gail said.

The staccato *beep-beep-beep* of a car horn sounded from outside. "That must be Karen." She hurried to the window and looked out. It was not a small blue car, but an aging black Mercedes that had stopped at the gate. Smoke drifted from the exhaust pipe, and Gail could just make out the face of a woman at the wheel. The horn sounded again, a long, impatient honk.

A second later Cobo appeared and swung back the chain-link gate. The car drove through and parked in a gravel area alongside the driveway. The door opened. Gail saw high heels, long legs, and a tight black skirt. The woman's eyes were hidden by big sunglasses. Blond bangs covered her forehead, and the rest of her hair was tied back in a long ponytail. She carried a portfolio under her arm. Something about her body—the heavy hips, perhaps, or the softness of her upper arms—revealed that the woman might be nearer to forty than she would have liked to admit. But sexy. Extremely.

Gail glanced at Anthony, who had come over to see what she was looking at. "Is that one of your cousins?"

"God, no. Her name is Olga Saavedra."

Gail prompted, "And?"

"I would guess that she's taking care of Janelle's party. That's what she does, parties. Olga Saavedra used to be a personality on television, very well known. Now she works for the Ministry of Culture. She plans dinners, entertainments, and so forth. There's always a party at this house. Fidel himself has been here many times. Marta likes to entertain, but she has no talent for the details."

Olga Saavedra walked toward the house, but Cobo was in her way. She moved left, then right; so did he. She flung out an arm and pushed past him. Cobo laughed, then watched her go. Heels clicking on the stone walkway, Olga Saavedra passed out of sight under the trees that shaded the front porch. Cobo went to the gate and closed it. He took some cigarettes from the pocket of his wind-breaker and lit one. Then he too disappeared.

"What was that all about?" Gail asked.

"She used to date him before she started working in television. She's ambitious, so it didn't last long. She hosted a talk show for several years."

"He's still obsessed with her," Gail said. "This is great. A soap opera right outside our window."

Anthony made one of his expansive shrugs, palms out, shoulders rising. "Love."

"Love Cuban style."

He laughed. "No, no. Love anywhere, *querida*. Come on, let's go downstairs."

"In a minute, I just want to ask you one thing. It's about Olga. Who is she, exactly? If you don't mind my asking."

Amusement played around Anthony's eyes. "More questions. All right, I'll tell you." He came closer and spoke in a low voice. "Olga knows everybody—artists, musicians. The guys who run things in Cuba like to throw parties, and Olga is the party girl. She has friends—I will call them friends—in the Ministry of the Interior, which is like our FBI and police department rolled into one. So. On one of my visits—before I met you, sweetheart—Olga invited me to go out with her. We went to a nightclub. She wanted to find out who I was, in addition to being Marta's brother."

"What do you mean, who you were?"

"Whose side I was on. Was I working for anybody? Could I be of some use to the regime? I wasn't on anybody's side, so I let her questions slide, and she stopped asking."

Gail laughed softly. "You're telling me that Olga Saavedra is a spy?"

"Not at all. She works for people who want to know things, and they probably asked her to find out. I am not immune from suspicion."

"Who wanted her to talk to you?"

"I have no idea. It doesn't matter."

"Are you sure Señorita Saavedra is here for Janelle's party?"

"Not for me, *querida*. She knows I'm not interested."

"Really. Did you do more than get drunk with her? Not that I *care*, I was just curious—"

With a small exhalation of surprise, Anthony said, "No. With a woman like that? You know what I like—skinny *americanas*."

Gail didn't smile at the joke. She held onto his arm when he turned toward the door. "Wait. Something's been bothering me. Bill Navarro and that other man came to your grandfather's house all the way from Washington, on the very eve of our departure for Cuba, and they want you to . . . how did you put it? *Invite* Ramiro to defect? Anthony, you never get involved in Ernesto's business— not *this* kind of business. Who was that guy, some kind of . . . undercover agent?"

"His name is Everett Bookhouser, and he's a congressional aide. Come on, Marta's waiting."

"An aide. Why do I not believe that?"

Anthony stared at the door a second, then looked back at Gail. "He said he's an advisor to the House Intelligence Committee. Is he more than that? Maybe he is."

"He's in the CIA! Oh, please, it's so obvious. What did he tell you?"

"Gail, I don't want to discuss it."

"Is this room bugged or something?"

"Of course it isn't. Gail, I told you before we left Miami, please stay out of this. I shouldn't have said anything to you."

"Excuse me, but I would like to know if we're in any danger here."

"We are not in danger, and neither is Karen, if that's what's on your mind. I will tell you one more time." He lowered his head to look at her directly. "You know nothing about it. I don't want to hear another word on this subject. Do you understand?"

"Yes. And don't fucking speak to me like that."

He raised both hands. "Jesus. I apologize. All right?" At the door he said, "Let's go. I could use a drink."

"Go ahead. I'll be right down."

"What's the matter now?"

"I'll be there in a *minute*, I said."

He went out, shutting the door hard, just short of a slam.

Gail exhaled to relieve the pressure in her chest. She headed for the bathroom to splash some water on her face. She jerked the pink towel off the rod. Through the small window, cluttered with bottles and jars and a vase of plastic daisies, a salsa beat came from the neighboring house. Gail wondered if she could stand this for ten more days.

5

The cool curve of aluminum slid under Anthony's palm. His footsteps echoed in the space below. Marta had moved most of the furniture out to make room for the tables and chairs that would be delivered for the *quinceañera*. He had been to a couple of his sister's events. She would have a five-piece band on the patio and people running back and forth to the kitchen with trays of food. The liquor would flow. But Janelle's birthday was about to be eclipsed by her father's promotion. Anthony expected to see the Cuban flag on a polished brass pole. A framed color photograph of Ramiro getting his new star, shaking hands with the *comandante en jefe*. Fidel looking pale in the photo, age spots on his forehead, beard getting thin. But still alive, still pissing on his enemies. Icon and scourge, as entrenched as Mao. The Cubans making a sly new pun: *coma-andante*, the walking coma.

Anthony was never sure how far Marta bought into the system. She had asked him to bring her some Johnnie Walker Black, but she wouldn't serve American liquor at her parties. There had once been a swimming pool in the backyard, but Marta had it filled in. She'd said it was a "bourgeois indulgence." Anthony's nephew had told him that the pool had started leaking and they couldn't afford to fix it. Anthony suspected that both versions were true.

Cuba itself was a contradiction, an impossibility. That it still functioned was a miracle. Not to see this was to shut yourself off from reality: You stay in a hotel on Varadero Beach and take a guided tour of Old Havana. Or you could see it but not care. Tell yourself it didn't matter. Like a missing toilet seat. That Gail had noticed this made him uneasy. With what? Her criticism? His own reaction to it? All right, maybe he had shown some irritation, but what had she expected him to say—that he liked having his family's shortcomings pointed out to him?

Anthony sat on a long teak bench by the front windows, the only piece of furniture remaining in this half of the room. He had wanted her to accept Havana on its own terms, the beauty and the misery, without judgment. But Gail Connor was the kind of woman who noticed things.

Gradually he recognized the noise that had worked itself into his mind over the past minute or so. An angry voice—his sister yelling at someone. Anthony had an idea who. He walked to the open archway in the long stone wall behind the stairs. Ramiro kept an office at home. Anthony stopped a few paces from the open door.

Marta was outraged. The food would be an embarrassment; the musicians were second-rate. This was not just any birthday party. Many important people had been invited. "I asked you for the best. Why are you giving me this shit? Is this what you think a man of my husband's rank deserves?"

Another voice said, "Maybe we should talk to Ramiro. He hired me, you know."

Olga Saavedra.

Marta retorted, "I don't care, you deal with me. And don't call him Ramiro. You will refer to him as General Vega. Such disrespect! Let me see that menu again."

With a sigh Anthony retraced his steps and headed for the kitchen. He opened a bottle of Cristal beer and carried it back to the living room. The voices were quieter. He was about to go back upstairs to see if he could coax Gail out of her mood when he noticed his mother-in-law in the front yard with her camera. Her red hair curled from under her wide straw hat. She flitted from plant to plant, zooming in on a flower, pulling back to capture a tree. She couldn't be still for a minute. Something like her daughter.

When he walked onto the terrace Irene saw him and waved. "Hi. I hope it's all right if I take some pictures of the house."

"Yes, it's fine." He sat in one of the metal rockers. "What do you think of Havana?"

"Well, I haven't really seen it yet, but you know, it's so much like Miami, the weather and the plants and all."

"That's why we Cubans settled in Miami. It's not so different."

He began slowly to rock. The motion soothed him. He drank his beer and felt the warm sun on his face.

Irene came up the steps. "Tell me, do we dress for dinner tonight?"

"We never dress for dinner," he said. "Wear what you have on, or shorts if you prefer. No, Cubans are very casual at home. If we go out to dinner, that's another matter."

"I'll just freshen up, then." She thought of something else and rested a hand on his shoulder. "Anthony, you lovely man, I'm so very grateful that you invited me along."

"My pleasure." He took her hand and kissed it.

She laughed. "Well. Guess I'd better check in with the gang. See you later. *Hasta luego.*" With a flutter of her yellow skirt, she vanished through the door.

Anthony closed his eyes and rocked. He heard the voice of the old flower-seller, singing his refrain: *"Flores, florero . . . flores, florero."* It was illegal, selling without a government license, but nobody cared. There were flowers on every table.

He thought about Gail. It had been unfair of him to expect her to adjust to the rhythms of Havana so quickly. He gave the chair another push. The metal rockers clicked on the tile floor like the slow tick of a clock. At the condo in Coconut Grove there were no front porches with rocking chairs, nor at his previous house, nor at the house where Gail had lived with Karen's father. In suburban America one could drive down the street and see one closed garage door after another.

The sound of an engine made him look toward the street. The kids had come home. Janelle got out and opened the gate so her brother could drive through. Angela waved from the backseat. Anthony lifted a hand. The car went under the portico at the side of the house. Nobody went back to close the gate. It didn't matter.

He settled back in the rocking chair.

Someday, when things changed, he would spend more time here. He could help rebuild the country. His country. Still his country, even after thirty years of separation. They could buy some property, he and Gail. A second home, a house on the water. The kids would visit. They would bring grandchildren. He would take them to Camagüey to see where he had grown up. He would teach them to fish in the clear streams, as his father had taught him.

The truth was an ache in his soul: He wanted to come back. As the grandson of Ernesto Pedrosa, he was here on sufferance. If Ramiro defected, what then? Who would be blamed? Whose name would appear on that long list of people who would never be let in?

He had thought of saying nothing. Let fate work itself out. If General Vega had skimmed money from the regime, he could pay for it. But there was Marta to think of. The children.

When would he talk to Ramiro? Soon. Tomorrow, the next day. Where? Not here. Someone in the household could be reporting to State Security. The housekeeper, the man who came to trim the plants. Even Cobo, who had lived here ten years. A part of the family. Gail had called him a house slave. She noticed things, and often out of context, but her vision was clear. Upstairs she had asked the question that had been rattling around in his own head. Why was Ramiro so important? It wasn't Navarro who wanted him; Navarro was only the messenger, useful because of his connection to Ernesto Pedrosa. Was it Everett Bookhouser who wanted him?

Gail had been on the mark about Bookhouser. Before leaving Miami, Anthony had told Hector Mesa to find out what he could. Hector had once been employed, unofficially, by the CIA. That had been years ago, when Oliver North and his pals were trying to topple the Sandinistas, but Hector had kept his friends. Hector had confirmed Anthony's suspicions: Bookhouser was a high-level spook.

Why did he want Ramiro Vega? Ramiro had just been made a general. His job was to oversee industrial facilities; he had nothing to do with strategic planning. Maybe Bookhouser was handing him a plate of bullshit. Using him to take a reading on loyalties at *las Fuerzas Armadas*.

Anthony felt the chair come suddenly to a stop. He looked around.

Olga Saavedra was holding on to the back of it. A bleached-blond ponytail spilled over one shoulder. She slowly shoved gold-trimmed sunglasses into her bangs. Her long nails glittered. She spoke to him in her own bizarre mix of Spanish and English.

"*Hola,* look who is here. *El norteamericano de Miami.* How you doing, *mi amor*? You looking *muy* handsome and rich, *como siempre.*"

"Life in America," he said. "You don't appear to be suffering either, Olga. Are you still traveling?"

"Oh, yes." She pronounced it *jess*. "To Barcelona last winter for the *festival del cine*." Her shiny pink lipstick filled in the brown pencil lines on her mouth.

He said, "You must have been a sensation."

"I wish so! I was es-stuck in the hotel pouring drinks for the Minister *de Cultura* and his buddy-buddies. I should have stay in *España*, you think? *Ay*, Cuba, *qué horror*, it's get so bad. The new year will bring good fortune, *si Dios quiere*. You never know."

"*No se sabe nunca,*" Anthony agreed, switching to Spanish.

Olga did the same. "So you got married to an American. Your sister told me."

"Her name is Gail. I brought her with me. My children as well."

"Is she as pretty as me?"

"How could I compare you to anyone, Olga?"

She laughed, showing a gap between her front teeth. "You are full of shit, baby." She touched his cheek with a forefinger, drew a line. "I still like you."

He jerked away from her hand as if it had been a mosquito.

"I tell you the problem with Americans," she said. "They lack passion."

"My wife doesn't think so."

"I didn't mean *you*. You aren't American."

"Part of me is."

"I hope not *that* part."

"Enough, Olga. I don't have other women."

"No?"

"No."

"How sad for you." She dropped her sunglasses back into place, hiding her eyes. She went down the steps, then came back. "Maybe we can talk sometime. Just to talk."

Anthony looked over her head and rocked in his chair.

She said, "I have to tell you something, love. You should be careful when you visit José Leiva. They're watching him. They take pictures."

"I know, from the house across the street. They probably have some of me."

Olga came closer, holding her portfolio tightly to her chest. She wore a gold bracelet with a heart dangling from one link. In the center of the heart, a diamond so small that Anthony was stirred to feel sorry for her. When she was younger, her lovers had been more generous.

She said, "If they come to his house, and you're there with him, they could take you too. There are rumors about getting tough on the opposition. I speak sincerely."

"Thank you for the warning."

"Anyway, you can't trust Leiva. I lost the best job I ever had in television because of him."

"An old complaint. You should let it go, Olguita."

Her teeth caught her lower lip before she said, "Anthony, love . . . I need to talk to you. A big favor. Please."

He shook his head. "As you say, may this be a better year for all of us."

She looked at him a moment longer through her sunglasses before turning away. He watched her go, swaying on her high-heeled red sandals. She walked like her hips had been dipped in hot oil. Each half moved independently—the glorious backside of the Cuban female.

Halfway between the house and her car, she looked over her shoulder and laughed. "¡Oye!" In English she said, "If you change your mind, you know my phone number."

He could only grind his teeth and pray that Gail wasn't still standing at the upper window. He put the beer to his lips and drank.

In a cloud of diesel smoke, Olga's car turned the corner and was gone.

It was hard to say what Olga Saavedra knew, much less what she believed in, beyond her own survival. She seemed to be surviving well enough, despite her complaints about Cuba. Everyone complained about Cuba. He considered the warning she had passed on to him. The dissidents had become a constant, low-grade headache for the regime, but he didn't believe that José Leiva would be picked up and sent back to prison. He was known by the international press. They would start howling if the political police dragged him down to Villa Marista for nothing.

He heard the door open. His daughter came out and held onto the scroll of decorative metal on the porch support. She swung out over the edge.

"Hola, mi angelita."

"Dad, does your cell phone work in Cuba?"

"*No, m'ija, no funciona aquí en Cuba.*"

"Oh, God, please don't make me speak Spanish. My brain is exhausted. That's all Gio and Janelle speak. I *know* it would do me good to practice, but I can't right now."

He held out an arm, and she came over to stand next to him. "Are you having a good time, sweetheart? Do you like it here?"

"I guess so. Yes, it's all right." She gave him a hug. "Thank you for bringing me."

"What do you think of your cousins?"

"They're fine. I like them, but . . . Janelle is so immature for her age. I can't believe she's fifteen. She just giggles and hangs on to me. It gets very tiresome. Danny and Gio are hitting it off great." Her beautiful, soft brown eyes went to his. "Papi, do you think I could use Tía Marta's phone to call the U.S.? I would pay for it."

"You want to call Bobby," he guessed.

"Please?"

"All right. I'll ask Marta for you. Don't worry about the cost. I'll pay for it."

"Thank you, papi." She put her head on his chest.

He smoothed her silken hair. "Angelita, life is long, and there are many opportunities, many adventures ahead of you. The Miami City Ballet isn't the only company in the world—"

"I don't want to talk about it."

"All right. Where is your brother?"

"He's with Giovany playing Nintendo. It's not even a new game."

"Danny comes to Havana to play Nintendo?" Anthony considered finding him, forcing him to come downstairs and behave as though he had a family.

The front door banged open, and Marta came out lighting a cigarette, which bounced on her lips as she said, "*¿Ya se fue esa chusma?*" Asking if the cheap slut was gone. Marta saw Angela and raised her hands to her brow. "*Ay, perdóname.*" She grabbed Angela and kissed her and apologized for not having noticed her before.

"I'm sorry, oh my God, what language, how terrible." She dropped her lighter back into her purse. "I thought you were with

Jani. Your papi and I, we'll be back soon. We're going to go get your grandfather." She put on her sunglasses.

Angela made a tentative smile. "May I come with you?"

Anthony took her hand. "You don't mind, do you, Marta?"

"Sure, sure, honey, you come too. Let's go, *apúrense*. Anthony, close the gate behind us, eh?"

Above them at the window in Gio's room, Danny watched the blue Lada back into the turnaround, kick up gravel, and head for the street. His father shut the gate, then got in the car, and they took off. He had a beer in his hand. He would never—not ever—do that at home.

Where is your brother?

Right up here, listening to every word you say.

With Giovany playing Nintendo.

Angela was such a suck-up.

She got to go with them to pick up their grandfather, but observe this: Nobody had asked Danny if he wanted to go, did they? It would have been nice. He could have seen where his grandfather lived, a hero of the Revolution, Luis Quintana Rodríguez. The other old men would have looked up from their dominos and asked each other, *Who is that young man?*

My friends, allow me to introduce my grandson from America, Luis Daniel Quintana. He was named after me.

"Luis." He spoke his own name aloud, then said it again, pronouncing his name as his grandfather would, the accent on the last syllables. "Luís Daniel. Luís . . . Daniel." All his life he had Americanized it. *Loo-is Dan*iel. It had been all right back in New Jersey, but here in Cuba, it sounded stupid.

Resuming his seat on the windowsill, Danny flipped his cigarette butt to the porch roof. The car went down the street and around the corner. Earlier he had seen the van leaving to pick up General Vega. He had seen the black Mercedes come and go with the blond woman in it. The general's driver had laughed at her. What was the deal with them?

Olga. Olguita.

She'd been down there on the porch with his father. They'd

been talking in Spanish, so Danny had missed most of it, but he knew one thing: His father had fucked Olguita. Maybe that's why he came to Cuba twice a year. Danny had watched her walk to her car. Her skirt was so short he saw her panties when she parted her legs to get in.

Before coming here, Danny had researched Havana on the Internet and found some clubs he wanted to check out. Gio was going to take him around, tonight if they could get away. Danny wanted to see if it was true, what they said about the women, how hot they were. They liked Americans, and they would do anything if you bought them some shoes or a dress and took them dancing.

Havana was amazing. The beer cost a dollar on the street, and the parties went on all night.

6

The late-afternoon sun threw an elongated image of the clay flowerpot onto the wall. Faded yellow wall, red flower, purple shadow. The bright colors had caught Mario's attention. An ant crawled along a crack in the pot, which was very old, green with moss.

Mario was aware that his mother was still looking at him. The pressure of her gaze was so intense he could feel his cheeks growing warm. A few minutes ago, when he had walked up the steps of the retirement home, she had stared at him wide-eyed, as if blinking might cause him to vanish. Then she had carefully set her broom against one of the columns and embraced him.

Mario asked her if he could speak to the old man, but she gave him no answer.

"Do you know that your father and I haven't seen you for nearly six months? *Six months.*"

"Well . . . don't I call you? I have called many times."

She shook her head. "Mario. What are you doing with yourself? Look how thin you are."

"No, no, you're always saying that. I'm eating. I'm doing okay."

His mother smelled of violets. There was always a bottle of cologne on her dresser. He had bought her some the last time he'd been home. She wasn't old, but her hair had been gray for a long time. Today it was tied back under a blue bandana. Over her shirt and slacks she wore an ugly smock with her first name on a plastic tag. She could have been a doctor, but she worked as a nurse in this place, changing diapers and sweeping the floors. Mario wanted to take the broom and ram it through every window in the building.

Behind her a row of old men sat in their rocking chairs watching the world, which consisted of a view of B Street and the houses on the other side. Under a tree by the sidewalk, four of them played cards at a folding table. They had put on their sweaters. By sunset it would be cool again.

Mario said, "I've been out of town a lot, playing with the band. We played at a club in Matanzas. I bought some new clothes. You see?" The word *bought* was close enough. A German girl had bought him the jeans and T-shirt at the Benetton in Varadero Beach after they had spent the day swimming.

"I see," his mother said. "And now you're back. Where are you staying? Not on the street again. Mario, I couldn't bear it."

"No, mami." He laughed. "I'm staying with a friend of mine on Oquendo."

"You could come home. We have room for you, my dear heart. Always."

"I know, but I like to have my own place. Do you know what? They have roof access. They raise chickens up there. We traded one last week for some gasoline and drove to the beach. But now my friend is gone for awhile, and he won't need his car, so. . . ." Mario shifted his weight and slid his hands into the back pockets of his jeans. "May I talk to Luis Quintana?"

"I'm not in such a hurry to give you up." Smiling, his mother put her arm through his and led him to the railing. They sat on it with the sun on their backs. "Guess who arrived today from Miami. Luis's son, Anthony. You remember him, don't you? He always asks about you. 'How is Mario?' 'What is he doing lately?' I have had so little to tell him these past months, but here you are. Today! God must have been listening to me, don't you think so? Anthony brought his family with him. He's married now—to an American. They're coming to our house for dinner tomorrow. They want to meet you. Mario, please come."

"We're practicing every night this week, but . . . I'll try to come."

She looked at him closely, shifting her eyes on his. She had beautiful eyes, brown touched with flecks of green. He saw with dismay the shadows on her cheeks. Had she looked so exhausted six months ago?

"Mario, tell me the truth. Have José and I done something to offend you?"

"What? No, mami. Don't say that."

"Are you afraid to come to our house? Is that it? José asks me every day where you are. What can I tell him? He's sure you're staying away because of him."

"That's not true. Not at all. Tell José that I send my respects. Tell him I'm sorry, I've been busy. I promise I'll come when I can." Mario took his mother's hand. "Please, may I speak to Señor Quintana?"

Her eyes lingered on his. Then she stood up and straightened her smock. "I'll take you to him."

One of the heavy entrance doors was open for the breeze. The house, which was of considerable size, had been owned by a single family before the Revolution. Now it was occupied by fifty veterans and used by the government as an example: how we care for our elders. Photographs had been taken, articles written. Inside, the tile floor shone from a recent mopping. Sofas and chairs were placed in groups around low tables. A double staircase with an ornamental railing led to the rooms upstairs—but only one side was usable. The other side had been roped off for repairs as long as Mario could remember. His mother had said they received enough food and basic supplies, but for anything else, they had to rely on the families. Clothing, bath soap and toiletries, aspirin and cough syrup, a TV for the game room. Relatives on the outside sent money.

The old men here were lucky. Mario had seen others who weren't. He and Nico had borrowed a car to drive south to San Antonio de los Baños to visit Nico's grandparents a couple of weeks ago, coincidentally the day of the pilgrimage to the church of San Lázaro. They had been stuck in the river of cars, horse carts, and people. Crippled men on homemade crutches, old women with their hands out for coins, blind children. Nico, whom Mario had always thought a cynic, had pulled into the parking lot and bought some candles for his brother. They fought their way through the crowds to get into the church. In an alcove to the Virgin, Nico lit his candles. He started crying, then saying to the people around him, *My brother is dead. He died in prison. For nothing. He said "Down with Fidel" in a parade, and they gave him ten years. Ten years!* Mario dragged Nico away. *Crazy,* he had told the people staring at them. *He's crazy. Mental problems.*

Mario followed his mother to a large room in the back where a man dozed in a chair at the window. He had probably placed it there to catch the afternoon sun, but the light had shifted. A soft breeze came through. He was bald on top. His chest was like a barrel, and his muscular right arm, with its curly gray hair, lay on the armrest. The other was a stump hidden under the sleeve of his blue cotton shirt. He had lost the arm fighting counterrevolutionaries sent by the CIA. Mario had heard the story many times.

Mario's mother bent over and spoke softly to him. "Luis? Wake up, love. My son is here. Look. It's Mario."

The old man's eyes came open. One was clouded, the other fully dilated, a pool of black. Through the clouds he could see shapes and color. He smacked his lips and dragged a hand across his mouth. "Mario. Where?"

"Right here, sir." He took Luis Quintana's arm and helped him sit up straight.

"Where the hell have you been, boy?"

"Out of town, playing with the band." Mario found a chair and sat facing him. "How is your health? My mother takes good care of you, does she?"

"She's a good girl. If she wasn't hooked up already, I'd marry her." He patted her hip.

"Señor Quintana, I have a favor to ask of you."

"What is it? I don't have any money."

"No, no, I want to be your chauffeur, to take you to your daughter's house and to bring you home. Your family could pay me a little if they want to. I would do it for the experience. If I get some customers, I can apply for a license. You see, I'd like to get into the tourist sector."

"Jesus, don't they all? What about your band? Not many jobs for long-hairs, eh?"

"Not so many."

"But enough to afford gasoline. Where'd you get a car?"

"It belongs to a friend, but he's on a three-month visa to visit his family in the U.S."

"Ahhh, going to La Yuma. He'll come back fat and lazy, you watch."

"What do you think of my suggestion, sir? May I be your driver?"

"It's all right with me. My daughter drives me now, but she talks too much. Ya-ya-ya-ya. Makes me crazy. Don't marry a woman who talks too much. If she doesn't come, then she sends the man who works for them. Cobo. He never says anything, which is just as bad. Yoli, honey, go get us some coffee."

She hesitated. "I'll try to sneak it past the cook. You know we're a little short of coffee."

The old man waved her on. She walked toward the hall but stopped so suddenly that Mario thought she had tripped. She backed up to let three people come in. Mario recognized the woman in front: Señora de Vega, the wife of the general. His skin tightened, raising the hair on his arms. He stood and moved out of the way.

The man in the group smiled at Mario's mother and kissed her cheek, then looked across the room. It had been a long time since Mario had seen him. Anthony Quintana looked no different, except for a little gray in his hair. He was tall and slender, dressed in ordinary brown pants and a knit shirt. His leather belt with the polished buckle gave him away. You could always tell the exiles from the real Cubans.

There was a girl with him who might have been fourteen. His daughter, who else? She was wearing a short skirt, and he could see the muscles in her legs. He remembered Luis Quintana telling him his granddaughter was a ballerina. Yes. There was a picture of this girl in a tutu in his room.

They came over to the old man. Mario watched Señora de Vega. If she was in a good mood, she might grant his request. He smiled at her but she walked past him and opened her arms to her father.

"Papi! Look who I've brought you!"

The family embraced each other. He heard the girl's name. Angela. The old man pulled her closer, exploring her face. His thick, callused fingers couldn't see what Mario saw: her straight teeth, the gold barrettes holding back her hair, the small crucifix on a narrow chain. The sleeves of her pink sweater were pushed to her elbows. Such slender white arms. This girl was not from here, anyone could see that.

Anthony Quintana said, "Mario! Don't you remember me?"

Mario looked around. "Yes! It's good to see you again, sir." He held out his hand.

"Come here." They embraced quickly, and Mario felt several firm pats on his back. He smelled the cleanliness of Anthony Quintana's clothing, the cologne on his skin. "What is this?" The beads at the ends of Mario's braids clicked through his fingers. He laughed. "No, I like it. It suits you. How old are you now, Mario? Forgive me. Time passes so quickly."

"I was twenty last month, sir."

"Imagine that. Please, call me Anthony, not 'sir.' We should greet each other as men. Let me introduce my daughter, Angela. Sweetheart, come over here."

Her hand was cool and delicate, but it closed around his fingers with surprising strength. "I am very pleased to meet you." She had an American accent. Mario was aware that her father was talking about other people. Danny. Gail. People he would meet soon. The girl's eyes were the color of milk chocolate. They moved over his face. "My father says you're a musician?"

"A flautist."

She didn't understand. He held his hands to one side and moved his fingers. "Flute."

"Oh." She smiled. "Flute." He revised upward his estimate of her age. Eighteen?

Just in time Mario heard the general's wife say, "Papi, get up. Come on. Are those pants clean? Why didn't you wear the new ones I bought you?"

He growled, "How the hell am I supposed to know the difference?"

"Let's go. Everybody's waiting for us at the house."

"Excuse me," Mario murmured. He went over to greet the general's wife. "Good afternoon, Señora de Vega. May I speak with you?"

She crossed her arms over her stomach. Her mouth was colorless and tight. "Be quick. We're in a hurry."

Everyone was watching. Mario's words tumbled out. "I have a request, in honor of your father, Luis Quintana Rodríguez, whom I respect and admire and have come to know in friendship. I would like to become his driver, to do him—and your family—the honor of taking him to and from your house. You're a very busy

woman, and . . . I believe this would help you. I have talked with
your father about it, and he said yes. He wants me to ask your ap-
proval . . . as a courtesy. I could start today. Or tomorrow, if you
wish."

The general's wife looked at her father. "His driver? He doesn't
need a driver."

"Yes, but we have talked, Señor Quintana and I, and he said it
would be agreeable to him."

She said, "Thank you, but no. We can manage."

"You don't have to pay me much—or anything. I would do it
for the experience. Out of respect for your father . . . who is a hero
of our nation."

She raised a brow.

Anthony Quintana said, "Why not, Marta? It would save you
the trouble."

But she was already pulling on her father's arm. "It's no trouble. I like coming here. Papi, love, put on your sweater."

He jerked away from her. "I can do it."

Mario's mother handed him his cane. "We'll see you tomorrow,
Luis."

"Thanks, beautiful." He straightened with dignity. "All right.
Where's that pretty granddaughter of mine? Angela!"

Anthony Quintana sent Mario a slight smile and a shrug. He let
his family go out the door first. "My sister likes to take care of our
father herself. She has nothing against you."

That was a lie. They all knew it.

Mario hid his frustration behind a smile. "It's all right."

"So . . . you are well, Mario?"

"I am, thank you, sir."

"We must see each other again," Anthony said. "I have something for you, but not knowing you would be here, I didn't bring it
with me."

His mother put her arm around him. "Mario is coming to dinner tomorrow. I told him about your marriage. He wants to meet
your wife. Don't you, Mario?"

"You will like her," said Anthony. "I am sure you will. She is
very American, but curious about everything Cuban."

"José and I will love her as we love you. We'll make a party to
celebrate."

"You needn't do that, Yoli."

"But we want to. It's a special occasion."

"All right, but allow us to bring some food. Steak. Would you like that?"

"No, no, no, Anthony, my dear, really, there's enough. We have some fish. Does your wife like pargo?"

"I'm sure she does, but . . . let us bring something. Some bread. Wine. Tell me."

"If you want to." Mario's mother smiled and lifted a shoulder. "A bottle of wine."

"Red or white? No, I'll bring both. And some Scotch for José."

"You will spoil us completely!"

Mario looked from one of them to the other. They seemed to have forgotten he was there.

His mother was saying, "Oh, there are flowers in our yard just now, carnations. I'll bring them inside for the table. Everything will be so festive, you'll see. José wants to give you a book, some essays he wrote."

"I would be honored," Anthony said.

Then she turned to Mario and took his face in her hands. She was happy. Her eyes were shining. "Well? Will you come? My darling one?"

He said, "I have nothing to bring as a wedding gift."

"There's nothing we need," Anthony Quintana said. "You. That's enough. Play your flute for us. I would like that very much. You will come, young man, or I will find you and thrash you." He took Mario in the crook of his arm and shook him. "You are not too old for this, are you?"

Mario laughed. "Stop. I'll be there!"

When Anthony left, Mario and his mother walked a little ways down the hall to see him out. The girl was waiting by the front door. She took her father's arm and they went onto the patio.

Mario knew what would come next.

She looked back at him over her shoulder.

There were benches in the park along Paseo de Martí. In the evening Mario would often find one that wasn't occupied, sit down, take out his flute, and play. People walking by would drop some money into his case, and when he had enough, he would buy dinner. He couldn't appear to be a beggar; the tourist police with their batons and gray uniforms were on every street corner in the old section. He always brought sheet music with him. He would politely say he was in the student orchestra at the University, and he was practicing. Sometimes the police told him to move on. Usually they left him alone.

Tonight he wasn't far from the Hotel Inglaterra. He had already collected four dollars and two pesos, not worthless *moneda nacional* but convertible pesos he could use as dollars. He was halfway through Lecuona's *Siboney* when he noticed that three women had stopped to listen. Tourists liked the old stuff. He wouldn't make as much playing his own compositions.

The women were whispering to each other. Mario picked out a word or two in French. One of them walked closer and smiled down at him.

He cut the tune short and lowered the flute to his lap. "Hey, mamita. You like Cuban music?"

She put a dollar in his case. "The music, very good."

"Thank you, beautiful," he said.

Her friends giggled.

The woman stood over him. He knew what she wanted: Where are you from, pretty lady? *D'où êtes vous, ma belle?* You French? Want to see the city with me? *Voulez-vous voir la cîté avec moi?* That was all he knew of the language. He would speak slowly to her in Spanish. She would understand. You want to have a party? We buy some rum, go dance? You pay for a taxi?

Her hair was very short, like blond fur. Skinny French woman in tight white pants with a food stain on the thigh. A black pullover that said ANTIGUA in fake diamonds.

Unfolding a ten-dollar bill, she sat beside him, and her hip touched his. "I like Cuban men." She slid the money down the neck of his T-shirt, and her fingernails scratched across his chest before she withdrew her hand.

He pulled the money out and looked at it. He tore it in half and let the pieces flutter to the ground. "Fuck off."

Her mouth opened, then a laugh came out. She cursed, shoved

him hard in the shoulder, then got up to find the pieces of the note. She said something to her friends, and they fell on each other laughing.

As they walked away Mario picked up his flute and fingered the keys. One of them was getting loose. The metal surface of the flute was scratched and discolored. He had been tempted many times to throw it over the sea wall. He thought that if he were standing on the Malecón this moment, he would do it. Pitch it into the darkness so far he wouldn't be able to see the splash.

Mario glanced around when someone sat on the other end of the bench. Tomás. He held a little cone of popcorn. He picked one out and tossed it into his mouth. The streetlamps outlined the wire frames of his glasses.

He chewed slowly. "You should have taken the money."

"It was only ten dollars, my friend. A woman like that, I want at least fifty." When Tomás stared at him, Mario smiled. "It's a joke, Tomasito."

"Was it?"

"Sure. Everyone gets screwed. The least I can do is set my own price."

Tomás shook some kernels into his palm. "Did you arrange things with the old man?"

"His daughter said no. She would rather pick him up herself. She doesn't want her family tainted by any connection to José Leiva."

"Ah. A problem," said Tomás.

"I can still get inside," Mario said. "I believe that I can. Quintana's son is here from Miami with his family. They're staying at Vega's house. I've known the son for a long time. He's a friend of my parents. If I go to the house to meet him, he'll let me in."

On his knee Tomás folded the cone into a flat square. "You're sure?"

"If not, then his daughter. Her name is Angela. I have a feeling about her. Yes, I think she would let me in."

"You and women. A talent I do not possess."

"Did you bring something for me?" Mario asked.

Tomás slid a bag across the bench. The bullets rattled as Mario dropped the bag into his flute case. He lowered the lid and the latches clicked shut.

"Contact me tomorrow, will you?" Tomás stood up.

"Tomás . . . I've been thinking. Maybe someone else should do it. I'm ready, don't worry about that, but I'm thinking what effect it would have, my doing it."

"Effect?"

"On José Leiva. On the movements that he's involved with. They would be suspected of helping me. It could be bad for them. Look, I'm not backing out, but we should consider these things."

Tomás looked along the avenue, and the trees shifted in the wind, sending shadows across the paving stones in the sidewalk. "The effect. I will tell you the effect. We show that we can cut the head off a snake. Listen. I hear things from Olga. The Ministry is talking about cracking down on the dissidents."

"Another rumor from Olga. Why do you trust her? She's not so smart, you know?"

"True, but she's useful, and I believe she's right about this. What I am telling you, my friend, is that they're going after the opposition whatever we do. Shall we cower like children for fear of what might happen? Think of Nico's brother, Carlos, who was our brother as well. They put our brother Carlos in prison for the crime of acting like a free man. The movement needs you, Mario. What you do will matter. The liberty of our people—"

"For the love of God, Tomás, will you shut up?"

Tomás blinked behind his glasses. "Raúl can't get close to him; you can. You're the only one who can."

Mario felt tired. Empty. "Yes. I'll do it."

"Good. I leave you to your flute, then. And don't be so quick to turn down the next tourist. Nobody said you had to starve."

7

Ramiro Vega sat on one side of the long dining table, knees apart, arms spread. He was a man who took up space, not because of his size, which was only average, but by the energy that surrounded him, radiating outward, throwing off sparks. His head was the shape of a melon, and his taut brown skin reflected the lights in the brass chandelier over the table. When he laughed, dimples appeared, and his cheeks would redden and push his eyes into two inverted smiles. His mustache was thick with gray wires, and his strong, square teeth flashed as brightly as a cloud hit by a bolt of sunlight.

He gulped his beer from the bottle, ate with both hands, and stood up to reach across the table for more. He speared fried plantains with his fork and poured beans directly from the bowl onto his rice. Unless one quickly said *no, gracias,* he might drop another chunk of roast pork on the plates of those who sat near him. He tucked a paper towel into the open collar of his short-sleeved plaid shirt, the same shirt that he had worn home from the Ministry. Gail had expected to see him in a uniform. She had expected to be half afraid of him.

The general was openly affectionate with his children. He had hugged Giovany and Janelle and kissed them before they had gone upstairs half an hour ago. They wanted to hear the music that Karen had put on her iPod. Anthony's kids had gone with them.

The older Vega daughter, Paula, and her new boyfriend, whose name Gail had already forgotten, sat at the far end of the table. Neither of them spoke any English. Their attention was on Paula's baby, who was ripping bread into pieces on the tray of an old wooden high chair. The boy's grandmother got up to brush the crumbs into her hand and complain about the mess on the floor. Gail had the feeling that Marta liked complaining. It showed who was in charge.

At first Gail had tried to keep up with the conversations in this boisterous family, which were almost entirely in Spanish. She had asked Anthony to fill in what she couldn't understand, but by then the Vegas were on to something else.

Ramiro grabbed his beer bottle in his fist. "Gail! Irene! Listen, I got a joke. It's complicated. I don't know how to say in English. Tony, help me out, okay?"

Gail and her mother waited while Ramiro took a swallow of beer and wiped the foam off his mustache. His black eyes sparkled, and dimples flickered in his round cheeks. *"Un tipo va al infierno—"*

Marta groaned. "Ramiro, please—"

"Un tipo va al infierno—"

Anthony translated: "A guy goes to hell, and he sees that every country has its own door. There is a hell for the Russians, a hell for the Chinese, a hell for the English, and so on. You have to pick a door. So first the guy goes to the American hell and asks what happens inside. The demon at the door says, 'Well, first they put you in an electric chair, then they put you on a bed of nails, and then they whip you with chains.' And the guy says, 'Oh, that's no good,' so he goes to the Japanese hell. He asks, 'What do they do to you in here?' "

Marta dumped the bread crumbs onto an empty plate. "My husband has the most stupid jokes."

Ramiro told her to be quiet. He resumed where he had left off. Anthony said, "The Japanese demon says, 'In here, they put you in an electric chair, then they put you on a bed of nails, and then they whip you with chains.' The guy thinks, 'That's exactly like the American hell.' So he goes to the other doors, and they're all the same. Then he sees a long line of people waiting to get into the Cuban hell, and he says to himself, '*Coño*, that's the place to be,' so he asks somebody in line, 'What do they do to you in here?' The man says, 'They put you in an electric chair, then they put you on a bed of nails, and then they whip you with chains.' 'But that's the same as every other hell. Why is everybody trying to get in?' 'Well, my friend, in the Cuban hell, the electricity is off, the nails have been stolen, and the guy with the whip comes to work, punches in, and then leaves.' "

"Haaaaahhhh!" Ramiro Vega slapped his hand on the table so hard the silverware bounced on the plates. He leaned back in his chair with his hand on his chest. "Oh, my God. I love it!"

Laughter echoed off the terrazzo floor of the dining room, and the boy in the high chair shrieked and pounded on the tray.

Gail had already heard the joke—it was a favorite among the exiles—but she laughed anyway, more from incredulity that a Cuban army general would tell it, much less tell it to Americans.

Her mother fanned her face. "That is hysterical!"

"Oh, sure," Marta said. "They're going to put him on a comedy show in Miami."

He wiped his eyes and let out a chuckle, then a sigh. "What's the matter, mamita?" As Marta walked by, Ramiro grabbed her around the waist and said something in Spanish.

Anthony translated. "He says Marta laughs at his jokes but not if there are guests in the house."

Marta told her husband to let her go, she wanted to clear the dishes. Ramiro gave her a one-armed hug and a slap on her backside. Gail started to get up with her own plate and Anthony's, but Marta told her to sit down.

At the other end of the table, Luis Quintana felt his way across the lace tablecloth until his fingers found the bottle of rum. He connected his glass with the mouth of the bottle and poured. He had barely spoken during dinner. Irene had tried with her phrase book to talk to him, but his Spanish was idiomatic beyond comprehension. Now and then he had asked Anthony to help him with his food, but otherwise he seemed content to lean on the stump of his left arm and become quietly drunk.

Gail noticed her mother hiding a yawn behind her napkin, the result of the wine or the hour. It was past ten o'clock.

Ramiro Vega leaned across the table. "Irene! What are the three most big success of the Revolution?"

Irene blinked and focused on Ramiro. "Me? I don't know."

He counted them off. "Education. Medical. And sports. What are the three . . . how you say, Tony?"

"Failures." Anthony had heard this one.

"Yes, yes, what are the three biggest failures?" Ramiro looked around at everyone. "Breakfast, lunch, and dinner!" He bellowed a laugh and clapped his hands together.

Marta stacked more plates. She said to Gail, "You see how we Cubans are. We laugh at our troubles. It's our national character. We're under siege, and we make jokes."

"Under siege?" Gail repeated.

"From the Americans," Marta said, as though three of them, including her brother, weren't sitting at her table. "Not you. I mean your government."

Gail was considering whether it would be rude to give her opinion, when Anthony said, "Marta, how about some coffee? And leave the politics in the kitchen, will you?"

Laughing at that, Ramiro went down the table to where his grandson sat in the high chair. He lifted the boy and tossed him in the air, babbling in nonsense verse and lifting his shirt to blow rude noises on his stomach.

Gail saw Anthony watching them. She could read his thoughts. How could Ramiro Vega possibly want to defect? To leave this house, this family? It was impossible. Anthony would return to Miami with bad news for Congressman Navarro and his mysterious friend from Washington.

A staccato click of heels came down the stairs in the living room. Janelle Vega swung around the railing at the bottom. She ran into the dining room wearing her new dress from the boutique in Coconut Grove. The dress was sleeveless, with a flounce at the bottom and a narrow waist. Too narrow. Gail saw with dismay that the buttons gaped, and the fabric rode up on her hips. The girl told everyone to look; wasn't it pretty? Her sister laughed, and Janelle told her to shut up.

Just then Marta came back with the tray of coffee. She set it on the table so she could look at the dress. She felt the fabric and tugged at the front. Gail guessed she was telling Janelle they could move the buttons over and let out the seams, and that Paula was saying no, *she* would take the dress because Janelle was too fat. Janelle's mouth turned down, wobbled, and opened in a cry of angry self-pity. The girls' father yelled at Paula, and their mother shouted at him to stop.

Gail murmured, "Oh, no. Anthony, I thought you told me the right size."

"I screwed up. How much did you pay for that?"

"Don't ask." Gail went to put an arm around Janelle, who was crying into a napkin. "Oh, Janelle, I'm so sorry. We'll buy you something else. We'll go shopping right here in Havana. Anthony, please tell her."

He did, and Marta said, "No, no, don't worry about it. You give this to Karen. She's small. Janelle has enough clothes."

Ramiro said, "Marta, it's her birthday. If Gail wants to buy a dress, okay."

The girl raised her reddened eyes to her mother. *"Sí, mami, por favor—"*

Another argument broke out. Marta not wanting Janelle to be spoiled; Janelle pointing to Paula's good clothes; Paula saying what the hell was wrong with looking nice? Ramiro stalking off to the kitchen for another beer, coming back with two, tossing one to Paula's boyfriend. Luis saying a woman had a right to wear a pretty dress.

Gail and her mother exchanged a look. Irene mouthed the words, *What is going on?*

Anthony motioned for Gail to lean closer. He said, "Tell her you'll take her to La Maison."

"What's that?"

"It's a store. Tell her."

Gail did, and Marta said no, they could go to the Carlos the Third shopping mall. That brought another sob from Janelle. Such terrible clothes there, everything so cheap and ugly. She wanted to go to La Maison.

Ramiro started yelling. Anthony said, "He's telling Marta to butt out, let Janelle go where she wants. You see, Gail, my sister doesn't think rich Americans should come in here and drop money on her kids. No, don't worry about it. She'll give in."

Gail slid back into her chair and whispered, "In about ten seconds I'm going to scream."

He shrugged and drank his wine.

It was decided: Gail could take Janelle to La Maison. Janelle threw her arms around Gail's neck and kissed her before running back across the living room, the sound of her pumps pounding, then diminishing, up the stone steps.

Ramiro said to Gail, "Thank you. You're very nice. My wife

don't want to spend money for Janelle, but she's making a big party. The biggest. I have to sell my teeth for this party."

Marta snatched empty serving bowls off the table. "He hired someone to do the party for us, and now he doesn't like it."

"No, no, it's a good party. My wife don't like who does it."

"Ramiro forgot this is a *quinceañera*. That woman will make it look like a show from the Tropicana if I let her. *Qué desgracia.*"

They switched to Spanish, talking about each other to their guests, throwing accusations like spit wads. Gail glanced at Anthony for some explanation. He made a slight smile and said, "You'll get used to it."

"Oh, really?"

Ramiro told his wife to go get the coffee. He stood up with the wine bottle and reached over to top off Gail's glass yet again, then her mother's and Anthony's. He began to relate an off-color story about someone in the army who had served in Angola and came back with an African wife and found her sacrificing chickens in the bedroom.

Irene wasn't following the translation. Gail saw her eyes drift along the narrow, horizontal pieces of stone on the opposite wall, an architectural touch from the 1950s. Hanging on this wall was a beveled mirror in a gold metal frame. Under the mirror was a chrome beverage cart, and in a German beer stein on the cart someone had planted a lace umbrella with blue roses. From Paula's baby shower?

Such utter bewilderment settled on Irene's face that Gail had to look away. She felt a bubble of laughter rising in her chest and bit her lips to hold it in. Her mother kicked her under the table. "*Shhh.*"

Gail cleared her throat and sipped some wine.

It wasn't the decor that threatened to knock her off balance; it was just being here. This wasn't her family, not her culture, not her city. It was Anthony's, not hers. And maybe not even Anthony's. She wasn't sure if he really *liked* staying in this house or could tolerate it because he wasn't stuck here. They would be back in Miami soon, living in their minimalist apartment with the leather sofas and blond wood floors.

She reached for his hand. He was still listening to Ramiro's joke, but his fingers automatically closed around hers, warm and strong. When she leaned against his shoulder, he disengaged his hand and put his arm around her. Before dinner he had taken her into their room and said he was sorry they had argued. He had kissed her and said he loved her. There had been no time to talk, but even if there had been, Gail wasn't sure she could have found the words for what she really wanted to ask: Why do you come here? Is it because you can be yourself in Havana? Who is that? Do you think of me the same way here as in Miami?

He would say: *Gail, what are you talking about?*

She wondered: Could love be true in one place and not another?

Marta came back with a battered *cafetera*. Holding a dish towel to catch the drips, she poured an ounce or two of coffee into each tiny, rose-decorated porcelain cup on the tray. She had put a plate of almond candy on the tray as well.

Gail wished she could apologize, but she wasn't sure for what. *Marta, I'm sorry for laughing at the umbrella. And for the missing toilet seat. You're a wonderful hostess.* Blinking to focus her vision, she put down her wineglass. She'd had too much of it already. Her head was starting to float.

A glow lit the windows across the front of the house. The glow became brighter, moved across the glass, then went out. A car, Gail thought. Someone had arrived. At the same moment she heard the front door open. Ramiro's driver appeared at the opening to the living room.

Interrupting himself in the middle of another story, Ramiro watched Cobo as he came around the table. Cobo leaned down and murmured in his ear. The family fell silent, and Marta turned her head toward the front of the house. She asked who was there.

"*Es García.*" Ramiro took his paper towel out of his shirt collar and laid it on the table. His back had straightened; his movements were quick and precise. He told Cobo to get the door.

Gail leaned closer to Anthony. "Who's García?"

Quietly he said, "General Abdel García. Very close to Fidel. I've heard about him, never met him."

Ramiro's grin returned. "He's my boss."

Luis Quintana roused himself from his fog and lifted his head, asking if it was true that General García was here. Here in this house? Marta told her father yes, yes, it was true, and be quiet. She brushed a hand across his shirtfront and straightened her hair.

Mumbling to himself, Luis found his glass and emptied it.

The door opened. Closed. The measured tap of General García's heels preceded him. His shoes gleamed. The olive-green uniform had knife-edge creases in the trousers and a rectangle of ribbons on the long-sleeved shirt. The collar was open. There were two stars on each shoulder. He held a green cloth cap, which he beat slowly into the other palm, a cadence that matched his stride. He stopped a few paces away from the table.

García was a man of medium height, mid-fifties, clean shaven, with clipped gray hair. His small black eyes glistened like onyx. He had an oddly shaped face, narrow at the brow, wide at the cheek-bones, which were high and sharp. There was something wrong with his jaw. His square, jutting chin was off center. When he slowly turned his head to look from one end of the table to the other, Gail saw a scar. It went from the underside of his chin to his left earlobe, which seemed to have melted to his face.

Chairs scraped the floor as the family stood. Paula put the baby on her hip. Anthony stood as well, but put a hand on Gail's shoulder, a signal to remain seated. Irene got up halfway, then slowly sat again.

Gail shivered; the temperature had fallen. Logic told her it wasn't because of this visitor. The sliding door was open to the terrace; the night air had come in. Even so, she was chilled. She detected, or imagined, as his tilted eyes passed over her, a predator's quick dismissal, as if she were a small animal not worth swallowing.

García spoke. An apology. He had just come from a meeting. It was so late. . . . This was followed by a murmuring among the family. Marta said it was a pleasure to see him again. Ramiro introduced everyone. Marta's cheeks were pink with pleasure. She asked General García if he had eaten. Would he like coffee?

The general declined with a slight wave of his hand and assurances that she was kind to inquire. His eyes moved toward Anthony. A smile lifted one corner of his mouth and sent his chin sideways. He spoke.

Gail understood most of Anthony's reply. *Here for my niece's birthday. My children . . . their first time in Havana.* When García spoke again, Anthony glanced at Ramiro, who nodded. Anthony said yes, if the general wished.

García made another off-center smile. He nodded rather formally to the women, turned, and went out. Ramiro went with him.

Irene whispered, "What was that about?"

Gail kept her eyes on Anthony. "What did he say to you?"

He pushed in his chair and for a moment tapped his fingers on the back of it. "General García wants to find out how I'm enjoying Cuba. We're going outside to talk about it. Maybe he'll offer to be our tour guide."

"I don't like this," she said.

He squeezed her shoulder. "It's all right. You stay here and have your coffee. I won't be long."

She got up. Walking as far as the living room, she saw Ramiro's driver holding the front door. Anthony went out. Cobo followed. Like snapping a photograph through the narrowing gap, Gail saw the men on the patio. A dark sedan in the driveway. At the gate, caught in the streetlight, a soldier standing guard.

Fighting back a little spurt of panic, Gail spun around and went over to Marta. "Where are they taking him?"

"They're not taking him anywhere. Abdel wants to meet him. It's an honor that he came to my house. Abdel García is an important man."

"Why does he want to meet Anthony?"

Resting the tray against her stomach, setting the cups on the table one by one, Marta didn't reply right away. Finally she said, "We are friends of Abdel, friends for many years. He came to Paula's wedding. He and my husband were in Angola together. They both received medals, and on the same day! Abdel has helped Ramiro in his career. He knows I have family in Miami. Who doesn't have family on the outside?"

She laughed, but to Gail it seemed thin and forced.

Paula held her cup without drinking. The boyfriend made a little cough into his fist and looked anywhere but at the American visitors.

Irene's blue eyes shifted to follow Marta around the table, then cut toward Gail before she said, "I suppose it must be hard for you, though, having a grandfather like Ernesto Pedrosa. I mean . . ." Irene hesitated. Marta was looking at her, one hand on her hip. "Well, I mean . . . you know how Mr. Pedrosa is, so completely . . . against what you and Ramiro believe in. It must be hard."

Luis Quintana laughed into his glass of rum. Apparently his English was better than he had pretended.

Marta shook her bronzed hair back from her face, which had gone blotchy and red. "I have nothing to do with Pedrosa or with any of those people. The Miami Mafia! They want to destroy us, to come back and take everything. My grandfather is part of that. He hates me. All of them do. That's all right. I don't give a damn for them. My brother is different. He's for us, for Cuba."

Gail had to reply. "Marta, I don't think he's on anyone's side, particularly."

Marta raised her chin. "Then you don't know him."

Silence followed this outburst.

Biting the inside of her cheek to keep from blurting out the first ill-considered retort that came to mind, Gail turned the espresso cup in its saucer and counted the roses on the rim. She wondered how fast they could get out of here. How early in the morning they could be on a flight to Mexico. Whether Anthony would agree to leave. Of course he wouldn't agree. He loved it here.

"Oh, Gail, I am sorry." Marta pulled out Anthony's chair and put her arms around Gail's neck. "Don't worry how I talk." Gail smelled the kitchen odors in her hair, the alcohol on her breath, and realized that Marta was more than a little drunk.

"It's not easy for us. Nothing is easy. For my husband, I'm walking on a rope . . . like the circus. A wire. I walk on a wire." She kissed Gail on both cheeks. "*Te quiero*. I love you, my sister. I'm happy you came. This is your house. Okay? Don't be mad at me."

Gail said, "I'm not. Really."

Marta reached across Gail to take Irene's hand. "I love you too."

"You're so sweet to say that. Let me help clear the table," Irene said. "No, I mean it, I want to help." What her mother wanted, Gail thought, was to be done with dinner and escape to her room.

Marta told Paula to get up and help. She took the bottle of rum from her father and said he'd had enough. She set the plate of almond candy in front of Gail. "Here, take a piece of the *turrón*. I bought it for you. It's from Spain, the best."

Gail bit into a small slice. Her mouth was so dry she could hardly swallow. She got up and went into the living room, stopping at the bottom of the stairs. An overhead lamp gleamed on the curve of the brushed aluminum balustrade. Gail looked through the windows, whose louvers were tilted open for the breeze. From this angle only the roof of the car was visible, but she didn't want to walk closer and risk being seen.

The wind shifted the shadow of a tree on the glass. She felt her body trembling.

8

Halfway across the yard, the branches of a tree extended over the walkway, dimming the light from the front patio. García stopped beside a poured-concrete bench and reached into a lower pocket of his shirt for a pack of cigarettes. He extended the pack toward Anthony. Camels, unfiltered.

"No, thanks."

A soldier stood by the gate. The streetlamp put a sheen on smooth black leather: a holster, a pair of boots. A second man leaned against the car. Cobo had walked out of sight in the direction of the garage.

If Ramiro knew what was going on, he didn't show it.

The cigarette lighter clicked and flared inside the curve of García's hand. Anthony smelled fluid before the breeze took it away. The glow at the end of the cigarette increased, then dimmed. Looking at Anthony, García exhaled to one side.

It was almost comical. The theatrics of it, standing out here in the dark, a couple of armed goons to impress him. Anthony waited to see what García had in mind.

"You have a beautiful wife. May I say that? Blond. Tall like a Swede." Abdel García compensated for his ruined jaw with slow and precise pronunciation. "Gail Ann Connor. A lawyer. Age thirty-six, born in Miami. One child."

Anthony felt the first push of unease.

The orange dot of the cigarette doubled in García's *chino* eyes when he brought it to his lips. "What does your wife think of Cuba?"

"After eight hours? I don't know. Maybe she needs a little more information."

The general daintily touched a knuckle to the left corner of his mouth. Moisture had leaked out onto his lip. "We will talk, but not now. Perhaps tomorrow." He tilted his angular head toward Ramiro. "You must tell Marta I am sorry for disturbing the family."

"It's all right. Marta is used to my leaving in the middle of dinner."

Anthony asked, "Could I know what this is about?"

"Of course. I am curious about you. Vega told me a little, but I wanted to see you face-to-face. You were taken away from your home, from your father, when you were very young, and by trickery, I understand. You grew to manhood on the other side. Most people don't come back, or not so frequently. I believe that you love Cuba. This is true, no?"

"True that I love this country, but my feelings don't extend to the regime."

"An honest answer." García turned to Ramiro to see his response. There was none. García smoked his cigarette. He said, "There is a park on Águila and Reina, near the Capitol. What would you say to meeting me at three o'clock in the afternoon tomorrow?"

"I think my schedule is full."

"Come on, Quintana, I'm not going to interrogate you. Consider it a conversation between friends. Or informal diplomacy, if you prefer."

"With regrets, general, I must decline."

Garcia blotted the corner of his mouth. "You should reconsider. If not, you and your family will be put on the first charter flight back to Miami. Directly, not through Cancún. You can explain to your State Department why you were in Cuba. Maybe you came to visit your family, maybe for other reasons. We could give them reasons."

Anthony glanced at Ramiro, whose face told him nothing. He said, "I'll let you know in the morning."

"No. You tell me now. Tomorrow at three o'clock in the afternoon I want to see you standing in the park on Reina and Águila."

"And then?"

"We'll walk to a place nearby, we'll sit down, we'll have a drink, and we'll talk." Abdel García spread his hands, showing how simple it would be.

"See you at three o'clock," Anthony said.

"Good night, then. General Vega, my apologies again to your wife."

He turned and crossed the yard to his car. The driver opened the back door for him. They picked up the other man at the gate, and ten seconds later the sound of the engine had faded away.

Ramiro said, "Don't ask me, because I don't know."

They looked at each other in the dark. Anthony said, "You have some idea."

"None. Maybe you do."

Anthony could feel Ramiro's distrust. "I'll let you know what your boss wants as soon as he tells me. Should I worry about it?"

"You're my brother-in-law."

"That isn't much assurance."

"Okay. I give you my word. You talk to Abdel, nothing will happen to you." Ramiro's eyes remained on him. "What are you doing here, Tony?"

"The CIA asked me to spy on your kid's *quinceañera*. They want to know if Olga Saavedra should be recruited to work for the White House."

That brought a laugh. "Olga. I regret getting her involved in that fucking birthday party."

"Why did you?"

"She asked me. Mother of God, you better not mention her name around here. Marta has good ears, that's the problem. She hears things that aren't there." Ramiro turned toward the house. "Come on, let's go."

"Are you sleeping with Olga?"

"Ayyy. Don't say that." Ramiro raised both hands. "I give her jobs here and there, so what? After this party is over, that's it. No more. I love your sister, but she's driving me crazy. Olga this, Olga that. I should arrange an embassy job in the Middle East. Put her someplace where she can't shake her ass."

"Even wearing a black bag, Olga would be noticed," Anthony said.

"Very true!" Stopping at the steps to the patio, Ramiro said quietly, "What are you going to tell your wife?"

"About what?"

"She'll ask you what Abdel wanted."

"I don't know. I'll tell her something." Anthony had already decided that he would give Gail enough of the truth to satisfy her curiosity, but not so much that she would worry and demand that they leave. Anthony still had a message to convey to Ramiro.

He wondered if Abdel García knew about that. The agents of State Security were good at their job. They had been trained by the best—the KGB. The man who defected to the Americans in São Paulo could be a double agent. He might have been planted by Cuban intelligence. If so, Ramiro was in even worse danger.

"You coming in, or are you staying out here to admire the stars?" Ramiro had gone up the steps.

Anthony went up after him. "Tomorrow night Gail and I are having dinner with friends, but afterward, you and I should go out."

"Why?"

"I'll buy you a drink. We'll talk."

"About what?"

"We should do that," Anthony said.

They stood in the lights of the patio. A slight movement of Ramiro's head toward the house showed he was aware that they could be overheard. "Okay. Tomorrow night." His mustache widened with his grin. "We'll leave the women here and enjoy ourselves for a change."

9

T he sheer white curtains belled inward, rotated, and fell back, and filled again and turned and fell as the cord knocked lightly, rhythmically against the metal frame of the door. It was as hypnotic as watching the sea. Beyond the curtains was the balcony railing, then the empty rectangle of black sky.

Anthony Quintana was sitting up in bed smoking a small cigar, the sheet to his waist. His left hand rested on his wife's bare shoulder. The faint glow of city lights fell on a table and four chairs, a television, a long dresser, and two king-sized beds. A big room. It had cost him one hundred twenty dollars cash, his American credit cards being worthless in Cuba.

He had asked his sister for the use of her car: He and Gail wanted to go out for a drink, and if it got late, they might check into a hotel. He had driven directly to the Habana Libre and handed the keys to the valet. On the way, he had told Gail about the conversation with Abdel García. There wasn't much. He didn't know what García wanted, but he would try to find out before tomorrow.

Downstairs in the lobby bar they had ordered a couple of club sodas, Gail staring at the fully decorated, twenty-foot Christmas tree in the atrium. For the tourists, he had told her. Likewise the leftover carols on the sound system, "Good King Wenceslas," "Silent Night." And the young women, such as the *negrita* at the next table in low-cut jeans and a denim jacket with silver studs down the front. Across from her, a besotted, white-haired Italian stroking her hand.

Leaving Gail in the bar, Anthony had walked across the marble floor to a room near the reception desk. He gave the girl a number in Miami and went into a booth. When the phone rang, Hector Mesa was on the other end. They spoke without using names anyone would have recognized. Anthony told him to call Room 1208 when he had some answers.

Now he was waiting to see what Hector came up with. Hector had a long list of people who owed him favors. There were others who might talk because they were afraid of him.

A puff of wind slid through the curtains and reached the bed. Gail moved closer and put her leg across his thighs. Anthony set his cigar in the ashtray and pulled the blanket around her shoulders. Even in the near-darkness he could pick out the gleam of gold in her hair. He curled a strand of it around his finger, like warm silk. Her body was not what he had ever thought he would want in a woman. Too thin, too small-breasted. But completely beautiful. Her skin was the softest he had ever touched. He could get drunk on the scent of her.

Disturbed from her sleep, she raised up on an elbow and murmured, "What time is it?"

"About two-thirty."

"Nothing from Hector?"

"Not yet."

"Do you think somebody intercepted the call?"

Anthony laughed softly. "They aren't listening on every line, sweetheart. Hector is taking his time. This hour of the night, his friends won't be too eager to get out of bed."

She scooted up until her head rested on his chest. Her voice was a warm touch on his skin. "Ramiro won't leave here, you know. I think Marta would kill him. She's such a dedicated socialist. Do you mind if I say that?"

"It's true."

"The system isn't working. Ramiro makes jokes about it. But Marta says it's great. Does she really believe that?"

"Absolutely. People don't like giving up illusions they've spent their entire lives creating. I used to sing the same song when I was a child. Oh, you would have loved me in my little Pioneer uniform, so cute. We all believed in heroes in those days. In magic. In the perfectability of man, which is even more fantastical."

"You're still cute." Gail made small circles on his chest with her fingernails.

"We have no gods anymore," Anthony said. "That's why people wanted the Cuban experiment to succeed. It was a rebuke to the idea that life can be boiled down to how much you own, and that owning is a measure of meaning."

"What's with all the philosophy tonight?"

He took a final pull on his cigar before snuffing the ember. He sent the smoke upward. "Havana does that to me."

"Politics and religion," said Gail. "It's all the same."

"Not really. Politics is easier to believe in because it doesn't seem as irrational. You don't feel naïve saying you're a socialist, you feel proud of yourself. I am talking about here in Cuba, of course, or anywhere you want to spit in Uncle Sam's eye. That's what makes Fidel a hero—he stands up to Washington. It's not his fault Cuba is poor, it's our fault. We're evil. We want to destroy Cuba because we can't have it. There are those who would die believing that."

"Marta isn't *that* extreme, surely."

"I doubt it." Anthony smiled. "She has a household to run. Dying is for young men and crackpots."

Gail's laughter tickled the hairs on his chest. "Oh, dear. We're such a corrupting influence. You know this, right? Bringing them all that stuff from Macy's. Promising to take Janelle to La Maison. Did you know that Gio likes hip-hop? Your son brought him about a dozen CDs, according to Karen, my chief spy. Eminem, Outkast—capitalist poison."

Anthony laughed too. "There isn't one Cuban kid who doesn't think the system is crap. They all want to go abroad to study. Paula would have, but she got pregnant. They are complete realists, these kids, on *both* sides of the water." He added, "But it's sad, you know? When I was Danny's age, I felt that I had a purpose."

Sitting up, Gail raised her knees and brought the blanket to her chin. "Marta said something funny tonight. I mean funny *weird*, not ha-ha. She said she was walking on a tightwire for Ramiro. What does that mean?"

Anthony thought about it. "I don't know. What else did she say?"

"Well, after my mother happened to mention Ernesto, Marta said she didn't have anything to do with *those people*, the Miami

Mafia, and so on, but she didn't include *you* in that group. She says you're on her side. Or for Cuba, which is the same thing."

"Marta creates her own reality," he said.

Gail shifted a little so she could see him in the vague light from the doors. "Really, Anthony, you're such a chameleon, aren't you? Abdel García doesn't know where you stand, either. He wants to find out, doesn't he?"

"I'm not on his side," Anthony said. "General García is out for himself. If not for the Revolution, he would be a provincial cop. And Ramiro would own Coca-Cola of Cuba. He's a capitalist at heart, if only he knew it."

"I guess Marta was embarrassed," Gail said. "Her husband's boss showed up, and there she was, caught in the act, entertaining a bunch of Americans in her house."

"We're not Americans, we're family." Extending an arm, Anthony felt around on the nightstand for his watch. Two forty-five. What had become of Hector? Had there been someone at the telephone desk who had recognized the name Anthony Quintana? And then called the security officer at the hotel? There was always someone on the staff with a connection to the political police—

He heard Gail halfway into one of her questions.

"—just an observation, the way they were talking about her. I don't mean to insult your brother-in-law or anything, but don't you sort of wonder what's going on there?"

Anthony said, "Going on?"

"She's sexy, she works for him, and Marta is jealous." Gail waited, then said, "Haven't you thought of that?"

"You're referring to Olga Saavedra?"

"That's what I just said. You weren't listening?"

He moved farther up on the pillows. "They're not having an affair."

"How do you know?"

"I asked him. He said no."

"See? You did think of it. Well, he's not going to tell *you*, is he? His wife's brother?"

"Gail, if he says no, that's where I'll leave it."

"Fine, then. I was just wondering." She stared at the ceiling. "Do you think this room might have a listening device?"

"MININT doesn't have the resources to bug every hotel room in Havana."

"Who? Minute?"

"MIN-INT. The Ministry of the Interior. State Security."

"This creeps me out," Gail said. "Like we're playing spies. They're following us, and the phones are tapped. God, it is *freezing* in here. Did you turn into an Eskimo?" She got out of bed and threw on the terry cloth hotel robe she'd left over a chair.

"No, I'm a hot Cuban," he said.

"You certainly are. I've got burn marks all over." On her way across the room, she turned around and walked backward, touching her hip, her breast. "Here and here. And here. Ouch." As she slid the glass door shut, the robe slipped from her shoulder, and she caught the front of the voluminous thing in one hand.

"I like you better in nothing," Anthony said.

Glancing over her shoulder, she opened the robe like wings, then let it slide down her back, down to the cleavage of her buttocks. "Is that far enough?"

"All the way off," he said.

The robe dropped to the floor, and her body was a dark curve against the window. Where the thin white curtains came together, she grabbed the edges and flung her arms out. "Here I am, Havana."

"Gail, don't do that."

"Why? We're twelve floors up. Nobody's looking. I thought people were supposed to go wild in this city, all the sex and salsa and rum. But if you ask me, Havana just looks kind of shabby and sad. Except for those women in the lobby with the European guys. What do you call them? I forgot."

"*Jinetera*. It's from the word for jockey."

"Oh, I get it. Bring on the whip." Gail stood in the gap between the curtains. The faint wash of light turned her body into a living white-marble statue. Her breasts were outlined by darkness, and a small V of light shone between her legs. "Havana," she murmured, then bent to pick up the robe.

"Leave it off," he said. "I like looking at you."

She hooked the robe by one finger over her shoulder. "If I were that girl downstairs, how much would you pay for me?"

"Nothing."

"*Nothing?*"

"You want me too much. You couldn't stop yourself."

"Well, that's true."

"Come here."

The curtains swung slowly together, and Gail crossed the room. When she reached the bed she lifted the sheet and crawled under it completely. Her hands on his body were like ice cubes.

He doubled over, reaching for his groin. "*¡Ay, qué frías las manos!*"

Her mouth was a flood of heat.

The telephone rang at half past three, pulling him out of a dream that vanished like smoke the moment he opened his eyes. He reached for the handset. Hector's voice could have been coming from the next room. "*Llámame de afuera.*"

When Anthony swung his legs off the bed, Gail asked him where he was going.

"Hector wants me to call him from outside. Stay here. I won't be gone long."

He turned on a light. She got up with him and went to the dresser, where she had laid her clothes. She said she had to get dressed. She couldn't lie naked in a hotel room while he went God only knew where.

"A few blocks down the street," he said. "There are some pay phones across from the park. I won't be long. Wait for me."

He took an elevator down and walked past the plainclothes security guard, who stood at the entrance to the elevator bank with a walkie-talkie.

Instead of going out the front entrance, Anthony cut across the lobby and into the restaurant, brightly lit and open twenty-four hours. He walked through and pushed open the glass door. The crowds were still heavy, and would be until dawn, but the marquee of the Yara theater was dark. The movie was *Spider-Man*, probably bootlegged.

Walking down the hill toward the Malecón, he zipped up his jacket to keep the wind out. A young *mulata* in tight pants and a blond wig walked alongside for a few paces, until he shook his head. She shrugged, and he noticed her big hands and narrow hips. A transvestite.

Anthony crossed the street, doubled back toward the Yara, and paused on the corner to scan the crowd. He doubted that anyone had followed. If they had, they were damned good at keeping out of sight. He went south to Coppelia Park and veered back across La Rampa.

At the Etecsa kiosk in the next block he paid twenty dollars for a phone card and dialed the number in Miami.

10

L eaving the nightclub on La Rampa, Nicolás walked backward and held out an arm to signal the drivers. Chachi was in his own happy world, singing out loud to anyone who would listen. They had to meet the others across town in half an hour. If they could catch a ride, they would make it. There were no buses at this hour, and it was hard to find a taxi that wasn't already taken, even if they had possessed enough dollars in their pockets to pay for one. They could usually find someone who would give them a lift for a few pesos, or for nothing. Headlights reflected on a tourist sign pointing the way to the Malecón.

"My friend, a ride!" Nicolás clasped his hands in prayer as the car came closer, but five or six people were already jammed inside. The car picked up speed down the hill and turned out of sight.

"Sexy lady, dance with me, *ayy*, look so good tonight—" Chachi stumbled over a break in the sidewalk.

Nicolás pushed him upright and put an arm across his shoulders. "I think you're drunk, baby."

A long line of streetlights shone on the Malecón. Lovers walked along the sidewalk or sat on the seawall, tiny figures at this distance. There weren't so many cars, and Nicolás began to worry they might have to walk all the way to Raúl's place in Cerro. The meeting was set for four-thirty, about the time Raúl would get there after a gig in Chinatown.

A black dog wandered out of an alley, a thin bitch dog with long teats and matted fur. It watched with yellow eyes as they walked by. A bad omen, Nicolás thought. He doubled his pace and gave Chachi a shove.

"Come on, let's cut over to Infanta."

"What's the rush? If we're late, we're late."

"Tomás will be on our ass."

"Screw him." Chachi stuck his hands in his jacket pockets and kicked a paper cup into the street. "Who crowned him king? He didn't start it, we did. It's our group, not his."

They went behind the Habana Libre on Avenue M, walking past the same trash containers where last month Nicolás had tossed a pipe bomb. He noticed something new and smiled: a security guard half asleep on the steps of the loading bay. Infanta would be a few blocks ahead, a street running due south, the direction they needed to go. Away from the activity of the Rampa district, the neighborhood was quiet, no one coming or going from the apartment buildings.

Nico slowed to a stop. Just ahead, in the cone-shaped glow of a security light, a gray concrete wall came out of the darkness, the side of a building whose front faced the street. A sign had been pasted to the concrete: the Beard in his green uniform. COMAN-DANTE EN JEFE, ¡ORDENE! Time had faded the colors and lifted the paper at the corners.

Chachi saluted as they approached. "Yes, tell me what to do, my leader, my commander. Order me, and I will obey."

"Chachi, wait. Give me the chalk."

"Not here, are you crazy? Someone will see us for sure."

"Who? You stand behind me. They'll think I'm taking a leak."

"All right, then. Piss on the sign while you're at it." Chachi reached into his pants pocket and handed the chalk to Nicolás, who turned to face the wall.

At waist level he signed the name of their movement, M28E. The birth date of José Martí, *Movimiento veintiocho de enero*. Poet, writer. Died in 1895, fighting to liberate Cuba. Nicolás thought it would be good to die in battle, like Martí. The concrete ate into the chalk, and white powder sifted to the ground.

"All right, let's go." Nicolás tossed the chalk back to Chachi.

"Not yet. You didn't *finish*." Chachi glanced around, then wrote. DOWN WITH . . .

Nicolás watched the street. "Hurry up."

"I'm telling you, Nico, we need to have a camera. Give the pictures to CNN. They would send a camera crew and a reporter."

"Unless they're right behind us, there won't be anything to film."

As soon as the sun came up, someone would report the graffiti to the block leader of the Committee for the Defense of the Revolution, and the CDR would wash it off. But people would see. They would tell their neighbors, and they would look out their windows. One of them might take a picture.

"Mother of Christ, will you hurry?"

"Almost finished."

Backing toward the rear of the building, Nicolás motioned for him to follow. "That's enough."

Chachi was writing the T in TYRANNY when they heard the sound of running footsteps.

"Shit! Let's go!"

In the instant before he hurled himself into the darkness, Nicolás saw two men, tourist police in gray uniforms and black berets. The shriek of a whistle echoed along the street.

Chachi took off at an angle, zigzagging through the cars and into some trees at the back of the parking lot. The police yelled for them to halt. Nicolás went up and over a chain-link fence, cut behind a high-rise, and came out on a street heading south. He tried not to panic. Where was he? Near the University. He thought of climbing the wall, hiding among the buildings, but that would be the first place they'd look.

He decided to keep going. They hadn't seen him clearly, maybe not at all. Chachi had gotten away, a piece of luck because he ran like a girl. Nicolás thought if he could put a few more blocks between himself and the police, he could slow down. Moving at top speed, his feet barely touched the sidewalk. He leaped over a box that had spilled from a trash bin. At the next intersection he flattened himself behind a tree to get his bearings. Twenty-seventh Avenue. He took a few breaths, stepped into the light, and walked along like anybody else going home from the clubs. He could feel the blood slamming through his veins.

At the next crossing he glanced left and saw someone in a bright green jacket running on a parallel path. Chachi! A building at the corner took Chachi out of sight. The two officers appeared, batons drawn, then vanished behind the same building.

"Please, God, don't let this happen."

With fear churning his stomach, Nicolás kept pace, shadowing them one street over. He saw them run past at the next intersection. One man. A moment later, two more. San Lázaro would be ahead. Traffic. People on the sidewalks. Harder for the police. Nicolás thought of drawing them away from Chachi. Run right in front of them. He had won the 1,000 meters in track. They wouldn't be able to keep up. He came out on San Lázaro and turned left.

They were nearly on top of Chachi, reaching for him.

Chachi ran into the street. A horn sounded, and a car swerved out of the way. The officers collided with the side of it.

Words screamed inside Nicolás's head. *Chachi, run. Run!*

Chachi vanished between two houses. The cops went after him. One of them lifted a radio to his mouth.

A truck cut him off, and Nicolás lost sight of them. He dashed into the road ahead of a car and crossed into a residential district. He chose the street where he thought the police had gone. The street was heavily shaded with trees, and he ran down the middle of it, afraid to risk a fall on the sidewalk where tree roots could snake unexpectedly out of the concrete. A dog began to bark wildly behind a fence.

He saw no one, heard no shouts, no footsteps. He turned right, went down another block, came back, and stood at an intersection turning around and listening. Chachi appeared at the next corner. A streetlamp picked up his bleached hair, his green jacket, and his white shoes.

Nicolás called his name and ran toward him.

Chachi looked around, and even a block away, Nicolás could see the terror on his face. "This way!"

The sound of a car engine grew louder, and the branches overhead lit up. Nicolás stepped behind a parked truck just as a white patrol car from the *Policía Revolucionaria* roared by, leaves swirling, brakes screaming as it neared the corner. Chachi was pinned in the headlights. The first two cops came from the other direction.

Nicolás hesitated, then dived into the gutter beside the front wheel of the truck. He hid the whiteness of his hands in the sleeves of his black pullover and lowered his face to his arm until only his eyes peered out.

He heard an engine at high speed, another car coming, blue light flashing, the letters PRN on the side. It braked and slid. Doors opened, men jumped out. Chachi went one way, then the other, then back. He looked small, like a kid in a nightmare game of tag.

He tried to slip past them at right angles. One of the cops grabbed him by the neck of his jacket, slinging him around. Chachi raised his hands and bent over, shielding his head. Someone kicked his legs out from under him. He curled into a ball on the ground. The men surrounded him and kicked him, and the sticks rose and fell in the glare of the lights.

Twenty meters away, Nicolás buried his face in the crook of his elbow and bit down on the fabric to keep from screaming aloud. When he next lifted his eyes, the men had Chachi under the arms, taking him toward the open door of the patrol car. His head rolled on his shoulders, and his feet dragged. Nicolás wanted a bomb, a pistol, a machine gun—

"Here! Look here! There's a man in front of my house!" The shrill cry came from the steps.

Nicolás looked around and saw an old woman on the porch in a nightgown. She was screaming, pointing at him, one finger extended.

"Thief! Murderer!"

One of the men shouted, and they started running toward the truck. Nicolás struggled to get out of the narrow space between the wheel and the curb.

A car door slammed shut, and tires spun on the pavement as one of the patrol cars took off and accelerated. Headlights raked the street and shone in his eyes.

Nicolás turned toward the shadows and ran.

The sun would not come up for an hour, but already the rooster in the courtyard was calling the night a liar. Perched on the back of a broken chair, the bird extended his neck and screamed that morning was here.

Mario Cabrera tilted a wooden slat in the window to look out. A single bulb by the stairs did little to relieve the gloom of the courtyard. Water dripped into an algae-slick wash tub from a spigot wired to the wall. Tomatoes and onions grew in a patch of earth where concrete had been taken out for this purpose. Above the patched tile roof of the second floor, darkness pressed down like a heavy black curtain. The rooster fluttered away to find another perch, and into the empty night came the low rumble and clank of a train.

The apartment was in Cerro, not far from the railroad tracks that went south from the city along the west side of the harbor. Raúl had rented it from the cousin of a man who had died several years ago. The death had never been reported, and the cousin had made some money on the place. To keep the neighbors happy, Raúl had brought them a pig in the back of his Fiat. It lived in a pen in a corner of the courtyard eating scraps, unaware that soon it would be stretched over coals, oiled, and basted with garlic.

The people here needed the food more than they needed to report strangers in the building. When the sun rose on this street, the men might set up little tables and earn a few pesos refilling cigarette lighters with hair spray; the women would walk to Vedado or Centro to sell the fruit they had bought on the black market. Criminals, all of them. No jobs, no licenses. They had to live. Nobody sent them dollars from outside.

"Mario, what are you doing?" Raúl asked.

"I thought I heard something."

Raúl's teeth flashed in his dark face when he grinned. "It's just the whores coming home from work." He turned off the gas stove and poured hot milk into the cups. He had already made the coffee, and Tomás had bought some loaves of fresh bread from the back door of a bakery. Mario went to the table to break off another piece for himself and spread it with butter.

The table had been dragged into the center of the room. An extension cord from the apartment next door allowed them to turn on a lamp. It shone on a row of photographs that Olga Saavedra had brought with her. The diagram she had made of General Vega's house, interior and exterior, lay in the pool of light on the table. Brushing away bread crumbs, Mario studied the layout of rooms, upstairs and down. The general's office. The bedrooms. The garage.

Olga sat on one end of the sofa with her eyes closed and her cheek in her palm. She looked like she wanted very badly to go home. She opened her eyes when Raúl waved a cup of coffee back and forth under her nose. With a shake of her head, she sank farther into the sofa. Raúl gave the cup to Tomás.

There were five of them here from the Movement. Mario did not include Olga Saavedra in that number. Aside from himself, Raúl, and Tomás, the others were friends of Nico's who knew electronics. Their job was to find some two-way radios or build them if they couldn't be found. This would be necessary if Mario wanted to get cleanly away after he shot General Vega.

Nico and Chachi hadn't showed up. It was possible they had been delayed, but with no telephone here, it was hard to guess what had happened.

Tomás said, "There are only eight photographs. Where are the others on the roll?"

Olga Saavedra said, "That's all I took. I couldn't get any more. His wife hates me. She has her eye on me all the time, so you make do with what I brought you."

Raúl grinned and sat heavily beside her, making the sofa creak. "If I were Vega's wife, I would hate you too."

Shoving him away, she wrinkled her nose. "Don't you take baths? You stink."

"You like it." He waggled his tongue at her.

"Disgusting." She got up and walked to the window. Her blond hair swung on her shoulders when she turned to look at Tomás. "Can I go?"

"Not yet." The light shone on his white shirt, his thin arms. "When was the last time you slept with the general?"

"I'm not sleeping with him."

"So you told us. When was the last time?"

She shrugged. "A couple of weeks ago. Why do you ask me that?"

"He has a wife, and wives are suspicious. You should stay away from him. Tell him you're busy."

From across the room Mario said, "Where do you usually go with Vega?"

"Go? A hotel. The house of a friend. Why?"

Mario looked at the others, the solution to their problems having become obvious. "If she meets him, we can be waiting, or she will let us in. He comes to us. That would be simpler, wouldn't it, than trying to go to him?"

"I won't do that," Olga said. She cut off the idea with a quick slash of her hand. "I can't. We aren't alone. The general has a driver who waits for him. He watches the street. I took the pictures, and that's all I do, no more."

Raúl started laughing. Mario glanced at him, then asked Olga, "Do you know this man, the driver? Can he be bought?"

"No."

"She knows him," Raúl said. "She used to screw him. A generous guy to share her with the boss."

"That was fifteen years ago! He's nothing to me, or I to him."

"Are you sure Vega's wife doesn't suspect you?" Tomás asked. "You said she hates you."

"She doesn't know, I tell you. She never said anything to me, not like that. Marta Quintana hates me because I wear good clothes, and I like perfume. You should hear what she says to me. I suck the juice from the Revolution and give back nothing. Such stupid things she says. Stop interrogating me, Tomás. I'm tired."

Peering through his glasses at the photographs on the table, he said, "Mario, what do you think? Can you work with only these?"

Mario moved the photographs onto the diagram of the house so they corresponded with the rooms. "I believe I can get inside the house at least once before the operation. I need some pictures of the neighborhood. I want to know the fences, the intersections. Where is the CDR located?"

Tomás nodded. "I'll see to it."

Sprawled on the sofa, Raúl put his hands behind his head. He wore a sleeveless T-shirt, and the muscles bunched in his arms. "Tell us more about this girl from Miami. Is she going to let you in her panties? If not, maybe you can put it to Vega's wife."

Mario remembered the girl's soft pink sweater, her flawless white skin, the small gold crucifix on the curve of her breast. "Shut up before I break your jaw."

"Ooooh! Do we like this little beauty?"

Tomás pointed at Raúl. "Enough. We are one heart, one mind. Remember that. All of you."

When the others began to argue how to take pictures of Vega's neighborhood in Miramar, Mario said he was going outside for a smoke. He went through the courtyard and pulled open the sheet-metal door to the street, careful not to let it squeak on the hinges.

He sat on one of the plastic crates on the sidewalk, took out his cigarettes, and remembered he'd left his matches inside.

Raking his braids off his face, he leaned against the wall, tired to his bones. Tonight his mother expected him for dinner at her house. The people from Miami would be there. Anthony Quintana and his family. His daughter. Mario needed to sleep for a few hours. To take a bath and put on some good clothes.

But first he had to see about Nico and Chachi. It wasn't like them not to show up. Tomás had suggested that somebody go around to their apartment and check on them. Mario had said he would do it.

Footsteps sounded, and two men dressed completely in white came across the narrow street. White shoes, coats, pants. They would wear white for a year as initiates in santería. Walking down Infanta a couple of hours ago, Mario had heard drumbeats and chanting. He had come nearer, and from the sidewalk had looked directly into a living room blazing with lights and color. A woman twirled in the center of the room, and the people shook gourds and shouted and sang. *Olofi-onise, onishe ko*— God grant us all good things—

The poor had to believe in something. Mario's parents believed in the Catholic God, or said that they did. Mario believed that this street and this dawn existed. Where they came from, no one could know. This dawn, and this day, and the next, would flow like a river. The people on this street would continue in their poverty. Whether the actions of one man would change anything, Mario didn't know. He expected no reward on this side or the other, but a man who saw and did nothing was already dead.

The door squeaked and moved inward. Olga Saavedra waited until the men had walked around the corner to come out. Her Mercedes was half a block away, visible under a dim streetlight. She reached into her fake Louis Vuitton bag for her car keys. "This place is terrible. I hate coming here."

"It's safe. Nobody asks questions."

"I'm not coming back. That's it."

Mario looked up at her, an odd view of breasts and chin and the point of her nose. Why had she come at all? Tomás had met Olga Saavedra when she'd done a TV documentary about the musicians at the Varadero hotels. She wasn't in love with him. She was older. She had a car, a job, money.

"Why are you in this, Olga?"

"Why do you care?"

"Because I'm not sure I trust you."

Her face turned down so she could see him directly. She smiled. "You have your reasons, I have mine." She tossed her keys in her hand, then sat on a crate next to him and slid a cigarette out of the pack he held on his thigh. "This isn't my favorite, Popular, but I'm getting desperate."

He said, "I don't have any matches."

Olga found a lighter in her bag, and Mario lit a cigarette for each of them. She crossed her legs and settled back. She was wearing tight black pants with a slit at the ankle, and as she swung her foot in its high-heeled sandal, her toe ring sparkled. "I'll tell you why. Someday, love, everything will change, and I'm going to be on the right side. I want them to know it."

"Them?"

"Those who take over."

Mario smiled, and smoke drifted from his lips into the still air. "We can't know who will take over. Your reason doesn't make sense."

"It's as good as yours. You want to send a message. Who is listening? Really, who?"

He gestured toward the doors and windows in the long, low wall of concrete across the street. "They are."

"They're asleep," she said.

"Not for long."

"Oh, my God." Olga Saavedra laughed quietly. "When you light that fuse, I want to be out of here." She was silent for a time, then said, "Do you really have to do this?"

"Yes."

"Why? He is not so important."

"He is the first break in the wall. Do you care about him?"

"No. I hate him. I only meant . . . how can you do it? You know . . . to kill a man inside his own house. Can you do that? What if his wife is there? Or his children? And if they see him die . . . all the blood—"

"Quiet! Are you drunk or only stupid?"

"Don't be mean. I like you. You're a nice person, I can tell. *Un ragazzo simpatico.* That's Italian."

"I know."

"I've been to Italy two times," she said. "Paris once, but only to change planes on my way to Rome. Paris is so pretty from the air. The Eiffel Tower was like a little toy, and I could see the river. What is that river called?"

Mario smoked his cigarette. "The Seine."

"That's right. You're very smart." Olga touched his hand and turned one of his rings around so she could see the head of the silver snake that lay across its own tail. "Such beautiful hands. Long fingers. Good for a musician, no? I bet you have lots of girlfriends." She nudged him with her shoulder. He could smell her perfume, feel the heat of her body.

At the east end of the street, the roofs of the buildings had become distinct from the sky. Dawn had pulled them back to earth. The tiles were no longer black, but their usual reddish gray. Birds on the electric wires had started their song.

Olga said, "Tomás says that you know Anthony Quintana, the son of Luis Quintana. He's a great friend of your family. Is that true?"

"My parents know him."

"So do I." The early light turned her eyes green as new shoots of grass. "We are friends for many years. His mother's family, they got out. They're very rich, very connected to the government. I might ask him to arrange for me to go to the United States. He could do it."

Mario put his elbows on his knees, moving away from her. "If you want out so badly, why didn't you stay out when you had the chance?"

Laughing, she replied, "Because how did I know? How did I know it was my last chance to get out of this circus of horrors? They locked the door. Maybe they think I will run. They are right." She played with one of his braids, then her breath was in his ear. "Mario, can I give you some advice? Let someone else take Vega. You get out of here. You could have a good life, a boy like you."

Tapping his cigarette, he watched the ashes fall to the sidewalk between his feet. He brushed off the toe of one dark blue canvas shoe. The rubber was peeling away from the fabric.

She leaned back against the wall. "Myself, I will get out too. I will. Have you seen Spain? I would like very much to live in Spain. Oh, my God, you would love it. I might go to Costa Rica. I'm sure I could find a job there. I used to be a TV journalist, did you know that? People would see me on the street. 'Oh, look, it's Olga.' "

A sudden and unaccountable fury clenched Mario's throat and sent the blood to his head. "Olga Saavedra, the famous Olga. You worked with my father. You accused him of selling videos to foreign journalists. You set him up, and they fired him. He spent four years in prison."

"That wasn't my fault." Bewilderment clouded her face, and unable to reach for anything more logical, she blurted out, "José Leiva is your stepfather."

"He's my father, and you betrayed him."

"I didn't." Olga shifted away.

"So if I don't trust you now, figure out why."

"Maybe you're not as nice as I thought."

"I'm not nice. Get out of here, Olga Saavedra, before somebody thinks you're for sale."

She stood and threw her cigarette at him. "Go to hell." Her eyes moved to the door. Tomás was there, a slight figure in wire-rimmed glasses. She shouted, "Mario called me a whore."

Tomás said, "Keep your voice down, Olga. Mario is sorry. Go on, apologize to her."

Mario made a tired laugh. "Tomás, shut up."

"Yes, Tomás, shut up." Olga turned and angled directly for her car. Her high heels clicked on the pavement.

"Let me have a cigarette." Tomás took one from Mario's pack, then pulled it through his fingers one way, then the other. "You've got to control your temper, my friend. We're at a critical stage. We can't start attacking each other. Our enemy isn't Olga." He leaned down to light his cigarette off Mario's. "Come back inside. We have things to discuss."

They heard the diesel engine crank, then clatter to life. The Mercedes pulled away from the curb and turned the corner. Its lights were off, but they weren't needed. Gray light filtered through the clouds.

"I don't trust her," Mario said.

"I know you don't, but she's all right. Olga . . . Olga wants to be important."

"That's not good enough."

"You trust me, don't you? Leave her alone."

"She betrayed José Leiva," Mario said.

Tomás sighed. "Olga was trying to survive. At the time, it was Leiva or herself. In a totalitarian state, we are expected to turn on our friends. Perhaps to help us now—to help you—is her way of redeeming herself."

"It is very strange, Tomás, to hear you, of all people, speak of redemption. Have you become religious?"

He allowed a thin smile. "I was only giving you my interpretation of Olga. Come inside."

Standing up, Mario extinguished his cigarette under his heel. He noticed a movement behind Tomás. A young man in black clothing was running toward them. His hair stuck to his forehead in dark, sweaty points.

"Nico?"

When Tomás turned to see, Nicolás fell on both of them. "You're here. I was afraid you'd already gone. They got Chachi. They took him. They beat him up. I was all over the city hiding until I was sure nobody was behind me."

"Inside." Tomás threw his cigarette away, and the two of them pulled Nicolás through the door.

Mario put a finger to Nico's lips as a warning. They hurried him across the courtyard. A woman on the walkway above watched disinterestedly over the railing as she drank her coffee. They took Nico into the apartment and closed the door. It was still dark inside except for the one lamp on the table.

Nico's friends came closer with their mouths open. Raúl limped over from the sink drying his hands. "So there you are at last." He frowned. "Mary, queen of whores, what happened to you?"

Mario pulled out a chair at the table, and Nico collapsed into it. "He says they got Chachi."

Tomás leaned down. "What happened? Why did they take him? Nico!"

"We wrote on a wall. Near La Rampa. We were on our way here. Someone saw us, and the police came. Sons of bitches! They caught him and took him away in a patrol car." Nico's voice shook. "They beat him. They used their batons. He was on the ground. They kicked him. They hit him in the head."

For a long moment the only reactions were contained in glances exchanged around the room. Then Raúl balled his towel and threw it. "Shit! I told you idiots to stop writing on the walls!"

Nico said, "I need some water." Mario went to the sink and came back with a glass. Nico emptied it, then started to cry.

Tomás told him to stop it, to be strong. "What did you write? Was it about the Movement?"

He wiped his face on his sleeve. "Yes. I went first, then Chachi was writing 'Down with tyranny,' and that's when they came. They caught him just south of San Lázaro. They didn't see me. Not well enough to recognize me. I'm sure of it."

"Where'd they take him?" asked one of Nico's friends.

Nico shook his head.

"Villa Marista, probably," said the other.

Raúl glared at the door. "Satan screw their mothers!"

Mario sat down next to Nico. "Nobody saw you. You're sure?"

"A woman. She came out of her house when they were arresting Chachi, and she saw me, but only for a second. It was dark. Nobody saw my face, and I got away."

"It doesn't matter," Raúl said.

"I got away. No one followed me here."

"It doesn't matter!" Raúl shoved the back of Nico's chair.

Nico's friend spun Raúl around and with both hands pushed him in the chest. "He said they didn't see him."

Raúl knocked his hands away. "You're as stupid as he is, then. It doesn't matter who saw him or didn't see him. They have Chachi."

"Chachi won't talk," Nico said.

Mario exchanged a glance with Tomás.

"He won't!" Nico grabbed Mario's arm. "We've discussed this. He knows what to say. He wrote the name of the movement for a joke because he sees it on walls. He doesn't know what it means."

"Of course they'll believe him." Raúl spread his arms wide. "He looks so innocent. Fairies don't throw bombs."

"No, listen," Nico insisted. "They haven't shown up here. If he had talked, they'd be here, wouldn't they?"

"They haven't shown up *yet*," said Tomás. He folded the drawing of the general's house that Olga Saavedra had made. "We'll know soon enough. The moment they start asking questions, we'll know. All right. We expected this could happen, and we have our plans. Other places to stay, places to meet, methods of communication. Nico, you'll have to disappear. Don't go back to your apartment. They will ask Chachi who you were, and he might tell them. I'll contact his mother. She might be able to find out where he is. In the meantime, we proceed. Our timetable has just been moved forward. Mario, take the diagram and the photographs and memorize them, then burn them."

Mario opened his flute case and put everything inside. He thought about Chachi. What they would do to him. The police wouldn't have him for long. They would turn him over to State Security. Mario had heard about their interrogations from José Leiva, who had seen strong men, brave men, come back to their cells, curl up on their concrete beds, and cry like children. Chachi wasn't weak, but the pain and fear might be too much. As that thought grew in Mario's mind, so did his anger. He wanted to kill them. He wanted to trade places with Chachi. He would find a way to kill at least one of them, to feel bones snap, to see blood spray across the walls. He would not fall on his knees and pray for them, as José Leiva had prayed for his interrogators.

He and the others picked up clothing and books, pillows and matches, any piece of evidence that could tie them to this apartment. They swept the floor and wiped off fingerprints. They were finished in less than ten minutes. Nico left first, and the others followed at intervals, each taking a different route out of the neighborhood.

11

They stood on the narrow balcony—a grid of aluminum, a pipe for a railing. Gail leaned against it with her take-out cup of coffee. On his way back upstairs, Anthony had brought *café con leche* and some rather soggy croissants from the all-night restaurant off the lobby. The coffee had gone cold.

When Gail bent to set the cup on the floor, Anthony paused and waited for her to come back within range of his voice. He had been speaking so quietly that no one more than a few feet away could have heard him, a precaution hardly necessary since the other balconies were empty at this hour. Gail thought they must be the only human beings on the entire northern face of the Habana Libre Hotel.

The sun had just come up, too weak to penetrate the overcast. Above the flat gray sea, clouds hinted at rain. Gail pulled her sweater closed and crossed her arms. She followed the progress of some seagulls gliding toward the center of the city, vanishing to small, flapping dots. Anthony's gaze seemed focused on the jumble of nondescript buildings below, some painted turquoise or pink, another with curved Art Deco corners. Several blocks away, waves rolled in, broke against the rocks of the Malecón, and turned to froth.

As he talked, he used his napkin to dust off the railing before leaning his forearms on it. He didn't want to get the sleeves of his windbreaker dirty. It wasn't new, but he could be obsessive in that way. As soon as they got back to his sister's house, he would probably have a shower and shave. Stubble darkened his jaw and upper lip, and lack of sleep made him squint.

Looking over the edge, Gail saw past the air handlers on top of the four-story building across from them, past the tattered green canopy of a restaurant, and then down to the narrow street below. Her stomach gave a lurch, and her hands tightened on the railing. It wasn't just the altitude giving her vertigo. While Anthony was making his phone call to Miami, she had wondered if he would be back. The scene had played out in her mind: men following him on the dark street, pushing him into an unmarked sedan, tying him to a chair in a room lit by a single unshaded bulb. *What are you doing here in Cuba, Señor Quintana?*

She'd heard a key in the door, and her heart had nearly stopped. When she told him her fears, he laughed. He gave her a croissant and coffee and a kiss on the cheek, and they went out on the balcony to talk. He told her that Hector Mesa had dug up the answers to most of his questions.

Well, of course Hector could dig them up. He had ties to God-only-knew what kind of spies, counterspies, and paramilitary fanatics. Such a shadowy little man, hiding behind a suit and black-framed glasses. He had spied for U.S. counterintelligence; he had assassinated leftists and organized raids into Cuba for Anthony's grandfather, none of which Gail was supposed to know about. Hector would fall on his sword for Ernesto Pedrosa. Gail assumed this meant that Hector wouldn't stab Anthony in the back with it.

It was true about Everett Bookhouser. He was a spy. No, more than a spy. He'd been seen in meetings with the president's national security advisor. Born in Morocco to an American diplomat. Graduate degree in international relations from Georgetown; fluent in Arabic, French, Russian, and Spanish. In the 1980s, stationed in Israel. Most recently in Pakistan, mission unknown. Also unknown: why Everett Bookhouser would be interested in Ramiro Vega.

As if scanning a list floating somewhere over the ocean, Anthony told her about the man he would meet today at the park near the Capitol. Major General Abdel Evaristo García. Never married, no children. Age fifty-six, deputy minister of MINBAS—the Ministry of Basic Industries. Member of the Central Committee of the Communist Party. Studied military science in Moscow. Served in Angola, then headed a military mission in Ethiopia. Injured in battle, taken hostage. His jaw had been broken during an interrogation. Awarded a medal: Hero of the Republic of Cuba. In the 1980s, in charge of getting weapons to insurgents in Central and South America. Rumors of contacts with arms dealers in states of the former Soviet Union and the Middle East.

"In 1988, García was promoted to general and in the same year assigned to the Cuban nuclear program. The Russians were financing a reactor in Cienfuegos province, but when the Soviet Union collapsed, construction stopped. Since 1996, García has been at Basic Industries. He's not well known by the public or popular among the rank and file, but very close to Fidel's brother, Raúl, who may be the next *líder máximo* when Fidel is gone."

Anthony glanced into his coffee cup, finished off what remained, and set the cup beside Gail's. "They say that on a clear day, if you stand on top of this building with a telescope, you can see Key West." He nodded toward the wider street to their left, barely visible around the side of the building. "That's La Rampa—the ramp. The street goes down to the Malecón. Before the Revolution, this area used to be wild. Gambling, strip clubs, prostitution, the Mafia—"

"I'll put it on my tour." Gail shifted her eyes back to Anthony. "I gather that you still don't know why García wants to see you."

"No, I don't. If he wants to go fishing, that's okay with me. Would you stop worrying?" Leaning on one elbow, Anthony reached out and pulled her to him. "I am sorry to have left you last night, even for one minute."

Sliding her arms under his jacket, she set her chin on his shoulder. He felt solid and warm. In the far distance a stone lighthouse and the walls of a fortress rose up from a promontory across Havana Bay. She said, "Do you have to go? I wish you wouldn't."

"Well, I don't want to make it tough for Ramiro. He works for him."

"That is so lame. Ramiro's career doesn't depend on what *you* do. There must be a better reason than that. Why?"

Anthony's lips found the tender spot under her ear. "*Cielito,* do you remember what we said about this trip? It's the honeymoon we didn't have time to take. Let's do something, the two of us. Why don't we rent a car and drive to Varadero Beach today for lunch?"

"Anthony—"

"The water is beautiful, like turquoise. You think Irene would mind watching Karen?"

She put her hands flat against his chest. "Why do you *have* to meet García?"

His brows made a little lift, matched by his shoulders. "Because if I don't, he will put us on a flight to Miami, and we'll have to explain to U.S. Customs what we were doing in Cuba. I don't want any problems, not for you and your mother, the kids—"

"Oh, God. I knew it."

"It's not a big deal, but I tell you something like that, you start worrying about it, getting neurotic, you know how you are—"

"You *lied*. Do you think I can't handle it? Or what, exactly?"

"Are you trying to start a fight with me? Sweetheart?" He tilted his wrist to check the time. "We should get back to Marta's before everyone wakes up."

"Wait," she said. "I have to ask you something. I asked you before, and I never got a good answer."

"*Coño.*" He let out a breath. "All right. What?"

"How did Bookhouser persuade you to get involved? No, not persuade, *force*, because otherwise, you wouldn't touch it." She hugged his arm tightly. "Anthony, I swear to God I don't want to fight with you, I just want to understand what's going on. I love you, and I'm worried, and if you think that's neurotic, too bad. Why are you doing this?"

Anthony took a few seconds to reply, "For Marta. For my family."

"What does that mean?"

She could see the thoughts assembling themselves into proper order in his mind. He said, "Last month a Cuban Army major named Omar Céspedes walked into the American embassy in São Paulo, Brazil, and requested political asylum. He was interviewed at length by the CIA, and he alleged that Ramiro Vega wanted to defect. Is this true? I doubt it. Céspedes got this alleged information from a source that Bookhouser refuses to name. Ramiro has never shown the least indication to me that he wanted to leave. I said to Bookhouser, forget it, I'm not interested. Then he told me that Ramiro is in danger. He has rivals who think he's gaining too much power. They want to get rid of him. They would accuse him of taking kickbacks from foreign companies. Theft from the state. If it's true, it could be serious for him."

"How serious?"

"Life in prison. If they were really out to get him . . . they could sentence him to death—"

"Oh, God."

"They haven't used the death penalty in a long time."

"But they could."

"They could, if they want to make an example."

Gail took a breath. "So you're going to tell Ramiro he has to get out."

"I'm going to try. Bookhouser could have made it up." A slight smile curved Anthony's lips. "He gave me a number to call after I speak to Ramiro." Anthony jerked his head in the direction of downtown Havana. "He's probably down there now with his cell phone in his pocket. This is what I will do: I will ask Ramiro if he wants to defect, he will tell me I'm full of shit, and I call Señor Bookhouser to give my report. If he wants anything else, he can go to hell." When his eyes moved to Gail, they held a challenge. "Does that answer your question?"

"Yes. Thank you." She kept the emotion out of her voice, but the flutter in her stomach had returned.

He continued, "I give you one other item of interest. Omar Céspedes was on García's staff at MINBAS. García has to be aware that Céspedes defected. I think he wants to find out what's going on, and that I can tell him."

"Wonderful. Abdel García thinks you're working for the CIA. Where's he taking you?"

The smile reappeared. "Don't worry. He won't tie me to a chair and beat me with a rubber hose. Maybe we'll go for a drink at the Hotel Inglaterra. It's not far from the park where he's going to pick me up. I should take your mother there sometime. Irene would like it, all the mosaic tile and the fountain and the indoor garden."

"How civilized."

Anthony took Gail's hand, and he must have felt her icy fingers. He curled them around his own and brought them to his lips, warm in the roughness of his beard. "Take a nap while I'm gone. We have dinner tonight with José and Yolanda. Remember?"

"God, I forgot all about it. Do be sure to tell General García about your friends in the opposition. We'll be lucky if he doesn't kick us out of Cuba for that."

"I am sure he's aware of it," Anthony said. "Remind me to give you some money. I want you to buy some wine for dinner, would you, sweetheart? Something nice. One red, one white. And a decent bottle of Scotch. Marta knows where." He picked up the cups and stepped toward the open sliding door.

Gail said, "How do you take kickbacks if you're a general in the Army? Not to say Ramiro *does*. I'm just curious."

He turned around. "Well, if you're dealing with foreign companies, you could make sure they get their electricity connected on schedule. You suggest that finding good workers might cost a little more. That sort of thing. The army controls sixty percent of the Cuban economy. They have turned into CEOs and bureaucrats. Fidel Castro put them in charge so that he, as commander-in-chief, can retain control. The generals don't do such a bad job. They aren't as corrupt as the rest of Cuban society, where larceny is a form of survival."

"Could it be," Gail suggested, "that the CIA wants Ramiro for his knowledge of the economy?"

"Hardly. The U.S. knows exactly what's going on. We know their banking system and their foreign debt, how many dollars they spend on frozen chicken parts from Texas, and how many dollars they collect from tourists at the Tropicana night club, everything."

"Chicken parts from Texas?" Gail repeated.

"It's called a special trade agreement," Anthony said. "The embargo is full of holes."

"And used for political purposes on both sides," Gail said.

"Exactly."

She said, "Do you think it's true that Ramiro is taking bribes?"

"That's not something he would confide in me, is it? I wouldn't be surprised if he's hedging his bets and stashing money offshore. He would be stupid not to, in these times. It may certainly be true that he has rivals. That I would not doubt."

"What is it? That he wants changes, and they don't?"

"It would be the other way around. Ramiro is not a reformer. He's a *duro*, a hard-liner. He makes jokes, but most of them do, at least in private. They don't want changes, because where else could they find a job? A very funny man, my brother-in-law. He voted to enshrine socialism in the Cuban constitution, forever untouchable."

Anthony held up his hands. "Enough. Let's get out of here." He tugged Gail inside and slid the door shut. The mechanical whir from the adjacent rooftop ceased, leaving near total silence.

"Then why do they want him so badly?"

"What?"

"Bookhouser and company. If Ramiro is so dedicated to Cuba, why do they want him?"

"Because he's a general. Because they think he will jump ship, and so few of them do. Because they have their heads up their asses. Get your purse. Did you leave anything in the bathroom?"

"No, nothing," Gail said. "What's he like, Everett Bookhouser? Does he wear a black suit and sunglasses?"

"Yes, and so does his dog." Anthony crossed to the table and dropped the cups next to the bag he'd brought from downstairs. The croissants still lay there, uneaten. "He looks like an accountant."

"Sort of harmless?"

Anthony glanced at her. "Sort of invisible. He's getting a little bald on the top, so he buzzes his hair. Pale eyes. He's about my age, a little shorter. Muscular. It doesn't show under the suit, but you see it in his hands."

Gail picked up her purse. "You know, Hector told you something that stuck in my mind. He said Bookhouser is fluent in Arabic." She watched Anthony scan the room for anything they may have left behind. He automatically patted his pockets. She said, "Don't you think that's a little strange?"

"What is?"

"That Everett Bookhouser speaks Arabic?"

"Strange?"

"Yes. What's he doing in Havana?"

"He is also fluent in Spanish."

Gail said, "Your grandfather told me that Castro is sending money to Al-Qaeda."

"My grandfather is a lunatic. He's sure that Castro is making a nuclear bomb. He promised George W. Bush half a million dollars for his reelection if he would invade Cuba. Listen. Tonight at José's, I might have to leave a little early. Ramiro and I have a date. Don't worry, José will see that you get back safely to Marta's. Take a taxi. Don't let the driver charge you more than five dollars. And make sure my son doesn't go anywhere. Danny thinks this is spring break in Cancún."

Opening the door, Anthony motioned for her to hurry up.

She grabbed the lapels of his jacket and glanced both ways down the hall. She whispered, "Anthony. If you're in more danger than you're admitting, I will break your neck. I swear I will."

He kissed her quickly. "No, sweetheart. We haven't yet had a proper honeymoon. I wouldn't deprive you of that."

"You're so full of it."

"And I love you too. Come on, let's get out of here."

12

Karen's eyes came open, and she jerked like someone had tried to push her down the stairs. She lifted her head, and for a minute she couldn't remember where she was, except on a narrow cot with her legs tangled up in the sheets.

Looking around, she saw Janelle's double bed and her arm hanging over the side of it, and her long, curly hair. She was breathing funny, first a little click in her throat, then a soft buzzing noise. Karen pushed up on her arms to see past Janelle. The other side of the bed was empty. Angela wasn't there.

The light coming through the lace curtains was so dim she thought that the sun was just up, or else it was going to rain today. She lay back down but the dream echoed in her head, too distant now for her to say what it had been about. She listened for sounds in the house and heard nothing. She wondered if her mother and Anthony were home. They had left last night after dinner, and her mother had said don't wait up.

Karen wouldn't have cared about it, their leaving like that, but she wanted to ask her mother what was going on with the general and his wife. They'd started yelling at each other in their bedroom, and somebody had thrown something against the wall. Janelle had acted like they did it all the time. Angela had given Karen a look, like *don't even ask*, so Karen hadn't. She'd wanted to put on her headphones and listen to music, but Danny and Gio had borrowed her iPod. Karen didn't know what they'd done with it. Probably taken it with them and lost it, with her luck.

The bed creaked as Janelle rolled over. Karen lay on the cot looking at the curtain slowly blowing in and out. She didn't think she could go back to sleep, so she got up and went to the bathroom, shivering in her T-shirt. It was her dad's, which he had bought at a Miami Hurricanes game. Janelle's brother liked it, and Karen thought she might give it to him, unless he'd lost her iPod.

She used the bathroom and cringed when she pulled the cord in the lid, it was so loud. She washed her hands, then turned the doorknob on the other side and looked in. They weren't home yet. Her mother's sandals were under one side of the bed, and Anthony's big sneakers were sitting neatly beside the closet. Their suitcases were pushed under the baby crib.

Back in Janelle's room Karen put on her jeans under the T-shirt. With her shoes in her hand, she went down the curving stairs into the empty living room, then through the dining room and into the kitchen with the old wood cabinets painted yellow.

Angela was standing at the counter making Cuban coffee. They said hello, and Angela asked if she was hungry. There were some eggs and some corn flakes and no bread except some left over from last night, but she could make toast with it. The only milk was in a box, was that okay?

"Sure. Is my grandmother up yet?" Karen asked.

"Nobody's up," Angela said.

"We are."

Angela smiled and said she wasn't sure if she was or not. She had bags under her eyes, and she looked so pale that Karen asked if she was sick. She said she was fine, and they were going on a tour today with her Aunt Marta, wouldn't *that* be fun. Karen knew what Angela wanted to do—find the house that her grandmother had lived in. Angela had asked her aunt about it last night, but her aunt wasn't interested. *Ay, Dios, that old house. I don't know where it is anymore.*

It sounded very romantic, having a beautiful grandmother who ran away with someone at age sixteen to get married, but Karen had seen the man she ran away with, Anthony's father, and she wasn't impressed.

Karen sat in a chair at the table to put her socks and shoes on. "I had this weird dream last night, but I can't remember what it was. Don't you hate that?"

Opening the refrigerator, moving stuff around, Angela said that dreams always get away from you, don't they. She meant she didn't get into the ballet. Or maybe she meant her boyfriend, Bobby. He was cute, but he wasn't as smart as Angela. All he knew about was dancing. Karen didn't think Angela would have trouble finding somebody else.

Angela poured some orange juice and set the glass on the table. She asked if Karen wanted toast and scrambled eggs. Karen said yes, thank you.

Just then the back door closed quietly, and Danny and Gio put their heads around the corner to see who was there. Danny asked if his father was up yet, and Angela told him no, they'd gone to a hotel, so Danny had lucked out. "You shouldn't have left," she said. "Dad told you not to go anywhere."

"What are you, my mother?"

"Don't be a jerk. Grandpa wanted to say good night. It was so rude of you to just leave."

"Hey, the old guy was so drunk he probably didn't notice." Danny grabbed a piece of toast as Angela was buttering it.

Karen watched him. He had a streak of badness. She had noticed that some people were just like that, and there was nothing you could do but stay out of their way.

Gio was pouring orange juice and trying to figure out what they were saying. He had studied English, but not enough. Janelle had said last night that she and her brother went to the Lenin School, the best school in Havana, where all the kids go who have important parents or who get super-good grades. They were supposed to spend time doing farm work, but Janelle said most of the time they got out of it. They ate in a special dining room, not with the regular kids. Giovany was about to graduate. He said he wanted to visit the United States, but was it as dangerous as they say? He was totally ignorant, and Danny didn't help much, telling his cousin that there were drug dealers in the schools, and everybody had alarms on their SUVs, and Danny's father let him shoot his .44 pistol anytime he wanted.

Danny finished his juice and left the glass on the table for somebody else to wash. "*Buenas noches,* ladies."

Angela said, "Don't expect to stay in bed all day. Marta wants to show us Havana."

"I've seen Havana."

"Well, you have to go. And you have to come to dinner with us tonight, too, so don't make any plans to go out."

"Dinner with who?"

"The Leivas. Dad's friend, José Leiva. You know very well who."

"I'll have my people call his people." Danny kept walking out of the kitchen, and Gio smiled as if he understood a word of it.

With a frown on her face, Angela went back to fixing the eggs. She lit a match and turned a knob, and blue flames popped out of the stove.

Karen said she would be back in a minute. She ran after the boys and caught up with them on the stairs. They were talking about going to Varadero Beach in the afternoon, how to get all the way out there, because Gio's mother wasn't going to let them use her car.

"Danny, what did you do with my iPod?"

Gio was telling Danny that he would call a friend.

"My iPod. Where is it?" She jerked on Danny's shirt, which was hanging out of his pants.

Danny looked over his shoulder and told her they were still using it, but she'd get it back when they were done.

"You'd better not erase any of my songs."

She followed them into the hall. They were whispering, trying not to wake anybody up, talking about some girl Gio knew, the same one who had dropped them off. Danny said he wouldn't mind seeing that chick again, then he had to say it over because Gio didn't understand the first time. They walked into Gio's room, and when Danny started to shut the door, Karen put her foot in it. He asked her what she wanted, and she told him to give her back her iPod or she would tell his father about it.

"Oh, you'll tell my dad," he mimicked. "I don't have your fuckin' iPod. It's hooked up to the computer, which crashed, so now we have to start over. As soon as we get the music downloaded, you may have it back. Okayyyy? And stay out of the general's study. It's off-limits."

The door closed in her face.

Karen clenched her fists a couple of times, wishing she knew karate. She went back to the kitchen.

Angela was sitting at the table with a cup of *café con leche* and her head in her hands, crying. She looked up and blew her nose on a paper towel. "Don't ever fall in love, Karen. It's just not worth it."

"Okay."

"But you will, of course. Everybody does, and then they suffer. I've never had any of my relationships work out. Is it my fault? Is there something wrong with me?"

"I don't think so," Karen said. "Maybe you pick the wrong guys."

"They're *all* shitheads."

Karen said, "I remember my dream now. Except it wasn't a dream. The window was open. I got up for some water, and I heard Mr. Vega's chauffeur crying. He was in the backyard. Didn't you hear him?"

"No. What was he crying about?"

"I don't know. He was drunk, I think. I heard him talking to himself, and then he would like roll over on the grass and start crying again. I don't know what it was about."

"A woman, probably. She broke up with him because he's a shithead."

"People in Cuba are so emotional," Karen said.

"I suppose." Angela put a plate on the table, only one, and Karen asked her if she was eating. Angela said she didn't feel hungry. She said she was going to walk around the corner for some fresh bread and more orange juice, since the boys drank it all. She checked to see she had some dollars in her jeans pocket.

"You want anything?"

"I guess not." Karen almost asked to come along, but Angela looked like she was in a hurry to leave. She rinsed her cup and went out the door.

Karen picked up her fork and ate the eggs. The refrigerator came on and started rattling. It was small with only one door and rust around the handle. Last night one of the shelves had fallen and spilled the food, and Mrs. Vega was yelling about that too.

She tried to think of anybody who got along with their boyfriend. Her parents had gotten a divorce, and Karen thought that her mother and Anthony would split up too someday. Karen didn't want to get married, except maybe to have a child, preferably a girl, and you could do that without getting married, so what was the point?

She finished and took her dishes to the sink. There was a bottle of something orange called CRISOL, and Karen squirted some out.

Detergent. She turned on the water, which was cold because Angela hadn't turned on the heater. Karen noticed Danny's and Gio's glasses and washed them too, and then the pan from the eggs.

The house was quiet. She dried her hands, hung up the towel, and turned off the light. She started to go back upstairs, but instead went through the living room to Mr. Vega's study. Her iPod was lying next to the computer, which was some model she had never heard of. A USB cable ran from her iPod to the back of the computer. She didn't see the earphones anywhere. She disconnected the iPod and went upstairs and down the hall, stopping at the door to Gio's room. He would probably tell her where the earphones were, but did she want to wake up his parents by banging on the door?

She went to her mother and Anthony's room. She took off her shoes and got in bed on her mother's side. She buried her head in the pillow. It held the faint scent of her mother's perfume.

13

In the tree-shaded park on Águila Street, concrete benches faced the sidewalks. Anthony Quintana sat on one of them. He had worn a cheap shirt and dark slacks to avoid being marked as a tourist. So far the hustlers selling cigars or sex had left him alone, but he assumed he was being watched, State Security checking him over before the general showed up.

On Sundays fewer cars jammed the streets of central Havana, but people were out shopping, and tourists were plentiful—sunburned blonds with cameras and leather sandals; a man in a souvenir Che Guevara T-shirt. Revolutionary chic. They would take their photos of the crumbling buildings and call them picturesque. Some attempt had been made at restoration in this district. Over the roofs soared the white dome of *El Capitolio*. A fading recollection from childhood: swinging from his parents' hands down the steps of the capitol, the wide thoroughfare and parks along El Prado at their feet. His mother, Caridad, laughing, the sun on her hair. The wind teasing the skirt of her polka-dot dress.

He checked his watch. 3:10 P.M. He looked toward the corner, where a long line had formed at the bus stop. A young man with a paper bag slowed as he passed Anthony's bench. He made quick eye contact and murmured *dulces, caramelos* as though he were selling drugs. Anthony shook his head. Farther along the sidewalk a mother opened her change purse, and the man slipped some candy into her boy's outstretched palm.

When Anthony turned back, a thin, gray-haired figure in brown pants and a plain white shirt stood at the other end of his bench. Sunglasses hid his eyes. Abdel García had not materialized out of smoke; he must have approached from behind, walking across the park.

The general said, "I'm sorry to be late. Thank you for waiting." He inclined his angular head toward the next street north. "I have an apartment a few blocks from here. Come. We can talk without interruption." He smiled, and his jaw slid to one side.

They walked out of the park and took a left on Dragones, plunging into a stream of tourists and neighborhood residents. García moved among them like a fish through sea grass. They had entered Chinatown. Restaurants lined the narrow street. A painted dragon stretched across a red canvas awning, and paper lanterns hung from the eaves. Anthony hadn't walked into this area in a long time. The government had splashed some paint around and opened souvenir shops. The blood of the Chinese who had come to Havana to work on the railroad more than a century ago had been diluted by intermarriage, but traces still showed in the tilted eyes of a waitress in a red silk tunic, and in the high cheekbones of an old man in a sleeveless undershirt looking down from his balcony.

Anthony followed García into an alley, around a corner, and under wooden scaffolding that kept walls from collapsing onto each other. They passed a CDR office with the sign taped to a barred window. At the next door, García led him into a small foyer whose mosaic-patterned tile walls were barely visible in the light of a bulb screwed into an ancient porcelain socket. García removed his sunglasses. He apologized that his rooms were on the fourth floor. Extending an arm, he let Anthony go first.

A skylight at the top lit the steps. Anthony heard children's laughter, and the sound seemed to float in the stairwell without source or direction. The soft, scuffling footsteps behind him mirrored his own heavier tread. Ramiro had assured him that nothing would happen. Even so, his senses were alert, and the skin on his neck tingled. The stairs turned, and he glanced around, catching his companion blotting his crooked mouth with a handkerchief.

The general slid it back into his pocket. "My mother's grandparents lived in this building. Their name was Chu. They owned a shop below. I remember coming here as a very young child. He restored furniture, and she made the upholstery. I still have some of the pieces. The workmanship is exquisite. They are buried in the Chinese cemetery. Do you know it?"

Anthony said that he had visited the cemetery. It was in Vedado, he thought, on Twenty-sixth Street.

"Exactly." The general smiled. "The former tenant of this apartment moved out, and I took it over. I am too sentimental."

At dawn this morning, standing on a balcony at the Habana Libre, Anthony had told his wife about General García. He had not told her everything. Hector Mesa had spoken to a woman whose husband had been a political prisoner in Combinado del Este in 1968. Then a young sergeant, García wanted names, and when the man wouldn't cooperate, García ordered him strapped to a table. He beat the soles of his feet, covered his mouth and nose with wet towels, and put electrical wires on his genitals. Unable to endure it, the man broke down. His friends were arrested and executed. The prisoner spent ten years in solitary, was released, escaped to Miami, and two years later hanged himself in his garage.

On the top floor García knocked lightly on a door at the end of the hall and pushed it open. A young man not far out of his teens rose from a chair. He was dressed in civilian clothes, but his erect posture and precise movements left no doubt he was military.

Anthony made a quick inventory of the living room: carved mahogany sofa with fringed, red brocade cushions, two chairs with cane seats, a brass floor lamp with a red silk shade. Oriental rug, bamboo screen. Bedroom behind a closed door. An opening to the kitchen. By the window, a wooden table and chairs. A black enameled vase with yellow flowers. Anthony noticed that the walls and ceiling bore no cracks, no water damage. That itself was as odd as the opulent red upholstery.

He detected the faint smell of incense.

García asked him what he wanted to drink. "Whiskey, a beer, coffee?"

"Coffee, thanks."

"And for me."

The aide nodded and went into the kitchen. García crossed to the window and pushed open the shutters, which were painted bright green. He touched one of the chairs, an indication that his guest should sit down. García took the other and crossed his legs.

Thin nylon socks left no skin exposed. He put an elbow on the windowsill, settling against the frame as though warming himself in the sun.

"I don't live in this apartment."

"I didn't think you did," Anthony replied.

"Whatever you and I say, you may repeat to Ramiro Vega. He's a good soldier, a loyal comrade. A friend." García's smooth gray brows lifted, something at street level having caught his attention. After a moment he said, "How is your wife enjoying Cuba? Your children?"

"They are sight-seeing today. I expect a report later on," Anthony said.

García folded his handkerchief and dabbed his mouth. His forearms were completely hairless. "When I was young I lived in the United States for a year. A large and varied country, no? I worked on farms in the southern states. Alabama, Georgia, Louisiana. There was great poverty and prejudice against the blacks, and myself as well, a foreigner who spoke so little of their language. I drove to Chicago with some friends. My God, the cold from hell. The American workers are naïve but good-natured, do you not agree? After the Triumph of the Revolution I returned to Cuba."

His jaw seemed hinged on only one side. His lips barely moved, but his speech was distinct, if slow.

Anthony said, "Why did you ask me here, General?"

He pulled his gaze away from the street. "I want to know who you are. Your grandfather, Ernesto Pedrosa, is an old enemy of Cuba. Your father lives here, one of our heroes. Your sister is here. You are a friend of General Vega and yet also a friend of the oppositors such as José Leiva. A puzzle. How do you explain it?"

Again Anthony heard the voices of children.

He said, "I'm not political."

García smiled. "Anyone with a brain is political."

Anthony said, "Yolanda Cabrera is an old friend of mine from Camagüey. She would have been a doctor, but she had the wrong politics. Now she's a nurse in my father's old-age home. Leiva is a writer. He and his wife have a lending library in their house. They aren't enemies of Cuba."

"Do you know that Leiva writes scurrilous articles about me and sells them to newspapers in the United States and other countries?" García laughed, and his hollow cheeks creased into deep folds. "These stories are so false as to be amusing. How could anyone believe them?"

"If that's the case, what is your objection? It looks bad, cracking down on journalists. You'll get the world press up in arms. Even the left might notice."

The smile faded, replaced by a sigh. "Don't call what he does 'journalism.' It's propaganda. José Leiva is supported and directed by the American Interests Section here in Havana. You must know this. The so-called dissidents receive thirty million dollars a year from the United States through charities and international aid organizations. They hide behind human rights, but what they *want*, Quintana, what they *want*, is to replace the gains of the Revolution with predatory capitalism, the same system that perpetuates inequality in your country."

"Forgive me for saying so, General, but if the regime didn't stop them, hundreds of thousands of your countrymen would head north on anything that would float."

Again the crooked smile. "But you understand the situation. Cuba has been in an invisible war with the greatest power on earth for more than forty years. We are poor and weak. We can't change. It is the United States that must change its policies, beginning with the blockade."

"Ah. Well, on that one point we might agree," Anthony said.

The aide came out of the kitchen with a tray. He set two small cups on the table and a linen napkin beside each of them. García told him he could leave. The young man backed away, pivoted, and went out, closing the door softly behind him.

The general turned the vase and plucked a misshapen petal from one of the flowers. "Quintana, I don't care to argue with you about José Leiva. We have differences, but I believe that you and I want the same thing, a normalization of relations. A prosperous Cuba. A free and independent Cuba. Yes, I want this as much as you do, and I'm looking for friends inside the United States who can help shape that future."

Anthony drank some coffee. He could guess where this was going. He was about to be propositioned.

García brushed the petal off the windowsill. "Vega tells me that you are the heir to Ernesto Pedrosa's wealth and also, perhaps, his influence, but you are not part of the Miami Mafia. I believe this is true. I believe you would help our fatherland if you were given the chance." García used the phrase *nuestra patria* as though already certain where Anthony's loyalties lay.

"Near the end of November, a major under my command went to Brazil with a group of technicians from the Ministry of Basic Industries. His name is Omar Céspedes Ruiz. I hesitated in sending him." The general made a self-effacing smile. "I should have listened to my doubts. Céspedes went over to the Americans. You may guess what agony of remorse I've suffered."

"My sympathies," Anthony said.

García eyed him, then continued, "Last week Céspedes arrived in Washington, where he testified in a secret session of the House Intelligence Committee. Congressman Guillermo Navarro is on the committee. Two days ago Navarro flew to Miami. He was met by a private car and taken immediately to the house of Ernesto Pedrosa in Coral Gables. There was a party at the house that night. I do not know if you were there, but I assume it. The next morning Navarro was on a flight back to Washington, and the same day, yesterday, you arrived here. I conclude that Navarro's trip to Miami was related to yours to Havana. In what way? This I do not know."

With care Anthony set his cup into its saucer. The back of his neck was prickling again. How in hell had Abdel García learned so much? He said, "You've come to the wrong conclusion. Navarro may have had business with my grandfather. If so, he didn't share it with me."

"Yes, yes, you will say that. Let me finish. I trusted Céspedes, but as I look back, his opportunism and his avoidance of sacrifice become clear. I see his lies. He would sell his mother for the right price. He will tell the Americans whatever they want to hear. And the exiles? He will build great castles of lies, and they will believe them. You know this is so. It has happened before. You might say, what has this to do with me? My friend, if Céspedes is lying, it affects us all, this country and the United States."

García paused to blot his mouth. "I would like very much to know what Céspedes said to the committee. And what you intend to do with that information here in Cuba."

"What do *I* intend to do? I've never heard the name Céspedes. I know nothing about this."

García stared back as though waiting for a confession. When none came, he said, "If you don't know what Céspedes said, your grandfather does. He would tell you, I think."

"He and I don't discuss Cuba." Anthony added, "The lie could be yours. You want me to take your accusations about Céspedes back to Miami to throw the Committee into a panic. This is exactly why I stay clear of Cuban politics. It's a swamp of lies."

The general gazed out the window through half-closed eyes. "I would like very much to know what he said."

"You won't get it from me. I will be very clear. If I did know anything, I wouldn't tell you or anyone else in Cuba."

"I understand. You have your principles." He sipped his coffee. "If you asked for money, I could find it, but you're already a wealthy man. What can I offer you? I can promise that when you come here, you will have our hospitality. A furnished apartment. A car and driver, a housekeeper. The most beautiful girls in Havana, if that's your fancy. To come and go as you please. Whatever you want. You can say no, but if you do, this is the last time you will walk on Cuban soil. I spoke to Vega this morning. You can ask him about it. Don't expect him to intercede. He has a good career. He won't risk it for you."

Anthony could feel the heat of anger and confusion building in his chest. He drummed his fingers on the table, then stood up. "Find someone else."

Pausing his cup at his lips, García said, "I don't want your soul, Quintana. I want to know what Céspedes said to the Committee. That is all. I believe you have that information, and I want it. You will do this for Cuba if not for yourself."

"I can't give you what I don't have."

"Then find out."

Anthony stepped away from the table. "Don't contact me again."

"What will happen when the story appears in the *Miami Herald*? You have been an agent of ours for years. You have given us information about Ernesto Pedrosa and the militant exile organizations. You have given us the names of American spies in Havana. You have told us about your meeting with Congressman

Navarro regarding Omar Céspedes. What will you do when the news is made public? Where will you go? You and your new wife?"

Anthony crossed the room to escape the image of his own hands sending Abdel García through the window.

"José Leiva. Your friend. What about him?"

Anthony turned.

García said, "Leiva is a mercenary of the United States. He's guilty of spreading enemy propaganda. If he goes to prison again, it won't be for four years like last time. What do you think the prosecutor should ask for? Twenty years? Life?"

The possibilities turned Anthony's words to sand in his throat. García leaned back against the window frame, and the sun flooded across his body, glowing on his white shirt. "I'll give you a day to think about it. Vega knows how to reach me. Don't try to leave Cuba. You won't be allowed on the flight. Any of you."

Coming onto the sidewalk Anthony Quintana staggered and put a hand to his eyes. The gloom of the stairs had momentarily robbed him of sight. Gradually the street came into view: pedestrians maneuvering around him, a bicycle taxi, a fifty-year-old Buick picking its way through the potholes. He wanted to leave here, to get back to the Capitol, where he could easily find a taxi.

He turned the way he thought they had come, remembered nothing familiar, and doubled back. Looking up to get a sense of north and south, he noticed a set of green shutters at a window on the top floor of the building. He followed the imaginary trajectory of the general's gaze across the street and into a courtyard, and through the open arch he could see children, bare-chested boys about ten years old, chasing a soccer ball.

14

Expecting to be followed from Chinatown, Anthony swerved into an alley, went through the back door of a restaurant, and merged into the stream of tourists. He mixed with a group of them outside the Partagas cigar factory. He walked with them as far as a souvenir shop, then went inside and bought a ball cap with a Havana Club logo. He found a matching black T-shirt, changed in the store, and tossed the bag with his old shirt into a trash can on the street.

There was a phone kiosk just north of the Capitol. He called Miami.

Using references Hector Mesa would understand, Anthony told him about the meeting with Abdel García and the general's curiosity about what Céspedes may have told the CIA. He had no plans to share anything with García, but he needed to know what was going on.

"I don't like working in the dark, my friend. See what you can find out from the old man."

"I already ask him. I say to myself, well, Señor Anthony is going down there and they want him to do this and that, and maybe it's all a plate of shit, you know how these people are, so I'm going to check it out."

"And?"

"He says it's top, top secret and they didn't tell him anything, but I never seen the old man so happy. Don't worry, I got some ideas. It might take some time. A few days maybe. You want me to come down there?"

"Not necessary, but thanks."

"Listen, you should get a cell phone. They got them for tourists, you know? I give you a number in Havana to call if you need to go someplace quick."

Anthony had to laugh. "You're amazing. Wait, I have a pen. All right, what is it?" He wrote the number on the back of a business card.

"Listen," Hector said. "What about that guy? The American. You going to ask him about all this stuff?"

"I already did. We're meeting in an hour."

"I can come down. It's no trouble."

Anthony told him, "No stay there, but if things change, I'll call you."

He calmed his nerves with a Scotch on the rocks at a bar near the *Plaza de la Catedral*. Sitting in a back corner, he could look through the window at the tourists aiming their viewfinders at the church, at the *mulatas* in bright scarves and long skirts, at the toothless old men playing their guitars, music straight out of Buena Vista, the whole scene right off a postcard. It occurred to him that he might see his family walking across the square, his sister impatiently beckoning everyone to hurry up.

He stared at each cobblestone and mildewed column, the iron rings on the cathedral doors, the bright blue trim on the balconies across the plaza. When would he see them again? Ever? He dragged them into his heart through his eyes and ordered another drink.

Everett Bookhouser was waiting for him at the end of the Malecón, where the road turned south to the port. The area was thick with tour buses, horse-drawn carriages, drivers hawking rides in old American cars. Bookhouser fit in: He had the camera and fanny pack. A map of Havana stuck out of the back pocket of his hiking shorts. They crossed the road and stood by the seawall to talk. Anthony did not mention his phone call to Miami.

Along the wall, the fishermen circled their weighted lines around their heads, then let them go. The monofilament spun out like spiders' webs. Across the harbor entrance, the age-blackened limestone walls of the massive *Fortaleza de la Cabaña* stretched along the promontory. Anthony had seen the inner walls; they were pocked by bullet holes from the hundreds of executions ordered by Che Guevara.

"The apartment," Bookhouser said. "What street were you on?"

"South of Dragones. I'm not sure. I could probably find it."

"You didn't see anyone else?"

"Just the aide. He made some coffee, then García told him to leave." When Bookhouser fell silent to ponder this, Anthony asked, "Is this how State Security operates? Or did the army set it up?"

"Don't know. The goons at State Security don't usually take people up to a fourth-floor nookie pad in Chinatown, but I'm willing to be surprised."

"I want García off my back," Anthony said.

Bookhouser didn't answer. A Panamanian freighter glided past, churning the green water, rocking the small boats tied to jetties along the seawall.

"Tell you what," he said. "I need to have a conversation with some people about this. You contact García tomorrow and tell him you'll look into it. Tell him you need some time."

"I see. You want me to feed García a story that someone in Washington puts together." Anthony straight-armed the wall and took a breath. "I should have told you to go screw yourself two days ago."

"I don't like getting civilians involved, but like I said, we need your help."

"Can you get my family out of here if I decide it's necessary?"

"That would look a little strange," Bookhouser said. "There's no immediate danger to Ramiro and certainly none to you or your family. Just talk to García. We'll give you something to throw to him, and that will be the end of it."

While waiting at the bar with his Scotch, Anthony had thought about the question on which Gail had fixated. *Why Ramiro?* He had never been able to give her an answer. "Let me ask you something, Bookhouser. You want Ramiro Vega. Why? Because's he's a general? No. There has to be more than that. I believe it's related to Céspedes and what he told the Intelligence Committee—whatever that is."

Bookhouser followed the freighter on its way toward the Straits of Florida. "What you want to keep your mind on is this: Ramiro needs to get out of Cuba. Otherwise, he's going to be in trouble."

"Who's after him?"

"Céspedes wasn't specific."

"Bullshit. He told you, and Ramiro will ask me."

"Ramiro will know, or he can figure it out." Bookhouser looked at Anthony. "I'm giving you as much information as I can. We need you to get back to García. Tell him you're working on it, and you think you can get the answers. Tell him you want an apartment on the beach. Tell him you want better Cuban-American relations. Whatever floats his boat. Let me know what he says, the questions he asks."

Bookhouser's gaze went back out to sea. "When are you going to talk to your brother-in-law?"

"I had planned to do so later tonight. Gail and the kids and I are having dinner with the Leivas. Maybe I should wait. After this with García . . ."

"No, I want you to go ahead. If Vega is interested in what we discussed, he can ask you to get back in touch with me, or he can do it himself. Give him my number. Either way, call me tomorrow. If you need to meet me, I'll be around."

Anthony gave a short laugh. "This is great. I love it."

Bookhouser said, "You're doing the right thing."

"How do I know?"

"We're not the bad guys, Quintana."

"In Cuba you are. If they found out I was talking to you, Ramiro would be suspected as a traitor for taking me into his house. I give him enough problems already, the grandson of Ernesto Pedrosa. They would like to put his head on a stake in the *Plaza de la Revolución*."

"Are you going to do this or not?"

"*Carajo*. Yes, of course I will do it. Of course. Do me a favor. You want me to play spy for you, okay, fine. I haven't asked anything for myself, but this is what I want. Arrange U.S. visas for José Leiva and his wife and her son."

"They want to leave?"

"They might."

Over the top of his sunglasses, Bookhouser's pale blue eyes studied him. "That won't make Navarro happy. José Leiva has been fairly critical of the exiles and of U.S. policy. Certain people in

Miami think he's a Castro stooge. Which I suppose you know about."

"Three visas. José Leiva, Yolanda Cabrera, Mario Cabrera. If it becomes necessary to get them out, I don't want any problems at the other end."

"All right."

Releasing a breath, Anthony leaned on the wall for a minute, suddenly aware of the tension that had twisted the muscles down his back. "I will be grateful for whatever you can do for them."

"You're welcome," Bookhouser said.

Anthony said, "When I talk to Ramiro, he will ask me about the informant."

"Informant?"

"The person who told Céspedes that Ramiro wants to defect, your 'reliable source.' Navarro wouldn't give me a name. It would add some credibility with Ramiro if I knew who it was."

Bookhouser hesitated. "His girlfriend. Her name is Olga Saave-dra. I wouldn't tell him about it unless I had to. She could be at risk. I'm sorry. Your sister probably isn't aware."

"Probably not." Anthony showed no reaction. "This woman. How does she know Omar Céspedes?"

"From MINBAS. She does some work for their public relations office. She and Céspedes had something going in the past, and he helped get her the job. Olga gets around." Bookhouser scanned the park across the street. "Well. I'm going to tour that fort before it closes. They've got some nice ceramics. Have you been in there?"

"Not lately," Anthony said. "Where are you staying?"

"A colleague and I are renting a room in a *casa particular* under the name Philippe and Sophie Dubois. You don't need to know the address. I'm reachable by phone."

"Dubois. Are you French now?"

"From Lyon. I manage a chain of photo supply stores. My wife is an artist who spends a lot of her time at the museums." A smile appeared fleetingly on Bookhouser's thin lips. "The owners no-ticed that we don't share the same bed. I think they feel sorry for me. We'll talk tomorrow."

Everett Bookhouser went back across the street and headed west, swallowed up by the crowds of people milling about the crafts fair, lines of booths with hand-carved ox carts and maracas and the other assorted trash that tourists took home.

There would be taxis over there. For a few dollars Anthony could find one to take him back to Marta's house. Gail would ask him what had happened this afternoon, and he didn't know what he would tell her.

The fishermen stood twenty yards farther down the sidewalk, a bottle of cheap rum or *aguardiente* next to their bait bucket. More men fished from small boats close to shore. A teenager floated on a truck inner tube. The fishermen on the sidewalk began to talk about whether to use the next fish for bait or keep it to eat. From their accents Anthony guessed the men had come from central Cuba, perhaps Camagüey.

He vaulted to the top of the seawall and sat facing the water.

The men's backs were wide, their long arms heavy with muscle, their skin dark as belt leather. Anthony remembered such men in the cane fields in Camagüey. He had seen them riding with their machetes in open trucks on the long, straight roads. His grandfather Quintana's mixed-race family had worked at the *central*, the sugar mill owned by a family so wealthy they had sent their sons to Harvard. The owners fled to Miami after the Revolution and settled in Palm Beach.

In elementary school, Anthony had gone with his classmates to the sugar collective. The kids provided no real help; the purpose was to teach them about work. It was summer, and they wore long pants and long-sleeved shirts and gloves to protect their skin from the sharp edges of the cane stalks. Carrying armloads of it, they sweated like pigs under their straw hats, and their red scarves quickly soaked through. The sugarcane had seemed twenty feet tall, and as the men swung their machetes, the steel sounded like bells, and the cane fell as though pushed over by the wind. Yolanda Cabrera had been there, too. When Anthony ran out of water in his canteen, she ran to refill it for him.

The steel clanged on the tough stalks, and the kids sweated and sang. *Barquito de papel, mi amigo fiel, llévame a navegar por el ancho mar*— Little paper boat, my faithful friend, take me sailing on the wide sea—

Smiling, Anthony shook his head, unable to remember any more of it. Yolanda had known all the songs, all the words.

He watched one of the fisherman pull in a fish, drawing it out of the water, rolling the line around his plastic yo-yo. He tossed the fish into a cooler, and it beat against the sides for a while, then was quiet.

Anthony had wanted to rent a car and take Danny to Camagüey with him, the two of them. He had wanted to show him the town, Cascorro, where he'd grown up, its dirt roads and concrete houses, the stream where he used to go fishing. The elementary school, how small it was. On a trip to Cascorro, they would have to carry their own food and take things to give away. It would be good for Danny to see that.

Would have been good. There wasn't any chance now that they would be going to Camagüey.

15

The lenses were scratched, and a bent wire held one of the hinges together. José Leiva took off his bifocals, revealing the deep lines at the corners of his eyes and dark pouches beneath. He unfolded the new glasses and held them up to the light. "Yes. Very nice."

Leiva slid the earpieces through his shaggy white hair and settled the glasses on his nose. He picked up a book from the side table, turned it over, and read the print on the back, tilting his head to bring it into focus. He lifted the book toward his visitors, a salute. "*Son perfectos.* Thank you, Anthony. Thanks to all of you." His smile went around the small living room to include his six visitors from America, jammed onto the sofa and sitting in chairs brought over from the dining table.

Sipping her wine, Gail watched with interest José Leiva's reactions to the things that Anthony took out of the bag: a notebook computer, a staple remover, a box of paper clips, ink cartridges for the printer, film for the camera. Leiva would look at whatever was put into his hands, nod politely, and explain how that this or that item would be helpful in his work. The more personal items—a shirt, some underwear, a package of socks—received the same solemn appraisal. He reminded Gail of her political science professor in college, a gentle but melancholy man past middle age, with a small white beard like Leiva's. The professor had been so conscious of the misery of human affairs that suggesting in his classroom the possibility of happiness would have been as much a *faux pas* as laughter in a confessional.

Leiva's wife, Yolanda Cabrera, walked from his armchair to his desk, stacking and arranging. There were CDs of classical music, double-A batteries, a can opener, a pack of 60-watt light bulbs, vitamin pills for him and calcium tablets for her. She set his old eyeglasses alongside the other gifts, perhaps saving them for the day that the new pair might break. Gail thought Yolanda would be the sort of woman who could make dinner from one egg and a carrot.

When she came back, Anthony handed her a set of Caswell-Massey bath products that Gail had bought for her. With a cry of delight, she bent down to give Gail a hug. She opened the hand lotion and rubbed it into her skin. "This is wonderful! Thank you, Gail. You are too good."

Trailing the faint scent of lilies, she put the box on the desk, then detoured by the front windows to pull back the lace curtain and look out at the street.

Reading her mind, Leiva asked, "*¿Mario no viene?*"

"*Me dijo que sí.*" Yolanda told him that Mario would be here. He had said he would. She let the curtain fall into place.

The house was located in the Santos Suárez district. Ramiro Vega's driver had brought them in the minivan just past sunset, not too late to view the run-down condition of the neighborhood. The house two doors down might have been built a century ago, with its Doric columns of poured concrete and its rusted metal railings. No one lived there. The roof had fallen in, and weeds grew in the cracked walls. Leiva's house was newer, perhaps from the 1940s, with a small front yard and a chain-link fence. Windows of frosted glass set in flat metal bars enclosed the porch, and potted flowers brightened the doorway.

José and Yolanda had given a tour of their library—three walls of books in what had once been the garage. Shelves made of old lumber went floor to ceiling. Anthony gave them the hardcover books he had brought: the latest Octavio Paz and Mario Vargas Llosa; Spanish editions of Milan Kundera, Alexander Solzhenitsyn, and Vaclav Havel. José Leiva examined each one carefully, running his hands over the covers, flipping through the pages.

In the last light of day, Yolanda had led them into the backyard. More flowers. A trellis. Folding chairs where one might sit and listen to the birds. A garden to supply fruits and vegetables. For twenty pounds of boniatos and a bag of mangos, a neighbor had repaired the brakes on their car. Yolanda tended the garden, worked at the retirement home, organized the library, and still managed to keep her floors mopped, the laundry done, and a smile on her face. Gail thought that she herself, put in Yolanda's shoes, would have wanted to cut her wrists.

Danny leaned over to take another ham croquette off the plate on the coffee table. He had already eaten half a dozen croquettes, two glasses of orange soda, and several crackers. Dinner would be served when Mario arrived.

"What's this for?" Danny picked up the end of a yellow extension cord that came through a window and dangled against the wall near the desk.

Leiva explained that it was in case of an *apagón*, a blackout. The cord ran to the house behind them, which was on a different power grid. If the lights went out, you plug in a lamp.

Anthony finished his translation, then said, "Danny, Angela. I have never seen an *apagón* in the tourist sector, nor in Miramar in all the years that I have visited my sister's house. Why do you think that is?"

"Because Aunt Marta pays her electric bills?" Danny's flip answer was met by a cool look from his father.

In the adjacent chair, Angela made a soft laugh. "There is no electric company. The government owns everything."

"Whatever," said her brother.

Anthony said, "You don't remember anything I told you about Cuba, do you?"

"Yes, I do. You just never told me about blackouts."

"Why do you *think* the lights stay on in the tourist sector?"

Danny glanced uncomfortably at the others in the room. "Because . . . they don't want the tourists to leave."

"Exactly. Start paying more attention. You might learn something." Anthony resumed taking things out of the bag. Danny stared at the floor. Gail almost felt sorry for him, being put on the spot that way. Anthony had been wrapped tight as a golf ball ever since coming back from his meeting with General García.

What Gail had wanted was not to rush over here but to talk with Anthony for more than five minutes about whatever in God's name had gone on with Abdel García. He'd come back to Marta's, turned on the hot water heater in the bathroom, and in the short time it took the water to heat up, he had told her that General García expected him to become a spy for Cuba. Worse: The CIA wanted him to play along. Gail said no way, are you crazy? She followed him into the bathroom, but he told her to leave him alone. He hadn't decided what he was going to do.

Anthony looked into the zippered bag as if he had forgotten something and pulled out a small, pale blue box tied with a narrow white ribbon. He said in Spanish that it was for Yolanda from both himself and Gail. It was nothing, not expensive, but they thought she might like it. Yolanda came over and took the box, opened it, and exclaimed, "*¡Ay, qué preciosa!*"

Gail had never seen it before: a hair clip with a floral design that looked very much like antique sterling silver. She knew the box: Tiffany. Yolanda thanked them both, then held the gift out to her husband. "José, look, isn't it pretty?"

"*Póntela,*" he said.

She hesitated, then laughed and pulled the simple plastic clip off her gray ponytail. She swept her thick, wavy hair back with both hands, fastened the silver clip, and turned to show them. The flowers curved gracefully around the back of her head. Her hair wasn't gray anymore; it was black and silver.

"That's so elegant," Irene said. "*Muy elegante.* Gail, did you pick that out?"

Gail sent her mother a little smile, then looked at Anthony. He sat back down on the other end of the small sofa and said quietly over Karen's head, "I noticed it when I was getting my watch repaired. You don't mind, do you?"

She reached across and squeezed his hand. "Of course not. It's perfect for her." Gail smiled once more at Yolanda, aware at the same time of a nudge of jealousy, which was totally irrational. There was nothing between Anthony and this woman. They had known each other from childhood. She took care of his father. They were lifelong friends, like cousins, one could say. Anyway, Yolanda was married to a man she clearly loved and admired.

On her chair next to Leiva's, Irene set her wineglass on his lamp table and picked up the paperback that he had given to Anthony, the collection of his writings. She dropped it on her lap and flipped through her phrase book until Angela showed her the place. Irene said, "*Señor Leiva, usted es escritor. ¿Qué . . .*" She bit her lower lip in concentration. "Wait, wait, I've got it. *¿Qué escrita?*"

Leiva's white brows rose quizzically before he nodded. "Ah. What I write."

Anthony translated: "José writes articles for the foreign press. The official newspapers in Cuba won't take them. An article of his was just published in *El País*, in Madrid. It will appear in *The Washington Post* next Sunday. He used to work in television. He made some videos about malnutrition in the eastern provinces and gave them to the BBC. He spent four years in prison for that."

José Leiva smiled. "I told lies. Nobody in Cuba is hungry."

"He was in a cell with murderers and thieves. He says it wasn't all bad. He lost twenty pounds. Unfortunately, he has put it all back."

"They think I am *contrarrevolucionario*. Maybe a terrorist." Leiva made his hands into claws and growled at Karen. "A very bad man."

Karen laughed.

He leaned over to give her an affectionate pat on the knee. "The Cuban people are educated and intelligent. *Somos seres humanos*— human beings, and human beings have from God the desire to be free. Anthony, *por favor*."

Anthony spoke Leiva's words: "Fidel Castro said that in Cuba there are no banned books, only the lack of money to buy them. The independent libraries started when people decided to take him at his word. They shared their books with anyone who wanted to read. When I was released from prison, Yolanda and I joined their movement. There is no censorship in this house."

Danny reached for another croquette. Anthony said, "Danny, *escucha*."

"I am listening, Dad."

From his armchair, the focal point of the room, José Leiva told them about the recent visits of a United States senator; a reporter from Italy; a group from Human Rights Watch. Anthony translated. Gail watched Danny stifling a yawn. His jaw stiffened, and his nostrils flared.

Finally, and more with gestures than with words, José Leiva told Danny to get up, walk to the front windows, and look across the street. After a glance at his father, he gave a little shrug and did as Leiva had asked. He stood by the window and pulled back the curtain.

"Okay. What am I looking at?"

"The house over there, you see it? *Con dos pisos.* Two . . . floor. Look at the tree. They cut it so they can see from the window on top of the house. The window that has no light. They watch us from there. They are looking at you right now. They are taking your *foto.*"

Danny stepped back.

"Don't be afraid. They want that, to make you afraid." He smiled and signaled to his wife. *"Es tarde, mi amor, se mueren de hambre."* The guests were getting hungry. She replied that Mario would be here soon, but yes, it was late, and they should eat.

"Let me help." Irene got up. Her earrings clicked and swung in her auburn curls. She had found the earrings in a souvenir shop in Old Havana, miniature tropical fruit in colors bright enough to compete with her green slacks and yellow pullover. Irene had said she wanted to look Cuban, but Gail hadn't seen any actual *cubanas* dress this way. Yolanda Cabrera wore flat shoes, black pants, and a sleeveless shirt of tiny black-and-white checks.

"I'll come too," Gail said.

In the kitchen, which was barely big enough for three women to turn around without bumping into one another, Yolanda rinsed a bowl in the sink. On the windowsill, placed where the afternoon sun would come in, plants in glass jars sprouted new leaves. Wooden shelves took the place of proper cabinets, holding dishes and spices and cloves of garlic and dried sausages on a string. Yolanda gave Irene the bowl for the rice and showed Gail where to find the oil and vinegar for the salad. She opened the oven door and took out a pan of six plump, crispy fish. She sprinkled fresh parsley over the fish and slid the *tostones*, the fried green plantains, into the oven to warm.

Her nails were unpolished, her hands roughened by work. She wasn't beautiful, Gail thought. She wore no makeup, except for a touch of red lipstick. When she smiled, wrinkles appeared around her eyes and mouth, and she was overweight. Immediately Gail felt guilty for noticing this, and revised her appraisal: Yolanda was voluptuous.

Irene left the kitchen with plates and knives and forks to set the table.

Gail sliced the cucumbers and tomatoes on a cutting board so old the center had been carved to a shallow bowl. "You speak English very well. Where did you learn it?"

"In school. I studied in the University, and I listen to the radio from Miami." Working at the stove, with her back to Gail, Yolanda tucked in a strand of hair that had escaped from the clip. The silver flowers gleamed in the light from the fluorescent tube in the ceiling, and the clip barely contained Yolanda's thick, wavy hair. Gail's own hair, blond and straight, was chopped level with her jawline. Anthony had said he liked it that way, but she wasn't sure he meant it.

"Does Anthony come often to visit you and José when he's in Havana? He doesn't talk much about Cuba. I really don't know what he does here."

"What he does? He comes to be with his family, you know, his sister Marta and the children. He has many friends here. He visits us, too."

"And when José was in prison?"

"Yes, Anthony was here, and he took me to see José. They put him in a prison in Ciego de Ávila, far away. That's what they do. They make it hard for the families to see the prisoners. Anthony tried to help. He talked to his sister's husband, but General Vega didn't want to do anything. Maybe he couldn't, I don't know."

Yolanda's warm brown eyes lifted to Gail's, and her lips parted in a smile. Her front teeth were slightly crooked, but this was hardly a flaw. "Two years ago, maybe more, Anthony told me about you, a beautiful American lawyer. He said he would marry you."

Laughing, Gail said, "Oh, well, then you knew before I did."

"I hope you come back many times, and that Mario will be a friend of Daniel and Angela. And your daughter, Karen. How funny she is. And your mother is so nice. I like her very much. This is your house. Okay?"

"That's very kind of you," Gail said. She could imagine how Anthony would want to return again and again to this house and these people, to walk through this tiny kitchen with its row of plants in bright jars in the window, to sit in the backyard with his friend José while Yolanda tended her garden. A thousand miles from the pretensions of Miami.

Yolanda lifted the lid off a battered pot and stirred what was inside, a mixture of red beans and ham and chunks of a yellow root vegetable that Gail didn't recognize. A cloud of savory steam drifted upward.

"How did you meet José?"

"He came to Camagüey City to work in the TV station, and he stayed in the building where I lived with Mario. We have been married for eleven years. My first husband was a soldier, and he died in the war in Angola. Mario never knew him. For Mario, José is his father."

A curious fact came into Gail's mind. Yolanda and Mario had the same last name. Cabrera. Why didn't the son have the name of his father? Yolanda had called him her first husband, but perhaps they had never married. How did one ask that question?

Irene came back in, and Yolanda gave her a bowl to fill with red beans. Irene said she would love it if Yolanda and José could come to Miami. They could stay at her house if they wanted. She had plenty of room. "Have you ever been to the United States?"

"No. I want very much to see it. I have a brother in Tampa, but I have not seen him since 1980. He went from Mariel in the boat lift. He wants us to come visit him, but they won't give us permission to leave."

"Who, your government?"

"Oh, yes! We are criminals." She laughed. "Not just José. Me too. In 1994 there was a *manifestación* . . . what do you call it? A demonstration, at the statue of Antonio Maceo on the Malecón. I was arrested with the others, and they put us in jail for a week. So when José and I ask permission to leave the country, they stamp our papers, '*no autorizado a viajar.*' 'Not authorized to travel.' "

"Well, I don't understand it," Irene said. "You'd think they'd be *happy* if you left, being dissidents and all."

"It's crazy, I know." Yolanda bent to check on the *tostones* in the oven. "Gail, do you like onions in the salad? I have some in . . . *el frigidaire.* I don't know how to say that in English."

"Refrigerator." Gail found the onion.

"Ref— Refri—" Yolanda laughed and gave up with a wave of her hand.

The lid clanged when Irene dropped it back on the pot. "Yolanda? I've got to do something to help you and José. I don't know what it is yet. When I get home, I could write some letters. Maybe you need donations. I know loads of people."

Setting the pan of *tostones* on the stove, Yolanda turned to look at Irene. "You can help us in Havana, if you want to."

"Fine. Just tell me what to do."

Gail's knife stopped halfway through the onion.

Yolanda said, "We have the new computer from Anthony. Now we can do e-mail, but we need Internet cards. We can't buy them, but you can. You're a tourist."

"What do you mean, you can't buy them?"

"They're for tourists or if you have permission from the government."

Irene's blue eyes widened. "You need permission to go on the Internet?"

"Yes, but if we have a card, we can do it. There is a code, and we use our telephone line."

"I'll buy your cards for you."

"Mother—"

"I'm going to help them," Irene said. "Yolanda, how do we do this?"

"It's very easy. We go to the commercial center, and you show your passport, and they give you the cards. They cost fifteen dollars. I want four, so I'll give you sixty dollars, and you buy the cards. They never ask questions."

"Okay, but you're not giving me any money. I'll get you as many as you need."

Gail said, "We should talk to Anthony first."

"But darling, *you're* not doing this, I am. They're not going to make problems for a sweet little sixty-year-old grandma. I'll take Karen with me. Yolanda just said nobody gives you a hassle."

How was Gail to explain that Anthony was caught between the CIA and *las Fuerzas Armadas*? What if his mother-in-law was seen illegally buying phone cards for the dissidents?

Yolanda filled the silence with, "Gail is right, Irene. She should ask her husband. If Anthony gives his permission, then we'll do it."

With a sigh, Irene said, "Gee, I forgot how much fun it is, being married."

"No, Mother, it's not that, it's . . . a courtesy."

"You're right. You're right." Irene picked up the bowl of beans to take to the dining table.

Gail noticed Yolanda's eyes move to the back door, where a panel of glass formed a window. She smiled and tossed her dish towel aside. There was a knock, then the door opened and a young man in blue jeans appeared. His long black hair was braided with beads and tied back with a leather cord.

"*Hola, mami.*" He picked Yolanda up off the floor in a hug and set her down again. She kissed him on both cheeks. Their speech flowed too fast for Gail to understand a word of it.

Mario Cabrera had melting brown eyes and full lips. His black leather vest hung open over a silky white shirt. A tiger was tattooed on his forearm, and a small silver earring in the shape of a crucifix shone in one earlobe.

With an arm still around his mother, he noticed Gail and held out his hand. He wore two silver rings and a small one of carved black stone. "Hello."

"This is Mario, my son," Yolanda said. "Here at last. *Muy tarde.* Why do you come in the back door?" She shushed his apologies. "Mario, this is Mrs. Connor, the wife of Anthony Quintana."

"How are you, Mrs. Connor?" He bent to put a quick, customary kiss on Gail's right cheek.

"Call me Gail if you like. I've heard so many nice things about you, Mario. The kids are in the other room. They'd love to meet you. But you've met Angela already."

He smiled and shook his head. "Sorry. My English . . . very bad."

"Mario!" José Leiva called out that he didn't believe it, was that boy really here?

In the living room he went to his father. "*¿Qué tal, viejo?*"

Leiva stared up at him for several seconds, then asked where he had been keeping himself. They had been worried. Did he need an invitation to visit his parents? Mario nodded and said he was very sorry. Leiva held out an arm. Mario helped him out of the chair, and the two men embraced.

———

At dinner the talk was of family, not politics. They wanted to know about Angela and Danny, about Karen. They talked about Gail and Anthony's wedding. Translating for Mario, Yolanda asked Gail to explain what an American lawyer did in the courtroom. Angela told them what she was studying at the University of Miami.

The dining table was barely big enough, but they all squeezed in, Mario sitting on a wooden box topped with books from the library. They put the kids at one end, adults at the other. The table was a garden of color: blue cloth, a green two-liter soda bottle for water, red and yellow carnations for a centerpiece, and a cheerful mismatch of plates.

Karen talked about her soccer matches at school and how she liked sports more than ballet, which she took for only two years. She wasn't any good at it, she said, not like Angela, who was great. Angela sighed and sadly admitted she hadn't made it into the Miami City Ballet. But she would take a job in another company, if one were offered. Mario asked if she had seen the *Ballet Nacional de Cuba*. Perhaps they could go together, if she had time. He smiled at her. They reached for the serving spoon at the same moment. She told him to go ahead. He said please, after you. Finally he heaped rice on her plate until she laughed and told him to stop, that was too much.

Angela's despondent mood over her faithless boyfriend in Miami wouldn't last much longer, Gail thought. She exchanged a glance with Anthony. He didn't seem displeased that this young man was paying attention to his daughter.

Mario asked Danny, *"¿Qué te parece Cuba?"* What did he think of Cuba?

Danny swallowed a mouthful of fish. *"Me gusta mucho."* In Spanish that his father patiently corrected, Danny said he and his cousin had been around the city yesterday, and he had seen everything. He liked the music, the people, the old buildings. He was surprised to see that nobody was starving, which wasn't the story he'd heard in Miami. "Gio says you don't have to pay to go to a doctor, and the education is free, too. Is that true?"

Mario laughed. "The doctor in this neighborhood drives a taxi because he makes only twenty dollars a month in the clinic. Education is free, that's true, but they tell you what to study. They send you to the countryside to do voluntary work, and if you don't go, they kick you out of school."

"My cousins don't go to the countryside," Danny said.

"Their father is an important man," Mario countered. "If you want to know how we live, you should stay out of the nightclubs and the tourist district. I'll take you to Cerro, to Guanabacoa, to Matanzas. It's not like Miramar, where your relatives live. We'll go out to the countryside. Open your eyes, and you'll see."

Danny was skeptical. "In Miami they were talking about people setting off bombs. I haven't heard any explosions since I've been here. I haven't seen any bomb damage or craters or anything like that."

Gail could see Anthony's irritation, but he let Mario answer.

"You don't hear about it because they don't put it on the news. People know. Ask your cousin. Ask General Vega."

"I did ask my cousin. He said it was mercenaries from Miami." Danny looked at his father. "That's what Gio said."

Mario shrugged. "No, I think they are from here."

"A gang of crazy kids," Leiva said. "They think violence is the only way. Good never springs from violence. We must follow the law and make our demands in a relentless but nonviolent way." He lifted a hand. "Argue with me if you like, but I am right about this."

Sitting next to Angela, Gail leaned close to hear her translations. Irene's eyes were fixed on the movement of Angela's lips.

Mario said, "I respect your views, papi, but some people don't want to wait another forty or fifty years. Change will come faster than we think. A great wave is building, and it will take one crack in the wall to bring it all down. One small crack."

Anthony said, "I understand your passion. When I was your age— Well, I was sure that I could liberate the world. I left Miami and went to Nicaragua to fight with the Sandinistas. It was bloody and useless."

"Nicaragua was not your country," Mario said. "Would you die for America?"

Anthony said, "Yes. If the cause were right."

"And I would give my life for Cuba." Mario spoke as though it was completely normal, talking of death and martyrdom. "I'm not afraid to die or to be put in prison for the rest of my life. My father told me that the day he became free was the day they turned the key of his cell. Why? He had nothing left to lose. It was in prison that he discovered his purpose. A man without a purpose may believe he is free, but he lives inside an illusion. That is the real death."

"Don't speak like that," his mother said. "You're scaring me."

Smiling slightly, Leiva stroked his fingers through his short white beard. "Mario. There will be a meeting here on Wednesday night, some independent journalists and librarians. We're going to discuss ways to work together. You should come."

He shook his head and said he was sorry, but he would be busy practicing with the band.

"Busy with the band. I knew it. Young men in Cuba are all talk. They're only interested in music and girls."

Yolanda broke in. "That's enough. Please, José. And you be quiet too, Mario."

"That meeting could be a mistake," Anthony said. "I've heard rumors that the dissidents are being watched more closely. If this is so, holding a meeting at your house would be provocative."

"Yes, we always hear rumors," Leiva said. "We're not doing anything against the law. Where did you hear these rumors?"

"This one comes from a woman with friends in the army. Olga Saavedra. You remember Olga."

"Ah! The devil take her. Where did you see Olga?"

Anthony explained that she was helping his sister Marta plan the *quinceañera* for her younger daughter. He had seen Olga at the house, and they had talked.

Tearing a piece of bread, Leiva said, "Nothing will happen. Do you know why?"

Angela translated: Arrests of peaceful dissidents would look bad for the regime. The international press would scream if the dissident movement were crushed. As long as they stayed within the law, Castro had to leave them alone.

Leiva dredged his bread through the liquid remaining on his plate. "Olga Saavedra is working for MININT. Look at what she did six years ago, how she betrayed me."

Yolanda objected. She thought that Olga had been pushed to do it to save herself from prison.

Leiva shook his head. "She is working for MININT, I am sure of it. She probably told Anthony because she knew he would pass it on to me. This is a way to disrupt our activities."

Yolanda said, "Shall I make some coffee?"

"My wife doesn't like this kind of talk."

Irene said she was going to help clear the table. Angela said no, to sit down, she and Danny and Karen would do it. Danny slouched in his chair. "Get up," she said.

He laughed when she poked him. "Men don't clear the table in Cuba."

"Get up! Dad, tell him not to be such a slug."

"Danny, help your sister."

Mario stood up with his plate and walked around the table collecting the others. He told his mother to stay with her guests. He would make the coffee.

Danny pushed out of his chair and laughed again. "I was kidding."

Elbows on the table, Anthony hid his smile behind clasped hands. When the boys were gone he said, "Mario is a good influence on Danny. He has turned out very well. You should be proud of him."

"We are," Yolanda said. "He's a good boy. I'm sorry to hear him talk about prison and dying. So serious!"

"It's his age," Anthony said. "I was the same way."

"*La juventud tiene su pasión,*" said José. Youth has its passion.

Yolanda steered the conversation from this gloomy topic by asking Irene what she wanted to see next in Havana, and Irene told her she hoped to spend some time in *Habana Vieja* looking for artists' studios. They talked about the new exhibition at the *Bellas Artes*.

Soon Mario returned with a tray of small cups, followed by Angela with sugar and spoons. When he reached Anthony's place he said, "Señor Quintana." He made a request that Gail couldn't follow.

Anthony said, "He wants to take the kids to see the *cañonazo*. They shoot the cannons at nine o'clock at La Fortaleza. The *cañoneros* are in costume, old Spanish uniforms." He checked his watch. "If they leave now, they can make it."

Gail said, "Wait. Is this all right? For Karen, I mean."

Mario said, "I have the car of a friend. I drive very good."

"They'll be safe with Mario. I think they'd enjoy it." Anthony smiled at his daughter. "You want to go, sweetheart?"

"Please."

Karen was bouncing up and down on her toes. "Mom, say yes. Please, can I go?"

"Okay, then. Sounds like fun."

Anthony said, "Mario, what about our flute serenade?" When he repeated the question in Spanish, Mario pulled in a breath.

"Oh! I am sorry!" Yes, he had promised to play the flute at dinner tonight in honor of their marriage. It was outside in the car—

With a smile, Anthony waved off the idea and told him they would have their concert another time. Then he stood up and reached into his pants pocket. "This is for you." Gail saw the envelope that contained two hundred dollars and a letter wishing him well.

Mario shook his head. He didn't need any money, thank you. He had enough. It was no problem. Anthony held out the envelope and said to take it. "No, no, *está bien*." There was an argument, which José Leiva ended. Take it, he said. Are you getting rich now, playing with your band?

He took the envelope. *"Muchas gracias, señor."* He embraced Anthony quickly, and Anthony gave him a pat on the back.

From the corner of her eye Gail thought she saw such venomous dislike on Danny's face that she had to look again, but it was gone, a flicker like lightning in a distant storm, and she hoped she'd been wrong.

The young people left through the kitchen door. Gail thought it was odd, but Mario explained that he had found a parking place around the corner, and it was shorter this way.

The night was clear and warm enough to sit outdoors. José Leiva suggested they bring out the Scotch and the wine and enjoy the fresh air. Gail pulled Anthony aside.

"When are you going to see Ramiro?"

"Later. I don't want to leave right now. I'll call Cobo to pick us up in a couple of hours. Ramiro doesn't usually go to bed until late."

"You don't know what to say to him yet, do you?"

Anthony shook his head.

"Listen, you were a little hard on Danny, don't you think?"

"What do you mean?"

"You shouldn't have given Mario that money right in front of him."

"Gail, please."

"I think it hurt his feelings."

"He could learn from Mario how to show gratitude."

"Never mind," she said. "Forget it. Let's open that other bottle of wine."

They sat in a ragged circle of five chairs on the small concrete patio. Irene sniffed the air and asked if that wasn't night-blooming jasmine. It reminded her so much of home, but Miami wasn't nearly this quiet at night.

Anthony filled Gail's wineglass, then walked over to fill Yolanda's and Irene's, then his own. José was drinking Scotch. He lit a cigarette and shook out his match.

They talked about the garden, the neighbors, the dog that kept them up all hours. Gradually the talk turned to the past. Anthony explained to Irene what the elementary school had been like in their little town of Cascorro. Yolanda said that Anthony had been very bad, always in trouble. Anthony denied it. His Spanish became faster, more colloquial, and Gail couldn't keep up.

Laughing about something he had said, Yolanda raised her arms and loosened her hair clip. Her arms and face and the V of her neckline shone white against the darkness. She raked her fingers through her hair, then refastened the clip.

Anthony fell silent. The light from the house was behind him, and Gail couldn't see his face. He resumed speaking, and she felt a pain in her chest, a heavy tug like a cord pulling across her heart.

16

Against the edge of the ocean, the city twinkled with gold lights. Across the harbor Karen saw some cruise ships, a park, and a small fort. The Malecón was behind the buildings, but she could see the bell tower of the church that Mrs. Vega had shown them today, and the dome of the capitol.

She looked around at Mario, who was putting his flute together, and at Angela, who hadn't taken her eyes off Mario. Karen jumped off the low rock wall and sat beside her.

Mario turned the pieces of his flute to get them to line up right. He ran his fingers up and down the keys, then put the flute to his mouth. His lips looked like he was kissing the mouthpiece, and the music came out beautiful and sad. His black eyebrows lifted, and he moved with the music. Angela stared up at him like this was the first time in her life she'd ever heard a flute.

Danny wasn't there. As Mario was driving through downtown, Danny said to let him out, he wanted to hook up with Giovany. Angela told him he was going to get in trouble, but Danny didn't care, as usual. After Danny got out, Mario continued through a tunnel under the harbor, then up a hill to *La Fortaleza de la Cabaña*. Mario paid their way in, pesos for Cubans, and dollars for tourists. There were loads of tourists, and everybody walked to the other side of the fort and watched while men came out wearing Spanish army costumes with silver breastplates and helmets. The commanding officer yelled the orders. They set the cannons off, then the soldiers marched back inside.

Mario asked if he could show them a good view of Havana, so they drove around the fort to another hill with a white marble statue of Christ at the top. They were laughing going up the hill because the car nearly stalled out, and Mario's seat kept sliding backward, and Mario had to hang on to the steering wheel and pull himself back up. A Cuban flag and strands of glass beads swung from the rearview mirror, and a bobble-head black woman smoking a cigar fell off the dashboard.

At the top Mario bought them a cola. He wouldn't let them pay for anything. He and Angela talked in Spanish, and Angela translated. After a while, they were just talking, like Karen wasn't even there. She wished that Mario was playing his flute just for her.

His fingers moved faster and faster. His silver rings sparkled in the light reflecting off the white marble statue. He opened his eyes and looked at Angela as he played. She smiled, then swivelled around like she was interested in the view.

People started coming around to listen. When Mario finished the song, they applauded and wanted him to keep playing. He bowed and shook his head. He took his flute apart and put it back into its case.

He helped Angela up, then held out a hand to Karen. He was being nice to her. She knew who he was interested in. When she stood up, he kissed her on the cheek and said she was pretty.

She laughed and felt her face burning.

Mario held Angela's hand, and Karen followed behind them as they walked back to the car. Their voices were low, and she thought Mario was asking if he could come pick her up tomorrow, and Angela was saying yes, she'd like that a lot.

17

By now his movements were as automatic as a machine's. He could do it with one hand. Pop the latches, remove the pistol, aim, shoot.

The long, narrow case had come with the flute, which he had purchased used. He could have had a more modern case made of heavy plastic, but he liked the feel of the leather and the faded green velvet. The forms that cushioned the flute had been removed, leaving a space just wide enough for the Makarov. The case hung horizontally at his right hip, and the strap went across his chest. He had just used some scissors to cut the strap to the proper length.

Pulling the hammer back before placing the gun in the case saved time and improved his aim. The trigger took only a feather's touch, so Mario put no pressure on it until he was ready. He put the pistol back into the case and snapped the latches. Walked across the garage, turned, came back. Raúl sat backward on a chair in a cloud of cigarette smoke with his bad leg extended. Mario walked past him, opened the latches, and let the pistol fall into his right hand. He pivoted, extended his arm, and placed the barrel behind Raúl's ear.

Click.

Raúl released some cigarette smoke toward the rafters. "I hope you can get that close."

"I will get that close."

The garage was in Guanabacoa behind the house of a friend of Raúl's, a toothless man of about eighty, with black skin and hair like cotton, who decorated his house with painted gourds and beads and candles. He lived alone. For a rent of twenty dollars he had given them the garage, which backed up on a vacant field. The floor was dirt, and the place smelled of oil and burned wood. The old man had a stone fire ring just inside the wide, sliding door. If it rained, he could perform his *Palo Monte* rituals without getting wet. There were some bones in the ashes, perhaps a chicken or a small goat. It was hard to tell. The only light was a kerosene lantern on the workbench.

Nico lay on the backseat of an old car getting drunk. Ever since the police had taken Chachi two nights ago, he hadn't been home. Raúl had brought him here.

The side door opened, and Tomás came in with some beers.

Mario dropped to one knee and put Tomás's startled face in the sights.

"Mother of God!"

"It isn't loaded," Mario said.

"Even so, please don't do that." Tomás dropped a beer into Nico's outstretched hand and tossed another to Raúl.

Raúl said, "Mario. Tell Tomás what you just told us."

Mario whirled around and aimed at the window, which they had covered with sheets of cardboard. He studied his silhouette. A man. A gun in his extended hand. "I saw Ramiro Vega tonight."

"Where?"

"At his house. Vega was just leaving when I returned with Anthony Quintana's daughter. I'd met her at my parents' earlier, and we went out—she and I and her stepsister. Taking them home, I saw Vega. We spoke to each other. He is shorter than on television, and even more ugly. He was wearing a blue-and-white shirt and a jacket. He looked almost like a normal man."

Nico's voice was sloppy. "Should've had the pistol instead of your fucking flute."

When Tomás held up a beer, Mario waved it off. He wanted to keep his head clear. His nerves were singing. He felt that he could run ten miles without stopping.

"Quintana introduced us. Hello, how are you, *et cetera*. Good evening, General Vega, an honor to meet you. Vega knows who my father is. He didn't shake my hand, but he didn't tell me to get out, either. I was still there when he left. I went inside the house with Angela Quintana to greet Vega's wife. What a cold one she is. She said I look like an American metalhead. The youth of Cuba

have no respect for the sacrifices of the Revolution. But . . ."
Mario tossed the Makarov to his left hand and shut one eye to
sight down the barrel. "But she gave Angela and me some coffee.
Before she threw me out."

"He's almost a member of the family," Raúl said. "The girl
likes him. She's going to sneak him into her bed, isn't she, Mario?"

"She isn't one of your whores, Raúl." Mario put the pistol into
the case left-handed and nearly dropped it. This would take more
practice.

"Did you get your tongue in her mouth, at least?"

"Would you like me to stuff yours down your throat?"

"Take it easy, both of you," Tomás said.

Nico rolled off the car seat and staggered to his feet, using the
workbench as support. He had worn the same clothes for two
days, and they were crusted with dirt. "Tomás! What about Chachi?
What did you find out?"

"Nothing." Tomás dragged a chair closer but seemed too dis-
tracted to sit. "I spoke to his mother. She can't find him. The police
say they don't know where he is."

"What the hell do you mean, they *don't know*?"

"She went to the station in Vedado, then to the main head-
quarters. The police say they never heard of him. She went to State
Security. Same story. Nothing."

Raúl lit a cigarette and shook out the match. "This is strange."
He looked at Nico.

"Do you think I was *lying*? I saw the car. It was the National
Revolutionary Police. They beat him up and they threw him in the
car, and they took him somewhere. He's in one of their damned
jail cells, I tell you."

Tomás opened a beer as he paced to the window and back. His
shadow moved across the wall. "No one has been asking questions
about us. No one has been to Nico's apartment looking for him. It
is possible that Chachi hasn't talked."

Raúl exchanged a glance with Mario, then said, "Maybe he
can't."

Nico stared at them, and even in the weak flame from the
lantern, the tears gleamed in his eyes. "I hope he is dead."

Mario said, "But where is he? No, he can't be dead, Nico. They
would have turned his body over to his family and told them a

story. Your son was hit by a car. He fell from a roof." Again Mario felt his nerves burn like electric wires in his body. He ejected the magazine from the pistol and slammed it back in.

Tomás was still pacing. "We can't delay any longer. If he is alive, he could talk. On Saturday there's the party at General Vega's house. Olga's handling the arrangements. That would be a good time to do it. Mario, if you go as the girl's guest, you could mix with the crowd."

Raúl grinned. "Half the army will be there. You can take them all out. To hell with the pistol. Let Nico make you some fireworks."

Nico whirled around so fast he nearly fell. "No. I won't do it. We don't bomb people, only *things*."

"It was a joke, my friend." Raúl downed some of his beer and wiped the foam off his mouth. He lifted his shoulders and smiled. "A joke. Come on."

"Cretin."

Still holding the pistol, Mario lifted his hands. "Wait. Should we do it at his house at all? I've been thinking that's a bad idea. His wife and children would be there. What would the world press say about us then? That we are brutal, that we have no morals. It could be counterproductive."

Raúl said, "Are you having second thoughts? Is it the girl? You don't want *her* to see you do it?"

"The girl means nothing to me. She is how we get inside. That is all she is."

"All right, all right."

"I will blow Vega's brains to the ceiling, and it will be the ceiling of his own house if necessary. I will be happy to put this pistol to his head, but if we kill him in the presence of his family, we make it worse for ourselves. Let me find out where he goes and when and with whom. I could follow or be waiting for him."

Raúl squinted through the smoke. "Maybe we should consider it, Tomás."

"Impossible. We've already planned everything. We have comrades who will help him escape. They have the route mapped out, a place where he can stay as long as necessary. If he needs to leave the country, I know someone who can get him out."

"I'm not leaving Cuba," Mario said. "Listen to what I am saying:

We can release all the statements we want, but if we kill the innocent, we will fail."

"Who suggested that? Did I? Mario, it's too late to alter our plans. We can move them forward, but they can't be changed. We have to proceed." Tomás finally sat down. "Please put that gun away."

Mario opened his flute case. He noticed that Nico had fallen asleep on the dirt floor. His beer had tipped over, making a puddle.

"When do we do it?" Raúl asked.

"Security will be tight at the party," Tomás said. "On the other hand, if he's a guest, no one would notice him."

"I will decide when," Mario said. He looked from one of his companions to the other. "I will decide and tell you in advance. Don't talk to Olga Saavedra about it. She knows too much already. My father is sure she's working for MININT. That could be true. She has friends there. Yesterday she told me to let someone else kill Vega. She said she liked me. Could it be a warning? I don't know. Consider another fact. She's Ramiro Vega's mistress. Why would she betray her lover?"

Cigarette smoke swirled as Tomás shrugged. "She wants to help us."

"Does she? You told me that she heard a rumor that the state is planning to arrest the dissidents. Who gave her that information? Who is she talking to?"

Tomás tiredly replied, "She gets it from Vega."

"Vega. Yes, that makes sense. But tell me again why Olga is helping us. Explain it to me."

"She wants to leave. I will use the word 'desperate' to describe how much she wants to leave. I told her that if she helps us, I can arrange it."

"Is this true?"

"She believes it."

"You lied to her?"

Tomás's narrow face turned toward him. He smiled, and the flame of the lantern shone in his glasses. "My friend and comrade, may I inquire where you developed this acute moral sensitivity? You who are planning to end a man's life."

"He's our enemy. We're at war."

"Exactly so. At war. When we have delivered our fellow citizens from tyranny, will you complain that in order to do it, we had to tell a few lies?"

Mario looked at him for several seconds. The words and arguments and counterarguments collided in his head. "Are you lying about getting me out of Cuba? I don't intend to leave, but were you lying about that too?"

"No, Mario. I can get only one person out. If it's between you and Olga, I would rather save your life." Tomás continued to look at him. "I have your trust or I don't. Tell me now."

"All right. Yes. I'm sorry, Tomás." He extended his hand.

Tomás took it. "I have to trust you too. Whatever may happen, they will remember us."

"Very sweet," Raúl said. "I might have to shoot you both if you keep this up."

Mario gave him a shove on the back of his head.

Raúl stuck his cigarette between his teeth and swung a leg over the chair. He limped over to where Nico lay sleeping. "Poor bastard." Lifting him under the arms, Raúl dragged him back onto the car seat and tossed a thin blanket over him. "He's going to miss his little friend."

Tomás took some dollars out of his wallet. "Ask the old man inside the house there to get him a change of clothes."

On the workbench lay the scissors that Mario had used earlier to adjust the length of the strap on his flute case. He turned up the wick on the lantern. "Raúl. I want you to cut my hair."

"Why?"

"Señora de Vega doesn't like it." He gave the scissors to Raúl and untied the cord at the back of his neck. His braids swung forward. He sat in the chair Raúl had just vacated and lit a cigarette.

"What a pity." Raúl lifted one of the braids by its end. "You must've been growing these things for years."

"Hurry up, before I change my mind. Not too short." Mario felt a slight tug. He heard the crunch of rusty metal and the beads dropping to the floor.

18

Water cascaded down coral rocks into the huge, free-form swimming pool. Underwater lights put a turquoise glow on the sleek curves of the balconies overlooking the pool deck. A woman swam slowly back and forth, the steady splash of her arms growing louder, then fading.

The waiter arrived with a tray, bringing Ramiro his fourth cognac. Rémy Martin X.O.

He turned to Anthony. "Nothing more for you, sir?"

"No, thank you." The melting ice had diluted what was left of his Scotch.

The waiter produced a cigar and a chrome-plated clipper. He slid the cigar halfway out of its cedar-lined tube and let Ramiro take it the rest of the way. Montecristo Especial. Ramiro clipped off the ends. The waiter held the lighter while Ramiro sucked gently, creating a soft orange glow. His eyes went slightly crossed.

The hotel catered to businessmen and wealthy tourists. The only black face within sight was across the table. If Ramiro Vega had not been a general in the F.A.R. he wouldn't have been let past the front doors.

Flicking an ash from the lapel of his sport coat, he settled into his chair. "Comrade, I have a joke."

The waiter smiled and waited. He was a young man with a black vest and bow tie. Anthony noticed that the cuffs of his shirt came nearly to his knuckles.

Ramiro grinned. "A schoolteacher asks her class, 'Boys and girls, if the sea between here and Key West were to dry up, and you could walk three miles in one hour, how long would it take you to get to Key West?' Pepito raises his hand. 'Yes, Pepito?' 'I could get there in fifteen minutes.' 'Fifteen minutes? Pepito, it's ninety miles. How can you get there in fifteen minutes?' 'Because I would run like hell before everyone else found out and ran over me.' "

With his smile frozen in place, the waiter glanced from Ramiro to Anthony and back again.

"What's the matter? You don't think it's funny?"

"Oh, yes, it's very funny, sir." He made a slight bow and backed up. "If there is nothing else you need. . . ." He returned to his post at the bar.

Ramiro reached for his cognac. "I thought it was funny."

"It was. Does he know who you are?"

"No, I don't come here. Only when I have a rich visitor from Miami. Don't tell Marta. She wouldn't like it. The other day I told her, Marta, my love, you know with my promotion we can afford to trade our house for one in Cubanacán or Siboney—that's where so many of your wealthy relatives lived before the Triumph of the Revolution, when they took off for Miami. It would be an irony, no? To live in their old neighborhood? She won't hear of it. Well, she's very happy about my promotion. Without Marta, I would still be a lieutenant. She is more ambitious than anyone I know. But she doesn't want to move to Cubanacán. She likes our house. I think it makes her feel proud that the roof leaks."

While Ramiro had been sipping his cognacs, Anthony had told him about the meeting in his grandfather's study; the CIA's offer to help Ramiro defect; and Abdel García's threats, made over coffee in the red-upholstered apartment in Chinatown.

So far Ramiro had made no comment. He propped a foot on an adjoining chair and stared through the royal palm trees and past the irregular line of low roofs along the shore, his gaze finally settling on the ocean, whose horizon was lost to darkness. A cool breeze rattled the palm fronds. There was a line of light several miles off, perhaps a cruise ship.

Anthony said, "Didn't you speak to your boss today? After his surprise visit to your house last night, I thought you'd be curious why he wanted to see me."

"I called him." The breeze took the smoke from Ramiro's cigar. "He told me he would ask you about Omar. He wanted to know what Omar said to your friends. I told him, 'Abdel, I also would like to know. When you find out, tell me.' He hopes that I can persuade you not to lie."

"Did García tell you he was planning to twist my arm?"

"Don't worry about it." Ramiro pulled his gaze away from the ocean. "It's your guys you have to watch out for. They can slice off your balls so cleanly you never know until you step on them."

"Your G-2 agents in Miami aren't so bad at it either."

"You would be surprised who we have working for us."

"To your credit, Ramiro, you've never asked me to become a spy for Cuba."

His teeth flashed in a smile. "Well, how would I be sure you weren't spying for the other side, too? Maybe you are. My friends ask me. They see your relationship with José Leiva, and they wonder. I tell them to talk to Marta. I say, 'If Marta lets him through our front door, he's okay.' "

Anthony said, "Your boss threatened to put Leiva in jail for life if I didn't cooperate."

"Really? He didn't mention it."

"I've heard the regime is planning to arrest the dissidents."

"If so, it's because they're stirring up trouble."

"Ramiro, how is it stirring up trouble to have a lending library in your house or to speak what your own eyes tell you is the truth?"

"You think it's so innocent?" He laughed. "If they weren't getting support from outside, we wouldn't complain about it. The Americans at the U.S. Interests Section have parties for them and invite CNN. The United States is using the so-called human rights movement as an instrument of foreign policy. They hope we'll arrest the dissidents because it will make us look bad. Who is pushing this policy? You know very well—the exiles. Congressman Navarro and others like him. They're looking for an excuse to invade. The oppression of the dissidents, harboring terrorists, imaginary bioweapons—"

"We're not going to invade Cuba," Anthony said.

"Are you sure? Your president will go into Iraq, and after that, Iran, and then what? Not North Korea, because they have nuclear weapons. Cuba! Yes, finally you can liberate the Cubans, and they will throw flowers at your feet—those who aren't throwing grenades. Navarro and his gang are playing a dangerous game. Leiva is part of it. He dares us to put him back in prison. He can be a martyr and gain the world's sympathy."

"Ramiro, you're full of shit."

He shrugged. "I'm telling you what people think."

"You make me believe the rumors of arrests are true."

"How in hell do I know? I'm not in MININT. Where did you hear it?"

"Olga Saavedra."

"She told you? Where did she get it? Never mind. She hears too much, that woman. Ay, yi, yi. Olga, Olga."

"She used to sleep with Omar Céspedes," Anthony said.

Ramiro lifted his brows. "Let me see. Your friend with the CIA told you. Yes, I know about Olga and Céspedes. So what? It wasn't yesterday."

"Are you in love with her?"

"God help me. She makes my blood run like a young horse." Ramiro hid his face, passing a hand over the bald dome of his head. "I'm sorry I lied to you."

"To Marta, you should say."

"Yes. I am sorry for that too. But Olga—" Ramiro peered through his fingers. "You know."

"Once. I was with her once. Before you started with her," Anthony added.

"I love Marta. I have a lot of respect for my wife. She is a good woman. A good mother. That too. But we have Revolutionary sex. I get it up for every national holiday. At your orders, commander-in-chief!"

"Please. She's my sister." Anthony said, "You will ask her to come with you, no?"

"Why would you think I'm going anywhere?"

The candle in the red glass candle holder caught the breeze, and the flame sputtered and flickered. Anthony sat facing the bar, which was tucked under a portico extending onto the deck. The sliding doors were open, and he could see people inside. If any of them was watching, he couldn't tell.

He turned his chair slightly, using Ramiro as a barrier. "Tomorrow I'm going to tell García that I have no idea what Omar Céspedes told the CIA—which is true, by the way. If I do find out—very unlikely—I'm not going to share it with him. What I am going to do is ask for more time. I want to keep him quiet for a few days so I can attend Janelle's birthday party, make my sister happy, and return to Miami as planned. Now, if you want to let García know about that, it's up to you."

Ramiro lifted the Montecristo to his mouth, pausing long enough to shake his head.

"I'm starting to look behind me when I go to the men's room," Anthony said, "and I'd like to know who's back there. Is García working for MININT? The Army? For Fidel himself?"

Smoke drifted in small puffs from Ramiro's pursed lips. It hung in his thick gray mustache. "You're getting too worked up, Tony. I told you. Don't worry about it."

"I've arranged a way out of here in case it becomes necessary. Marta won't like my taking the family home before the party. You'd have to explain it to her."

"Listen to me. If García causes trouble for you, he knows he has to deal with me too. And I will tell you something. He has lost many of his friends in the regime. People don't like him."

"He has no sense of humor," Anthony said.

"That's right. He can't tell a joke."

"What do you want to do, Ramiro? I've got to tell Bookhouser something."

The only reply was a slight shrug. Ramiro reached for his glass. He closed his eyes and rolled the cognac around in his mouth before swallowing.

"You do what you want." Anthony withdrew his pen and a small notebook from his coat. "I'll give you the number. You call him or not. It's your choice."

"Put it away," Ramiro said. "My wife goes through my pockets. That's one part of her job that she takes very seriously. Have another drink."

"I've had too much."

"Relax. Let's enjoy the night. I want to finish my smoke and this excellent booze."

Ramiro's eyes drifted halfway shut. "Answer a question for me. Why do you come back here? You have everything in Miami. If your sister and your father were not here, you would still come back. Why?"

"I like the music."

Ramiro extended an arm to deposit some ashes into the ashtray. "I'll tell you why you come. You're looking for the past. It doesn't exist anymore, my friend. All we want is to make it from one day to the next. My kids don't care about sacrificing for the fatherland. Giovany wants to go to college in Paris. Janelle wants to get a ring in her navel like . . . what is that girl on MTV? Britney Spears. It makes her mother crazy."

"Does Marta still believe? Or does she only pretend to?"

"Well. You know Marta. She's like you, I think. She's an idealist." Ramiro slid down farther in his chair, his jacket bunching at his neck. "So was I. You remember. History was on our side. We were good people. Virtuous. We were making a new world, a new man. To get there you had to follow the rules, and you made sure everybody else did too. Now? Socialism, capitalism, globalism, who gives a shit? The new hotel in Trinidad is delayed because we can't get the electricity hooked up. People keep stealing the wire out of the warehouse."

Ramiro's head turned toward the pool. The swimmer had splashed her way to the edge. She grasped the ladder and climbed out, water streaming down her body. She wore a white two-piece, and her blond hair reached halfway down her back. She spoke in German to a man lying on a chaise, and he handed her a pack of cigarettes.

"If you decide to leave Cuba," Anthony said, "you will have to persuade Marta to come with you, the kids too—at least Gio and Janelle. It wouldn't be easy for them here. I'd like for my father to get out, but you know what his answer would be. No, no, and no. He's happy here. I think his blindness will protect him—that and his combat medals."

"Don't assume I'm going anywhere, either," Ramiro said.

Anthony asked, "What do you have that we want? I keep coming back to that question. How are you important?"

The woman bent over to pick up her towel. She wrapped it sarong-style over her breasts. The glow of the cigar brightened as Ramiro pulled on it. He tipped back his head and let the smoke out in a long plume.

"I am happy that the United States government considers me such a big wheel."

"Big enough to bring Bill Navarro and the CIA rushing to Miami.

It's connected to what Céspedes told them, and I think you know what that is."

"No, I don't. It could be many things. Your friend Mr. Bookhouser knows. Why don't you ask him?"

"I did."

"Aha." Ramiro grinned. "He won't tell you. Or maybe he told you a lie. And you will give this lie to García, and maybe he'll believe it, but probably not."

"Olga told Omar Céspedes you wanted to defect. Did she invent that story, or did you really say it?"

Ramiro considered the soft orange glow at the end of his cigar. "I admit I've considered leaving. Who hasn't? Even Abdel García wants to get out."

"He told you that?"

"Well . . . not in those words, but I know him. He plans for contingencies. If the airplane is running low on fuel, it's a good idea to locate the parachutes."

"What about Olga?" Anthony repeated. "Did you tell her you wanted to leave?"

"I may have mentioned it, but I never told her definitely yes. Olga has her dreams. Spain, the Costa del Sol, a little house by the sea. She wants to grow olives and lie in the sun and become as fat and brown as a gypsy. Not a bad life, eh?" The alcohol was making Ramiro's words slide together.

"Ramiro. Look at me." His companion's eyes shifted to settle on Anthony's face. "You want to sleep with her, that's your business. But you have a wife. I think I might want to break your neck if you try to leave without her."

A puff of smoke escaped Ramiro's lips. "Who's leaving?"

"I saw Olga yesterday at your place," Anthony said. "She came by to talk with Marta about the birthday party. Olga wanted to speak to me privately, to ask a favor. I turned her down. Do you have an idea what favor she's talking about?"

"Let me guess." He took a sip of cognac, then rested the glass on his stomach. "She'll ask you to help her get out because I wouldn't do it. After her last trip, I made sure her exit visas were refused. Why? Why did I chain her to Cuba? I didn't want her to go. I'm a selfish son of a bitch. Go on. You can say it."

Exhausted, Anthony rubbed stiff fingers across his forehead, then lifted his hand to signal the waiter.

"Have another drink," Ramiro said.

"It's past one o'clock. I got three hours of sleep last night."

"You should have stayed in Cuba, my brother. We could have used you. If more men like you had stayed, maybe we could get good coffee in this country. It's a scandal."

"I was thirteen at the time, Ramiro. I didn't have a say in the matter."

"You could've come back. You *do* come back. You like it here, don't you? Yes, you do. Why does anyone want to live in the north? You are rich, but you work like slaves, you put metal detectors in your children's schools, and the world hates you."

Anthony said, "We like making choices, even bad ones."

The waiter came, and Anthony took out his wallet. The bill was for $175. He said, "Mother of Christ."

A smile dimpled Ramiro's cheeks. He tugged on the waiter's sleeve. "You want to hear another joke?"

The young man glanced around, then said, "All right."

"Pepito says to his teacher, 'Teacher, my cat had five kittens, and they all believe in the Revolution!' The teacher is so impressed, the next day she takes Pepito to the director and says, 'Tell the director about your kittens.' 'Oh, my cat had five kittens and three of them believe in the Revolution.' The teacher says, 'Pepito, yesterday you told me that all five believed in the Revolution.' 'Yes, I know, teacher, but last night, two of them opened their eyes.' "

Ramiro broke into giggles, and the waiter laughed. "Very funny, sir." He took the money and left.

Anthony shook his head. "Who's going to tell me jokes if you're in prison?"

"I know who my enemies are. That keeps me ahead of them." He finished his drink.

Pushing in his chair, Anthony said, "Come on. Give me your keys. I'll drive."

Ramiro looked up at him. The whites showed under the dark brown irises, and his forehead furrowed. He gripped the front of Anthony's jacket and pulled him closer.

"When you call your friend, say I'm thinking about it. I've got some conditions, which he and I can discuss. Don't tell Marta. I'll tell her. Maybe. She might try to kill me. What's the matter? You look disappointed."

"I'm surprised."

"So am I. They make me a general, and I kick them in the teeth. My God. What am I doing? I must be crazy. My heart wants to break. I am going to cry." Tottering slightly, Ramiro stood up. He put a hand on Anthony's shoulder to steady himself. "It's not such a bad country, you know. Cuba. I love it. How I love it so."

19

Years ago, a narrow road from Havana wandered southeast through hundreds of acres of orange groves. Taking this route, Abdel García had always slowed down and put his head out the window. In the spring the orange blossoms had filled the air with their sweetness. When the ripe oranges were processed, that was another sort of perfume, rich and heavy with citrus peel.

The land was part of a military base now, no access by civilians. The trees still bore fruit, he supposed, but the processing facility had been shut down for lack of parts. Weeds had invaded the place, and birds nested in the rafters. The equipment had been removed, leaving only the empty concrete shell, rusty metal, and broken sorting tables.

The half moon sent a shaft of pale blue light through the window. García stood in what had once been the factory's office. The others were in an adjoining room. He couldn't see what was happening but he could hear it. Screams had become moans, the moans had turned to grunts. García had been present at many sessions like this one. The variety of sounds could be astonishing.

He lit another cigarette.

As a boy he had worked in the groves. It had been hot, heavy work, and the thorns on the branches had torn his flesh, but he had done it without complaint because it needed to be done, and he, like everyone else, had been filled with the spirit of the Revolution. And then it was gone. Not all at once. It was like coming slowly awake in a strange bed and seeing a calendar that did not correspond with memory. All one could do was to find a way out.

How had it happened? What had caused the old to forget and

the young to become social deviants? Young men like this one, with his bleached hair and his clothes bright as a bird. He had soft hands. He played the keyboard in a rock band. And he had made bombs and burned a police car and set trash bins on fire.

His identification booklet revealed his name: Camilo Menéndez Rojas. Age twenty-one. Place of birth: Regla, Province of Havana. Occupation: student. Menéndez had told them his father was deceased, and his mother was a translator at the Italian embassy. He had two sisters, one married. He had given their names. *Fuck your sisters. Who are your friends, faggot? Your friends in the Movement?* He said he had no friends. *Who is your boyfriend?* He denied he was a homosexual. *Who was the boy who ran away?* He had been alone. He didn't know what boy they were talking about.

They had started with a bucket of water, submerging his head, holding him there. He had passed out several times. García would have done the interrogation himself, but he didn't want the boy to see his face. It was still possible they would take him back to Havana and let him go.

The sounds coming from the other room made García's skin tighten. He grasped a piece of broken glass stuck in the window frame and tugged until it came out. Like a tooth. He smiled to himself. He had left several teeth in Angola.

He wondered how long the boy would last. The sounds said that he was getting close. Dusting his hands, García turned away from the window. He quickly wiped the moisture from the corner of his mouth and returned his handkerchief to the pocket of his tunic. On the base he was always in uniform.

He walked to the doorway of the next room. White light fell into the corridor. He could smell the repulsive, animal odor of feces. The two men stood at a metal table. They had tied the boy to the four corners, and García could see only his bare feet, which jerked and arched and pointed. The men blocked the view of his body. His clothes, the white pants and green jacket, lay on the floor.

Give me the names of your friends in the movement. If you want this to stop, you have to help yourself. It's in your control. Give us the names.

One of the men must have felt García's presence. He looked around.

From the doorway, García motioned for him to proceed.

It had been pure chance that the boy had arrived at the Vedado police station at the precise moment when García's contact had been there. He had turned the boy over to him instead of to State Security.

García returned to the office. He watched the clouds drifting across the pewter-colored moon, the many shades of gray and dark blue and purple. The points of the moon seemed to snag the black mass and break it into tumbling fragments. For several minutes his thoughts drifted pleasantly to a beach on the Pacific coast of Mexico. Night. A house overlooking the sea. His house. A terrace, open windows, a piano concerto. The wind cooling his body.

He heard footsteps, then a voice. "General."

"Yes?"

"He's talking."

"Is he?"

"He admits he belongs to the Movement. He's giving us the names."

García blotted his mouth. "That isn't enough. I want to know how and when. Who will carry it out?"

The footsteps retreated, and a minute later there came an odd sound, like the yipping of a dog.

García remembered his own interrogator, a UNITA captain in a ragged green uniform, a big black man with enormous nostrils and a face shining with sweat. The man beat him ceaselessly, untiringly, then bent over him and spoke in Portuguese. "I don't like to hurt you. I don't like it. Please let me stop." There was blood on his uniform. García's own blood, he realized later.

García had tried to spit in the captain's face, but there was no saliva left, and he could only laugh. He had been lying in the dirt. The captain stood up and kicked him in the face with his boot. García heard the bones in his jaw snap. The men left him lying there for two days, and a week later they traded him and some others for UNITA hostages. If they hadn't given up so soon, would he have talked? García thought that the answer was probably yes.

"General?"

García looked around.

"He says they're going to kill Vega with a pistol."

"I *know* that." García imagined bringing a stick down on this idiot's face. "I don't want to see you again until he tells you when and how."

"He says he doesn't know."

"Of course he knows. Go ask him again."

When the man had gone, García rested his forehead on the window. He had hoped not to do this. He had hoped the boy would just tell them. He wanted the truth, a simple thing, but he wasn't getting it. The Movement had been infiltrated, but García didn't trust the people he had put there. They were incompetent. They lied. Everyone lied. It was a miserable fact that only pain could sort it out.

After a while, the noises stopped. The soldier came back. His boots stopped halfway into the room.

This time García didn't bother turning around. He let go some smoke through the broken glass. "Tell me."

"He says Mario Cabrera is going to enter Vega's house with a pistol hidden in a flute case. He will shoot him in the back of the head."

"Go on."

"Cabrera knows a girl at the house, Vega's niece. She's going to let him in."

García dabbed at his mouth with a knuckle. He felt his hand shaking. He had been told that Cabrera would become a chauffeur for the Vega family. Now there was another plan. It could be a lie. Or not a lie. How could he be certain?

"And then? After he shoots Vega?"

"Cabrera will leave the house, and the others will be waiting nearby in a car. Menéndez doesn't know the details of the getaway or where Cabrera will be taken. He doesn't know when. He thinks it will be in two weeks."

"Not true."

"No, General."

"They advanced the date after Menéndez was arrested."

"But Menéndez doesn't know that, sir."

García waited, then said, "Is that all?"

"He gave us everything."

"Make sure."

"I am sure, General."

"Is he dying?"

The man paused. "I don't know."

García threw his cigarette out the window. "Let me see him."

He left the office and stood at the door of the other room. The two soldiers placed themselves at the ends of the table. Except for the blood, the boy's skin was smooth and pale as ivory. He walked closer. The boy made no indication that he saw him. His hairless chest moved quickly, and a high-pitched wheeze came out with each breath.

"What shall we do with him?"

"Dress him. Take him to Lenin Park." García stroked the boy's head. His hair was still wet. "I hate doing this, you know?"

20

Gail didn't know what time it was. Three o'clock? Four? The streetlight at the corner sent a wash of pale gray into the bedroom, reducing its contents to colorless shapes: rectangle of closet, grid of lines on the baby crib, curve of mirror. A fan whirred by the door. Anthony had put it there to mask the sound of their voices, although it was hardly necessary. They shared the same pillow, and his mouth was inches from her ear.

Would Ramiro tell Marta that he wanted to leave? When he defected—however those things were accomplished—would he bring his family? Or would he come alone? Ramiro was capable of leaving Marta a note or calling her from outside the country, or something equally as shabby. Anthony was torn between his duty to his sister and the certainty that if anyone found out, Ramiro would be imprisoned for the rest of his life, if not blindfolded and put against a wall.

Gail might have given an opinion but Anthony didn't pause long enough to ask what she thought. He was almost vibrating with tension. If Marta knew, would she be so angry that she might betray her husband to his superiors in the army? Ramiro had to be considering that possibility.

With Anthony's arm around her, Gail held on to his hand and kissed his fingers. She turned his wedding band so she could see the row of diamonds, which sparkled even in the low light.

The rest of the Vega house was quiet. The girls had played music until midnight, when Marta had yelled at them to turn it off. Danny and Gio had sneaked in around one-thirty, and Marta had gone into another tirade. Finally the men had come back, and Ramiro, singing off-key, had staggered down the hallway to bed.

No screaming had come from behind the marital door, so Gail assumed that Ramiro was putting off any discussions until tomorrow or possibly never.

She brought her attention back to what Anthony was saying. A deal with Everett Bookhouser. Anthony would give García whatever story the CIA invented, and Bookhouser would arrange U.S. visas for José Leiva and his family. At that point, Anthony's involvement in this mess would be officially over.

"They aren't allowed to travel," Gail remembered.

"I could get them out," Anthony said. "A boat. That's easy. The problem—and I shouldn't characterize it as a problem—is that José Leiva believes too much in his causes. The regime is getting fed up with the dissidents, but José refuses to see it, and Yolanda won't argue with him. José will continue giving interviews to the foreign press, and she will continue typing his essays and writing his letters, and the informants across the street will continue watching. Maybe the changes we've seen lately will take hold. I pray they do. If José goes back to prison, he will probably die there. I shouldn't be telling them to leave. I should be standing with them."

"But you are, in your way."

"How? I give them money. I bring them office supplies."

"Do you want to go to prison for them? You have a law practice. A family. Me?"

"Yes. So I do." He stroked her cheek. *"Mi rubia linda."*

"I love you," she said.

"Te quiero mucho." He kissed her, then continued his thoughts where they had left off: "My grandfather taught me a word when I was very young. *Hombría.* It means you have fear, but you conquer it. I will tell you what Yolanda said to me. It was many years ago, but I remember her words: 'You lose your fear when you enter the struggle for freedom. They can come for me at any time, but they can never imprison my spirit.' "

"That's . . . very brave," Gail said.

"Yes, she's an amazing woman." Anthony said, "The first time I came back to Cuba, I had just graduated from college. I wanted Yolanda to leave. I said I could get her out, but she wanted to go to medical school. It didn't happen. Too many negative reports in her file, so instead—"

"They kept a file on her?"

"On everyone. They keep records starting in elementary school. Are you with the Revolution or against it? Here's an example. We were ten or eleven years old. Some neighbors had their visas approved to go to the U.S. Everyone ganged up on their son at school the next day. Pushing, shoving, calling names. Yolanda told the teacher it wasn't right. They wrote it in her record. I was ashamed because I had taken part. Yoli got another black mark for wearing her crucifix to school."

"She wears a crucifix now," Gail observed.

"They don't care about that anymore," Anthony said, "but years ago, it was a sign of disobedience. In high school she didn't attend the meetings of the Communist Youth, and they said she was unreliable. In college she asked why, if Marxism was so perfect, the Japanese prospered. She read the wrong books. She refused to march in the demonstrations. They wrote in her file, 'Yolanda is *una persona contraria al sistema.*' Against the system. The file followed her, and when she applied to medical school, even with grades at the top her class, the answer was no."

"And so she became a nurse," Gail finished.

"It wasn't easy, because by then she had a child. They sent her to the smallest towns, but somehow she found other people in the movement, and she spoke out. The police would pick her up and drive her twenty or thirty miles into the country and tell her to find her own way home. Mario had a hard time of it. Kids calling his mother *puta, gusana, escoria.* Whore. Worm. Scum. He was beaten up regularly." Laughing, Anthony said, "I remember I wanted to teach him how to go for the other guy's nose, and Yoli said don't teach him that, we're nonviolent. I took Mario for ice cream and showed him on the way back home. She never pushed him to join the movement. She said he was free to make up his own mind. He respects his mother and José, but he doesn't take part in their work. Even so, he was kicked out of the university because of his connection to the opposition movement. One good thing came of it: The army didn't want him. He didn't have to do his two years."

Gail threaded her fingers through his. "Why did Yolanda marry José?"

"Why? He's a good man. Maybe she didn't want to be alone, raising a son by herself. They were friends already. But you know, he didn't care about the movement. Not at first. Then gradually, a little time with her, and he became more of an activist than she ever was."

Anthony lifted their joined hands and put his lips to Gail's knuckles, kissing each one, leaving a little spot of moisture that quickly cooled. He didn't speak for a while, and when he did, it was as though he was thinking aloud.

"Ramiro told me that what they do is a provocation. If they're arrested, it's their fault. Ramiro is wrong, but I didn't argue with him. Why not? Whenever I get to Cuba, I put tape over my mouth. Even in Miami I don't speak out. If I did, Ramiro Vega would be ordered not to have me in his house."

"It isn't your fight," Gail said. "Not really."

"They're my friends. That makes it my fight."

"If they won't leave, what can you do?"

"Nothing. *Carajo*. They are both crazy. But what about their son? There's no opportunity in Cuba for a young man like Mario. I'm going to have a talk with him. He could go to college. I would pay for it myself. Yes, why not? If Mario will come to the U.S., Yoli might persuade José to reconsider leaving."

"Anthony—"

"José is playing with fire. What if he's arrested again? What would Yolanda do on her own? Does he think of that?"

"Anthony, please."

"What, *querida*?"

Gail had to take a slow breath to ease the tightness in her throat. "I'm sorry for your friends. Help them if you can. They deserve it. I wish I could be as brave as Yolanda. I wish I could fix everything for you. But I don't want to talk anymore."

"You're right. It's late. I'm sorry, sweetheart. You want to go to sleep."

"No. I want you to make love to me." With a ferocity born more of fear than desire, she clung to him and buried her face in his neck.

There was another word: *añoranza*. It wasn't nostalgia; it was more than that. It was the memory of the past, of childhood friends, of innocence and hope, of all that a man had loved and left behind but still dreamed of.

First seeing Yolanda Cabrera, Gail had not thought, "She is beautiful." She had not thought, "A woman like this—middle-aged, overweight, gray-haired—might be my rival." No, it was worse than that. Yolanda wasn't a woman, she was the earth and sky, the fields of his childhood, the rivers, the blue sky and fragrant blossoms. Yolanda was the balm that would cure the ache in his soul.

He loved her. He loved her and didn't know it. Gail thought that if they could just leave, go home, it would be all right. He would forget her. Until the next time he came back, looking for the other half of his heart.

Gail held him and stroked her hands down his back. If he left her, how could she stand it? She loved him beyond words, and she had none good enough. She was mute and stupid. There was more eloquence in the simple gesture of fastening a hair clip.

But I am his wife, she thought. *That has to count for something.*

21

D anny drank his *café con leche* alone in the kitchen. No one spoke to him. He was invisible. The girls had taken their toast and juice to the dining room. Mrs. Connor, Gail's mother, had come down for coffee a minute ago and left again. She looked ridiculous. Red pants, yellow Hawaiian shirt, and a fanny pack. All ready to go buy some more souvenirs.

This was the last of his two days on house arrest. He'd been grounded for not going to the *cañonazo* on Sunday night with his sister.

He left his dishes in the sink and walked into the dining room. Angela and Karen and Janelle were sitting at one end of the table eating their breakfast and talking about the dress that Janelle was going to get from La Maison today. What color it should be. If it should have sleeves. The table was full of centerpieces for the party—fake flowers and candles and yellow and white ribbons. It made him want to gag.

Hearing footsteps, Danny turned and saw the general coming down the stairs. He wore his olive-green uniform with the red stripes on the epaulets. He said hello to the girls, then gripped Danny's shoulder as he passed by. "*¿Qué tal, Daniel?*" He pronounced his name right: Dan*iel*. They were the same height, and the general looked directly into Danny's eyes.

"*Bien, y usted, señor?*"

The general nodded as he walked toward the kitchen. His back was square and straight, and his heels tapped on the tile floor.

Danny had decided that he wouldn't mind coming back to Cuba—on his own. He could share Gio's room. Aunt Marta had told him he was welcome to stay with them anytime he wanted.

He wondered if he could graduate from high school in Havana. As a nephew of Ramiro Vega, he would probably go to the Lenin Vocational School, like Giovany.

Someone knocked on the front door. Danny could see through the windows. A rusted-out green car was parked in the driveway.

"Oh, my God, he's early," Angela said. She brushed toast crumbs off her T-shirt and ran across the living room.

Mario Cabrera. He looked different. His hair. He'd cut his hair. Angela laughed and ran her fingers through the black curls before she pulled him inside. His flute case hung on a strap over his shoulder.

The general came out of the kitchen sipping his coffee.

"*Buenos días*, General Vega," Mario said, and held out his hand.

The general just looked at him and nodded once. Mario's hand dropped, but he kept smiling. Janelle came over and hung on her father's arm and stared at Mario Cabrera like he was a rock star. She asked him where his braids went. He said he was going for a new look. He held up his instrument case, opened it, and showed Janelle what was inside. His flute. He said he always carried it with him.

Janelle giggled and asked if he was going to play for her birthday. He said he would if she wanted him to. The general's eyes were on Mario. He finished his coffee, put on his hat, and told everyone to have a good day. A car from the army was waiting by the curb. A soldier got out, saluted, and opened the back door for him.

Mario was watching this, staring through the window until the general's car was gone. When Mario turned around, Danny was behind him. Mario smiled and said, "Hello."

Angela gave Mario some coffee and said she hoped he didn't mind, but Danny was coming too—their father's idea. Mario said yes, he would be happy to have Danny with them.

Liar. Suck-up. Danny wondered what he was doing here. General Vega didn't like him; that was obvious, and Mario was pretending it didn't matter.

Angela said she had to change her clothes; she'd be right back.

Drinking his coffee, Mario walked around the living room looking at the photographs on the walls. There were some family photos, but he didn't look at those, only the ones of the general with his staff. He stopped in front of the photo of the general with Fidel Castro.

Danny said, *"Mi tío es uno de los generales más importantes de las Fuerzas Armadas."* Telling him that his uncle was one of the most important generals in the army.

Mario nodded.

"Mira." Danny pointed to the photograph. *"Ahí está con Fidel Castro."*

"I see it," Mario said.

Danny turned when he heard his father saying good morning to Mario. He'd come downstairs. He walked over and shook Mario's hand and looked at his hair and said he liked it. They talked for a minute about how much Angela wanted to find the old house, her heart's desire, bringing back some photographs. In Spanish he said, "I remember it as a child, but I grew up in Camagüey, where my father was born. I am afraid Angela will be disappointed. The last time I saw the house, several years ago, it was in very bad condition."

They walked to the windows, and Mario put his cup on the windowsill. Facing the wall, Danny watched their reflections in the glass of a framed black-and-white photograph. His father asked Mario if there was a time they could get together. He wanted to know what Mario was doing these days, wanted to make sure he was all right. Then he told Mario he'd rented a cell phone at the tourist center. He gave him a piece of paper with the number on it.

Mario said yes, he would call. He thanked him again for the money. He would use it carefully.

"No es tanto. Cualquier cosa que necesites, me lo dejas saber." It isn't much. Whatever you need, let me know.

"Gracias, señor." Thank you, sir.

What an ass-kisser.

Mario took his coffee into the dining room to wait for Angela.

Danny's father came over and said, "Son, I'm going to be busy today, and I want you to stay with your sister. Do you understand? Unless you're with me, you will either be in this house or with Angela. Are we clear on that?"

"Yes, Dad. I understand. I sincerely apologize for leaving them before. It's just that I was so excited to be in Cuba, and Giovany expected me to come to the club with him—"

"Listen. Gio is older than you, and he has his own friends. He doesn't want you tagging along all the time. Give him some space."

"Sure, Dad. So where are you going? Do you want me to come with you?"

"Not this time. I'm going to see some old friends. People you don't know. We'll do something together before we leave Cuba."

"Okay. I'd really like that."

"I'm glad to see that your mood has improved." His father gave him a quick hug and told him to take care of his sister. Danny stood in the open front door as his father got into the Toyota he'd rented. He backed out from under the portico, turned in the yard, and drove away.

"Oye, joven. ¿Tienes un cigarrillo?"

Cobo lay on one of the lounge chairs at the other end of the porch. He hadn't taken the general to work because he was supposed to take the women shopping. He looked like shit. He was probably hungover from last night, Danny thought. He and Gio had sneaked out to the garage to find some rum, and Cobo was already halfway through a bottle of Havana Club.

Danny reached into his pocket for his Marlboros. His pants were so loose the outline of the pack didn't show. Cobo cupped his hand around the end of the cigarette while Danny lit it for him. He had weird reddish-brown hair that he slicked down with some kind of grease.

"Thanks."

Cobo didn't speak much English, but enough. Danny said, "Do you know that guy who just came in? He's the stepson of José Leiva. The dissident."

"Yeah?" Cobo pulled his knee up and draped a hand over it. His blue jeans were rolled at the cuffs, and he wore brown lace-up shoes.

Danny sat on the end of the next lounge chair and lit a cigarette for himself. "My father took us to their house the other night."

"Leiva's house?"

"Yeah, we listened to him talk his shit."

Cobo took a drag off his cigarette. "He's an *opositor*. They want to kill Fidel, to make the control by the rich, like before. You gonna see blood in the streets if they do that. Leiva is a friend of your father?"

"No, my father just knows him. He's not really his friend, per se. I wonder what his stepson is doing here? I mean, he's here to see my sister, supposedly, but they hate the army and the generals and everybody who runs the country, so it's kind of funny that Mario would come here acting all friendly and shit. General Vega can see right through him."

Cobo shrugged.

Danny said, "I think José Leiva asked him to come here. You know. He walks around, he sees how a general lives, and then they write about it and sell the story to foreign newspapers. That's what I think."

"Maybe. I don't know."

Cobo looked past him to the street. An old black Mercedes was turning into the driveway, parking behind Mario Cabrera's car. A blond woman in gold sunglasses got out and went around to open the trunk. Danny recognized her from last weekend. Olga something. She wore tight black pants and a red jacket with gold buttons. Last night Cobo had been crying over her, calling her a whore. Danny had tried to find out what was going on, but Cobo had been too drunk.

"Your girlfriend is here."

"Don't say that. Is not true."

Olga crossed the yard with a box, trying not to trip in her high heels. Coming up the steps, she saw Cobo and told him to help her. She had more stuff to bring in.

Cobo just looked back at her.

Danny flipped his cigarette into the bushes and went to open the door.

She said, "*¿Cómo andas, mi amor?* You speak Spanish? Not so good, eh? You are Anthony Quintana's son, no? Tell me, honey. Where is he?"

"He just left."

"*Ay, qué pena.*" Frown lines showed over the top of her sunglasses. "When he is coming back?"

Danny told her he didn't know when. "Is it important? Maybe it's something I can assist you with?"

"Assist?"

"Help?"

"No, no, *gracias, mi amor,* is okay. Maybe I see him later. You don't know what time he is coming?"

"Sorry, I don't." He decided not to give her the cell phone number. "I'll tell him you need to speak to him. Does he know how to contact you?"

"Yes, he knows." She smiled. Her front teeth had a gap between them. "You are so sweet." *Joo are so esweet.* "And very handsome, like your father." She took the box inside and set it on the bench near the stairs. Aunt Marta came over to see what was going on. Olga took off her sunglasses and said, *"Buenos días, compañera."*

Aunt Marta asked her what was this stuff, and what was she was doing here today? Wasn't she supposed to bring this tomorrow? They didn't have time for this right now; they had to go shopping. She opened the box and took out some plastic cups and plates. The wrong color, completely wrong. They had wanted yellow, not blue.

Olga was sorry, but nothing else was available.

Aunt Marta asked her when the chairs and tables would be delivered. Olga said Friday. Aunt Marta said that wasn't soon enough, and they argued about it. Finally Aunt Marta went out on the porch and told Cobo to get off his butt and carry the stuff in from the car. Danny said he would help.

Walking across the yard, Cobo asked Danny what Olga had said to him on her way into the house.

"She said I was hot. She wanted to see me alone."

"She want to do it with you?"

"Yeah, man. She says she likes young guys. She's really sexy."

"*Coño.* Don' go with her. She's a woman from hell."

Danny laughed. They brought in boxes and some forms that looked like Greek columns, which they put against the wall in the living room. Gail Connor and her mother were coming down the stairs. Olga noticed them, and when Gail got to the bottom, Olga said, "You're Anthony Quintana's wife, no? And your mother? Hi. Hi. My name is Olga Saavedra. I am doing the party for Janelle. I am also a friend of Anthony, maybe he tell you about me? I used to be on TV, a show called *Aquí la Noche.*"

The women shook their heads.

Olga took hold of Gail's arm. "Can I talk to you, if you got a minute, honey?"

She went out on the porch, taking Gail with her, and Danny

could see them through the window, Gail nodding, acting like she wanted to get away at first, but then standing there and listening. Olga wrote something on a piece of paper, and Gail put it in the pocket of her shorts.

They helped Olga carry in some more stuff. When she had left, Marta told Cobo to go get the minivan and bring it around. They were about ready to go. She would drive. Since all this shit had just been dropped off, Cobo had to stay here and unpack it. And sweep the floor in the dining room—get rid of all that glitter. And after that, do the kitchen. The housekeeper wasn't coming in again today, and Marta didn't know why in hell they kept her around. What was the matter with people? Didn't anyone care? Like these damned plates. Blue? This was horrible.

The women stood there listening to her complain. The girls and Mario were in the dining room pretending not to hear it.

Aunt Marta finally dropped her hands by her sides. "Gail, thank you for offering to buy Jani a dress at La Maison, but I don't think it's right. No. We're not going to La Maison."

"¡Mami!"

"Ssst! Jani, be quiet. What I want to say, Gail, is that my children aren't used to luxury. It's bad for them. Like that woman who was here. Did you see her? What is she teaching the young people of this country, dressing that way, showing off her gold jewelry and her designer shoes?"

"¡Mami, por favor! ¡Gail quiere comprarme un vestido!"

"¡Jani, cállate!" Aunt Marta waved at her to be quiet. She said to Gail, "The children of Cuba don't have fine clothes, but they have their self-respect! Jani isn't better than anyone else. This isn't Miami. She isn't going to be like Olga Saavedra. What a parasite!"

Gail said, "Well, all right. We don't have to go to La Maison. Is there somewhere else?"

Janelle's fat face was turning red. She told her mother that Gail had promised to buy her a dress. Aunt Marta said all right, all right, you can have a dress, but from La Época or Centro Náutico or Carlos Tres.

"Carlos Tres? ¡Mami, no!"

Danny saw Karen go over to her mother. She spoke softly, but Danny could hear her. "Mom. Please don't make me go shopping. Can I go with Angela and Mario instead? Please?"

They barely fit in the car, a rear-engine Fiat with no shocks or muffler. Danny had to sit behind Mario and hold the front seat with his knees to keep it from sliding backward. Karen sat as far over on her side as possible. She hadn't known Danny was going. Too bad for her, the little bitch.

They went east on Fifth Avenue heading for the bridge over the Almendros River. Danny was getting to know the city pretty well, having been around with Gio. Angela opened her purse and took out a photograph of a house and set it in a crack on the dashboard, propping it against the windshield, which was also cracked.

She told Mario, "This is what the house used to look like. It's on Twenty-first Street. My family lived there for a hundred and fifty years. They came from Spain."

"*¡Qué grande esa casa!*"

Angela told him to speak English. He had to learn. If he wanted to come to Miami to visit them, he had to practice.

Come to Miami?

Mario shifted gears and glanced at the photograph as he drove. "A big house. Is you gran'mother house?"

"That's right. The house of my grandmother. *Mi abuela.* My father's mother. Her name was Caridad Pedrosa. A very beautiful woman."

"Beautiful like you?"

Angela smiled. "Caridad fell in love, *se enamoró,* with Luis Quintana. That's my grandfather. You know him. He was a soldier, very poor. His family worked in the sugar fields. Caridad's family was very rich."

Karen put her chin on the back of Angela's seat to listen. Danny had already heard this story a thousand times. He tuned it out and looked at the scenery. Fifth was a wide boulevard with flowers and trees in a grassy median. A lot of the embassies were on this street.

Angela finally got to the end of the story. "Her father said no, forget it, you can't marry this poor soldier, but one night Luis came to her window and threw a little rock to let her know he was there, and she ran away with him."

"Okay. You gran' mother, the beautiful rich girl, is in love . . . with the poor soldier, no? *Muy romántico.*"

"Yes. A romantic story. But very sad too. After the Revolution, she went to Miami with her parents, *sus padres,* and she died there. My grandfather stayed here in Cuba."

Mario picked up the photo again. "I think . . . I think I see this house. Maybe . . . *derrumba'o.*" He shook his head sadly. "You know what is that?"

"You mean it collapsed? *¿Se cayó?*"

He squeezed her hand. "Maybe another house. I don't know."

Danny wanted to put both feet on the driver's seat and shove. He wanted a smoke too, but his sister would tell their father about it. He shifted to make some room for his legs, and his knee accidentally brushed Karen's. She pulled away and shot him a bird. He shot her one back.

She tossed her stringy hair out of her eyes. "You broke my iPod, you jerkoff. You did it on purpose."

"It was broken already."

"Liar. It was in perfect condition before you got your grimy hands on it. You're going to buy me another one. Your father said you had to."

"Well, Karen, if we see a Macintosh store in Havana, I will be happy to buy you another iPod."

Angela turned her head to look at him. "Danny, leave her alone." She asked Mario if he was going to his parents' house Wednesday night. She was thinking of going. His mother had invited her. Mario didn't know what she was talking about, so she explained it in Spanish. The meeting of the independent librarians. Would Mario be there?

"If you're there, I'll come too," she said. "It would be interesting. We could go out later. Go out? Dancing?"

"Okay. I will like to dance with you."

Jesus, what a suck-up, Danny thought.

Angela said, "Danny, come to the meeting with us. You might learn something. You've heard so much shit from Giovany, all his lies."

"Sorry, Angie. I'm only grounded through tonight. On Wednesday me and Gio are going out."

"Fine. Be stupid." She scooted around in her seat to look at Mario again. "So. When are you coming to Miami?"

"To Miami? Never. They don't let me go."

"Yes, they will. My uncle knows everybody. He would fix it for you."

"Okay. You ask him. Say Mario Cabrera wants to go to Miami. And we see."

"All right, I will!"

"No, no, no."

They started arguing in Spanish, and Danny picked up that Mario didn't think the general would do anything for him, the son of dissidents, please don't even ask. He made her promise not to bother the general with it. Angela said she wouldn't, but she was going to speak to her father about it, whether Mario liked it or not. She smiled at him.

"Okay. For you, beautiful, I will come to Miami."

Danny stared at the back of Mario Cabrera's head, at his curly black hair. He was using Angela to get to the United States. It was obvious. He didn't give a shit about her, he just wanted out.

Mario turned south on Twenty-sixth, and they started going back and forth on the side streets. He pointed at one big house, but Angela held up the photo and shook her head. After about half an hour of this, she yelled, "Stop! Mario, stop, that's it!"

Trees made a tunnel of leaves over the street. Mario parked the car outside the wrought-iron fence, which had mostly rusted away. They walked to the bottom of the broken, weedy driveway and looked at the house. It was completely gray. All the paint had faded or flaked off the concrete blocks and wood trim. Electric wires sagged across the front of it. Two of the columns had fallen down, and metal scaffolding held up the balcony. A woman with curlers in her hair was hanging laundry up there. Glass was missing out of most of the windows, and strips of wood had been nailed over two of them. Some black guys sat on the front porch. Another man, wearing no shirt, came out of the house and looked at the four people at the end of the driveway. The others turned to see what he was looking at. One of them smiled and waved.

They looked happy. They probably were happy, Danny thought. They didn't pay rent. They didn't have to work some crap job, fifty hours a week. They could stay on the porch all day and not bother anybody, and nobody would bother them.

Mario told Angela he would go ask permission for her to take some pictures. He would explain that she was American, and her family used to live here.

"Mario, wait. Come back."

"This is the house, no?"

"Yes, but . . . I don't want to take a picture. Let's just go."

He smiled at her and took her hand. "Okay. I understand." He touched her forehead. "The beautiful house is here. *En tus sueños*."

"In my dreams." Angela made a little laugh. "I guess that's true."

"You can tell everybody you couldn't find it," Karen said.

"Damn. It's so *awful*."

"Well, what are we going to do now?" Karen said. "Do we have to go back?"

Mario put his arms around the girls. "Come on, ladies. I take you to Lenin Park. We going to have a good time."

They headed back for the car. Danny walked behind them. Invisible. He could feel the hatred for Mario Cabrera like a force inside him, pushing on his ribs, making his neck hot. His hands were sweating. *User. Parasite.* His father had given Mario money, and Mario was going to try to screw Angela to get out of Cuba.

Danny imagined his forefinger sending a red laser beam that focused on Mario Cabrera's head. *I have the power to destroy you. I have the power, and you don't even know it.*

22

From the city, the best route to *Las Playas del Este*, the beaches east of Havana, is the tunnel under the bay. The road emerges near El Morro and becomes the Vía Monumental, a four-lane highway going past the sports stadium, then south of Cojímar, where Hemingway kept his fishing boat. Anthony Quintana had not been this way for several years, but his recollection was clear. He turned onto Vía Blanca, drove for another mile or two, then headed north to Santa María del Mar.

He left the rental car in a lot, gave the grizzled attendant a dollar, and crossed the street to the beach. Traffic was sparse, and the flat-roofed houses and shops wanted paint. The sun went in and out of heavy clouds, and the wind tossed the fronds of the palm trees. It would rain before evening. He saw a man in khaki shorts at a pizza stand, the only customer. The man wore a black Che Guevara beret with a red star on the front.

Anthony walked to the farthest of the thatch-roofed tables. A cat with half its tail missing streaked out from under the bench seat and looked back at him, ears flattened, before vanishing into the weeds.

Everett Bookhouser came over with two red cans of Tu-Cola. "Ever since they cracked down on the prostitutes, this beach has taken a nosedive." He set one of the sodas in front of Anthony, who pushed it aside.

"No, thanks. Where'd you get the hat?"

"I bought it off my landlady's kid for three bucks." Bookhouser removed the beret and tossed it to the table. He sat on the other bench. His short hair was the same gray as the clouds, and by contrast his eyes, set in their bony sockets, seemed intensely blue. "Vega and I had a talk yesterday. Did he tell you about it?"

"No."

"You don't know what he's asking for?"

"No."

"A million dollars. As soon as it's in an account in Grand Cayman, he'll talk to us. He says he can find his own way out. When he gets wherever it is he's going—and it won't be the United States—he'll call." Bookhouser looked at Anthony a while longer before saying, "Was that your idea?"

"What do you mean? The million dollars? I wish I'd thought of it. Depending on how much you need him, it could be a bargain."

"Was it your idea that he avoid U.S. jurisdiction?"

"It didn't come up."

"We're not going to pay him to thumb his nose at us from Argentina or Beijing or wherever he plans to surface."

"What do you expect me to do about it?"

"Change his mind."

"I did what you asked me to," Anthony said. "I put you in touch with him."

"Let me remind you," Bookhouser said, leaning closer. "If he stays here, somebody's going to try to set him up for crimes against the state. For a man of his rank, that means a life sentence—or worse. Vega is aware of this. We're making a good offer, but he has to cooperate. He contacted me. We talked. He's ours now. If he backs out, there have been suggestions made about dropping hints to State Security that Vega is on our side. I personally don't like that kind of squeeze, but there it is."

With a laugh, Anthony said, "I think you like it a lot."

Bookhouser's gaze remained steady. "I want you to convince me that Ramiro Vega isn't going to scam us."

"He's being careful. He'd be crazy not to. What about my sister? Did he say he had talked to her?"

"Nope. He didn't say." Bookhouser pulled back the tab on his soda can. "I assured him of safe passage for the family. He said he'd handle it. The guy has a set of balls." Bookhouser held his soda without drinking it. "Did he tell you he might ask Olga Saavedra to go with him? Is that going through his mind?"

"I don't believe he would do that," Anthony said. "Why do you ask?"

"Céspedes doesn't trust her. She's terrified of prison, and she wants to get the hell out of Cuba. Put those together, and you have someone who could be persuaded to turn on Ramiro Vega. I told Vega about it. He didn't seem too worried—but he doesn't reveal a whole lot, does he? You said she wanted to ask you for a favor. Why don't you go ahead and talk to her? Find out what it is. And tell Ramiro to keep his mouth shut, even with his wife, until we get the details figured out. What's he got against coming to the United States?"

"We're the enemy," Anthony said. "He doesn't like us. If he leaves Cuba, it's because he's sick of watching it rot. I believe he'll talk to you, but he'll give you as little as he can. Whatever that is, it must be worth a great deal to someone in Washington."

"Not a million dollars, it isn't. We could offer two hundred thousand and his freedom."

"Tell him yourself," Anthony said.

Swiveling around sideways, Bookhouser squinted at the long stretch of deserted white sand and the waves curling and falling back. The bridge of his nose had a break in it. He said, "Please don't get cute with me. You tell your brother-in-law that I want him where I can find him, whether that's Times Square, Disney World, or one of our embassies overseas. His choice. Otherwise, we can and will make it so hot for him that he will be wearing his flak jacket indoors. Are you hearing me?"

It took some effort for Anthony not to reach across the table and grab a fistful of Everett Bookhouser's shirt. "I'll pass him the message."

"Good. When are you meeting García?"

"Tonight, providing I have something to give him."

Bookhouser looked around. "I'm trying to keep Ramiro Vega out of harm's way. Believe that or not." Putting his back to the pizza stand, where some teenagers had lined up at the window, he said, "This is what I want you to tell García. Admit that Navarro talked to you about Omar Céspedes. Tell him that Navarro wanted you to find out if Céspedes was planted or if he decided on his own to defect. You told Navarro to go screw himself. If you started asking Ramiro questions like that, he would kick you out of Cuba. You came to Havana and forgot all about it. Then García showed up asking what Céspedes had told the CIA.

You didn't know, but you said you'd find out, so you called your grandfather."

Bookhouser paused for a sip of his cola. "The following part is true. What Céspedes told us has to do with the Cuban oil shortage, which is chronically bad. There's no cash to buy oil on the open market, and with twenty billion dollars' worth of unpaid foreign debt, loans are out. So Castro is getting a cut rate on Venezuelan oil in exchange for supporting Hugo Chávez. Cuba has already sent medical doctors and technicians. The next step is to send agents to infiltrate the opposition. Naturally the United States is interested in keeping Venezuela from turning into another Cuba."

"And interested in Venezuelan oil," Anthony added.

"Aren't we cynical? You can tell that to García if it helps your case, but oil isn't our motivation. The Venezuelan economy is going to hell, thanks to Chávez, and if Castro keeps meddling, it could destabilize the entire region."

Anthony smiled. "García won't buy it. Anyone who reads a newspaper could come up with that story."

"Probably, but Céspedes is giving us the details. We're getting the names of Cuban agents and where they're being sent. Your grandfather doesn't know who they are, or he would have told you. I think it's enough to satisfy General García."

"Who is he doing this for?" Anthony asked. "Himself? Or the Cuban government?"

"That's a damned good question," replied Bookhouser.

The teenagers had taken their pizza and sodas to the beach. The sun was dodging the clouds and dropping patches of light on the ocean. One of the boys pulled his T-shirt over his head. His ribs showed in his skinny torso. A girl ran down to the water and shrieked when a wave splashed her bare legs. The wind carried their laughter to the palm grove on shore. Anthony wondered where Danny was, if he was having fun. It was a strange thing, but Danny rarely laughed. Anthony didn't know why.

He felt his headache coming back and pressed his fingers against his temple. "What does Ramiro know that's worth so much to you? He has no contacts in the Cuban intelligence service. He's a bureaucrat who keeps the electricity turned on."

"Well, it's this way. We get a guy like Céspedes, and maybe we can

believe him, maybe not. Some people—some even in Washington—
will accept anything that fits their idea of what's going on in Cuba. I
for one don't like acting on sketchy information." Bookhouser swung
a leg over the bench. "I need to get going."

"Just a second." Anthony looked up at him. "Did you check
into the visas I asked about? For the Leivas."

Bookhouser dropped his beret over his gray buzz-cut. "First
you get me a reasonable answer from your brother-in-law, then I'll
see what I can do."

"Forget it. I'll put them on a boat. As long as they reach U.S.
soil, they don't need a visa."

"They could also be intercepted by the U.S. Coast Guard and
turned over to the Cubans."

Anthony let out a short laugh. "You're a son of a bitch."

"Maybe, but I'm *our* son of a bitch, not Fidel's." Bookhouser
poured the rest of his soda into some weeds at the base of a palm
tree. "I'm constrained in what I can tell you. Nobody really knows
where you stand. Bill Navarro didn't want to use you for this at
all. He thinks you're a closet communist. What I think is, you're
trying very hard to have it both ways. There will come a time
when you can't do that anymore. In this game, everybody has to
choose sides."

Bookhouser flattened the Tu-Cola can between the heels of his
thick, muscular hands. Holding the mangled aluminum basketball-
style, he flexed his knees and aimed the can at a rusting trash bin.
It clattered inside. "Keep in touch."

Anthony left his car in the lot and walked to the blue Etecsa
booth outside a boarded-up tourist hotel down the street. The
wind was coming in from the north, and he felt the chill. He inserted his phone card, dialed a number, and counted the rings on
the other end. He was about to hang up when Hector answered.

Anthony asked if he had talked to the old man.

"Yes, but he doesn't know anything. I was able to contact a
friend in the company."

Meaning the CIA.

"What did he tell you?"

"Omar is talking about that restaurant in Juraguá. You know.

The vodka drinkers were building a big restaurant, but they ran out of money and went home. So it's sitting there for fifteen years. That place."

Hector was being more obscure than usual: vodka drinkers. The Russians. The uncompleted nuclear reactor outside the town of Juraguá in Cienfuegos province.

"I know the place," Anthony said. "What about it?"

"They say Omar is talking about it. He's a cook. He went to a famous cooking school. What's that city that starts with an M? He went there and got an advanced degree in cooking, and he used to work at the restaurant. That's why he knows about it."

Anthony had to think before he deciphered Hector's meaning: Omar Céspedes went to Moscow and studied . . . what? Nuclear engineering? "Hector, don't worry about the phone. I'm on the beach, and no one's around. Let me understand you. They want to finish Juraguá?"

There was a long pause, then a sigh, as though Hector would rather be talking in circles. "That's what I heard."

"It would be suicidal." Three U.S. presidents had promised dire consequences if the Cubans ever attempted to finish the Chernobyl-style reactor. "Are they taking Céspedes seriously?"

"I don't know. What did they do with the stuff for the oven? You know, to make it hot?"

"The Russians never shipped it."

"There isn't any?"

"If we can believe Vladimir Putin, there isn't."

"They have some in the hospitals, no?"

"It isn't the same."

"You can make a dirty bomb from that stuff. Señor Ernesto says the Beard would give it to the terrorists for free—"

"Do you believe that?"

Hector hesitated. "He might. He's getting old. If he could make a final strike at the Americans, he could die happy."

"I've heard that theory already on Radio Mambi in Miami," Anthony said. "Did Céspedes mention Venezuela? The Cubans helping Chávez in exchange for oil?"

"My friend didn't say anything about that."

Anthony wondered if Hector's friend simply hadn't mentioned it, or if Céspedes hadn't talked about Venezuela at all. Anthony didn't mind lying to García, but the best lies lay close to the truth. Otherwise, something would invariably get screwed up. If García knew he was being lied to, the consequences could be serious. Anthony could sense rumblings, the ground shifting, about to crack open. He needed to know which way to jump.

Leaning against the phone booth, he noticed a few wet circles appearing on the dusty sidewalk. A drop of rain hit the plastic side of the booth. He asked Hector, "So that's all you have for me?"

"It's not easy." Hector's tone said he was miffed that his efforts weren't appreciated. "Everybody's got their mouths shut. No interviews, nothing on TV or in the papers. They don't even admit Omar is in town. Usually people talk to me, but this? *Ooof*. Do you want me to keep trying?"

"Only if you can get it to me soon. I'm meeting the Chinaman tonight. Hector, I need a favor."

"Anything."

"Find me a boat and a captain, will you? Something fast. I can't say we'll need it, but I'd like to have the option."

"Yeah, yeah, no problem. Maybe two, then if you want to go south, you can."

"Thanks."

"I should come to Havana."

"That's not necessary. Not yet."

"Señor Anthony . . . I'm worried. García is a bad man. Very bad. I heard that he has a place he goes to in the Sierra Maestra, where he keeps the bones of the people he killed. He has over twenty skulls lined up on a shelf."

"Who told you that?"

"A friend of Señor Ernesto."

"Oh, Jesus, Hector. Why do you listen to those maniacs?"

Patiently, slowly, Hector said, "The guy that told me knew a sergeant who used to be in the Chinaman's unit. He saw things. He wouldn't lie. Señor Ernesto knows him a long time."

Anthony remembered the general's small, tilted eyes, cold as stones. Even if he were a necrophiliac, it wouldn't interest the CIA. If they wanted Ramiro Vega, it was for some other reason. Not to ask if Castro had found the billion dollars necessary to finish a nuclear reactor that the United States would bomb before the switch was turned. And not even to confirm the existence of Cuban spies in Venezuela. That there were spies, Anthony had no doubt, but it was not why they wanted Ramiro.

After lunch in the veterans' home, most of the residents sat in the main salon to catch the news on television. Luis Quintana, who could see only the vaguest outlines of his world, found a chair by a window. He had put on a sweater. The sun was too fickle to warm his shoulders.

Anthony had come to have lunch with his father. Not to burden the kitchen, he had picked up some cold cuts and cheese at a dollar market. The old men at the table had shared the food, asked him about his kids, and wanted to know if it was true that Liván Hernández would sign with the Expos.

He had hoped to see Yolanda, but they'd kept her busy in another part of the building. He wanted to ask about coming by her house later to talk to José. On his way back to the city, he'd recalled that José Leiva had written articles about Abdel García, and at least one of them had mentioned Juraguá.

More information might come from Olga Saavedra, who used to sleep with Céspedes. Olga wanted something, but Anthony had brushed her off. After talking to Bookhouser, he knew what it was: a way out of Cuba. He could give it to her, but she would have to tell him what she knew about her former lover. Tonight he would see her. After dinner at his sister's house, he would drop in on Olga Saavedra.

On Tele Rebelde the big story was the debate in the United Nations on using military force in Iraq. The U.S. ambassador believed they were hiding weapons of mass destruction; the Iraqis denied it. President Castro was opposed to war. The picture occasionally flipped into a horizontal roll, and one of the men would get up to adjust the antenna. Through the window Anthony heard laughter and glanced out to see a foursome on the porch playing dominos. There was a bottle stashed under the table in a bag.

He leaned toward his father, elbows on his knees. "Papi, what time do you want me to take you to Marta's? I'm not rushing you, but I have something I could do later."

"I'm not going to Marta's today," his father said.

"No?"

A smile appeared. Luis groped for Anthony's arm and finding it, pulled him closer. "It's my day with Zoraida. Her uncle lives here. She comes from Matanzas every two weeks to visit him. She pays her respects, then she waits for me in my room. What breasts she has. Her skin, like rose petals. And the perfume between her legs! She's a goddess."

"How old is this woman?"

"Thirty. So what? I'm not as old as you think."

"Do you give her money?"

"Don't make it sound ugly. I like helping her out. She has a child to support. She's a good girl, very clean. What do you want me to do, go out in the streets?"

"Just be careful."

"Pah! Don't worry about me. And don't tell your sister." With a finger to his lips, Luis leaned back in his chair to listen to the television. One of the men must have been deaf, because the sound was turned up so far it threatened to shake the plaster off the ceiling.

Anthony set his empty cup on the window ledge and told his father he would be back.

He found Yolanda upstairs mopping the floor. The blue paint on the walls had disintegrated in patches, showing yellow beneath, and pink beneath that, creating an abstract pattern of decades of paint. Light streamed in from the open doors to a balcony. Her reflection shone on the wet tiles, fading out slowly as the floor dried.

"Yolanda."

She turned around.

"Did the housekeeper tell you I was here?"

"Yes. I'm sorry, Anthony. I had to finish this."

"They make you mop floors instead of having your lunch?"

Laughing, she said, "No, it was my idea. I'm leaving a little early today."

He walked closer. There were doors open along the hall, but he saw no one in any of the small, tidy rooms. "You don't have to work at all, you know."

"I don't mind. Really."

"Your husband gets enough money from outside, doesn't he? You could stay home and help him."

"You sound just like José."

He said, "Don't accuse me of that."

"I like it here," she said. "It's very peaceful. And they depend on me. The doctor at the clinic can't be found when you need him. They say he drives a taxi." With a laugh, she tucked some hair into her ponytail. He saw that she wasn't wearing her new silver ornament. Well, no. Not here. It was too much. She was not a woman who showed herself off. Her scent was the simple violet water sold in every Cuban market.

Dropping the mop into the bucket, she said, "Let me finish this. I'll come downstairs before I leave."

Anthony looked at her sideways, appraising. "Are you avoiding me?"

"No. Why would I?"

"I don't know."

She pushed on the mop handle to roll the bucket a little farther down the corridor. The wheels wobbled on the tiles. "I'm in a hurry because at three-thirty I'm going to meet your mother-in-law. She wants to buy us some Internet cards. I'm grateful to you for letting her do it."

"Of course. If Irene wants to help you, that's all right with me." Anthony walked alongside Yolanda. "Whatever you need, you have only to ask."

She glanced at him, and the light filtering through the trees just outside put flecks of emerald in her eyes. Her brows were pure black; silver framed her face. "That's very kind of you."

"It isn't kindness, Yoli. You and José have been my friends for many years." He stopped himself from putting an arm around her, and slid his hands into his pockets instead. "Come downstairs and see me before you leave. I brought you something to take home."

"Oh, please, you shouldn't."

"Something edible."

"No, we don't need . . . what is it?"

"Apples from Oregon. They're delicious. I had one."

"Where is that? Oregon?"

"A state north of California."

"So far! It would be rude to say no." She smiled and pushed down on the lever that squeezed the mop head. "I'll be there in a while. Go on."

He watched the mop move across the floor, making a wide, shining arc.

"I've been thinking about Mario," he said.

"Mario?" She looked at him, surprise fleeting across her face.

"He's a brilliant young man. Well-mannered. Ambitious. Tell me, what is his future in Cuba? What opportunities are there for him here? Very few. You must know this."

"We've talked about it," she said. "Mario doesn't want to leave."

"Of course he doesn't. He thinks he would be on his own, no friends or family. But Gail and I would help him, gladly. If he wants to enroll in a university, I would take care of his tuition. It's no problem. He could join a band if he wanted to. There are many young Cuban musicians in Miami. He could go to New York if he wanted. Anywhere. When things change here, he could come back and have something important to contribute."

Yolanda's eyes were focused on the bucket and its gray water. Anthony wanted to take it to the balcony and pitch it into the yard.

"He wouldn't be lost to you, Yoli. He'd come every year. As often as you like. I'd make sure of that."

"He's twenty years old," she said. "Not a child. It's not my decision."

"But he will ask for your advice. I want you and José to discuss it before I talk to Mario. Will you? He loves you. He would stay for your sake. You shouldn't let him."

"I know that." She pressed her lips tightly together, and for a second he thought she might cry.

"Yoli?"

She cleared her throat and turned away, dropping the mop once more into the bucket. "If he asks me, I'll say he should go. Now, would you please let me finish? I'll be down later."

Anthony walked a few paces before pivoting and coming back. "I almost forgot what I came upstairs to ask you. Will José be available later this afternoon? I need to talk to him. It's not about your son. It's something else."

"I don't believe that José has to go anywhere." She looked past him down the hall. "What's it about?"

He made a noncommittal noise, then said, "We'll talk later. I'll be there around four, all right?"

"I might not be home."

"Ah. You'll be with Irene."

"And after that I have some things to do."

Anthony clamped his teeth together to keep from blurting out, *What are you afraid of? That I might force you to admit how much you hate mopping floors?*

After José's arrest, Yolanda had called Miami, waking Anthony in the middle of the night. She had raged and wept. How could José have been so stupid? He'd known what he was doing. He had *wanted* them to put him on trial, as if the world would even notice. Such pride, such egotism! She didn't want to be married to a man who loved martyrdom more than he loved his wife. On his next trip to Cuba, Anthony rented a car and took Yolanda to the prison in Ciego de Ávila, more than 250 miles away, to visit her husband. Halfway there he pulled off the highway and told her she didn't have to stay in Cuba. She could come to Miami. He would find her a place to live, a good apartment. He could support her until she found work. When José was released, he could join her. Or not, if he preferred to suffer. She said she would think about it, but the subject never came up again.

"I'm leaving now," he said. "If I don't see you today, then some other time."

She held out her cheek to be kissed.

As he walked away, she said, "Don't eat all the apples."

itting on the terrace with her mother, opening a granola bar lifted from Karen's stash, Gail heard car tires on gravel, then an engine go off. She tore the cellophane with her nails and watched the front of the house. Through the open terrace doors she could see into the long, empty living room, which was still waiting for delivery of tables and chairs for the party. The stairs were a curve of floating horizontal lines.

Marta had rushed out more than an hour ago, saying she had to pick up some things for lunch. This threatened to screw up Gail's plans to meet Olga Saavedra at two o'clock. She had hoped that Marta could take her downtown. She would have asked Cobo, but God only knew where he'd disappeared to. Gail was afraid that Olga would leave before she got there. She had tried to reach Anthony, but he wasn't answering his cell phone, and the damned thing had no voice mail.

Irene squeezed a wedge of lime into her rum and Tu-Cola. "Is Marta coming back? You should put that snack bar away, darling. It will hurt her feelings."

"Where has she *been*? An *hour* to pick up a loaf of bread?"

"I offered to fix you some leftovers."

"Oh, please. That chicken last night was so vile."

"It wasn't that bad."

"It was all skin and fat! I saw you blotting it on your napkin. My pants are getting loose. Look! I'll have no butt left."

Irene scooted down in her chair and turned her face to the sun. "Don't be so grumpy, Gail. You should have eaten breakfast before we went shopping."

She heard a car door slam.

The morning had been spent crisscrossing Havana, Marta chain-smoking her Hollywood cigarettes, clutching her vinyl handbag under her arm like a holstered weapon, parking in VIP spots with the *Fuerzas Armadas* sticker on the minivan, looking for a dress for Janelle that wasn't so expensive she'd feel guilty about letting her have it. Finally at a shop in the *galería* at the El Comodoro Hotel, Janelle spotted a little two-piece outfit with rhinestones on the straps. Eighty dollars. Under threat of more tears, Marta surrendered. Gail put four twenties on the counter, thinking that at least the dress was the correct political hue—red.

Driving home, relieved it was over, Marta had been in a marvelous mood, recalling that she herself had never had a *quinceañera*, not in those days, when the Revolution required so much sacrifice. But Janelle deserved a party. It would be a statement of how far they had come. It would be a celebration for the family and most of all, for Ramiro. You don't know, Marta had told them, how hard he has worked for this promotion.

Gail had sat in the front passenger seat staring out at the street, realizing with perfect clarity that he hadn't told her. General Vega had not told his wife that he was going to defect. She didn't know. *Would* he tell her? Or was he planning to take someone else? Like Olga Saavedra? Gail didn't know why Olga wanted to talk to her, but she expected to come away with something of use.

Glass louvers rattled as the front door closed, and voices echoed in the living room. A moment later a skinny figure appeared, dodging around the dining table, coming onto the terrace. "Hi, Mom. Hi, Gramma." Karen wore a screaming pink T-shirt and a matching South Beach ball cap. The wind had tangled her hair, and dirt smudged the knees of her jeans. She gave Gail a kiss. "Mwah!" Gail said.

"Hello, sweet pea." Irene set down her drink and reached out for a hug. "Did you have a good time?"

Karen looked at both of them, her eyes shifting under the bill of her cap. "There was a dead guy in the park."

"Excuse me?" Gail said.

"I am totally serious. We went to Lenin Park, and we were walking to the stables so we could ride the horses, and there were police everywhere. Mario went over to see what was going on. They found this dead guy in the woods. He'd been there for like two or three days."

"Oh, honey." Gail reached out for her hand. "I'm so sorry. You didn't see him, I hope."

"No, the ambulance was driving away when we got there, but the police were still investigating. Mario talked to some people to find out what happened, but they didn't know who the guy was. Mario wanted to bring us home, so we left." Karen added, "I don't know why he thought we should come home."

"He was being considerate," Gail said, pulling Karen onto her lap. She hugged her tightly. "What an awful thing to happen!"

"Mom, we didn't *see* anything."

"Yes, I know, but still—"

"It was kind of exciting, actually."

"My God, Karen."

Irene said, "That's what you get when they watch so much violence on TV. Kids become inured to it." She reached over and patted Karen's cheek. "I bet you're hungry."

"Not really." She scooted off Gail's lap. "Mario bought us some pizza. Can I have a cola, please?"

"May I?" Irene corrected. "Why don't you have some juice instead?"

"You're having cola." Karen leaned over and sniffed her glass. "Aha! And what else, Gramma?"

"Have some juice, Karen," said Gail, looking toward the living room. "Is Mario leaving? I wonder if he could give me a lift downtown."

She got up and went inside the house. The wide roof overhang cut the sunlight, and she blinked in the cool semi-darkness. When she came around the corner toward the front door, the long row of bright windows reflected on the floor and in the framed photographs on the wall.

The living room was empty, but she saw Anthony on the porch talking to his daughter. His back was to the house. He turned his head slightly, and she saw his long nose and full lips and the familiar angle of his jaw. He wore a tight blue shirt she didn't recognize . . . and a silver earring.

She stopped and stared. It wasn't Anthony at all. In a split-second her mind had played a trick, filling in the image of the man she had *wanted* to see. This was Mario Cabrera. Of course it was Mario. He had just brought the kids home. He was shorter than Anthony, and his hair was black, not dark brown.

Angela's soft voice came through the open windows, and she stood on tiptoe to touch her lips to Mario's cheek. He tilted his head and kissed her on the mouth, then flashed his gorgeous smile and turned to go down the steps.

Unable to breathe, Gail walked closer to the windows.

This morning she'd hardly recognized him without his braids. The beads and long hair had been a distraction. Now she could see the shape of his head, the curve of his neck, the slim hips and easy motion of his long legs. Mario got into his car, a tiny European model of some kind, spray-painted lime green. A cloud of smoke rolled from the exhaust. He stuck a lean, muscular arm out the window. The tiger tattoo was a flash of orange and black, and gold winked at his wrist.

"*Ciao, mi ángel.*"

Angela waved. "*Ciao.*"

Gail put out a hand to steady herself on the pillar dividing the windows. Her heart thudded in her chest. She murmured, "You're wrong. You're being completely stupid. It's not possible. Stop it."

But the image of Anthony's face, superimposed over Mario's, had incised itself into her mind. She sank down onto the low, tiled window ledge and took another breath. She counted backward. Anthony was forty-four years old. Subtract twenty—

The door swung open. Angela noticed her sitting there, and her smile faded. "Gail? Is anything the matter?"

"No, not at all." She stood up. "I've been waiting for Anthony, but I guess he's still having lunch with your grandfather."

"You saw Mario kissing me, didn't you? Don't worry, I'm not going to let it go too far." Her smile reappeared. "But I am over Bobby. So over him."

"Karen says you had an experience at the park."

"They found a body. He was a teenager, they said. Isn't that awful?" Long lashes gave Angela's velvet-brown eyes the look of a fawn, but her body was not that of a child. Her bare shoulders glowed like honey. A camisole top skimmed her waist and revealed the curve of her hips. A pink stone on a gold stud sparkled in her navel.

Angela said, "Mario was very upset. They think it was a murder. We didn't tell Karen. That is just so unheard of in Cuba. Someone that age, you know? Someone *any* age."

Gail asked, "Where's Danny? Did he go up?"

"He's not *here*?" Angela rolled her eyes. "My brother. He said he didn't want to walk around in the sun all afternoon so we left him downtown. He said was going to get a taxi and come back here."

"I haven't seen him," Gail said.

"Oh, is he going to catch it." Angela held up her hands. "Fine. I'm tired of dealing with him. If Dad grounds him for the rest of our trip, I couldn't care less. Gail, do you think Aunt Marta would mind if Mario came over sometime? Like Thursday night? I invited him already. I know his father is sort of *persona non grata* around here, but Mario isn't part of all that, I mean not publicly. If he said what he really thought, they'd put him in jail. That's what it's like in Cuba. You have to lie. Your whole life is a lie. Mario says it's like being dead already. Isn't that depressing? People are just waiting for Fidel to croak. Mario wants to get out. He says they won't give him an exit visa, but there are ways. There are definitely ways. I think Dad would help him. Don't you?"

Barely able to follow this torrent of words, Gail finally said, "Well . . . I don't know. Maybe. Listen, about Mario coming over for dinner. Let me talk to your father about it. Okay?"

"Okay. Thanks. Maybe he can soften Aunt Marta up." Angela kissed Gail's cheek and ran toward the stairs, swinging around the handrail, taking the steps two at a time.

Alone in the living room, Gail brushed back her hair with trembling fingers and noticed that her forehead was damp. She said quietly, "You could be wrong. You *are* wrong, you dunce. He would have said something. He would have."

Last night Anthony had made love to her. He had kissed his way up her body from her heels to her forehead, taking his time doing it, and any thoughts of his being with Yolanda Cabrera had flown out of her brain like leaves on the wind.

We will be home in six days, she reminded herself. *He will forget, and it will all be normal again.*

How? How was it ever going to be normal? Anthony wanted to bring Mario to Miami. And Yolanda and her husband—assuming José wasn't in jail. And all the better if he was!

So why don't you just ask him?

Gail's laughter echoed on the terrazzo and the stone walls of the living room. What in the name of God would she say? What if it *was* true, and he didn't know? Better to leave it alone.

But it couldn't be true. Meeting Mario's mother, Gail hadn't seen the least sign of guilt, shame, or duplicity. Nothing. Not from either of them. After ten years of watching courtroom testimony and paying attention to the most subtle clues of body language, Gail thought she could spot a lie. Anthony might have unresolved feelings for Yolanda Cabrera, but that didn't mean he had ever slept with her.

Gail went through the kitchen, fixed herself a cola, cracked some ice from the metal freezer tray, then poured a little rum into the glass. She returned to the terrace. Karen was gone, and Irene appeared to be dozing.

A recollection swam into Gail's thoughts. Olga Saavedra had known the Leivas for a long time. Had she known Mario's father? Not José, his biological one. Gail wanted to clear this up before it started taking root in her mind. Olga would say she'd known Mario's father quite well, a short, fat man with blond hair, nothing like Anthony Quintana. Olga Saavedra would tell her—

"Shit," she said.

Opening her eyes, Irene said, "What's the matter?"

"I forgot to ask Mario to take me downtown."

"Well, Marta will be home soon." Irene turned her wrist to check the time. She was wearing a tropical-green Swatch. "I might go with you. I'm supposed to meet Yolanda at three-thirty. Don't worry, I won't get in your way. My guidebook says there's a perfume factory somewhere in the old town."

"Mother, I don't want you wandering around *Habana Vieja* by yourself."

"Why not? The worst that could happen is I'll get picked up by a hot young *cubano* trolling for female tourists." She smiled. "Wouldn't that be fun? If I called you from Varadero Beach? 'Hi, darling, I met this wonderful guy named Fernando, and he wants to show me his maracas.' "

"For God's sake, Mother, please."

"You're in a strange mood."

A movement at the corner of the house caught Gail's attention. For a brief second or two, a burly man in a plaid shirt and blue jeans appeared in the portico that separated the kitchen from the garage.

"Was that Cobo?" her mother asked.

"Unless he has a twin."

A door closed inside the house. Gail turned around to see her sister-in-law walking at a quick pace toward the stairs. Marta had arrived. She'd come in through the kitchen. Evidently she had gone to pick up Cobo, which explained the phone call she'd received just before she left. What was it, the Lada had broken down? Why not just say so? Why lie about needing groceries?

With a wave toward the two on the terrace, Marta vanished upstairs.

"Do you think she's all right?" Irene asked.

"I don't know. Should I go find out?"

"Yes, why don't you?" Irene got up. "I'll see what's for lunch."

By the time Gail reached the top of the stairs, Marta was nowhere in sight. Gail passed the girls' room, hearing low murmurs of conversation. At Marta's door, Gail turned her ear toward the crack. Water was running in the bathroom. "Marta? It's Gail. Are you okay?"

Her muffled voice said, "Yes! Fine!"

There was something wrong. Gail turned the knob.

"¡Momentito! Don't come in!"

She pulled her hand back. "Are you sure you're all right?"

"Yes." Marta laughed. "I'm not dressed. You want to hear what I did? In the market, I made such a mess! I dropped a box of yogurt on the floor." Jo-gurrr. "It splashed on my pants. New pants. Such bad luck."

Gail leaned against the wall and stared idly across at the framed print of some Cuban abstract artist who liked a lot of brown and black.

The water was still running in Marta's bathroom.

She spoke through the door again. "Mother said she'd start lunch."

No reply.

"Marta?"

The water went off. There was silence, then a long moan. *"Ay, Dios, se me olvidó el jodido pan."* She had forgotten the f-ing bread.

Gail decided that if Marta could still curse, she was probably all right.

"I was thinking of going downtown. There's something I want to get for Anthony. Do you think Cobo could drop me off?"

"Cobo?"

"You brought him home. Didn't you?"

More silence. "Yes. He can take you after lunch. I'll be there in a few minutes."

Gail mouthed the word *damn*. She didn't have time to wait. Olga Saavedra might be gone. "Do you think I could borrow your car? I have a map of Havana—"

"No! The traffic. Call a taxi. Wait for me. I will do it." Marta was getting annoyed. "Please wait downstairs."

In silent slow motion, Gail pounded her fist on the wall.

"Mom?"

She turned to see Karen standing in the hall. She had come out of Janelle's room. "Where are you going?" Karen asked.

"Nowhere special. To get something for Anthony."

"May I go with you?"

"No, sweetie, not today. I'll be back soon. Go talk to Angela. I think she needs company after what happened in the park."

But Karen followed her to the stairs. Halfway down she stopped and held on to Gail's elbow. "You're not going shopping for Anthony, are you? I wish people would stop treating me like a child."

"I don't, Karen."

"You most certainly do." At times Karen could look older than her twelve years. Her thin, straight lips would compress, and her eyes would focus like a pair of blue laser beams.

Gail sighed. "I'm sorry. I can't explain right now."

"Jeez-us, Mom. What is going on around here? You and Anthony stay in your room and whisper all the time, and Mr. Vega didn't even come home last night until like two o'clock."

"Karen, my God."

"I wasn't spying. I just couldn't sleep."

"There is nothing going on." Gail lifted her hands and said quietly, "All right. The woman who was here this morning, the one doing the party for Janelle? Her name is Olga. Here's the truth, I swear. She's trying to get in touch with Anthony, and she can't, so she wants to talk to me."

"Why?"

"I don't know why. She just said show up at two o'clock."

"So . . . how are you going to get there?"

"Marta's going to call a taxi."

"It takes a long time for a taxi. Janelle says you can wait an hour."

"Oh, no."

"What you do is, you walk over to *Quinta Avenida*. You stand there and hold up a dollar. You don't have to call a taxi. People just give you a ride." Karen arched her brows. "I could show you."

Gail looked at her a second, then went back to Marta's door and told her thank you, but she could find a taxi on her own, not to worry. She used the telephone in the kitchen to try Anthony one more time before they left. After six rings, she hung up.

24

They sat in the back of a maroon 1950 Plymouth with bulbous fenders, a split windshield, and truck tires. The windows were cranked down to get rid of the diesel exhaust coming through the floorboard. Karen had changed into a fresh T-shirt and jeans. She sat in the middle with her backpack between her feet. She and Irene would find something to do before meeting Yolanda Cabrera at the *Centro Comercial*. Gail didn't know where that was but had no doubt Karen could find it.

The driver said the ride would cost five dollars. Karen had argued with him, shaking her head, holding up three dollar bills until he finally snatched the money out of her hand and told them in fast Spanish to get in before the police saw them. Gail began to object, but Karen pushed her toward the open door and told her not to worry about it.

Leaning over the seat, Gail showed the driver a piece of paper with an address on it and said to go there first.

The address was Olga Saavedra's apartment. Gail understood that Olga dropped in several times a week at the Ministry—the publicity office, Olga called it—but she ran her party-planning operations out of a government building near *El Palacio de las Convenciones*, the convention center. She drove there every day, except when she had other things to do. She lived near the University. Sometimes she didn't get home until very late, as she was forced by the nature of her work to attend many cultural functions, musical events, and the like. She knew many important people.

Olga had explained all this in very bad English, and Gail supposed she had missed some of it. What she hadn't missed was the woman's hand gripping her wrist, her darting eyes, her jittery insistence that she *had to speak to Anthony*, very important, but she couldn't get in touch with him, and if she explained everything to Gail, maybe Gail could help.

Ordinarily she would have stayed out of Anthony's business, but she'd felt Abdel García's presence like cold fingers touching her neck, so she had smiled at Olga Saavedra and said all right, what time?

Irene's guidebook was open on Karen's legs. Obrapía Street here, the perfume factory there. Karen had brought from Gail's law office a dispenser of transparent page tabs. She peeled one off, laid it on the map, and drew an arrow on it.

Irene grabbed her digital camera out of its case. "Oh, tell him to slow down, Gail, I want to get a shot of that statue. It's José Martí. *Señor, un foto! Lentamente, por favor.*" She took off the lens cap as the old car slowed to a crawl.

"Mother, hurry up," Gail said. "I'm going to be late."

"No file?" Irene stared at the blue screen of her camera. "What does that mean, 'no file'?"

Karen glanced over. "Is the memory stick in it?"

Irene clicked open a panel and looked inside. "Oh . . . *drat.*"

The driver shifted gears, and fresh fumes blew through the holes in the floor as he hit the accelerator. Karen leaned over and unzipped a pocket of her backpack. She took out her PDA and removed a slim blue piece of plastic. "Here, Gramma. This fits your camera. I downloaded some games, but it's still got loads of room on it. Just don't use a high-res setting."

Irene said, "I am amazed. You're the smartest girl in the known world."

"It's not that hard," Karen mumbled. She went back to the guidebook.

Taking a route Gail had no hope of remembering, the driver eventually stopped his wheezing automobile on a street with a three-story apartment building on one side and a mildewed colonnade on the other, through which Gail could see shop windows with tape pasted over the cracks. The car behind them gave a few sharp toots of its horn.

Gail scooted forward to ask the driver, "Where is it? *¿Dónde?*"

He pointed at the address written on the paper, then at the apartment building, which had no numbers on the front. With some difficulty, Gail pushed open the car door, then leaned in to tell Irene and Karen she would see them at Marta's place later on. Miraculously, she had arrived early by ten minutes.

The Plymouth rattled away on the uneven pavement.

Gail studied her destination. An arch of decorative ironwork extended across the entrance of the apartment building. The lower windows were framed by twisting, bas-relief columns; the upper windows had been retro-fitted with glass louvers, ugly in the late-nineteenth-century facade. A concrete walkway led into a courtyard, which contained a profusion of greenery. Olga lived in apartment three, which Gail assumed was on the ground floor. Air conditioning units hung over the alleys that separated the building from its neighbors.

Her eye was momentarily captured by an enormous sign on the blank wall of the adjacent building: the flag of Cuba above the words EN CADA BARRIO, ¡REVOLUCIÓN! Revolution in every neighborhood.

An old black Mercedes was parked about halfway down on the left side of the alley. Gail recognized it: Olga Saavedra's car. How many of those could there be in Havana? With a few minutes to spare, Gail stepped under the colonnade. She had dressed in a plain black pullover and jeans, but as people walked around her, she felt their eyes. With her leather shoulder bag and expensive walking shoes, she looked like what she was: a foreigner.

She walked to the end of the colonnade and back again, passing a state-run pharmacy and a hair salon with a sign taped to the window. *Moderno, eficiente y siempre socialista.* Gail wondered what a socialist haircut looked like. The doors of a lunchroom were open to the street, revealing stools at a long counter but not much in the display cases.

Finally, checking her watch, she walked across the sidewalk and waited for traffic to clear. She was about to go across when she saw a slender young man in a blue shirt. He was coming in her direction, walking alongside the row of cars in the alley. He wore sunglasses, which seemed odd, given the heavy cloud cover.

Mario Cabrera.

Gail moved quickly behind a utility pole. She waited for him to walk through and turn one way or the other, but instead he suddenly went between the parked cars and disappeared. There had to be a side entrance into the building.

Perplexed, Gail wondered if Mario knew Olga Saavedra. This

morning at Marta's house, when he and Olga had been standing within ten feet of each other, neither had given any sign of recognition. But he had to know her, Gail thought. His father had worked with Olga Saavedra at a television station, and Olga had let José Leiva take the blame for the documentary that had sent him to prison.

Gail thought of confronting him. *Why are you here? Who are you? Yes, who are you, Mario? Tell me about your alleged father, the soldier who went to Angola and died there.*

As she debated with herself what to do, Mario reappeared in the alley and went back in the direction he had come. The alley intersected with another that went behind a building on the next street. He turned right and was gone. Gail hesitated, then ran across and got to the end of the alley in time to see Mario turn at a building whose windows were mostly sealed up with sheets of metal or plywood. She hurried to catch up, then stopped and looked around the corner. This passage led to a wider, busier street. Mario paused at the sidewalk, glanced each way, then turned right. He walked half a block, took some keys from his pocket, and got into his small green car. He pulled away from the curb in a haze of exhaust fumes.

Why she had let him go, Gail couldn't say. It would have been so easy to catch up. *How do you know Olga Saavedra?*

She retraced her steps, stopping at the line of cars in the alley and the opening through which Mario had vanished and reappeared five minutes ago. A rusty iron gate, no longer functional, leaned against the wall.

A dim passageway led her to the courtyard, a pretty area with palm trees, some plastic chairs, and a fountain. But no water. She looked at the numbers on the plain white doors and found number three back where she had started, in the passageway near the side entrance. The windows were closed, and no light or noise came from within.

She knocked. Waited. Knocked again.

"Damn it." Gail opened her shoulder bag for a notepad and pen. *I was here at 2:05. Call this number.* She flipped through her notebook until she found the number for Anthony's cell phone. She folded the paper and wedged it in the crack between the door and the frame.

She heard the noise of traffic. The muffled beat of a salsa tune from one of the other apartments. The rain. It had come at last. Rain whispered on the dry grass of the courtyard and slanted onto the sidewalk. It ticked on the long black hood of the Mercedes at the end of the passageway and dripped off the fenders.

For a full minute Gail stared at the door before deciding to give the knob a turn.

L ater on, she would say she had a feeling. A presentiment. The police detective, a man named Álvaro Sánchez, who had studied English and had spent a year posted at the Cuban embassy in London, did not have that word—presentiment—in his vocabulary, so Gail would explain that she didn't like knocking on doors and getting no answer when she knew that someone was inside waiting for her.

The knob turned, and Gail pushed the door inward.

This was an apartment of some luxury, as Havana apartments go. A functioning air conditioner; a sofa and armchair upholstered in leather; a black laminate cabinet holding pieces of ceramic and pottery; a new 36-inch Sony television with DVD player; a brown-and-cream area rug of Scandinavian design; walls without cracks in them.

Gail had no eyes for any of that, no immediate notice of the overturned armchair or the patterns on the walls and ceiling, the streaks of red flung across the white surfaces like paint from a paint brush. She was focused on Olga Saavedra, in her black pants and red jacket, lying crumpled on the floor as if someone had thrown her there. The left side of her forehead was misshapen, and strands of blond hair, matted and sticky red, stretched across her face. Her mouth was smashed, and her nose, and there was blood, so much blood, a great pool of it, bleeding into the rug, running along the cracks between the tiles, everywhere.

Gail had completely forgotten about the note. When she came in, it fell, and her shoe pushed it across the threshold. Sánchez, who missed very little, saw the paper on the floor. He picked it up and unfolded it. He used his cell phone to call the number, and a man answered.

25

H eavy clouds blotted out the sun. The rain had stopped, but water dripped from the roof and echoed in the dim passageway. The hour seemed much later than four o'clock.

Standing just outside Olga Saavedra's apartment, Anthony could see his wife on the opposite side of the courtyard. They had put her in a chair, and a policeman was with her, a reminder that she remain where she was until permitted to move. The residents and the curious were being kept away from the activity at the rear of the building. They watched from windows and gathered at the entrance near the street.

The detective, who had introduced himself as Álvaro Sánchez, was a tall, fair-haired man in the gray uniform of the PNR. Behind his glasses, his eyes were patient and probing. He was the senior officer sent for when the municipal police realized what they had on their hands.

Not knowing what Gail had already told the detective, Anthony gave him the truth: "I was not aware that Miss Saavedra contacted my wife or that my wife agreed to come here. Gail probably tried to call me, but I had my phone turned off most of the afternoon. As for Miss Saavedra's purposes . . . I haven't the least idea. Detective, my family must be wondering where we are. My sister lives in Havana. She is married to General Ramiro Vega."

The name produced a nod. "Your wife told me. Because of your relationship to General Vega, I was compelled by procedures to report this case to my superiors."

"May I make a phone call? It won't take long." Anthony held up his cell phone.

"I am sorry. Telephone calls must wait until after we are finished."

"It's your job," Anthony said.

"Exactly so," Sánchez said. "Why do you think Olga Saavedra wanted to see you?"

"I told you, I don't know."

"You must have a theory, at least."

"I can give you a guess. I believe that Olga wanted to see me because she thought I could get her out of Cuba."

"Could you have done it?"

"It can be done," Anthony said.

"Would you have, if she had asked?"

"No. It isn't legal."

The detective made a brief smile. His teeth were dark from nicotine. "Did Miss Saavedra tell you that she wanted to leave?"

"Not specifically."

"Then in what way?"

"In the way that most people express it, by telling me that life is not easy in Cuba."

With a slight shrug, Sánchez said, "How long had you known Miss Saavedra?"

"We met about eight years ago at a reception for the director of the Cuban National Orchestra. I went as the guest of my sister and General Vega. Miss Saavedra was working in television at the time. She knew a great many people in the arts."

"And what was the nature of your relationship with her?"

"We were acquainted."

"Friends?"

"No, I wouldn't say so."

"There was nothing between you but . . . an acquaintance?"

"This is correct."

"Have you ever been in her apartment?"

"Never."

The detective crossed his arms and rested his chin in his fingers, then said, "I don't understand why she would ask *you* to help her leave. You are a relative of a high-ranking officer in the armed forces. Wouldn't she be afraid that you would inform him of her request?"

"I don't know what she intended to ask me."

"Ah, yes. So you said." Sánchez glanced across the courtyard.

Gail was intently watching their conversation without being able to hear it. "Your wife says that you and Olga Saavedra have talked recently, within the past few days."

Anthony was compelled to admit, "We saw each other at my sister's house on Saturday, the day after my family and I arrived in Cuba. Miss Saavedra was there to talk to my sister, Marta, about the fifteenth birthday party for her daughter."

"What was the subject of your conversation with Miss Saavedra?"

"Nothing in particular. She said hello. I said hello. She congratulated me on my marriage. That was about it. She may have kept my name in her head as someone she could use, if the need arose."

Sánchez considered the response, then said, "Do you know any of her friends?"

"No, I don't."

"Do you know, or have you heard, of anyone who would have wanted to harm her? Someone who may have been jealous? Someone seeking revenge?"

"I am not aware of anyone."

"Did she have a lover?"

"I do not know," Anthony said.

As if suddenly remembering, Sánchez said, "A woman in the CDR for this zone has told us that Miss Saavedra has traveled several times to Europe. If she was free to travel, why would she ask for your help in leaving Cuba?"

Anthony shook his head. "It was only a guess, detective. I couldn't read her mind."

"Of course not." He lifted his head to look at Anthony directly, and his glasses reflected the fading gray light from the courtyard. "Where were you at noon today?"

"In Vedado. I had lunch with my father, Luis Quintana. He lives in a home for veterans on B Street."

"When did you arrive there?"

"Around eleven o'clock."

"And you left at . . . ?"

"I was with my father until one-thirty. Call the veterans' home if you like. I drove back to my sister's house in Miramar and arrived about a quarter before two. My wife wasn't there, and my sister said she had gone downtown to do some shopping. I was with my sister until shortly after four, when you called."

"We will have to confirm it, of course." Sánchez clasped his hands briefly in thought, then extended an arm toward the open door of the apartment. "Would you like to come inside? Your wife told me that in Miami, you're a renowned criminal defense lawyer. She says you have handled many cases of murder. Perhaps you could look at the scene and give me your impressions."

"I'm a lawyer, not a detective."

"It doesn't matter. Come."

Anthony had the thought that this man wanted to hear from someone outside his own world. He followed Sánchez, and they stopped a few feet past the door. Men in plainclothes were taking photographs, opening drawers, coming out of the bedroom with a box. One was at the desk going through an appointment book. The men stopped, glanced at each other, then returned to their work.

He knew nothing about Cuban crime scene procedures, but he had heard that officers from the Department of Technical Investigation had a double role. They also acted as secret police, reporting directly to State Security.

Anthony looked quickly around the room and finally forced his eyes to the body on the floor. He could not recognize Olga Saavedra. The bones of her face had been smashed. She lay, with her head toward him, her twisted legs beside an overturned chair. A large amount of blood had pooled around her, drying to purplish brown at the edges. With his teeth clamped together, Anthony followed the spatters of blood that went up one wall and across the ceiling. He felt a heaviness in his chest and at the same time a burn of anger.

"A terrible death."

"It was," said the detective.

"How long do you think she has been dead?"

"Between three and five hours. Your wife arrived at two o'clock. One of the neighbors saw Miss Saavedra go into her apartment at noon." Sánchez gestured to the ruined face. "There was anger in the attack. Do you not have that impression?"

"Anger or thoroughness," Anthony said.

An oddly shaped piece of wood lay on the leather sofa. It was perhaps two feet in length with curves extending from a heavy base. Anthony took a step toward it, and the curves resolved into the elongated, nude figures of a man and woman carved from mahogany. "That wooden statue. Was it the murder weapon?"

"Probably. We haven't moved it. The base appears to match an indentation in her skull. There, above her left eye. The amount of force required for a fatal blow would not be great if the point of the base struck at the correct angle. The other blows appear to have been made after she fell, but we'll know more when the coroner arrives. There will be an autopsy tomorrow at the Institute of Legal Medicine."

Anthony looked around the room once more, avoiding the body. "How did the killer get in? Was the door forced? Are there any broken windows?"

"No, there are no indications of a break-in. She probably knew him."

"Perhaps. Or he followed her and forced his way inside when she opened the door. He could have been a stranger."

"In Cuba, such crimes are rarely committed by strangers," said Sánchez.

"She knew him, then." Anthony asked if they had examined the statue for fingerprints.

"Unfortunately, the killer wiped it clean of fingerprints. There are smears on the floor by the desk as well. He obliterated his shoe prints."

"Where is the cloth he used?"

"We have not yet found it."

"Miss Saavedra's hands appear untouched," Anthony said. "There are no . . . *defensive wounds*." He said it in English.

Following in English, Sánchez said, "Yes, yes, we have the same way to describe it. *Heridas de defensa*. She was probably dead or unconscious at the first blow."

"*Menos mal*," Anthony said. At least this small thing. He leaned over the body. Returning to Spanish, he said, "She's wearing a gold necklace. Are there abrasions on her neck?"

"No. The killer didn't attempt to take her necklace, nor is the money missing from her purse."

"Then it wasn't a robbery," Anthony said. "She's fully dressed. That would seem to rule out an attempted rape."

"That was my thought as well," Sánchez replied. "On the other hand, perhaps he did intend such an act and left after realizing she was dead. He could have become frightened that he would be discovered."

"Frightened? No, he was very cold," Anthony countered. "Not only violent, but intelligent. He took the time to get rid of the evidence."

"What do you infer from this?" Sánchez asked.

"That the crime could have been planned in advance."

"It is impossible to say until we find the person responsible."

"That is true." Anthony brought his eyes back to the woman on the floor. "Did she have any family? I never asked her."

"No children. There is a sister in Holguin. Her mother died in prison."

"In prison? What had she done?"

"She was profiteering from the black market," Sánchez said. "Her sentence was ten years, but she died of a heart attack after six. That is what we have been told by the CDR. Miss Saavedra has no criminal history, and she attended the block meetings. Not all of them, but enough not to have been marked as uncooperative. There were no unknown visitors coming and going from her apartment."

"But with the side entrance so near her door, they might not have been seen."

"Exactly so."

Anthony accompanied the detective back to the passageway. The buzzing fixture in the low ceiling did little to keep out the encroaching darkness. Lights shone in the other apartments.

Sánchez said, "Before I reunite you with your wife, I would like to ask an unrelated question, if you would allow me. A police chief from the Bahamas was here last week. He told me about the crime laboratory in Miami. He says they use it for their difficult cases. Even the FBI uses it. Is this so?"

"He means the laboratory that belongs to the county," Anthony said. "But yes, it is nationally recognized, as is the medical examiner's department. They do death investigation for many of the islands."

"It would be something to see." Sánchez nodded, then said, "I have a brother in Miami. He left twenty years ago. His daughter is about to graduate from medical school. It won't be easy, all the red tape, but I am thinking of going for a visit. I would be there at least a month."

"Keep in touch with me," Anthony said. He took one of his cards out of his wallet. "If you come, I'm sure I could arrange a personal tour of the crime laboratory and the morgue."

"I would like that very much." Sánchez put the card into his shirt pocket. As he did so, his attention went to the courtyard. The people milling around the entrance were being ordered back by one of the police officers. Three men appeared, walking in a V formation of square shoulders and lace-up boots. The Army had arrived. Two other men followed in sport shirts and dark trousers.

Those two continued into the apartment. The men in uniform stopped just short of the passageway. The officer in the lead, a *mulato* in his late thirties, had two red stripes and a small star on his epaulets. His eyes fixed on the detective.

"Inspector Sánchez? I am Major Orlando Valdez. This investigation is now being handled by State Security. You will assist them by giving a full report."

Sánchez glanced at the door of the apartment, then nodded. "I am at your orders."

The major shifted his attention to Anthony. "Mr. Quintana, you and your wife will come with me."

"May I ask where?"

"To the Ministry of the Interior to answer some questions. General Vega has been notified. It's completely a matter of routine."

He motioned in the direction of the officer across the courtyard, who leaned down to Gail's chair and spoke to her. She picked up her purse and started walking toward them. Even in the diminished gray light of late afternoon, Anthony could see the apprehension in her eyes.

26

T he face of Che Guevara looked out from the smooth stone facade of the Ministry building. This was not a photograph but a line drawing made of steel, amazingly accurate: the firm mouth and flowing hair; the piercing eyes fixed on the inevitable, glorious future; the beret with its star. Under the face, Che's words were written as if scrawled by an immense hand: *Hasta la Victoria Siempre.* Onward to victory forever.

Che presided over several acres of cracked asphalt in the *Plaza de la Revolución*. A seated José Martí gazed back at him from the low hill across the plaza. Dozens of utility poles with floodlights and speakers had been erected between them to carry the speeches and music at the rallies and mass demonstrations, a million Cubans waving flags and carrying banners, screaming, "Fidel, Fidel, *¡estamos contigo!*" We are with you, Fidel.

On one or another *Dia de los Trabajadores*, a Workers' Day celebration several years ago, Anthony Quintana had marched with the crowd to the plaza to find out what it was like in that sea of bodies and emotion. From his own pocket of silence he had seen an old man with tears of love pouring down his face, a girl fainting from the heat, a teenager listening to his Walkman, and a man taken away by undercover police after he had cupped a hand at his mouth and shouted, *"Palabras, no. Pan, sí."* Words, no. Bread, yes. Dripping sweat, Anthony had gone back to his hotel room, turned the AC to its lowest setting, and opened a beer.

The face of Che Guevara grew larger as the driver sped across the plaza. Anthony was in the back of a small white Renault. The army major who had come for him sat in the front passenger seat. There wasn't much conversation. Turning around, he could see the

other car following close behind. They had separated him from
Gail. It was procedure, the major had said. So far Anthony had
kept a grip on his anger. Gail would be afraid, and he hated to
think of it. But she was more intelligent than they knew. She had
run across the courtyard, the distraught wife, throwing herself into
his arms too fast for the soldiers to stop her. She had clung to him,
hiding her face against his neck. Her lips were at his ear long
enough to whisper, *I didn't say anything*.

The car turned under the portico past the main entrance, then
went around back and stopped with a slight squeal of tires on the
damp concrete driveway. Soldiers came to attention. The driver
opened the rear door.

Getting out, Anthony looked back to see one of Valdez's men
extending a hand to help Gail from the other car. Her eyes connected with Anthony's. She was all right.

"This way," the major said. "Your wife will wait for you
downstairs."

Two soldiers fell in behind them. They went up some steps and
through a door, where a guard saluted. As they walked, the tap of
their heels went into and out of cadence.

Anthony was aware of what he had to do: protect Ramiro
Vega. Sometime between his conversation with the CIA spook this
morning and staring down at the body of Olga Saavedra, the answer had come into focus. He knew what Céspedes had said. No,
better to call it a theory. Anthony needed a couple of details from
José Leiva. Another phone call to Hector. He wanted to toss his
theory at Bookhouser and see if fireworks went off.

They entered an elevator and avoided looking at themselves in
the polished metal doors. No one spoke. The elevator opened onto
a terrazzo-floored hall lined with flags and photographs. Through
a set of glass double doors across the hall, a thin figure appeared.
Abdel García.

His off-center jaw shifted when he spoke. "Thank you, Major
Valdez. I will take Mr. Quintana from here."

Valdez hesitated, then said, "Yes, general." He motioned to one
of his men, who pressed the elevator button. The doors slid open.
Valdez and his men entered and were gone. At the end of the long
corridor a group of officers walked out of one office and into
another.

As the voices faded, García said quietly, "You were brought here because of your family relationship with General Vega. That was explained to you?"

"Yes. My wife discovered a murder victim. Am I here to talk to you about it?"

"No, you will speak to Lieutenant General Efraín Prieto. As Vega's superior officer, I was notified. They are waiting for us. We don't have much time." García moved so close that Anthony could feel the other man's breath on his cheek. "Do you have something for me?"

"You're referring to your friend who took the trip to Brazil?"

"Quickly."

"I have some information. I'm not certain how accurate—"

"Good. We will talk later. Prieto doesn't know you're working for us. For reasons of security, I couldn't tell him. His staff has been infiltrated with traitors. I report to his superiors. Say nothing. Do you understand?"

Anthony stared down the empty corridor. *Efraín Prieto.* The name stirred a memory. Prieto was near the top of the Cuban power structure. A member of the Politburo, he thought. There were not many men senior to Prieto. The Interior Minister himself. The commander of the Armed Forces. And the *comandante en jefe* at the top of the pyramid. Which one—if any—was Abdel García reporting to?

His mind grabbed at a possibility: Abdel García was reporting to no one but himself.

"Do you understand?" The words hissed in García's mouth. "Do not speak of this, or you and your wife will never leave Cuba. Answer me."

"Yes. I understand."

García moved toward the glass doors. "Come, they're waiting."

A smaller corridor led to an anteroom with a soldier at a desk. He stood and saluted. García walked past him to a door and knocked lightly before opening it and motioning for Anthony to go first.

He quickly took in the details: brown carpet, teak furniture, a flag in a small spotlight. Aluminum-framed windows looked out on the plaza, which was quickly fading to darkness. A glow came from the floodlit monument to Martí. Two men in plainclothes sat in chairs along the back wall, pretending to be invisible.

The general stood behind his desk. He had the shape of a concrete block. His uniform fit so trimly that it could have been stitched into place. There were three stars on each shoulder, gold leaves on the lapels, and a rectangle of campaign ribbons.

"I am Lieutenant General Efraín Prieto. Please have a seat, Mr. Quintana."

The width of the desk, or the occasion, prevented a handshake. Among the various files and papers and bound reports on the desk lay a thin folder, dead center.

Anthony said, "Is this about Olga Saavedra? We've told the police everything we know."

The light over Prieto's desk glowed on his white hair and deepened the pockmarks on his cheeks. "I will read the reports, but I would like also to have the information directly from you."

Evidently someone from the DTI team at the apartment had already briefed Prieto. For the next hour Anthony answered the same questions that Detective Sánchez had asked him. How do you know Olga Saavedra? Why did your wife go to her apartment? Why did she want to see you?

Unlike Sánchez, the general had not much interest in Olga Saavedra's possible desire to leave Cuba. His questions went toward Anthony's relationship with her. Anthony said they had gone to the clubs a few times, but he denied he had slept with her. As he talked, he could see Abdel García out of the corner of his eye. Occasionally García blotted his lower lip. The toe of one polished shoe rotated slowly. Other than that, he remained perfectly still.

On the wall behind Prieto hung the usual portrait of Fidel in his green uniform and cap. Beside it, a framed black-and-white photograph showed bearded soldiers in open trucks, the jubilant crowds mobbing the procession, throwing flowers. The triumphal entry into Havana, 1959.

The questioning closed in on Anthony's background. How he had left Cuba. His first marriage, his law practice, his children, his marriage to Gail Connor. Her background, her opinion of Cuba.

"She was enjoying Cuba a great deal until this afternoon. General Prieto, how much longer is this going to take? My wife has suffered an emotional trauma, and I would like to take her back to my sister's house."

"Of course." Prieto made a brief smile of apology. "You are a frequent visitor to our country, Mr. Quintana."

"I like to keep in touch with my family."

"You are breaking the laws of the United States." When Anthony acknowledged that this was so, Prieto said, "How many times would you say you have been to Cuba in the past ten years?"

"I'm not sure. Several. I don't keep track."

Prieto lifted the cover of the folder. There were some sheets of paper inside. Anthony saw what looked like a list.

"Ramiro Vega must obtain clearance before you are permitted to stay at his house. It is unusual that an American would stay with anyone in the armed forces. He vouches for you. As does your father, Luis Quintana Rodríguez, a hero of the Revolution." The general's finger moved down the page. "Nine visas in ten years."

The list should have been twice as long. Anthony guessed that it failed to pick up the routine tourist visas he had acquired at the Cuban airline counters in Mexico, when he had flown to Havana or Camagüey without telling his sister about it.

Prieto turned a page. Anthony saw some photographs. "You have friends in Cuba."

"Yes."

"Some of them are dissidents. José Leiva?"

"His wife is a friend from childhood. She takes care of my father. I have already explained this to General García."

"Do you agree with their demands?"

"Most of them, yes."

He turned another page. "Do you bring them money from the United States?"

"Not from the United States, from friends. If your government allowed José Leiva to work in his profession, he could earn his own money."

"What is General Vega's opinion?"

"We don't discuss it. We share views on some issues. Not this one."

Prieto lifted his eyes. They had the warmth of ice cubes. Anthony glanced again at the picture of the soldiers in the back of the truck and wondered if Prieto had been among them. Too young. Maybe he'd been that kid hanging onto the running board.

"You come into our country, you stay in the home of one of our generals, and you support the opposition."

"Ramiro Vega is my brother-in-law. Leiva is my friend. Politics doesn't interest me. I don't let it interfere with my personal life."

"Politics does not interest you." Prieto drummed a slow beat on the pages. "You are a man with no defined loyalties, is that it? A foot in each camp. As a soldier, I couldn't do it. If I were a lawyer . . . maybe. You are trained to hold more than one position at the same time. No, I couldn't do it." The cadence of his fingers slowed.

"When was the last time you saw your grandfather, Ernesto Pedrosa?"

Even expecting this didn't prevent Anthony's pulse rate from picking up. "Why do you ask me that?"

"Was it the night before you left Miami?"

"Did you have spies among the caterers? My grandparents gave my wife and me a party to celebrate our marriage."

"There was a guest at the party. Guillermo Navarro, the congressman."

Anthony momentarily lifted his hands from the arms of his chair. "Yes. He was there."

"Are you a friend of Mr. Navarro, that he was invited to celebrate your marriage?"

"Navarro isn't a friend. My grandfather invited him."

"Did he and Ernesto Pedrosa have a meeting that night?"

"I don't know if they did or not," Anthony said. "Please don't expect me to discuss my grandfather with officials of the Cuban government. He wouldn't like it."

"Did you speak to Navarro?" Prieto asked.

"Yes. He gave me his congratulations, and that was the last I saw of him."

Prieto's gaze went to his two guests at the back of the room, hung there a moment, then shifted to Anthony. "I will give you a name. Omar Céspedes. Do you recognize it?"

"No. Who is he?"

"He was a major in our armed forces. He is now in Washington testifying before the House Intelligence Committee. Navarro is a member of the Committee." Prieto waited as though Anthony might reply. When he did not, Prieto said, "You are aware of this?"

"I know that Navarro is on the Committee. I didn't know about Céspedes. What are you trying to say, general?"

"Tell me again why you came to Cuba."

"To visit my family. It's my niece's birthday." Anthony smiled. "Ah. I see. You think I was sent here because of Céspedes. The Committee wants to know if he's lying. How likely is it that Guillermo Navarro would trust *me* to find out?"

Again Prieto's gaze shifted toward the other side of the room. Anthony felt a tightness in the back of his neck. Disdain flickered across Prieto's face before he said, "If you wish to remain on good terms with Cuba, I suggest you maintain this exemplary lack of interest in politics." His chair rotated slightly before Prieto followed its motion with his head, then his eyes. "General García? Do you have anything you wish to add?"

He touched a knuckle to the corner of his mouth. "No, general."

Prieto closed the folder and shoved it aside. "When is your return flight to Miami, Mr. Quintana?"

"On Monday morning."

"There may be other questions regarding the death of Miss Saavedra. You and your wife will not leave Havana until you are notified by State Security." Prieto rose to his feet. "Good evening."

In the elevator on the way down, Anthony cleared his throat a couple of times. It felt like he'd been swallowing sand. When the doors slid shut, he could see Abdel García in the polished metal.

"What do you have for me?" García said.

"Juraguá."

"What?"

"Céspedes is talking about Juraguá. He says you want to finish construction as soon as possible. You need the energy, and you believe the United States is in no position to object. With world attention diverted by the situation in the Middle East, the time is ready to push forward."

The digital red floor display counted down.

García said, "Do they believe him?"

"They think he's probably lying. If he were correct—if you resumed construction on the reactor—it would be bombed to rubble. Your government is aware of what could happen."

"The Americans have made it quite clear. What else?"

"He's naming the agents you're sending to Venezuela, but I couldn't get a list."

"What else?"

"There is nothing else."

"That can't be all." A light flared in García's narrow black eyes.

"That's all I was given."

"Who is your source for this . . . information?"

"I regret that I can't divulge the name."

"You're lying," García said. "I can hear a lie. Yes. I can smell a lie."

"Can you? I don't have that ability. What does it smell like?"

The doors opened on the first floor, and Anthony stepped out of the elevator.

"Quintana."

He turned around.

García's mouth slid into a moist and tilted smile. His lips parted on one side to reveal small, discolored teeth. "This is not our last meeting."

The doors closed, and Anthony was looking back at his own reflection.

27

The police were still working at Olga Saavedra's apartment. From the backseat of Ramiro Vega's minivan, Gail could see two small white cars with blue lights on top. She caught a brief glimpse of a uniformed officer in the courtyard. And then the minivan continued down the street to where Anthony had left the rental car.

Sitting with Gail for nearly an hour at the Ministry, Ramiro had told someone to bring her some coffee, someone else to find food, a sandwich, *inmediatamente*. He had let her use his cell phone to assure her mother they'd be home soon. Aside from telling Ramiro what she had seen at the apartment, their own conversation had been filled with long silences. What could she have said? *I know about you and Olga. You loved her, and I'm so sorry.*

"*Ese carro ahí,*" Anthony said, and Cobo stopped alongside the blue Toyota.

Ramiro got out to slide back their door. Gail gave him a quick embrace. "Thank you for taking care of me."

When Anthony spoke to him, Gail understood most of it. They would talk at the house. What a horror this day had been. Ramiro got back in, and Cobo drove on.

Darkness had made the street narrower, emptier. The pavement was still wet from the rain. Gail recognized the colonnade and glass storefronts where earlier she had waited to go across. The dim streetlight on the corner outlined the gray arches and put shadows on the wall. She saw a man standing against one of the columns. Except for the light that touched one sleeve, she wouldn't have seen him at all.

"Gail, come on." Anthony was holding her door.

She felt vulnerable and exposed in the interior lights. They went off when Anthony closed his door. He started the engine and hit the wiper control to clear the windshield of mist. After another car went by, he made a U-turn. The headlights passed across the colonnade. The man who'd been standing there a few seconds before was gone.

It wasn't cold in the car, but Gail crossed her arms and rubbed them briskly. The muscles in her chest quivered, and her jaw was tight. "When will they let us go? I hope my law practice is still there when I get back to it." She laughed. "Why don't we just confess everything to the American Interests Section and beg them to help us?"

Anthony looked over at her. "If it's more than a couple of days, we can ask Ramiro to intervene. Don't worry."

"Don't worry. Well, at least my mother and the kids aren't stuck here. We aren't either, damn it. Why don't we just have a boat pick us up? I'm serious, Anthony. To hell with State Security."

"We're not going to do it that way," he said.

"God, no, they'd never let you come back here, would they?"

After a few seconds of silence he said, "If we left without permission, they would ask Ramiro why. I can't allow that. He needs to stay completely under the radar."

Leaning over, Gail put her forehead against Anthony's shoulder. "I know. Sorry for my bitchy mood. I can't think straight."

Without looking away from the street ahead of them, he picked up her hand and brought it to his lips. "*Todo va a salir bien*. It's going to be all right. I promise you."

"Poor Ramiro. Poor Olga. What a rotten, rotten thing to happen to her. He's not going to tell them about her, is he?"

"It's his *duty* to inform them, but—" Anthony shook his head. "I hope he's out of the country before they find out."

"Do they know yet who could have done it?"

"If so, they didn't share it with me."

"Why did Olga want to see you?" Gail asked.

A wedge of light fell across his eyes, and he glanced into the rearview mirror. "I believe she wanted me to get her out of Cuba. After Céspedes defected, she may have thought it was too dangerous to stay. She'd been sleeping with him, before Ramiro. Céspedes spilled secrets to the CIA, and she might have known about it. But if you want my guess as to who killed her . . . I don't have one."

Gail sat sideways in the seat. "Yes, you do. You just told me it's connected to Omar Céspedes."

"I'm not sure," Anthony said. "Her attacker could have shown her a badge to get in, but the Cuban government does not send agents into women's homes to beat them to death. It doesn't happen. It's messy."

"What would they do?" Gail asked. "I mean, assuming . . ."

"She would disappear. Or have an accident in her car. A drowning." Anthony checked the rearview again. "The problem with someone like Olga is, too many people knew her. There would be questions."

Gail shuddered, remembering the blood, the smashed bones in Olga Saavedra's face. "Maybe she had other lovers."

"If so, the police will find out," Anthony said. "With the CDR, eyes are everywhere. No, I wouldn't say it was a crime of passion. Except for the violence, it didn't fit the pattern. The killer was methodical and cold. He took the time to wipe the murder weapon clean of fingerprints. He mopped up footprints from the floor. He even took the cloth with him. No, most killers who do it in a jealous rage aren't so smart. They get rattled. They forget something. This guy knew what he was doing. He was careful."

Anthony's route took them up a hill past the Colón Cemetery with its long wall of peeling ochre paint. Even here, the streets were dark. There were no flashy signs, no floodlit billboards. Gail had noticed this the first time they'd driven through Havana at night—how the city surrendered to darkness. Even the modern streetlights on the Malecón seemed to be on a dimmer.

She said, "Tell me what happened at the Ministry."

Anthony checked the mirror, then slowed and turned right into a residential district. "Not much. I was questioned by Lieutenant General Efraín Prieto. Three stars. They want to handle it at the top because you and I are staying with Ramiro, and you walked into a murder scene. They want to be sure nothing more comes of it. Prieto went over the same ground Detective Sánchez had already covered. There was nothing I could tell him. He finally said okay, but don't leave town."

Gail waited for him to go on. "Anthony, that isn't *all*. You were up there for an hour and a half."

"Prieto was thorough. He wanted my life history. He even wanted to know about you. 'Is it true what they say about American women? Are they all as pretty as your wife?' "

"Right. I'm sure you guys had a grand time."

Anthony's eyes went back to the rearview mirror. "Abdel García was there too. We had a talk afterward. He asked if I'd found out what Céspedes was saying to the CIA, and I gave him the story I got from Bookhouser."

Gail remembered that Anthony was supposed to meet the agent this morning, but she hadn't spoken to him since then. "Well? What story?"

"That Cuban spies are going into Venezuela to help prevent a recall election, so that Cuba can keep getting cheap oil. Céspedes is also telling the Americans that Fidel wants to finish the nuclear reactor at Juraguá, which the Americans think is bullshit. García asked me if there was anything else, and I said no."

Gail let her head fall back on the headrest. "Great. For once the Cubans and the CIA are on the same side. They will both want to kill you if you screw up."

"No one is going to kill me. Label me as a spy? Maybe. Have me banished from my grandfather's house? Destroy my career? That's more likely. You might have to support me."

"You don't have to see him again, do you? García, I mean. You said you had to meet him tonight."

"No. I won't see him again."

"Thank God. The man gives me a major case of the creeps." Gail twisted her mouth sideways and made her hands into claws. In an exaggerated accent she said, "Good eeeee-evening. *Saludos a la familiaaaaa—*"

Anthony's grim expression gave way to a smile, then a laugh.

They were traveling on Twelfth Street. Gail saw the sign on a low concrete marker on the corner. They were in Vedado. She was beginning to know her way around. To get to Miramar, Anthony would go north, then turn left on Calzada.

She said, "Anthony? I have to tell you something. This afternoon, Karen and Mother and I hitched a ride downtown. The driver let me off at Olga's apartment."

He was watching something in the mirror. "You hitchhiked? I was wondering if Marta took you."

"No, she was busy. Anyway, the driver let me off, and I was a little early—"

"Hang on." Anthony slammed on the brakes and turned the wheel left just in front of an oncoming car. Gail's body was pressed against the door, and she heard the screech of tires and a high-pitched horn. "Anthony!"

He accelerated. The headlights made a tunnel of light in the trees. At the next corner, he swung left again. The tires skidded into a pothole, and Gail's breath jolted out of her lungs. She looked back and saw headlights sweeping around the trees behind them. Anthony took a quick right, then another, and came out on a larger street, where he joined the flow of traffic heading west.

"My God!"

He looked over at her. "Are you all right?"

"I am having a heart attack! Someone was following us? Who?"

"I don't know. It's probably nothing."

"Nothing? You were driving like a madman. Was it the police?"

"Well, if it was, they know where we're staying. They can sit outside Ramiro's house and wait for us."

Gail closed her eyes and pressed her forehead into her hands. "You make me want to scream."

They went into the tunnel under the river, and someone ahead tooted to hear the echo. The road descended, then quickly came up again.

"Are they still behind us?"

Anthony looked in the rearview. "There's no one there. I'm sorry to have frightened you. It was nothing."

Gail stared across at him. "You thought it was Abdel García. Didn't you?"

"No. Why would I think that?"

"He killed her because she knew about him and Omar Céspedes. That's what's going through your mind. Isn't it?"

Anthony watched the road. Streetlights shifted the shadows inside the car. His face went in and out of darkness. "Abdel García wants me alive. In exchange for a house on the beach and my choice of women, I'm going to report on exile activities in Miami."

"That makes me feel so much better." Gail huddled into the

seat as the road split into a wide boulevard divided by grass and flower beds. The trees were clipped into cylindrical shapes. "What's going on, Anthony? When Sánchez was questioning me, I didn't know what to tell him. I had to play so dumb he must have thought I was retarded."

Anthony smiled and rested a hand on her knee. "I would trust you with my life, sweetheart, but I don't want to put you in the position of having to lie. You don't do it very well."

"Is that supposed to be a compliment?"

"What I want you to do, if you don't mind, is to let me take care of this. All right? It's not your problem. In a few more days, we'll be on our way home."

She stared through the windshield.

"Gail. Don't be that way." He lifted his hands and let out a breath through his teeth, then took the turn into the Vegas' neighborhood.

She looked over at him. "No, I was just remembering what I meant to tell you, before you started sliding around corners back there. Detective Sánchez doesn't know about this. Just before I went across the street to knock on Olga's door, I saw Mario Cabrera going into her building."

"Mario?"

"Yes. He went through the side entrance. But he came out again a minute later—less than a minute. I think he knocked on the door, and when she didn't open it, he left. That's what I assume because I almost did the same thing."

"Coño. What the hell was he doing there? Did you talk to him?"

"He didn't see me. I followed him to the next street. I was curious. He got into his car and drove off, and I walked back to Olga's. What's odd about it is that he parked so far away . . . but he couldn't have killed her. It's not possible. If I had told Sánchez, they would have jumped to all sorts of conclusions. It was Olga Saavedra who remained free while José Leiva spent four years in prison."

Anthony stopped the car in front of the gate. "You may not be the only one who saw him. I need to find Mario."

The headlights shone on the chain-link fencing and picked up the reflectors on the back of the minivan in the driveway. Through the long windows across the front, Gail could see her mother walking across the living room.

She wanted to tell Anthony the rest of it, but she was afraid that if she gave voice to her thoughts, they might become real. And Cobo was already walking toward them across the yard, and it was too late.

Anthony, there's another reason I didn't tell them about Mario. Because . . . he might be your son.

When the men vanished into the study to talk, locking the door behind them, Gail went upstairs. She wanted a hot soak in the tub and some clean clothes, preferably flannel. She got as far as taking off her shoes. Sitting on the edge of the bed, she pivoted around and threw both pillows against the headboard.

In something of a fog, she stared at the peeling veneer on the built-in armoire and counted the cartoon characters over the baby crib. She heard the thud of hip-hop coming from Gio's room. Gio was out with friends, but Danny was in there playing CDs. God knew what else. Drinking. Blowing Marlboro smoke out the window. Lying low.

Karen sat cross-legged on the other side of the bed keeping Gail company. Her thumb moved over the controls on the back of Irene's digital camera, deleting photos she judged too boring to be worth saving.

"Mom, do you think Mr. Vega would let me have a blank CD? I didn't bring any with me. He has extras. I saw them."

"You could ask him. What do you want it for?"

"For photographs. Gramma is filling up her memory sticks. If I burn them to a CD, she'll have more room. I brought my PC interface, and I'm pretty sure it will work with his computer. Check these out. We took these today." Karen turned the screen so Gail could see it. "That's where we bought the Internet cards. There was this lady behind the desk who was really nice. You should've seen her panty hose. They looked like black spider webs. All the women in Cuba wear them. Gramma spent a hundred and fifty dollars! Yolanda was all like, no, no, please, but Gramma said, well, Yolanda, *darling,* allow me to be selfish. If you can't get on the *Internet,* how can you stay in *touch* with us?"

Gail reached over to hug her. "I love you."

Karen scrolled through, and Gail saw various doors, buildings. A park. A huge *santera* in a flouncy white dress and bangles on her earlobes, reading Irene's fortune. Street performers in bright costumes, walking on stilts. Then a shot of Yolanda Cabrera and Karen arm in arm, squinting in the sunlight. Yolanda's hair gleamed. She was beautiful. Saint Yolanda.

Gail said, "They're all good. You pick, Karen. It doesn't matter to me."

If Karen hadn't been there, Gail might have rolled over and wept into the pillows. She had to make a decision, and whatever it was, it would hurt. Should she bring it up or not? Maybe Yolanda had never told him. But it was so obvious! Was he blind? Anthony had said she wasn't a good liar. He should know, Gail thought bitterly to herself. He's an expert. She had come to Cuba to find out who he was, and she knew less now than before.

On the nightstand was the book Anthony had been reading in bed. The essays by José Leiva. Gail leaned over and picked it up. *Memorias y esperanzas*. José Benito Leiva. Memories and hopes. She flipped through. Published in Spain, 2001. A scrap of paper marked a page. "Crónicas de una isla semi-hundida." Anthony had told her it meant "chronicles from a half-drowned island." He had said don't expect to find these essays in any bookshop in Cuba. A friend had brought Leiva some copies in his suitcase. A box sent by the publisher had been confiscated by customs.

Dangerous contraband. A bomb made of paper and ink.

Gail wished she knew enough Spanish to understand it.

When she heard Marta Quintana's voice at the door, Gail returned the book to the nightstand, facedown.

"Hello! I brought you a little surprise." Carrying a tray, Marta pushed open the door with one foot. "Irene says you like warm chocolate milk. I have some toast, too, with grape jelly."

"That's so nice of you, but you didn't have to bother, really."

"Shush, shush, it's not a bother to me." Marta set the tray on the end of the bed. "Irene is making dinner. Noodles and tuna and cream sauce! A new dish for us, for sure!" She laughed and pushed her streaked bronze hair off her forehead. "Dinner will be ready soon. You want to eat up here or come downstairs with us?"

"Marta, I'm *fine*. Ramiro had someone bring me a sandwich at the Ministry. Thank you, though."

"Well." She picked up Gail's bath towel and smoothed it, then folded it neatly.

Karen looked up. "Mrs. Vega? Are you going to cancel the *quinceañera*?"

"No, honey, I wouldn't do that! Janelle would be so disappointed! Everything is almost ready. Your grandmother says she will help me. I love Irene. Oh, Gail if my own mother were still alive! I miss her so much, you know. She left us, but I always loved her."

Marta's face reddened, then crumpled. She wiped away tears and laughed at herself. "Oh, I'm sorry. There is so much to do! Everyone is coming to the party. We are going to have a beautiful party!"

Karen glanced at Gail, then went back to staring down at the display on the camera.

"It's too bad about Olga Saavedra, eh? I wish it had happened next week. *Ay, Dios, discúlpame,* I don't mean to say that. Gail, what did the police tell you? I talked to Anthony, but he says they don't know anything."

"They don't. I can't add to what Anthony told you."

"I am very sorry, but a woman like that, she probably had friends in the black market. Thieves and profiteers. Even drug addicts. Don't listen to me, Karen. You shouldn't be hearing this talk."

"That's okay."

"No, honey, we don't have murder here like other places. I don't know what to say. It doesn't happen."

"Two murders." Karen looked up. "They found a boy at Lenin Park today. We were there."

"Yes, that's right. Angela told me. A young man. It wasn't on the news. They don't put things like that on the news." Marta went around and took Karen's hand. "So now you know that Cuba isn't perfect, eh? We have murders here too—but not many. No. We don't have crime like most other countries. I think that we respect life more. Most of us do. Not everyone. There are criminals in Cuba, like any place on the earth. There are people who do drugs, who are a drain on society, and they don't care. They are useless. But that isn't normal. Don't think bad about us. We are not rich, but we try to give equally to everyone, even in our hard times. We live simply, but we have enough. We take care of each other. I try to tell that to my children. You know what I mean, don't you, sweetheart?"

Karen nodded.

Marta kissed her. "I am so happy that you and your mother and Irene came to see us. My brother made a good choice this time. Oh, Gail, the trouble we go through to bring you here. Did Anthony tell you? Every time he comes, we have to get permission. Maybe you didn't know this. It's because Ramiro is in *las Fuerzas Armadas*. Some people tell me, no, don't let them stay with you because it would be bad for your husband's career, but I don't care. He is not a little low-rank sergeant! He is respected. I tell them, if my husband wants to have my brother and his family here with us, it is Ramiro's decision, so go to hell."

Marta smiled. "Gail, I tell you the truth before God. Ramiro is a good husband and father, a good man, and he and the children are my life. I'm sorry that Ernesto hates us. He doesn't know us. If he came here, he would see. I wish it could be changed. When you go back there, tell them to tear down the walls. You speak to them, eh? You are a woman with a voice, and you must tell them the truth."

Marta enveloped Gail in a hug, gave her a kiss on the cheek, leaned over to do the same to Karen. Her knee pressed into the mattress, and the tray tilted, sending the milk close to the rim. "My beautiful sisters. *Las quiero mucho, mucho, mucho*." Wiping her eyes, Marta went out.

Karen looked around at Gail. "Is she okay?"

"She's under a lot of stress right now," Gail said.

"I've noticed that. This family is very strange. Janelle cries a lot too. And so does that man who works for them. He cries every night in his room. I'm not, like, going up there to listen or anything, but you can hear him if you walk in the backyard late at night. Is everyone like that in Cuba?"

"No. Not everyone." Gail looked up at the ceiling. The horrible fluorescent fixture was buzzing again. "Listen, sweetie, I'm going to take a soak in the tub. Do you know how to turn on the heater?"

"Sure." Karen scooted off the bed.

Gail wished Irene would come see her. She wanted to talk to her, but what would she say? Whatever Gail said, the answer would be the same: *Darling, of course you must tell him. Secrets between husband and wife will destroy the best marriage. . . .*

Yes, Mother, but it isn't my goddamn secret, it's *his and Yolanda's!*

She was up to her neck in water, which had gone tepid, when a soft knock came on the bathroom door. Anthony put his head in.

"Marta wants to know if you're coming downstairs for dinner."

"I suppose I should." She whispered, "How's Ramiro?"

Anthony shut the door and sat on the edge of the bathtub. "All right. He's getting drunk."

"Is he going to tell her?"

"He says he will. I don't know."

Sitting up, she gave Anthony the washcloth and soap. "Do my back."

He swirled the washcloth in the water and squeezed it out. The muscles moved in his forearm, and the dark hair lay flat on his skin. "I have some things to do tomorrow," he said.

"Really. Who are you meeting? The spook?"

"That's a little later. I want to check out a couple of things with José. And if they know how to get in touch with Mario, I want to talk to him."

"Angela says she and Mario are going over there tomorrow night for the meeting."

"What meeting?"

"The librarians and journalists?"

"Ah, yes. Good. I'll see him then."

Gail leaned her head against his thigh. "Am I invited?"

"Of course."

She said, "You're wrong to keep me in the dark. I've been thinking about that."

"Let's not argue about it tonight."

"It's not an argument. This is important, Anthony. There are things that we both need to talk about, and if you won't be honest with me, how can I have confidence that what I say to you will be listened to—"

"We'll talk tomorrow."

"Will be listened to with the same degree of attention. Oh, we'll talk tomorrow. Fine. You said that yesterday."

"I promise. *Te quiero, bonboncita.*"

"I wish you wouldn't call me that. It's so . . . cute."

"*Abusadora. Bruja.*" Abuser. Witch. The washcloth went slowly up her leg. "*Malcriada.*" Spoiled brat. Anthony lifted her hair and put more words in her ear that made her skin burn.

She laughed. "Now? Are you serious?"

He reached over and pulled the chain for the plug. "Hurry up. Where's your towel?"

In the bedroom, he put the fan by the door and turned it on high so no one could hear them.

28

Standing at the window with the baby in her arms, Jennifer gazed down at the brick alley behind her townhouse. It was just past midnight. Frost twinkled on the tops of the cars. Snow lay along the wood fences in the narrow backyards. By morning the temperature would be in the teens again. A week of this! A record for D.C.

The alley was dimly illuminated by a single streetlamp fifty yards farther on, where another alley bisected the block. Jennifer wanted to see a gold Saturn turn the corner. Her husband had gone to a dinner at the Grand Hyatt. Health insurance providers, she thought. Jeff was a lobbyist, and there were so many parties this time of year.

She rocked the baby side to side, feeling his warmth and the pleasant pull of his weight on her arm. Sometimes for no reason other than this she would come into his room at night and pick him up.

There would be no place for Jeff to park except right behind her Range Rover. The neighbors were always arguing about parking spaces. With so many SUVs, there was less room. Whoever got home late would have to park alongside the back wall of the minimart, which left hardly any space for a turnaround. Jeff had gone ballistic when he'd seen the scrape on the side of his Saturn. He had found gold paint on the bumper of the Ford Explorer that belonged to the new neighbor.

The man lived in one of the town houses on Twelfth Street Southeast, perpendicular to C. He had appeared a couple of weeks ago, but nobody had seen a moving van in the alley. He was gone most of the day, then would come home, park his Explorer, unlock

the gate on the wood fence, go inside his town house, and never answer his door. Jeff had gone around to Twelfth to leave a note, but
there had been no reply.

The housekeeper had explained it: The man didn't speak English
at all. Maria had come across him one day as she was taking out
some trash. When Jeff complained that he hadn't gotten an answer
to his note, Maria told him that he should have written it in Spanish. *Why the fuck should I have to write it in Spanish? Why can't
Manuel fucking speak English, if he's going to live here?*

Manuel. Not his name, but Jeff called him that, and they had
begun referring to him in that way. *Looks like Manuel came home
ripped again last night. He knocked over the Kovaks' trash can.*

The baby squirmed and sighed, and Jennifer shifted him higher
on her chest. Maria would stay if Jen had to work late, which happened frequently. She was a fourth-year at Kanner Wainwright, a
boutique firm specializing in international tax law. She earned a
blow-out salary, but 150K a year didn't go that far, even with Jeff's
hundred added to it.

The house was bleeding them dry. It was a 1905 town house on
C Street. She and Jeff had paid $525,000, offering fifty thousand
more than the list price, because the market was going crazy. Last
year they had squeezed out the equity for a new roof and windows. They still didn't have a dining room table and chairs, but it
didn't matter, because there was no time to entertain. The Capitol
Hill area used to be fairly sketchy, but renovators were coming in.
People could ride bicycles through the neighborhood and walk
their dogs without feeling like they'd get mugged. A Starbucks had
opened on the next block.

She and Jeff planned to work in Washington for three more
years, then find jobs in northern Virginia. The pay wasn't as good,
but by then their law school loans would be paid off. They would
have four bedrooms and a two-car garage. Jackson would be starting kindergarten. That was the dream.

Jen kissed his warm, soft hair and walked a little closer to the
window to lay her hand against the glass to check the temperature.
It was double-paned. Even so, the electric bills were insane this
month, with the endless cold.

She saw the glow of headlights coming from the left, picking up
the crevices between the bricks, shining on the dead clematis vine

on the utility pole. She thought at first it might be Jeff's car, but the lights were too high. A dark green Ford Explorer came into the alley and swung right. Colors leaped from the darkness: a yellow VW, a small red pickup truck.

The double-paned glass made the big engine sound far away. A front tire fell into the hole where the bricks were missing and cracked the ice. His favorite place behind his town house was already taken. The Explorer sat there unmoving for a few seconds, then the white backup lights went on. After a couple of tries, he got his SUV against the wall. Looking down, Jennifer saw the light go on. The door opened.

He was short, and he had to slide off the seat, an awkward figure in a down jacket. He slammed the door and pressed his keychain to lock it. His breath was a cloud of white. He pulled his cap down on his head and wrapped his muffler around his neck as he hurried across the alley.

Someone came out from behind the pickup truck.

It happened so fast that later, when she talked to the police, Jennifer would not be able to say what the man looked like or what he was wearing, not his height or weight, or the color of his face.

The man stepped out from behind the truck and walked quickly across the alley. Three, four steps. His shadow moved ahead of him on the brick pavement. His arm lifted.

Two flashes of light. Manuel held up his hands, stepped backward, and stumbled over the bricks. He crawled on his knees. The other man followed. More flashes of light. Manuel reached for the back of his neck as though to pull out a thorn. He dropped and lay still. The man stood directly over him. A light reflected on his face for a split second. He crouched down and felt under Manuel's coat as though he was looking for something.

Then he walked away.

Jennifer couldn't remember which way he'd gone. She didn't know how many gunshots. She hadn't even known she was screaming until she felt the baby struggling and thrashing in her arms.

29

The light came through the wooden louvers in stripes. Gail had been watching their slow progress across the bed when Anthony's cell phone rang. She nudged him. His hand came from under the pillow, found the phone, and pressed it to his ear. He listened for a minute, then murmured in Spanish. She heard the soft beep of a disconnect button.

"Who was that?"

"Hector. He's in Havana."

Gail laughed softly. "What?"

"He just arrived at the airport."

"Under what phony name and false passport did he manage that?"

Anthony sat on the edge of the bed and raked his hair off his forehead. The light curved across his back. "He says he needs to see me. Something's come up."

"What is it?"

"I don't know. He didn't want to talk about it on the phone." Anthony reached for his robe.

"What's he doing in Havana?"

"I asked him to come."

"Why?"

Tying the belt, Anthony said, "He might be needed."

"When are you going to tell me what's going on?"

By now Gail was out of bed. Anthony looked across the room at her. "Let's have brunch at the Nacional. I'm dying for a cheese omelet."

When Gail came into the kitchen, her mother was putting on her sun hat and refilling her water bottle. She and Marta were going shopping together.

Anthony poured espresso into mugs and used an old towel to take the pan of hot milk off the stove. Angela moved around him to turn off the gas broiler and take out the toast. She said they would all be leaving for Varadero Beach after breakfast, just to see it, because it was too cold to swim, unless you were Norwegian or something.

"Gail, Karen can come with us, can't she?"

"Sure, that's fine."

Rinsing out the *cafetera* in the sink, then tossing it into the drainer to dry, Marta said she was sorry about what had happened to Olga Saavedra, but the food and drink still had to be purchased, the tablecloths and napkins picked out, and somehow she had to track down the agency that had arranged for the band. And the house needed a thorough cleaning. The housekeeper was useless, so the kids would have to spend the last day of their vacation from school helping out, like it or not.

"*¿Me entienden?* You understand me?"

Five sets of eyes looked at her from the kitchen table. Giovany and Janelle said in unison, *"Está bien, mami."* Marta pointed at their American cousins. "Hey! You are in this family too." They quickly nodded. So did Karen.

Marta put both hands on her heart, then blew kisses across the room. "I love you!" She grabbed her purse and held open the door for Irene. It closed behind them.

Gail and Anthony took their coffee to the patio.

The air was still slightly chilly in the shade of the trees, so they pulled the old metal chairs into the sun. Shafts of light wavered as the breeze moved the branches. On the patio, puddles of rainwater darkened the mossy tiles. Anthony stood silently staring out at the backyard for so long that Gail tugged on the sleeve of his shirt and asked him what was wrong.

He quickly smiled at her and sat down with his coffee. "Nothing. It's beautiful this morning, no?"

"You're afraid this is the last time," she said.

"No. We'll be back. I am sure of it. My father is here."

Gail whispered, "Can't you talk to Luis about coming to Miami?"

"I have. He refuses."

"But if he knew that Marta was leaving. He could live with us. Okay, a condo isn't what he's used to, but we could find a house with a cottage in the back."

Smiling, Anthony reached over to squeeze her hand. *"Te quiero."* He looked around when his daughter came out of the house. He held out his arm, and Angela leaned against him.

"Papi, could I ask you a favor? I'd like it if Mario could come over tomorrow night. Not for dinner. He would just come by to say hello."

Gail said, "Oh, Angela, I'm so sorry. You wanted me to mention it to your father, and I completely forgot."

"That's okay. You had a lot on your mind after . . . you know, finding that woman. I would've been catatonic all night. So, Dad. What do you think about Mario coming over?"

Anthony set his *café con leche* on the side table. "It's up to your Aunt Marta, don't you think?"

"I know it is, but she'll probably say no unless you ask her. You're such good friends with Mario's parents. They're critics of the regime, but why must that fact be held against Mario? It isn't right that if Mario wants to see me, or you, we have to go somewhere else to talk to him. He's polite and educated. He won't start any arguments. He avoids political discussions completely. Aunt Marta and Ramiro don't *know* him. If people would just put aside their prejudgments, the world wouldn't be in the state it's in."

"He has an excellent advocate." Anthony smiled and took her hand. "I'll talk to Marta tonight."

"Well . . . he needs an answer this morning. He's trying to arrange his schedule. Band rehearsal and so forth."

"All right. Tell Mario to come over. I'll deal with your aunt."

"Thanks, Dad." She kissed his cheek and turned to run back into the house.

"Angela! How are you going to get in touch with him?"

"A lady in his building lets him use her phone. She takes messages."

"Before you leave, sweetheart, would you write the number for me?"

When Angela had gone, Anthony picked up his coffee. He said to Gail, "Even his mother doesn't have that number."

"Will you ask him about Olga Saavedra?"

"If I can find him, I will." Anthony closed his eyes and tipped his head back. The sun put gold lights on his skin and mahogany in his hair. "Mario should leave here. I'm going to ask him about it. Help me twist his arm, will you? I spoke to Yolanda yesterday on the subject."

"Oh? You didn't say you'd seen her."

"I had lunch with my father, and she was there. I said, 'Yoli, if you love your son, let him come to Miami.' She knows it's for the best. I believe that in the back of her mind, she wants to leave here, too. It's crazy to risk arrest and imprisonment when they could do their work from Miami. Yolanda wouldn't leave without her husband, of course, but she's saying to herself, 'Oh, to be away from here. If I could just persuade José to leave. If I could do that.' "

Anthony's eyes came open. He squinted, and the sun cut across his lashes. His lips slowly parted in a smile. "I am his devil. José organized a union of independent journalists, and I would tempt him with the easy life in Miami. Wouldn't it be funny, if José and Ramiro ran into each other in Little Havana? Ramiro would be waiting tables at Versailles Restaurant, and he looks down, and there is José Leiva, ordering a big plate of *puerco asado*. José says, '*Oye, compañero*, so how is life in America treating you?' "

Gail smiled. "And where would Yolanda be?"

Anthony thought about it. "Getting her hair styled at a salon in Coral Gables. Yes. She wants to look nice because Mario has a concert on South Beach with his band."

Seen from the limestone bluff behind the Hotel Nacional, the Malecón was a long curve of concrete laid across the spoil rocks in the shallows. Waves broke on the rocks and exploded into froth. In the distance, sea mist diffused the pastels of Old Havana's crumbling colonnades.

Gail wore sunglasses, though the sun was more hazy than bright. After having a late breakfast on the veranda, where no conversation could go past the trivial, she and Anthony had found a bench in the back gardens. The wind snapped the Cuban flag, which flew over an antique cannon pointed at the sea.

She shivered, but it was more than the wind sending a chill through her body.

Anthony had posed a question. What if the Cubans had uranium at Juraguá?

"Someone's going to assume that Castro would use it. He's sliding toward eighty years old. He can't save his Revolution, but why not strike a final blow against the enemy? The U.S. would invade, without a doubt. Would the President ignore a potential terrorist threat on our doorstep? At last we have an excuse to take out the *hijo de puta* who has been making us look like idiots for forty-four years."

"Insanity," Gail said.

Anthony's brows rose over his sunglasses. "There are people who would believe it."

"Of course there are. Your grandfather. And Bill Navarro. And half the population of Miami. They would dance in the streets for a month if we invaded."

"It won't happen without proof. That's why they need Ramiro Vega."

Gail said, "How would he know? Ramiro never worked on the nuclear project."

"He worked with Céspedes. He's at the Ministry of Basic Industries. Gail, I don't have the answers. Céspedes could be telling Navarro what he wants to hear in exchange for money, for prestige. There have been defectors who have told falsehoods, and we believed them. It could be that Céspedes is a double agent. Castro wants to draw us into another embarrassment. He's good at that. It keeps him in power. We demand that he turn over his nuclear material, and this provokes a confrontation. Once again, he stands up to the mighty Americans."

"I'm getting ill, thinking of it," Gail said.

"It's only a theory." Anthony put his elbows on his knees. He seemed to be watching the endless horizon, blue and calm. "Maybe in a few months, Ramiro and Marta will fly to Spain with the kids for a vacation. They don't come back. He tells the CIA that Céspedes is a liar, and everyone is happy."

And you can keep returning to Cuba, Gail added silently.

She leaned forward and put her arm against his. The dark green fabric of his sleeve was warm from the sun. "What does Ramiro have to say about your theory?"

"Nothing. He's being very sly. He doesn't trust me. I'm working for the CIA. How does he know I'm not trying to set him up? If he told me too much, they wouldn't need him, would they?" From Anthony's pocket came a muffled ringing, and he shifted to get to it. "Ramiro is right. He shouldn't trust anyone. He should wait until he's safely on the Costa del Sol with money in the bank." He put the phone to his ear. *"Hola, dígame."*

He listened, then said they would be there in five minutes.

"That was Mario, returning my call."

They picked up the car from the valet, drove out the long, palm tree–lined entrance of the Nacional, then took a left and parked at a run-down snack bar outside the Servi-Cupet gas station. The yellow-and-red striped awning shaded the tables underneath. Gail saw a phone booth and assumed that Mario Cabrera had used it for his call.

He stood up as they approached. There were handshakes. Anthony went over to the window to buy some sodas, and they moved nearer the street, where the noise of traffic would muffle their conversation. The sodas remained unopened, pushed to one side.

Mario wore jeans and a black knit shirt that stretched across his broad shoulders and clung to his lean torso. He sat directly across from Anthony at the square table. Though she tried to avoid it, Gail found herself comparing their faces. Mario's eyebrows curved; Anthony's were thick and straight. Mario's eyes were lighter, with flecks of green. His ears were smaller, the lobes different. His earring was the shape of a crescent moon. When he clasped his hands on the table, Gail noticed the long fingers and square palms. She counted four silver rings and a heavy link bracelet. She saw two chains around his neck. They were cheap gold, but gold nonetheless. Anthony liked jewelry. Gail thought of the leather jewelry box in his bureau, Anthony taking off his rings and bracelet the night before they left for Cuba.

When Mario spoke, she studied his mouth. Full and symmetrical, the upper lip making two defined points. Lines that curved at the corners when he smiled. The lines around Anthony's mouth were deeper, but he was older by twenty-four years.

Mario spoke English to include the American at the table. He
thought that Anthony had come to warn him to keep his hands off
his daughter. "Señor, I am a friend of Angela. I have much respect
for her and for your family—"

"I am glad to hear it," Anthony said, "but that's not why I
wanted to talk to you. *No es eso, Mario.*" He went on to say it
had to do with Olga Saavedra. He asked Mario if he had heard the
news. "*¿Supiste que está muerta? Un homicidio.*"

"Yes. Yes, I know it. I am sorry for her."

"My wife went to see Miss Saavedra yesterday on some business. She found her body."

"That is true?" Mario glanced over at Gail, surprise on his face.
Anthony explained that shortly before two o'clock, Gail had been
waiting to cross the street. She had seen Mario go into the building
and come out again. She had said nothing to the police because she
was sure Mario had only knocked at the door. That was the case,
was it not?

Mario stared at him, then said yes. Speaking quickly, he raised
his hand as if to knock on a door.

Anthony asked him why he'd gone to see her.

He didn't answer for several seconds. Then he shrugged. "She
make the party for Janelle. They have . . . *un conjunto.* A band.
Me too. Mercurio. That's my band. So . . . maybe . . . Olga Saavedra wants Mercurio for the parties. I say, okay, talk to her."

"You thought Olga Saavedra might hire your band to play for
other parties."

"Maybe. Yes." He smiled. "Is a very good band."

Anthony nodded. "Another question. *¿Por qué dejaste el carro
tan lejos, en la otra calle?*" Why had he left his car so far away on
another street?

Mario answered, finishing his reply with another shrug.

"He wasn't sure where Olga lived." Anthony's glance at Gail
said he wanted her opinion on whether this made sense, but it
wasn't her language, and the subtleties were lost. She gave her
head a little shake.

Anthony spoke slowly, and his next question was clear: Did Mario
have any other reason for going to Olga Saavedra's apartment?

"No." Mario's brows rose, and he shook his head, looking at
Anthony, then at Gail. "No. To ask her for the band. *¿Qué otra*

razón?" What other reason could there be? And he was sorry she died. "Very terrible thing, no? Maybe *un ladrón*. A thief? The police find him?"

"Not yet," Anthony said. He leaned on his elbows. "Mario. *Escúchame bien, m'ijo."*

Listen, my son. But this meant nothing, Gail thought. Men used the word all the time with boys they didn't even know.

Anthony explained to Mario that in the United States, he was a lawyer. Mario knew this, didn't he? In the United States, Anthony advised people who were in trouble with the law, and sometimes not in trouble, but the police suspected them for the wrong reasons.

Nodding, Mario said to Gail, "I know. In Cuba, the police . . ." He quickly touched his eyes. He meant they were everywhere, always looking.

Anthony continued. If Gail had told the police Mario had been there, they might have asked questions. Mario's father and Olga Saavedra had sold videos to foreign reporters, but only José went to prison. Olga saved herself by turning against José. Anthony hoped that Mario didn't know about that. If the police ever asked him about it, well, of course it would not be good to lie to them, but in this case, he wanted to protect his father. Didn't he?

Mario nodded. He would do anything for José. He would die for him.

Anthony smiled. *"No es necesario.* No, Mario, you must live a long time. Do you understand when I speak English slowly? I want Gail to hear this too."

"Yes. I understand."

"It's all right," Gail said. "Please say it in Spanish. I can understand most of it."

Anthony said that there was something else he wanted to discuss with Mario, and since they wouldn't be in Cuba much longer, he would bring it up now. Anthony explained how close he had always been to the family, how he respected and admired Yolanda and José. He was sure they would want their son to have a future. Had Mario ever thought of coming to the United States? Anthony listed the benefits—work, education, a career. Anthony said he would help him. He said that Mario should think of him as his *padrino*, his godfather, his friend, a part of his family. Someday Mario could come back to a free Cuba, and he would have the tools to help rebuild his country. If he stayed here, what would he have? How could he hope to support a wife and children?

Mario lowered his eyes. He had thick black lashes. Several seconds passed. He said he would think about it. Yes, he certainly would. It was very generous.

Anthony said they would see each other tonight at his parents' house, at the meeting of independent journalists and librarians. Mario nodded and said that Angela wanted to meet him there, but he couldn't stay very long, as he had things to do. A rehearsal with the band. They hoped to find work soon.

Mario stood when Anthony did, and the two men embraced quickly. Mario put a soft kiss on Gail's cheek. His smile dazzled. "I see you later."

He walked over to his tiny green car and got in. The engine coughed into life, and Mario drove up the hill and around the corner.

Anthony checked his watch. "Let's take a walk. Hector's on his way."

They took the sidewalk that Gail had seen earlier from the hotel. It went under the same limestone bluff where the flag blew in the wind.

"You're very quiet," Anthony said.

"I'm fine."

"Good."

Gail said, "Mario didn't seem enthusiastic about living in Miami."

"Well, it's a big decision for him."

"You'll have them all in Miami, won't you? One way or the other, you'll do it."

He looked at her as they walked. "Do I sense an objection?"

"Maybe they think of Cuba as home, miserable as it is. Maybe they don't want to leave, and you're interfering."

"If they don't want to leave, they don't have to. I'm not putting a gun to their heads."

Gail laughed. "Oh, sweetie. You severely underestimate your ability to persuade."

"What are you trying to say, Gail?"

She turned to him, and they stopped in the middle of the sidewalk. "I want you to think about something. Maybe you don't have the answer now. Or maybe you do, but you have to think what to say to me."

"Do I hear an argument coming on?" He put a hand to his ear.

"It's an observation, all right? I believe you're in love with them. All of them. With José for his courage, his ideals that you think you've lost. In love with Mario for being young and innocent. You're in love with Yolanda most of all because she's what you left behind."

"Oh, Jesus." He looked up at the sky, then back at Gail. "Where do you get these ideas?"

"I listen to what you say. I watch you."

"Is that so? Did you notice someone making love to you last night? Who was that?"

"I have to ask you something. I don't want to, but I will. Did you ever make love to Yolanda?"

"Ah. So that's the problem. You're jealous. I should have known."

"Did you? When you and she were young, and you first came back to Cuba—"

"No. Never. It is beyond belief that you would ask me such a thing. Yolanda is . . . she's like a sister."

"A sister? You don't buy sterling silver hair clips at Tiffany's for a sister! How much did you pay for it?"

"I don't remember."

"Don't lie to me! How much?"

"It was nothing. Two hundred something."

"What, two hundred ninety-nine?"

His anger erupted, and he shouted, "It's a goddamned hair clip, not a fucking ring. Why don't you add up what I've spent on *you*?"

A woman in tight capri pants and a sleeveless top approached around a curve in the sidewalk. Not a tourist, a middle-aged Cuban woman who had to be wondering why these people were screaming at each other. She glanced at them apprehensively.

Hands on his hips, Anthony let out a breath and stared across the road at the Malecón. When the woman was gone, he looked back at Gail. "I'm sorry for yelling at you. The answer is no, I did not sleep with Yolanda. Now let's drop it."

"And I'm sorry I brought it up."

He put his arms around her neck and looked into her eyes. "Sweetheart. I love you. Only you. Don't you believe that? Gail?"

"Yes. I know you love me."

"How can you doubt it? *Te quiero,* Señora Quintana. Well?"

"Te quiero," she said, and kissed him.

He laughed. "I'm in love with José Leiva too. I'm glad he wasn't around to hear that. Come on."

Taking her hand, he pulled her toward the street. They waited a moment for traffic to clear, then hurried across three lanes to a monument in the center of the road. Two bronze cannons pointed east and west, and two Greek columns rose to support a narrow platform with nothing on it. Ahead of them, across the westbound side of the road, the wind whipped the spray over the Malecón. Gail could taste the salt on her lips. They walked around to the other side of the monument and sat on one of the steps facing the ocean.

Anthony put his arm around her. "I'm crazy about you."

She smiled. "And I'm just crazy. Please forget what I said."

"I have already forgotten."

Within a few minutes a small, gray-haired *mulato* came into view. He carried a plastic sack with some large green fruits in it. He called out, *"Mamey. Señora, mamey rico, dos por un dólar."* Mamey, two for a dollar.

Gail had to laugh. "Hello, Hector."

Hector Mesa stood a few steps down from them, a slight figure in dusty trousers and a faded plaid shirt. He had even traded his black-framed glasses for a pair with clear plastic frames, convincingly scratched.

"Señora." He made a little bow in Gail's direction.

"You look like a farmer," Anthony said.

"I am Eusebio Pérez from Pinar del Rio, visiting my relatives in the city."

"I hope you have your identification card."

Hector acknowledged that he did.

Anthony said, "You know they'll arrest you, selling mamey on the street to tourists."

"You are not tourists," Hector said. *"Señor Anthony, necesito hablar con usted."* He nodded again at Gail. "You will excuse us, señora?"

"It's all right, Hector. I've told her everything so far."

The little man made a regretful grimace.

Anthony sighed and patted Gail's knee as he got up. "I'll be back."

They walked out of earshot, and Gail watched traffic, a sparse procession of old American cars and rusted-out Eastern European models, a double-humped bus crammed with riders, a shiny Mercedes tourist bus with tinted windows. The waves broke on the Malecón. She could see the spray as it rose and fell behind the concrete barrier.

The men finished their conversation. Hector glanced her way, bowed slightly, and ambled off with his sack of mameys.

Anthony came back up the steps. The sunglasses hid his eyes, but something was wrong. Gail stood quickly and reached for him. "Anthony, what happened?"

"Omar Céspedes. He was shot to death last night."

30

Everett Bookhouser said to meet him at the Colón Cemetery. After the murder of Omar Céspedes, Anthony thought this might be the CIA's idea of a macabre joke. He took Gail back to the house in Miramar. She didn't argue when he said he had to go alone. It was close to three o'clock when he walked under the triple-arched stone gate of the cemetery. Above him, Lazarus rose from the dead, and saints in their classical robes stared out over the graves.

Anthony paid his dollar entry fee and walked along the main road with its double row of meticulously clipped ornamental trees. At midweek, the place was nearly deserted. A groundskeeper trimmed the grass beside the low iron fences. An old woman moved slowly among the monuments, vanishing and reappearing.

The necropolis was laid out like a small city with streets on a grid. Bookhouser would be at the intersection of 5 and G, east of the central chapel. Standing in the shadow of the church, Anthony looked around. The road was empty. He had taken a different route leaving Ramiro's house. If anyone had followed, they had been extremely good at it.

He walked east. Even through his sunglasses, the glare off the white marble tore at his eyes. The memorials and tombs and family vaults fought a silent battle of architectural excess. Just past a baroque tomb of carved doves and angels, Bookhouser stood with one sneaker-shod foot on a low wall, reading the tourist guide. The bill of his Yo ♥ La Habana cap turned when Anthony stopped alongside him.

"It says here a million people are buried in this cemetery. Isn't that something? The more important you are, the closer you get to the chapel. Nobility over there, common folks in the back. And the ordinary rich somewhere in between. Like this one. An excellent example of the classical Greek influence popular in the late nineteenth century."

Bookhouser glanced up from his tourist guide to gesture toward a tomb built like a small Parthenon. He read, " 'The family vault of Julio Amador Pedrosa, 1814 to 1892, who founded the national railroad system of Cuba.' Do you want me to take a photo?"

"No, thanks. There's one hanging on the wall in my grandfather's study."

"I saw it," Bookhouser said.

With the toe of his shoe, Anthony gently nudged Bookhouser's foot off the wall. "Ernesto carried hopes for many years that this would be his final resting place. Now he wants me to wrap his body in a Cuban flag and bury him in a field. Red earth, he says. Make sure it's the red earth of my homeland." Anthony was halfway through crossing himself before he realized he had fallen into this old habit again. He finished, put his fingers to his lips, and reached over the iron fence to touch one of the columns.

Bookhouser watched without comment.

"Tell me about Céspedes," Anthony said.

"How did you find out, by the way?"

"You aren't the only one with friends."

Bookhouser closed his tourist guide. "At one-fifteen this morning, Omar Céspedes was shot five times with a .22-caliber pistol. The round in the back of his head was fired at close range as he lay on the ground. A neighbor happened to be awake checking on her baby and saw the whole thing from a third-floor window. Céspedes parked his vehicle in the common alley behind the town houses. He got out, walked toward his back fence, and a man came out from behind one of the cars and shot him. The witness said it was very fast, very neat. The man took Céspedes's wallet and walked away. The D.C. police initially classified it as a robbery-homicide, but the FBI monitors all murders in the District. The name Omar Céspedes rang a bell, and they called us."

"Not a robbery," Anthony said.

"No. And it's going to affect your brother-in-law in two ways. First, we need him more than ever, because Céspedes was only halfway through his sworn testimony before the House Intelligence

Committee. And second, Ramiro should get out as soon as possible. Céspedes is dead. Olga Saavedra is dead. Unless you can think of some reason why not, I'm going to say that the same person is behind both murders and that Ramiro Vega is next."

Anthony said, "Do you want me to tell him to call you?"

"Please." Bookhouser checked some readings on his camera, then raised it to his eye and focused on a weeping angel across the path. Her hand hid her eyes, and her wings drooped. "Look at the skill in that carving. Did you know that Cuba has its own marble? I thought all this stuff was imported from Italy. No, most of it was homegrown and carted over from the Sierra Maestra." *Click*. "Tell Vega we'd like him to leave on Friday night. That gives him a little over forty-eight hours."

"Marta won't like leaving Friday. Their daughter's birthday party is on Saturday."

"Yes, I'm sorry about that," Bookhouser said. "Are they coming? Vega hasn't told me. We can accommodate as many of the immediate family as he wants to bring with him, but he has to let me know who they are."

"I'll see him tonight," Anthony said. "How do you plan to get him out?"

Bookhouser aimed his camera west. "See that white marble cross over there? It marks the grave of 'La Milagrosa.' Woman of the miracles. She died in childbirth, and they buried her and her baby in separate caskets. When they opened hers for some reason, who knows why, the baby was in her arms. Faith is required, Mr. Quintana." He squinted through the viewfinder. "Faith in the resourcefulness of your friends in the United States government."

Click.

Checking the photo's image in the viewing screen, Bookhouser said, "If you would, let Ramiro know that additional compensation has been approved. He and I can talk about it."

"Are you taking my family out, too, or am I supposed to arrange my own miracles?"

"No, we'll get you out." Bookhouser snapped the lens cap back on. "What I need you to do is stay in Havana through Friday night so the house doesn't look empty. You leave on Saturday. I can give you final details by tomorrow. Do not—I repeat this—do not attempt to leave Cuba on your own. I know you have ways of doing it, but we need you here. You and your family are not in danger."

"That's good to know."

"The people behind this aren't after you."

"People? How about Abdel García?"

"García? Maybe. García and a few others."

"Does Ramiro agree with that?"

"Ramiro wouldn't say."

"Ah. Well, that's Ramiro." Anthony noticed that on the pediment of the Pedrosa mausoleum, a small tree had taken root in a crack. The roots reached through and hung in the air below it, seeking earth. A crow flapped away, cawing loudly, and the noise echoed across the cemetery.

Anthony said, "García was at MININT last night when I was being questioned. Afterward we had a talk, a brief one, in the elevator on the way down. I gave him your story, that Céspedes was talking about Cuban spies in Venezuela. I found out—through one of my friends—that Céspedes had also talked about finishing construction on the nuclear reactor at Juraguá. I told García. He didn't buy either story. Let me give you my theory. Céspedes told you that the Russians made an unaccounted-for shipment of uranium. Someone in the regime—if not Fidel himself—wants to put it to good use by selling it on the arms market. It could wind up in a backpack bomb on the New York subway or at the next Super Bowl game."

Bookhauser's ice-blue eyes moved to look at him. He smiled. "Please don't. I myself think you're just trying to figure it out, but if your actions were to affect the outcome adversely, there are some people who would get a lot of satisfaction in labeling you as an agent of the Cuban government."

"It would be a lie."

"Since when does that count? Don't take the risk. Friendly advice, okay?"

"I should be getting back," Anthony said.

His companion followed a few paces behind. They passed a low crypt where someone had laid yellow carnations, some beads, and a handmade doll dressed in blue and yellow. The colors of Yemayá.

Bookhouser aimed his camera. Anthony kept walking.

He heard Bookhouser say, "We erect crosses and we leave beads and flowers. The afterlife. How badly we want it."

The wall of the cemetery ran alongside a narrow sidewalk. Sections of iron fence interrupted the long stretches of concrete and white, bas-relief crosses. Anthony had left his car across the street in a line of them at the curb. Trees cast heavy shade, and the side streets angled past low apartment buildings. He saw no one standing nearby, but as he was reaching for his keys, he heard car doors opening. Two men got out of a car ahead of his. One leaped out of the driver's side; the other hurried around the rear bumper. They wore sunglasses, and their shirts hung over their trousers. If they were armed, the guns would be on their belts.

Muscles tensing, Anthony shifted his weight to the balls of his feet. Another car door slammed. A third man came from the other direction. It was useless to run, even if he'd had the chance. One of them was a muscular black guy in his late twenties; the other was a little older, a *trigueño*, white with a touch of *café* in his blood.

The younger man said, "Anthony Quintana?"

"Who the hell are you?"

"Get in."

His partner opened the rear door of their car. Small brown model, no markings, typical of undercover police.

The third man followed close behind. The *negro* had a hand on Anthony's upper arm. He limped. Anthony registered this fact, and as they shoved him into the backseat, he wondered who they were. State Security wouldn't use a man with a bad leg.

The *trigueño* drove. The *negro* sat in the backseat. He took out a cell phone and told someone they were on their way. The car did a tight U-turn and headed east.

"Where are we going?"

The pair of sunglasses in the seat next to him turned slightly, but the man behind them said nothing. A young guy, mid-twenties, a smooth brown face. Big arms. A scar across his knuckles. They drove down the hill past the university, then farther into the old part of the city. The dome of the Capitol drew nearer.

Anthony was not surprised when he began to see Chinese characters on the buildings. The car slowed in a river of pedestrians, bicycle taxis, and exhaust fumes and went under some wooden scaffolding. The driver turned onto an even narrower street rutted with potholes. The car stopped. Doors opened.

When they told him to get out, Anthony looked up and saw the bright green shutters of Abdel García's apartment.

This time, the shutters and the windows were closed. The darkness of the room was relieved by a floor lamp. The light glowed on the gold silk fringe and painted large yellow circles on the floor and ceiling. Everything else was the same, the red upholstery and carved wood and lingering smell of sandalwood.

The general stood by the opening to the kitchen as one of his thugs put a hand between Anthony's shoulder blades and shoved him inside the apartment. The heavy door closed, and Abdel García crossed the room, his steps silent on the oriental rug. Cigarette smoke trailed behind him. He carried the ashtray in his other hand. Not a sound entered the room from the street below.

It might have been the quick walk up four flights of steps that made it hard to breathe. Anthony drew in some air, then said, "You're in uniform. Did you remember to punch out at the office?"

The light from the floor lamp was doing strange things to García's uneven bone structure. He smiled slightly and paused his cigarette at his lips. "Please, sit down. I have a favor to ask you."

"I've already done you a favor." Anthony pivoted as the general walked over to his little table by the window. "Tell me. Who shot Omar Céspedes last night?"

"Who knows? Washington is a dangerous city. There's a lot of crime in your country." The general settled into a chair and crossed his thin legs. He crushed out his cigarette and put the ashtray on the table. Anthony saw that the black enameled vase held a fresh arrangement of flowers. "Do you have ancestors in the Colón Cemetery, Mr. Quintana?"

"Yes. My grandfather's family, the Pedrosas. I drop in to say hello when I'm in town. What do you want, general? I don't like being followed."

García lifted the flap on his uniform shirt and took out a small tape recorder. He pressed a button, and Anthony heard someone speaking. After a second he recognized the voice: his own.

—Céspedes is talking about Juraguá. He says you want to finish construction as soon as possible. You need the energy, and you believe the United States is in no position to object. With world attention diverted—

García stopped the tape and slid the recorder back into his pocket. "You don't want this tape to show up in Miami, so please listen and do not interrupt. For many years, Ramiro Vega and I have been friends and fellow officers. I have tried to contact Vega for two days, but he won't talk to me. This is not only rude, it is insubordinate. I could have him arrested. But I don't. For the sake of that friendship, I will be patient. I could cause him harm, but I'd rather not. I admire Vega. And his wife. Your sister, no? Marta. And their children. Paula. Giovany. Janelle."

He took his handkerchief from his side pocket. He refolded it and dabbed at his mouth. "A lovely family. For many years I felt a part of it. No longer. This is not a complaint. It's how life is. People are loyal, and then you feel the blade sliding into your heart."

The room was overheated, and sweat ran down Anthony's back. He said, "Tell me what you want."

The small black eyes lifted slowly. "Some information . . . a collection of lies. Vega knows what it is. He will give it to you, and you will deliver it to me. I will tell you where. If he refuses, I will have him arrested and charged with treason. My duty would require me to ask that he be executed. You will give him this message . . . and my regrets. It isn't easy for me, because I am fond of his family. Tell him that. Ask him to think about who will suffer. My pain, his pain. That's not so much. We are men. What about his wife? His children. If he went to prison . . . if he were executed . . . what would happen to them?"

Abdel García's thin body appeared to be floating, and his face was a mask of old ivory. A trick of light, of perspective.

"What is it?" Anthony asked. "This information you want."

"Vega knows. You get it for me, Quintana. I trust you. Get it for me."

31

A long porch went across the front of the veterans' home, and afternoon sunlight brightened the flowers in clay pots on the stone railing. The old men watched from their chairs. Gail gave the taxi driver an extra ten dollars and told him to wait.

She had come to pick up her father-in-law for dinner. No one else could do it. Marta and Irene were still out shopping, and Anthony hadn't come back yet. Cobo had gone who-knew-where. So Gail had called Marta on her cell phone and said she'd take care of it, not to worry. Gail didn't want Luis to sit there wondering if he'd been forgotten.

What a lie, she said to herself, scanning the shady yard and crumbling stone columns. She hadn't come for Luis, though soon enough she would be helping him into the taxi, telling the driver to take them back to Miramar.

She had come because of Yolanda.

Not to talk. No, they would talk tonight at the meeting. They would chit-chat about their kids and politics and how terribly brave it was to open a library in a dictatorship. For now, Gail just wanted to walk through Yolanda Cabrera's magnetic field and watch the needle swing. *Did she sleep with Anthony or not?* No, that wasn't it either. What Gail really wanted was to push Yolanda into a chair and make her answer the question. But Yolanda, being noble and good, might tell her the truth. Gail would rather hear a lie she could believe in. Anthony could do it so well. He would just drop certain untidy pieces of his life into a box and throw it away. If he didn't have to think about it anymore, it didn't exist.

There was a flaw in that reasoning: Mario. He did exist.

Gail had played with the idea of being good. If Anthony and

Yolanda still loved each other as they had as children, if culture and language, and now blood, fated them to be together, wasn't it wrong to stand between them? Gail did not think she could be that unselfish. She doubted if Yolanda's husband could either.

Crossing the street, Gail kept her eyes on the cracks in the pavement. She would find Luis and get the hell out of here.

It didn't matter what Anthony had done twenty years ago. Maybe Mario wasn't his son. If Yolanda denied it, Gail would only have succeeded in making an ass of herself. And Anthony would go off like a rocket. *You went behind my back! Why don't you call me a liar to my face?*

Gail's mother had once told her, somewhere during a pitcher of martinis, that Gail's father had not been faithful. Irene had overlooked a lot of it. Had to. By the time she found out about yet *another* little indiscretion, it was in the past, so what good would it do, dredging it up? No good at all except to ruin the fragile truce they'd reestablished after she had taken him back. *Darling, sometimes a woman just has to pretend it never happened.*

Gail went up the steps to the porch. The row of rocking chairs came to a stop.

"Hello," she said. *"Buenas tardes. Yo soy . . ."* She had forgotten the word for daughter-in-law. *"Soy la . . . esposa de . . . el hijo de Luis Quintana."* The wife of the son. Is he here? *"¿Está aquí?"*

A man with a Yankees ball cap, and a back as bent as his cane, shuffled over and kissed her hand. The others laughed and told her to watch out, he was a devil. He opened the screen door for her, and they went inside. Painted tiles brightened the floor with stylized flowers of red and green, and two staircases with wrought-iron balustrades curved to an upper hall. One of the staircases had some missing steps and a rope across it.

He pulled her by the wrist to a door framed in carved mahogany, gone gray from age. There was a cardboard sign: OFICINA. The old man knocked, then rapped with his cane.

Gail said, "No. Upstairs." She pointed. "Señor Quintana is upstairs—"

The office door swung open, and Yolanda Cabrera appeared in a white smock and a blue bandana. She seemed slightly out of breath. When she saw Gail, she smiled. "Hello!"

Gail took a step forward, still out of range for a kiss of greeting.

"How are you, Yolanda? It's nice to see you again. I'm here for Anthony's father. Everyone else is busy, so I volunteered."

"I think that he is taking a nap. Do you want me to tell him you are here?"

"Yes, if you would." Gail turned and thanked the man who had brought her inside, then said to Yolanda, "I'll just wait on the porch."

But Yolanda took her by the elbow. "Gail, are you in a big hurry?" She glanced at the door closing behind the old man, then said, "I have to make some copies. It will take five minutes. Can you help me?"

"Well . . . I suppose so."

She followed Yolanda through the outer office, then into a smaller room whose ornate plaster molding hinted at a history as a music room or library. Its current function was more practical. Molded chairs faced a large wooden desk, on which sat a computer and ledgers and paperwork. Filing cabinets took up one wall. Opposite, Fidel Castro in his green uniform smiled placidly at a poster of Monet's water lilies. Under them was a copy machine on a stand. Pieces of paper formed a semicircle on the floor.

Yolanda went over to look through the uncurtained window. "I pay the manager ten cents each to let me make copies. I bring my own paper and leave the money in the drawer. If I do it when he isn't here, he can say he didn't know."

She showed Gail what had to be done. Unstaple this, make twenty copies, staple, put with the copies already on the floor. And twenty copies of this other page.

"It's lucky you came! A supervisor from the Ministry of Health is on her way," Yolanda lifted the cover, laid a sheet on the glass, and pressed a button. "She is not so nice about it."

"Should we do this? Are we going to get in trouble?"

"Not if we hurry." A strand of silver hair moved across Yolanda's cheek as she worked. She wore no makeup, and forty-four years had sketched lines on her forehead.

Gail took the copies and laid them on the stacks. Yolanda opened and closed the lid as the copier hummed and clanked, and the light moved slowly from one side of the glass to the other. "You should have a Kinko's in Havana," Gail said.

"What is that?"

"It's a place where you do this about fifty times faster. What are you copying?"

"It's for the meeting at our house tonight, lists of all the independent journalists and libraries in Cuba and all the opposition groups."

"Oh, my God. Is this legal?"

Yolanda laughed. "Yes. What is not legal is to make copies on this machine."

Gail ran out of staples, and Yolanda went to the desk and found more in the top drawer. She got back in time to whisk out one sheet and put in another. "We used to have a copy machine, but they took it when José was arrested."

"They took your copier?"

"They took everything. Our computer. Our books. Letters from my parents. Photographs of the family. A certificate from Mario's school when he won a prize for music. I will never know why they took that." Yolanda ran to help Gail lay the stacks on the desk to be stapled. "It's changing. Not much, but a little. We don't think they will arrest José again. There are too many of us now, too many groups." Yolanda turned off the machine.

Adrenaline was pumping through Gail's body, and her hands moved effortlessly. Collate, staple. Collate, staple. Yolanda found another stapler, and soon they were in a race, laughing and tossing the finished sets into a pile.

With the last one, Gail said, "Are we finished? Is that it?"

"Yes. The angels are watching us." Yolanda ran across the room for her purse and calculated aloud in Spanish as she took money out of her wallet. She grabbed an envelope and stuffed some bills and coins into it. Licking the envelope, she walked to the window again.

"She is coming." Yolanda put the envelope into the bottom drawer of the desk and closed it with her knee. "Hurry."

Gail scooped up the copies while Yolanda turned out the lights. They bolted across the office and out the door. Yolanda closed it and inserted a key in the lock. "Put the copies in your bag. Walk to the stairs. Wait there."

The supervisor came through the door a few seconds later, a woman with frizzy blond hair, a tight red sweater, and a black skirt too short for her stubby legs. She glanced at the two women standing at the bottom of the stairs, one with a shoulder bag out of sight behind her back, the other with nothing in her hands.

Yolanda said, *"Buenas tardes, compañera."*

The woman smiled pleasantly, took a key from her collection, and opened the door to the office. It closed behind her.

Gail's eyes met Yolanda's, and her lips tightened to hold in her laughter. Yolanda stared at her. When air erupted through Gail's lips, Yolanda's face reddened, and she pressed her hands to her mouth. They ran. Gail followed her, holding the heavy bag with both hands, running through the hall and out the back of the house, where they turned the corner and collapsed against the wall, laughing. Yolanda put a finger to her lips. "Shhh."

Gail wiped her eyes and whispered, "Oh, my God. I haven't done anything like that since we tee-peed the principal's car."

"What?"

"Tee-pee. T-P? Toilet paper. All over his car. Next time I come back, I'll bring a few rolls. We can tee-pee Fidel's car." She broke into giggles.

"Shhhh!" With a hand on Gail's elbow, Yolanda took her around the corner, where a wire fence had grown so thickly with vines that the next house could not be seen, except for its mildewed tile roof.

Rakes and a shovel leaned against the wall. Gail set her bag on the bottom of an overturned wheelbarrow and reached under the copies for the bottle of water. When Yolanda said she didn't need any, Gail finished it. Yolanda's face was still flushed. She took off her bandana and retied it behind her head. "Gail, can you take those with you and bring them to my house tonight?"

"Of course. If the police stop me, I don't even know you."

With a laugh, Yolanda said, "Don't worry. No one will stop you. I don't want *her* to find out. She saw me making copies a few weeks ago, and she said if I did it again, I would lose my job. The manager is with the CDR, and *he* doesn't care, but this woman—" Yolanda shook her head.

"I shouldn't have started laughing," Gail said. "It isn't funny, what you have to go through. I'm sorry."

Yolanda's smile lit her eyes. "Don't say that. I'm too serious. I need to laugh a little more. We are a good team, no?" Then her smile faded, and she took a breath before saying, "I was thinking to talk to you at my house tonight, but here you are. God brought you to me. My friend. I wanted to see you because . . . Anthony says he will ask Mario to come to Miami. I don't know if he means that Mario would live at your house. Maybe until he can get a job and his own apartment, or go to a university. Anthony didn't tell me that. I want to be sure, very sure, that you approve. You are Anthony's wife. Sometimes men can forget that a decision is not only for them."

Without hesitation, Gail said, "I approve completely, if that's what Mario wants. Anthony and I talked to him this morning. I'm not sure Mario would leave, but if he does, I have no objection." She added, "I will help in whatever way I can. I mean that, Yolanda."

"Do you think Angela and Danny will accept him? I think Angela yes, but maybe Danny wants his father to himself."

"He should be very proud of Anthony for helping you. Anyway, he lives in New Jersey. Don't worry about Danny."

"Thank you." Yolanda put an arm around Gail's waist. "I don't want Mario to leave. I know we wouldn't see him for a long time, but it's better. I'm worried about him, Gail. One of his friends in the band is dead. The police found his body yesterday at Lenin Park. He was gone for three days, then they found him. His name is Camilo. They called him Chachi."

"That was Mario's friend?" Gail said, "Mario dropped off the kids yesterday, and they said they'd been at the park, and the police were investigating. I'm so sorry. Do they know how he died?"

"He was beaten. It was very bad. A friend of their family told me last night. Olga Saavedra also is dead. Killed like Chachi. They beat her. Do you know about this?"

Gail said she knew but stopped herself from revealing anything else.

Yolanda said, "Someone called us, because José used to work with Olga. News like that travels very fast in Havana." Moving closer, Yolanda spoke in a whisper. "Chachi's mother is afraid that he was doing things very dangerous . . . against the state. You know about the bombs in the tourist district? No one was injured, but the police are looking for who put them. They say it's a counterrevolutionary group, *el movimiento veintiocho de enero,* twenty-eighth of January. The birth of José Martí. I don't believe that Mario would be in such a group, because always, always José and I have told him the only way for change is nonviolence. José made him read about Gandhi, Martin Luther King, Jr., Lech Wałesa. He *knows*, but . . . I'm afraid for him. He should leave. I'm going to tell him, 'Mario, you go with Anthony. He will take care of you.' "

Yolanda pulled away to look at Gail fully, and her eyes shifted on Gail's as if trying to see into her heart. "You'll be good to my son. I know it. Anthony is very lucky to find you, Gail. You are perfect for him."

"Not perfect at all," Gail said. "I'm not easy to get along with. I'm not as good as you are. You're the kindest women I've ever met. You are. I'll bet you've never done anything bad in your entire life."

"You are being funny again." With a smile, Yolanda shook her head. "I am not so good. When I was a girl, no one could control me. It's true. I was selfish. I would do anything I wanted. When you are that way, and you hurt the people in your life, you pay for it. But God does not turn his back. He never abandons his children. You can have a great sin, but God gives you something good with it, too. It's always there if you look."

Gail felt she was watching a great wall of water approaching, the truth coming toward her, and there was nothing she could do but stand there and hold on as it flowed over and around her like a wave. When the wave flowed away, it took her fear with it.

"Anthony is his father."

Yolanda's eyes widened. She blinked slowly, then nodded. "How did you know?"

"I saw the resemblance."

"Yes. It is there."

"You never told Anthony?"

"I couldn't. He was married."

"That's true. He was," Gail said. "Even so, you should have told him. Why didn't you?"

"Many reasons. For myself. Because it was easier. When could I tell Anthony that Mario was his? When Anthony was with his wife and their two children? I was afraid that Anthony would take Mario away, like his grandfather took him away. I would have to go too, and I couldn't do that. My work was here. I am needed here. Could I tell Anthony when José was in prison? Could I do that to my husband?"

"But at the beginning, when you were pregnant—"

"Yes, it was wrong. I know. I can't change that."

"You have to tell him now," Gail said.

"Listen. When Anthony left Cuba the first time, I cried for a week because he was so much a part of my life then. I loved him as girls do, you know, when you are twelve or thirteen years old. He was the first boy who ever kissed me." She laughed a little, then said, "One day he told me he was going to Miami to see his mother and he would be back. It was a trick. They never let him come back. I didn't see him for more than ten years. I was living in Camagüey City and studying at the nurses' school. I walked from my class, and he was waiting for me. He was visiting his father and wanted to see me too. We were very young, and I didn't care about his wife in the United States. He was here for almost two weeks. I said to him, Anthony, stay. Don't leave me again. What do you want to go back there for? You are Cuban, you will always be Cuban. He said he would talk to his wife, he should not have married her, it was a big mistake, but . . . well, he left and I didn't hear from him. He was young, so now I don't blame him, but then! My anger made me very cold. When I knew I was pregnant, I said to myself, this child is *mine*, and someday, when the boy is grown up, I will show him to Anthony, and I will say, look at him. This is your son. You abandoned me, and now we are equal. No, I was not a good person.

"My mother saw my stomach, and she knew. She hit me and called me a whore. My mother hated everyone. She was not like your mother, Gail. I was so mad I told her the father was a soldier with a wife already, and I met him at a bar. She told me she wouldn't speak to me until I had an abortion. We didn't see each other again until my father told me she was very sick. She died when Mario was four years old.

"Anthony heard about my mother's death, and he wrote to me. I told him I had a child, and I told him the story about the soldier, because I had said it so many times I believed it. When Anthony started coming back again to see his family, I was taking care of his father. Anthony and I became friends. He was very good with Mario. We never spoke of the past. Our lives went on. I joined the movement, and I met José, and we got married. And Anthony found you."

Yolanda took Gail's hand. "Each time he is with us, I say, well, maybe the next time, I will tell him. But I don't. And now it isn't for me to decide. I will give Mario the choice because he's not a boy anymore. I will let him go with you and Anthony, and you'll take care of him. He will learn what life is on the outside. When my son comes back to Cuba for the first time, in one year or two years, I will tell him, and he will make the choice, not me. And not you.

"Please, Gail. Let Mario decide. I think I know Anthony. He would want to be Mario's father completely. Whoever Anthony loves, he loves completely, and he wouldn't give Mario the freedom to find himself. Do you understand?"

"I do," Gail admitted. "You know him very well."

"Mario is my son, the only child I will ever have, and José is my husband. I will talk to José when the time is ready, but not now." Yolanda took Gail's hand and pressed it to her cheek. "Please. I ask you for a little time. For my son."

Gail put her arms around Yolanda. "I won't tell anyone. I promise."

32

Three pairs of shoes, one pair of rubber thongs. Black jacket, two sweaters. Shirts, pants, jeans. Five pairs of sunglasses. Socks, underwear, condoms. Razors, hair brush, toothbrush. Soap from a Marriott Hotel, unopened. Beach towel. A box of beads and woven cords. Nail clippers. Blue-and-white cap from the Chelsea Football Club. Four bottles of cologne. Earrings, a watch, bracelets, neck chains, rings. Biography of Che Guevara, guidebook to the Prado Museum, poetry of Martí. Three stamps and one envelope. Postcard from Oslo. Address book. Wallet and identity card. One hundred twelve dollars, six Euros, eighteen pesos. A portable CD player and radio. Twenty-seven CDs. A folder of sheet music. Notes from music composition class. One flute case. One flute. One pistol, thirty-six bullets.

When Mario had finished putting everything on his cot, he began making three piles. One for clothing and jewelry to be put into plastic bags and left on the street tonight. One for things to be thrown out. And the last for what he would wear or take with him to General Vega's house. If by remote chance the police did come to this apartment, they would find nothing of his, not so much as a hair.

From his wallet Mario took a hundred dollars and put it into the box of detergent. The woman would find it. She had no relatives out of the country. Her husband was dead, and she took care of her grandson. The boy's mother worked nights at the train station. They let Mario sleep in the laundry room for ten dollars a week. His door was a sheet pinned to a wire. He washed his clothes in the concrete laundry tub. A window and a short drop gave access to the neighboring roof, and Mario could sit there at night and look at the city.

He turned to get a plastic bag from a hook on a wire shelf. Raúl was in the way. There was no chair, so Raúl moved some shirts aside and sat on the cot, straightening his bad leg. The room was so narrow his foot reached the doorway.

Raúl was telling him what his cousin had found out, the cousin who worked in the records department of the PNR. She had looked up Chachi Menéndez's name and couldn't find it.

"So she asked some questions, being very nonchalant about it. 'Do you remember that kid they brought in here the other night for writing graffiti? Where'd he go?' Like that. They told her the army took him. Would you like to guess on whose orders this was done? Come on, Mario. Guess!" Raúl's eyes darkened.

"Vega."

Raúl lifted his hands and spread his arms wide.

Mario said, "That means he knows about us."

"It means he suspects, at least. But he doesn't know *who*," Raúl said. "If he had that information, we'd all be where Chachi is right now." Raúl's fist came down on the cot so hard the toiletries bounced on the thin mattress. "Sons of syphilitic whores."

Snapping open the plastic bag, Mario started throwing his underwear inside it. "If Chachi didn't talk, who did? Olga?"

"Probably. That bitch. My cousin says the police were investigating Olga's murder, but the army took over. Why? It's obvious, no? They're covering up for Vega. I think he killed her. She wouldn't let him touch her again, and he killed her. Beat her face in. That's what I heard. What a monster. Mario, these people are worse than you could believe. I know. I was in the military, and they made us do things that would make you sick to your stomach. You have to pass an exam in sadomasochism to get promoted. It wouldn't surprise me if Ramiro Vega buggered our little friend before he killed him and dumped his body in Lenin Park."

Mario tied the bag at the top, set it under the mattress out of the way, and reached for another. He had already imagined Chachi's death. The images had numbed him, slicing through his nerve endings. The knowledge that Vega was responsible brought no sensation at all.

With a shudder, Raúl sat up and looked around. "Is there anything to drink? Some rum, whisky? A beer?"

"They don't drink."

"That's pathetic. Mario, we have to know when you're going to do it. I asked you, and you never answered me."

"I told Tomás I would let everyone know twenty-four hours in advance."

"That doesn't give us enough time."

"All you have to do is pick me up when it's over."

"Listen to me, my friend," Raúl said. "It isn't as simple as you think, an operation like this. You aren't the only one involved. You can't leave us standing around with our thumbs in our asses."

Mario was careful not to wrinkle his shirts getting them into the bag. They were good shirts. Someone could use them. He shoved the bag under the cot. "The less notice you have, the less time there is for someone to screw up."

"Listen, you arrogant shit. I do not screw up. If it weren't for my leg, *I* would be doing it. You're not getting nervous, are you? We're counting on you."

"I'm fine."

"How about Sunday? Do you remember? Olga told us he's always home on Sunday night."

Mario glanced over at Raúl, whose weight threatened to collapse the narrow folding legs of the cot. "I'll do it tomorrow."

Raúl laughed. "My God, are you joking? Good. Tomorrow. We can be ready. What time?"

"Probably as soon as it gets dark."

"When? Seven o'clock?"

"I haven't decided," Mario said. "Tomás and I will meet later today to talk about the communiqué. By then I'll have the final details. He can pass them on to you."

Raúl sat up so fast the cot nearly went over. He grabbed Mario's arm and brought him close. Mario could feel a fleck of spittle on his cheek. "You forget yourself, Mario. This is a military unit, and I am in charge of the logistics of this operation, not *you*."

Mario looked into Raúl's eyes and without fear said, "Do you want to kill him yourself?" When the fingers released, he said, "I will give Tomás the exact time. I will shoot Vega and go over the fence at the rear of the property. What you must do for me, Raúl, if you please, is to be on the street behind the Vega house ready to pick me up. I will signal with a pocket flashlight, as you told me to. The signal is one . . . two . . . and a longer three. Then again. If I don't appear within sixty seconds of the time we establish, you can assume that I didn't make it out. You leave without me."

Huffing, Raúl leaned against the wall again. "You'll make it out. That watch you have on. Is it accurate?"

"Yes, it's a Seiko," Mario said.

"Give it to me. I'll set it with mine to the exact second." He held out his hand, and Mario dropped his watch into it. Raúl pulled out the stem and made an adjustment. "The street behind Vega's is a long one. I'll go slowly, looking for the signal. Don't forget to test your flashlight. Are you sure Vega will be there?"

"He will be there," Mario said.

"How do you know?"

"Angela says he's always home for dinner." Mario laid a white shirt on the cot, folded one arm inward, then decided to wear it to his parents' house tonight. He wanted them to remember him in good clothing. He would wear it with his black pants.

"Here, put this back on." Raúl tossed him the watch, then leaned over to pick up the Makarov. "What about the gun? Did you clean it after the last practice?"

"Yes. And oiled it."

He broke it open to check the spring and the barrel. "This little sweetheart likes you, Mario. She will do as you say. You won't miss. Hell, you're getting to be a better shot than I am!" Tilting his head to listen for something, Raúl said, "What's the matter with the child?"

Mario flipped through his composition book. "He has bronchitis. I gave his grandmother some money. That's where she is now, at the pharmacy." There was nothing in the composition book that had his name on it, but he went slowly through the pages. Ideas for songs. Some lyrics. He hummed a few measures.

"Mario."

He ripped the compositions out of the book, tore them in half, then again. He stuffed the pages into the trash bag. "What?"

"Don't you want to know how you're getting to Mexico? We have everything in place."

He smiled. "Do you think I will make it to Mexico?"

Raúl looked at him, then said, "You might."

"You should clear out your apartment," Mario said. "Tell the others to do the same. Destroy all your papers. Nico should go to his relatives' house in Las Tunas. Put him on a bus."

"He's part of the team to get you to the boat." Raúl took a cigarette out of his pack.

"Nico can't help us," Mario said. "He's useless after what happened to Chachi. Don't smoke in here. The boy has bad lungs."

"I'll go over by the window."

"Put it away."

Raúl wedged the pillow behind his back and leaned against the wall. "I wish I could come with you. I would use a knife. Cut his throat like a pig. For Chachi and for Olga. It's too bad about Olga. She was stupid, but I liked her."

"You tormented her," Mario said.

"That's my nature. I torment everyone."

Mario had not told Raúl that he had gone to Olga's house yesterday. He had gone there because knowing about Chachi had pushed him to want to ask her a question. She had told him, *Let someone else take Vega.* What had she meant?

Mario tossed his jewelry into the bag with the toiletries.

"What are you doing?" Raúl said. "You might need to sell it." He dragged the bag closer and looked inside. "Don't throw this away. It's the necklace you got off that Brazilian woman last summer. She's one to remember."

"Take it."

Raúl shook his head. "Bad luck."

"Leave me alone, Raúl. I have to be by myself so I can think."

Raúl pushed himself off the cot. "If you're throwing me out, I'll go." The two men embraced, and Raúl slapped him on the back. "Don't forget. We have a final meeting tomorrow morning, ten o'clock sharp. Is there anything you need?"

"Nothing. Except to get it over with."

He went with Raúl to the front door, checked the dark stairwell for anyone coming up, then let him out and locked the door behind him. From the bedroom came the sound of coughing, and Mario looked in. The boy, called Pipo, was holding on to the bars of his crib. His face was red, and his shoulders and belly shook with his coughs, but he seemed bored by it, as accepting as an animal. Mario wiped off the boy's face with a clean diaper and took him into the kitchen. The refrigerator was full of plastic bottles of water to be used when nothing came out of the pipes. One of them contained boiled water for the boy. Mario couldn't figure out which it was, so he gave him a little orange soda.

He carried Pipo into the laundry room and put him on the cot. "Stay there." He hid the pistol and the bag of bullets under the mattress.

The only thing left to be done was the letter to his parents. Mario thought he would let Anthony Quintana deliver it. He would give it to him tonight and tell him to keep it until Sunday.

If Quintana was at Vega's house tomorrow, and if he saw the pistol, he might try to go for it, but Mario would have the barrel at Vega's head first. He could shoot Vega, run for the back door, and probably escape. He would be faster than Quintana. But he couldn't do it that way. Not in front of Vega's family. He would tell Vega to go into his office. He would close the door. He wouldn't make it to Mexico.

Mario sat down and used his flute case as a desk. He thought about what to say. *I am not gone. You will know I'm with you . . . when you feel the wind of liberty on your faces . . .*

No, that wasn't any good. The words sat in his brain like heavy rocks. This would take some time. He wanted to say it correctly.

The boy crawled over to see what he was doing.

Mario used to think about dying, and his insides would become cold, and he'd have to take a breath to make his heart go again. But not now. He felt clear and strong. He would be remembered. When Pipo grew up he would talk about him. *Mario Cabrera stayed with us. He was a quiet man. We never knew about his mission—*

The boy coughed a few times, then sighed.

Mario put down his pen. "Do you want to go outside, Pipo? Come with me."

He set the boy on the windowsill, jumped down, then reached to get him. Holding the boy on his arm, he walked to the edge of the roof. He heard voices from one of the apartments. A soap opera from another. A truck changing gears, five floors down. The sun had set, but the sky was still blue. He told the boy to look, and he pointed at the stars coming out and the lights of a ship on the horizon.

33

The voices of the women drifted through the kitchen window into the backyard. Anthony sat with José Leiva under the trellis, drinking beer and watching the sky fade to indigo. Vines curled around wires stretched between metal posts. The garden was beyond in neat rows, and the lights of the house next door shone through the mango trees.

José said, "If Mario wants to leave Cuba, I won't argue against it. He has no job here, and he's not likely to get one. I had hoped that he would become interested in what his mother and I are doing. Nothing interests him but his band. If he leaves, he can develop a career. But should he go to the United States? Philosophically he isn't suited. He has no love of money or what it can buy. On the other hand, that is how the world works everywhere nowadays—except here. Cuba is a time capsule. Yolanda says that if he leaves, we will double the size of our library to compensate for his absence. I asked her why she waited so long—Mario moved out a year ago. Two of our friends—you'll meet them tonight—want to start a library in Miramar. It would be near your sister's house! Do you think she and General Vega would visit? A few of our neighbors are coming tonight. Most of them are supportive. Most of them. Somebody left a bag of dog shit on the porch the other day. We get hang-up calls and death threats. The CDR knows who does it, but we don't bother complaining. Their days are coming to an end. What an amazing thing. People are losing their fear. There are a thousand small movements, and we're joining into larger groups. We are librarians and journalists, independent economists and trade unionists. Yes, I am very hopeful."

José Leiva was a person who could carry a conversation entirely on his own back. This had allowed Anthony time in which to form his thoughts. He looked at the house and saw Gail moving across the bright kitchen window. She turned to someone out of view and smiled.

Anthony set his beer on the patio. "José, before your guests arrive, I want to ask about some recent articles of yours. They had to do with General Abdel García. What were they about?"

Leiva pulled at his short white beard. "Ah. I mentioned García, but the subject was the copper mines in Pinar del Río Province."

"Copper mines? What connection does García have to mining?"

"The mines are under the control of the Ministry of Basic Industries. García is a deputy minister."

"Yes, but did you write any articles about García that also mentioned the nuclear reactors in Cienfuegos Province, at Juraguá?"

Slowly shaking his head, José said, "In the past I've written about nuclear energy. I said it was expensive and unsafe, and we should abandon it. I didn't mention García in those articles. He was involved in the nuclear industry, but that predated my interest in it."

Their chairs were drawn closely together, and Anthony kept his voice low. "Let me ask another question. The Russians deny sending any uranium to Cuba. Is it possible that they did? And if so, could any of it have been diverted?"

"No. We never had any uranium."

"You're certain?"

"Absolutely certain. Castro invited scientists from the International Atomic Energy Agency to have a look. The United States was threatening to bomb the reactor site, so he wanted to prove that we had no uranium. What's the matter? I gave the wrong answer?"

Leaning back in his chair, Anthony looked up through the vines that wound through the trellis. He had thought that Céspedes had told the CIA about uranium, but if there was none, the theory didn't hold up. Had García ordered Céspedes's death to silence him? Anthony believed this was so, but why?

"José, I need your opinion." Quickly he wove the events of the last days into a narrative that omitted any mention of Ramiro Vega. He began with Abdel García's demand that he find out what Omar Céspedes, the defector, had said to the CIA.

"García apparently thinks I have a direct connection to the CIA through my grandfather. When I told García I wasn't interested, he threatened to frame me as a Cuban agent. So I called some people I know and asked about Céspedes. This is what I found out. Among other things, Céspedes was talking about finishing the nuclear reactors. The Americans know it's bullshit, but it's the story I gave García. He said I was lying, and what else did Céspedes say? I told him that was all I could get. Last night Céspedes was shot dead outside his apartment in Washington. I believe that García was behind it."

"Mother of God," said José. "Why are you still in Havana?"

"State Security won't let me leave until Olga's murder is cleared up."

"Ah, yes. That's right. Ramiro Vega could help you, no? He's not without power in the government—"

"Don't worry, I have a way out if I need it. José, what did García expect me to give him? What am I looking for?"

José lifted his glasses to rub his eyes. He remained motionless with his eyes closed, then said, "The last time the police searched my house—a year ago?—they confiscated all my notes. I had a source, a friend, with Geominera, the company in charge of the mines. They're part of MINBAS. Geominera was participating in a copper mine with a Canadian company, and my friend told me that the Canadians were always complaining about sloppy procedures. Very bad inventory system. Incompetence. It's what you get when you put military men in charge of industry. That was the point of my article. I mentioned Abdel García by name. The story was published in France, then picked up by the *Miami Herald*."

With a slight smile, José added, "And I was picked up by State Security and interrogated for two days. I thought I was on my way back to prison. If you're looking for radioactive material, you can find it in testing equipment. That was one of the complaints made by the Canadians. The stuff kept disappearing."

"It was stolen?"

"Stolen, lost, unaccounted for. Who knows?"

"What kind of tests do they do?"

"If I can remember. In mining, you mix crushed rock with water and send it through pipes to get it to the machines where they extract the ore. To know the percentage of rock, you send a beam through the pipe, like an X-ray. The instruments contain radioactive

materials. Cesium-137? I'm not sure. Anyway, equipment and parts
went missing from the zinc mines and a metal fabricating plant in
Rancho Boyeros, too. That's what I heard from my sources. I couldn't
prove it, so I simply wrote it down as a rumor. I'm a journalist, not
a fabulist. The government is supposed to keep a careful account-
ing, but in truth, they don't pay much attention."

"Why? Because the stuff isn't that potent?"

"No, because they're negligent. It's potent, all right. You don't
want to drop it down your shorts."

"What does it look like?" Anthony asked. "Is it powder? A
solid? Liquid? How would you get it out of the machine?"

José held up his hands. "I don't know, but the quantities are
small, and it isn't so very dangerous, not like plutonium. You
couldn't make an atomic bomb out of it."

Anthony remembered his conversation with Hector Mesa. Dirty
bombs. A small amount of radioactive material could be wrapped
with TNT in a bag and left in a place where crowds gather—
Grand Central Station, the Boston metro, a shopping mall in the
Midwest. Anywhere. Bombs could be detonated at the same time
in a dozen different cities. Scores of people could be killed. Or very
few. Its purpose was not destruction but terror. If radioactivity
were detected, the device could shut down the city.

"Ahhh," he murmured softly.

"What is it?" José asked.

He put a hand on José's shoulder. "I could be wrong, but assume that a group of officers at MINBAS, led by Abdel García,
have been stealing the radioactive materials used in industrial testing equipment. They disguise the losses as sloppy record-keeping,
then sell it on the black market."

Even in the dim light of the backyard, Anthony could see the
astonishment on José Leiva's face. "But . . . how could they accomplish that?"

"Easily. Abdel García used to be in charge of sending arms to
Africa and Central America. He would still have the contacts, no?
Céspedes was a nuclear engineer. He worked with García at Juraguá. Céspedes was in the process of telling the Americans about it
when García had him killed."

"Mother of Christ," said José. "If this is true—"

"It doesn't have to be true," Anthony said, "as long as people believe it. There was a report a couple of years ago that alleged the existence of a bioweapons laboratory east of Havana. A defector—someone like Céspedes—said he had worked there. The CIA found no credible evidence, but there are people who believe it. They will tell you that Cuba harbors terrorists. They will show you Castro's own words. In Iran he said that Cuba and the Ayatollah would bring the United States to its knees."

Glancing again at the kitchen window, Anthony saw a woman he didn't recognize. "Your guests are here." He picked up his empty bottle.

"A moment. What are you going to do now?"

"I hope you will introduce me."

José stopped him at the edge of the patio. "Leave Cuba as soon as you can. Go to your State Department with this information and tell them to make it public. They should confront Castro directly. That's what must be done. If they suspect, why haven't they made it known already?"

"Because, José, they aren't sure who's involved. They won't accuse García if Fidel Castro is behind it, nor will they tell Castro anything until they know what is going on." It was clear now to Anthony why the CIA wanted Ramiro Vega, but he would not discuss that with José. He added, "I assume that the Americans are looking for proof. They won't move until they have it."

"Everything comes from the top," José said. "Castro is a spider at the center of the web. Nothing happens in Cuba without his knowledge."

"I don't believe that Castro would sell radioactive materials to terrorists. He may be getting old, but he's not crazy. It's García. That's why he had Céspedes killed."

"You're wrong," said José. "Castro is behind it. Look at him. Look. He lives to confront the great enemy to the north. You see the damage terrorism has already done to your country, not only to steel and bricks, but also to the spirit of the people. They are afraid. Your president reacts with belligerence, and the world is turning against you. Would Castro want to keep this momentum going? My friend, you know the answer."

Anthony shook his head. "I have no answers. You live with these ideas too long, you get paranoid. All I want, José, and maybe it's impossible, is to chart a course that doesn't take us into the rocks on this side or the other. I'm going to turn the information over to whoever I think can hear it and not go crazy. Who is that? I don't know. I have to think about it. But for now, let's go inside. Fix me a drink, and introduce me to your friends."

"Come on, then." José took the beer bottles and went over to rinse them out in the rain barrel he used for watering the yard. The rectangle of light from the window lit their way. "Mario called me this afternoon. He's going to pick up your daughter and bring her with him tonight."

"Angela mentioned it."

"I must thank her," José said. "He says he can't stay long because they're going dancing, but that's all right. We'll be happy to see him. If he does go to Miami, a pretty smile would get him there faster than the hope of a job."

José was setting the bottles on a rack to dry when Anthony heard a shout, then men's voices in the kitchen. A moment later the back door opened, and two men in plainclothes came down the steps. Their eyes searched the darkness.

They had come for José Leiva.

It was quick and efficient. No guns were drawn, no handcuffs used. The plainclothes men were from State Security; the uniforms from the *Policía Nacional*. There were a dozen in all, some to wait outside and keep the neighbors away, others to search the house and take the suspect into custody.

They let José Leiva sit in his chair in the living room while they showed him the warrant and did some paperwork. Everyone else, including his wife, was told to wait on the front porch. Yolanda stood by the door with her eyes locked on José. Her friends formed a barricade around her and glared at the police. When Gail's mother broke into tears, Gail found a chair for her. Anthony wiped sweat off his neck and ground his teeth together. When asked, he gave State Security their names and explained why they had come. He asked why the police were there. The officer said it was none of his concern.

Anthony said, "Do you like doing this? Does it make you proud to be Cuban?"

Yolanda looked around and said, "Anthony. It's all right."

By then, the guests were arriving for the meeting. Some saw the police cars and kept going. Others parked nearby and stood in the yard. There were shouts, accusations. The police saw a flash and took away someone's camera.

Looking in through the front window, Anthony saw a face he recognized. Álvaro Sánchez came into the living room from the hall. A policeman behind him carried a stack of equipment, including the notebook computer Anthony had just brought from Miami. He went to the door and called to Sánchez.

The detective's manner was less cordial than before, but their acquaintance from two days ago was enough to provide a connection. Sánchez said that José Leiva would be taken in for questioning in the Saavedra case. However, that was not the reason for his arrest. They had also received information about contraband items in his house. If Leiva had no permit for the computer, it was illegal. The fax machine, the Internet connection—

Anthony asked who had given them this information. A neighbor? The spy in the house across the street? Sánchez said he was sorry. He told Anthony to wait with the others. When Anthony continued to look at him, Sánchez turned away and went back into the library.

State Security opened desk drawers and dumped papers into a box. From the door Yolanda argued with them. José Leiva told her not to worry about it. They could take what they wanted.

Anthony heard yelling and crossed the porch to see a young man in a white shirt struggling to get past the police. Gail said, "Is that Mario?"

One of the officers raised his baton. Anthony got there in time to pull Mario out of the way. The officer's baton glanced off Anthony's shoulder, but he felt nothing. He put his arm across Mario's neck and pulled him backward. "They will take you too. Stop it! Mario, your mother needs you."

The boy suddenly went still, but his breathing was fast, and his eyes shot fire. The officers lowered their sticks. When Anthony turned Mario toward the house, Angela ran from the crowd and put her arm around his waist, clinging tightly, so that they held Mario between them. Her lips moved with silent profanities.

Mario stopped walking. He reached into his hip pocket and took out a sealed envelope, folded in half. "Mr. Quintana, I don't want to forget this. Would you please give it to my mother on Sunday?"

"She's inside. You can give it to her yourself."

"No, she would open it now, and I want her to read it later."

Anthony nodded and took the envelope. When they reached the porch, Mario went to his mother and embraced her. She took him to the front door, and he spoke to his father. A few minutes later, one of the men from State Security told Leiva to get up. The police directed everyone to move back.

Leiva kissed his wife and son and told them he would be home in a few days. He smiled at Anthony. "Take care of them for me, my friend."

34

Ramiro Vega sat behind his desk shifting papers from one pile to another, putting some aside but tossing most of them into a cardboard box, which was already overflowing. Anthony had watched the level in the bottle of Canadian Club go in the other direction. The bottle and a shot glass sat at a precarious angle on some folders. Leaning around them, Ramiro reached for a stack of mail, but instead picked up a small white stone glued to a piece of varnished wood.

"Ha! Look at this." He showed Anthony. "It's from Pico Turquino, the summit. My Pioneer group made the hike. I was fourteen. It rained. The only good thing about the trip was I lost my virginity. Should I take this with me? Why not? It would fit in my pocket." Ramiro slammed the piece against the edge of his desk and peeled away the stone.

"When are you going to make the disk?" Anthony said.

"I'll do most of it tonight. I won't be getting much sleep, that's certain. Marta is crying with her head under the pillow. If we had a dog, I would be sharing his blanket. The kids don't know we're leaving. They think mami and papi are having another fight."

He swung his chair around toward the computer on the table behind him and fumbled with the drawer of a small plastic cabinet. He removed a blank compact disk. "Most of my notes are here. Some at my office. I'll finish it there and clean out my computer. This one too."

"Make an extra," Anthony said.

"Why? It's safe with me."

"Ramiro, if the disk is damaged, you will have only your word that this goes no higher than García. I don't think that will be enough."

"The disk will be next to my heart. Very safe." As Ramiro propped it against the monitor, he noticed a cable draped over the keyboard. He picked it up and squinted at the end of it, then followed the cable to a USB port. He pulled it out. "The kids have been in here again with their games and their music. I hope I don't press the wrong keys and make a collection of rap songs." He looped the cable and handed it across the desk. "This is Karen's, I think."

"Ramiro, let me have a copy to give to Bookhouser. A thousand things could happen."

He finished the whisky in his glass. *"Cin-cin."* As he drank it down in one gulp, the light slid over his bald head. He wiped his wiry gray mustache with the back of his hand. "Anthony, my brother, I am sorry, but . . . no. You, I trust. It's the people around you that make me think twice. Ernesto Pedrosa. Forgive me. And Bill Navarro. God save us, what a disaster that would be! Don't worry. I'm going to take very good care of it."

The whisky had not cut off Ramiro's ability to understand what he needed to do. Get the proof out of Cuba that Abdel García, not the Cuban regime, planned to divert radioactive materials to the international black market. The files had to reach the Intelligence Committee.

About a year ago, Omar Céspedes had made Ramiro an offer: evidence against García in exchange for $50,000 in an offshore account. Céspedes had worked under García; he had documents, notes, and records. He told Ramiro that García wanted to be ready when the *comandante* made his final departure. If events turned against him, he would have enough money not to worry about it. Ramiro recognized the motivation—he had it himself. He had observed García becoming more unstable, but he didn't believe the general would become involved with terrorists. Céspedes assured him it was so.

To confirm this story, Ramiro quietly investigated his boss through his own connections at the Ministry. He put the information into encrypted files and waited for the right time to use it. And then Omar Céspedes defected. He betrayed Cuba, and Ramiro lost his best ally. Who would believe a story that had come from a traitor? The documents wouldn't be enough against a master of innu-endo like Abdel García. The general had friends who didn't like Ramiro Vega's quick rise to power. Unfortunately for Ramiro, he was not innocent. He had profited by doing favors for his business associates: over a quarter of a million dollars in an account in the Caymans—minus what he'd paid to Céspedes for the files on García.

Anthony asked him why he'd accepted the money. He couldn't spend it; Marta would have noticed.

It's a key in the door, Ramiro told him. It gave him freedom. It gave him the confidence to push, to criticize, to move ahead. And it had made him a little too reckless. García had found out. And now, to save his skin, Ramiro had to make a deal with the Ameri-cans. All he had to offer them were the files. To make only one copy was a risk, but Ramiro didn't trust anyone. Anthony couldn't say that his brother-in-law was entirely wrong.

Spinning his chair around, Ramiro grabbed the desk and abruptly came to a stop. "What a mountain of shit. I can't be ready to go in two days. It would take two months." He picked up the stack of letters, glanced through them, then flung them into the trash box with such violence that it tipped over. Ramiro got out of his chair and kicked it across the room. He stared at the papers scattered across the floor. "Let them find it this way." He picked up the box, set it back by his desk, and opened another drawer.

He laughed. "I am reminded of a joke. Capitalism is a trash can filled with useless material objects. TVs, Cadillacs, Rolex watches. Communism is the same trash can, but it's empty."

When Anthony only looked back at him across the desk, Ramiro pulled out another drawer and lifted out more papers, which he threw into the box. "I should have let Olga leave Cuba when she asked me. You say she was unconscious at the first blow. Should that make me feel better?"

"She wanted me to help her get away," Anthony said. "I'm sorry I didn't, but we can't blame ourselves."

"Then you have no conscience." Ramiro looked into an enve-lope, then tossed it into the box. "She thought someday we would have a house in Spain. That was her fantasy. She was mine. I am Marta's fantasy. Everyone has a fantasy. It's hard to exist without one. I should be grateful for Olga. You know, if not for her, I would not have my little savings account."

"Did you tell Marta?"

"Are you crazy?" Ramiro smiled. "It's bad enough she thinks I'm a traitor. If she knew I was a traitor *and* a thief, she would kill me. What a trap I've made for myself! If I stay, the army will kill me. If I leave, my wife will kill me." Ramiro sighed. "No. Marta wouldn't do that. She loves me. How did your parents produce such a foolish woman? I knew she would come with me. But telling her! I've been less terrified in combat. 'My love, would you and the kids like to see Disney World?' "

With the lip of the bottle at his glass, Ramiro said. "I should make some coffee." He screwed the cap on. "Go to bed, my brother. Why are you still here? Your wife is waiting."

"I want you to do something for me. Have José Leiva released from jail."

"What? I can't. He's under preventive detention in a murder case."

"He didn't kill Olga Saavedra."

"He had a motive. And where was he? The police say he wasn't home when she died. No alibi."

"What happened between him and Olga Saavedra was six years ago."

"I can't tell the Ministry of the Interior what to do. Besides, there are other reasons to hold him. Leiva is a provocateur, a mouthpiece for the Americans. He whines about human rights as a cover for what he really wants—a Wal-Mart on the Malecón."

"That is not funny," Anthony said.

"I am so sorry."

"Are you the one who informed on him? The detective told me that they had a tip. Was that you?"

"No. It wasn't." Ramiro started leafing through the papers again.

"Do you want me to beg? All right. I am begging you, Ramiro. On your way out of Cuba, do one last, decent thing. Have him released. You can find some way to do it—"

"If he's released, they will only lock him up again sooner or later."

"I believe I can persuade him to leave. I can have a boat here within hours. Bookhouser said he would get U.S. visas for them.

I'll have no trouble with that, but I can't do it if Leiva is in custody."

"He *should* be in custody. He and his lot are dangerous because of their phony pacifism. They would be more honest if they had mortars and rockets."

"It is *you* who are defecting, and *Leiva* is dangerous?"

"Why do you come here? Marta and I feed you and give you a place to stay, and you go behind our backs to help the opposition. I may be a traitor, but I'm not a hypocrite."

Anthony was around the desk in three steps, his fists on the front of Ramiro's shirt. "Make your jokes. No one is laughing. If you weren't drunk, I would kill you myself." He dropped Ramiro back into his chair.

Ramiro knocked his hand away. "It's a funny world. I will tell you who informed on Leiva. Your son."

"You're lying!"

"I wish that I were. He asked Giovany what to do if he had information about a murder. Gio took him to the police. Tonight, after Gio heard your daughter crying, he came to me and asked if he had done the right thing. I said he should have come to me first, but yes, he and his cousin had a duty to report it."

Anthony took a step away and nearly stumbled. He righted himself on a corner of the desk. "Danny. Oh, God."

Straightening his shirt collar, Ramiro returned to his stack of papers. "I'm sorry that I had to tell you. Leave me alone now, my brother. It's late."

The feeling of helplessness was as heavy as grief. Gail lay on her side and stared at the cartoon faces over the baby crib. She had tried to read José Leiva's essays, thinking she might know enough words to understand his meaning, but her eyes wouldn't focus on the page.

After the *jodido* State Security cops had taken José Leiva away, they had taken his books. Not *all* the books. Not the encyclopedias and old *National Geographic* magazines in Spanish, or the children's books and medical texts. Not the boring stuff. They'd taken the books it would be hard to replace. The bastards had cleaned out the library, which they had no goddamn right to do because it wasn't illegal to have books. They had kept throwing things into boxes and carrying the boxes out to their van. Gail had demanded that Anthony ask them what they thought they were doing, but he told her to stay out of the way. Yolanda said she didn't mind if they took the books, if they would just read them. They showed Yolanda a receipt and told her to sign it. They gave her a copy. She closed the door.

The house was full of their friends, and everyone stayed around talking, trying to decide what to do next, what foreign news organizations to contact, what the strategy should be. Finally Yolanda asked them all to go. She was tired, and Mario would be with her. In the morning she would look for a lawyer for her husband.

When they got home, Angela ran upstairs sobbing, and Irene went to her room with a bottle of wine. The house was too quiet. Nothing from the boys' room. Marta had her door locked, and Ramiro had closed himself in his study. Karen said they'd been screaming at each other, and Janelle had worn herself out crying about it. Gail told Karen what had happened to José, but she didn't have much success making Karen understand it. She told her to go back to bed; they'd talk in the morning.

Gail reached over and turned off the lamp on the nightstand. A minute later, she got out of bed, turned on the overhead light, and started rearranging their clothes. She couldn't pack the suitcases. Although they would be leaving on Saturday, everything had to appear normal until the last minute.

Pulling out one drawer after another, Gail filled them in order of priority, reserving the top left drawer for things they'd need to grab if they had five minutes to get out of the house. It was a grim variation on what she did every time the Miami TV stations posted a hurricane warning.

She heard footsteps in the hall. The door opened. Anthony came in and put a coiled computer cable on the dresser. "Karen left this in Ramiro's study. I think it goes to her PDA."

After he had stood there without moving for several more seconds, Gail asked him if he was all right.

He looked around. "Ramiro says that Abdel García is working on his own."

"Thank God. How did Ramiro find out about it?"

"Omar Céspedes told him, in exchange for fifty grand. Ramiro was looking for something on García, because García had something on him." Anthony sat on the end of the bed and took off his shoes. "Ramiro was moving up quickly in the ranks, and García doesn't share his power willingly. Their friendship is a pretense. García had Ramiro by the throat. He knew he'd been taking kickbacks. Ramiro got some of them from the copper mines, if you can believe that irony. Omar Céspedes helped Ramiro with dates, shipments, lists of what came in, what went out. People would look the other way while technicians stole radioactive materials out of the storage rooms. Ramiro has proof of what García and his group were doing. It's on encrypted files. He'll put everything on a disk, then he'll destroy the hard drive."

"I suppose he told Marta they're leaving," Gail said. "She hasn't come out of her room, but Karen said there was a lot of yelling and screaming a few hours ago."

Anthony nodded. "He told her."

"Well?"

"She'll go with him."

"The kids too?"

"He didn't say. Probably." Anthony wearily let out a breath.

Gail stood between his knees and smoothed his hair off his forehead. "You want to take a shower? There's some hot water left. I saved it for you."

"Thank you. Come here, *bonboncita,* give me a kiss. I need one."

She laughed a little and put her mouth to his. She felt some of the tension let go from his shoulders. He buried his face in her stomach for a second, kissed each breast through her nightgown, then gently moved her aside and stood up.

He saw the open drawers of the built-in closet. "What are you doing with our clothes?"

"Pre-packing," she said. "In case we have to run for it."

He smiled. "Don't worry. That won't happen." Squinting toward the ceiling, he said, "That light is ripping my eyes out."

"Turn it off, then."

The room was dark for a moment. Gail turned on the lamp by the bed, and a soft golden glow fell on the nightstand and the pillow on her side. Anthony pulled his shirt out of his pants and unbuttoned it. "I asked Ramiro if he would use his influence to get José Leiva out of jail. He won't do it. He says Leiva is a threat to the state."

"Does he really believe that?"

"Yes."

"*Why?*"

He replied with a shrug, lifting his hands.

"Anthony, I couldn't believe what was happening. They just pushed in there and took everything! I wanted to scream or hit somebody. It was worse for you, wasn't it? You're always rushing to the rescue, and there wasn't anything you could do."

His shirt was open, and when Gail put her arms around him, she felt the warmth of his skin through her silk nightgown.

He said, "Tomorrow morning I'm going with Yolanda to find a lawyer for José. There are some good ones, but they cost more. I want to make sure she gets the right person and that she has enough money for pay for it."

Gail could feel the pressure on her heart, the ache that radiated into her throat. She didn't want to be jealous. Not now, when Yolanda had just seen her husband taken by police for something he hadn't done. On the way home in the car, when Anthony had said nothing, and the silence had been broken only by Angela's weeping from the backseat, Gail had thought: *Oh, God. If José Leiva dies in prison, Yolanda will want Anthony, and he will go back to her.* Selfish, stupid thoughts. Gail wanted to be better than that, but she wasn't.

Through the window she heard the branches of a tree move across the house. A bird fluttered, and its call faded away.

Anthony's arms were around her, but his attention was somewhere else. "It's a pretty night. I used to sleep outside in the winter when I was a kid. You wouldn't believe the stars in central Cuba. Like the sky was dipped in milk."

She wiped her cheek and cleared her throat before she said, "I'll be glad to get home, though. Won't you?"

"Yes. Very glad. I will never come back here."

His words were so flat, so unexpected, that she had to ask, "Why? I don't understand."

"You won't believe this, Gail, because I'm going to sound like my grandfather. By being here, I support what they do. I tried to walk in the middle, to understand both sides of it, to be fair. Well, I do understand both sides, but I can only choose one. Tonight was too much. I won't be back."

Shifting so he could look at her, he turned her toward the light. "Hey. What is this? Don't tell me you want to stay."

She laughed. "No. Listen, Anthony, if you don't mind, I'd like to come with you and Yolanda tomorrow. Would that be all right?"

"Of course. It's going to be boring. A lot of waiting around. I thought maybe you had things to do."

She sobbed once, and put her head on his shoulder.

"Sweetheart—" He lifted her face. "What is going on?" His brows came together, and his eyes were so dark she felt she could float into them like opening her arms and falling slowly into the sea. He turned her toward the light and looked at her, then held her face in his hands.

"What are you thinking? No, no, no." He kissed her slowly, softly. "*Mi rubia linda.* Gail, it's you I love. It will always be you."

anny was on an errand with the Brat. As they walked, Karen stayed about ten feet behind him. At the corner he checked to see if she was still there before he went across. He got to the median and waited under a tree. It was like waiting for a dog, except worse because Karen was doing it on purpose to piss him off.

They had to pick up some bread and a cake from Pain de Paris. Mrs. Connor had given them twenty dollars and a list. If there was any money left, they could have it. The problem was, the twenty was in the pocket of Karen's jeans.

On the other side of Fifth, Danny stood on the sidewalk while Karen caught up. She was almost as tall as he was, but skinny as a straw, and her bangs hung in her eyes. She got within a few feet and stopped, only starting again when he did.

Danny looked over his shoulder. "So, Karen, what kind of cake are you going to get?"

"A Charlotte. Why?"

"I hate that cream stuff. It has no taste."

"I like it."

"Nobody else does."

"Yes, they do. It's Mrs. Vega's favorite."

"A Charlotte costs like twelve bucks. If you buy a Charlotte, we won't have enough money to get something for ourselves."

"Look, Danny. You're only coming along because my grandmother wouldn't allow me to go by myself. It isn't your money."

"You're so fucking selfish. I can't believe you," Danny said.

The day had started out bad. His father had knocked on the door at eight o'clock in the morning and told Gio to leave. Then he reamed Danny out for telling the police about José Leiva. *Deeply disappointed in you. Why did you do it?* Danny hadn't seen him so mad in a long time. *Put you on a fucking plane right back to New Jersey.* Danny had started crying. He hated that, crying in front of his father. It wasn't because he felt sorry for calling the police. It was knowing that whatever he did, he and his dad would never get along. His father went out and slammed the door. A minute later a car started. They were going to find a lawyer for Leiva. *To try to repair some of the damage you have done.*

Angela overheard it, naturally, and now she wouldn't speak to him. Gio took off with his friends, didn't even tell Danny he was going. The general was in his study with the door locked. Janelle was freaking out because nobody was paying attention to her party. Aunt Marta was just freaking out, screaming at whoever spoke to her. Was Danny responsible for all of that?

Cobo was supposed to drive Karen, but when Mrs. Connor went up to knock on his door, he didn't answer. Drunk again, probably. And so Danny got stuck with escorting Karen to the bakery. She didn't like it either.

They walked on Nineteenth Street like that, with him in front and the Brat behind him. A few blocks later he saw the yellow-and-white striped awning of the bakery. He opened the glass door, held it, then let it go just as Karen got there. She caught it with her sneaker.

There was a crowd picking up sandwiches for lunch, and the place smelled of coffee. Behind a window, a guy in a white jacket was making espresso. Finally they got to the front of the line, and Danny told Karen to give him the list. He read it in Spanish to the lady behind the counter. Baguette, rolls, two croissants, and a Paris cake. Plus two of those eclairs and two boxes of orange juice. "Karen, you want a juice, right?"

"Sure. Did you order a Charlotte?"

"Yes, Karen, I ordered a Charlotte. Give her the money. It's nineteen-fifty."

Danny looked around the bakery. There were a couple of blond tourist girls at a table by the window. They were from England. He could hear their accents.

When Karen saw what the clerk was putting in the box, her face screwed up. "That's the wrong one!"

Danny reached over and stuck his finger in the icing and licked it off. "Too late."

"I didn't want that cake!"

"Come on, it's better than a Charlotte. Look, I bought you a chocolate eclair."

"*You* bought it? That wasn't your money!"

"Well, do you want this or not? I can eat both of them."

She grabbed the bag out of his hand and looked into it to make sure he wasn't lying. He handed her the orange juice and she jabbed her straw through the hole in the box.

"You could say thank you," he said.

"For *what*?"

When he took the bag from the clerk, Danny rolled his eyes toward Karen. The lady smiled at him, and he told her to have a good day.

They were in the parking lot when he noticed his orange juice wasn't in the bag. "Oh, shit, I left my juice. Hold this."

Karen took the bag over to the curb at the edge of the parking lot and sat down to eat her eclair. Danny went back in, said excuse me to some people in the way, and got his juice off the top of the glass case.

One of the tourist girls motioned for him to come over. "Do you speak English?"

"Yes."

"Great. You look like you do."

"What does that look like?"

The girls giggled.

"They gave me this cappuccino, and I really wanted ice in it." The way she was sitting, he could look down the front of her shirt and see everything. The other girl had a tube top, and marks from a bathing suit cut through her sunburn.

"I can fix that for you." He took her cup to the window. He told the man the English lady wanted it *con hielo*, with ice. He waited, then took the glass to the table.

"Thanks, it's perfect. Are you American?"

"Cuban. I live near New York, but a lot of my family's here. My uncle's a general in the army."

"A general!" They giggled again.

He glanced out the window, but a car was in the way, and he couldn't see the other side of the parking lot.

The girls asked where a good beach was. They didn't want to drive all the way to Varadero. Danny told them to go to *Playas del Este*. "It's not far."

"Could you just show us on this map?"

He leaned over and traced the route with his finger. "There are like three or four beaches, but this one is best."

"Thanks." She drew a circle with her pen.

"Well, nice meeting you."

"Bye," they said in unison.

Danny picked up his juice and went outside. The curb was empty. He saw a small white bag on the ground. He walked to the corner of the building, but there was nothing back there but a steel door and some cans.

"What the hell?"

He walked out to the sidewalk and looked up and down the street, but he didn't see any skinny girls with long hair. He went next door to the video store, but it was closed.

Danny stood on the sidewalk with his hands on his hips. There was only one answer. The Brat had taken off without him. He wasn't worried. Havana wasn't New York City.

He went back inside to help the English girls with their directions.

36

Gail noticed that Anthony's knuckles had turned white. He held on to the steering wheel as if he wanted to rip it out. He was furious with himself for not being able to help José Leiva. Eighteen years of practicing criminal defense law in the United States meant nothing. He had $1,000 cash in his wallet, the amount Yolanda had said would buy a good lawyer. In the U.S. this wouldn't have paid for a D.U.I. defense.

"Do you know there are only *one hundred* defense lawyers in Cuba?"

"I didn't know that," Gail said.

"And they're all working for the government."

"Well . . . so are our public defenders."

"Our P.D.s don't roll over," Anthony said. "They're a pain in the ass to the system, as they should be. This is useless. Yolanda won't find a lawyer who will take the case, not for a thousand, not for ten thousand."

"Why not?"

"Because there's not a fucking thing that can be done."

"Being here is something." Gail touched his face. "Don't let her see you like this."

He blew out a breath through his teeth and guided the car through the tunnel under the river and out the other side.

The lawyer Yolanda would talk to was part of a *bufete colectivo* in Central Havana. The building, once the home of a wealthy merchant family, had been converted into law offices in the 1920s. After the Revolution, lawyers became employees of the state. In theory they would charge all their clients the same low fee in Cuban pesos; in reality, the best lawyers demanded a premium in dollars.

The friends of José Leiva had gathered in a corner of a waiting room that Gail found astonishingly luxurious. Air conditioned, quiet, lots of polished wood. Stained glass above the windows put curves of blue and red on the tile floor. Yolanda Cabrera sat between two women whose own husbands were in prison. Gail asked what for. One had put an X through Fidel's face on a poster. The other had handed out copies of an Amnesty International report.

It was unreal, impossible. Gail had heard of this; she'd lived in Miami all her life hearing such things, but now she felt she had walked into a surreal play, and these people were actors. No one really went to prison for drawing an X on a poster, not in the twenty-first century.

Her chair was next to that of a robust man in his late sixties named Carlos Portal. He had presented Anthony with his card: *Comité de Derechos Humanos.* Committee on Human Rights— one of many such groups that the government tolerated. Portal held a straw fedora on his knee. His English was lousy, but he insisted on speaking it so that *la señora de Quintana* would understand.

Portal had found out that José Leiva had not yet been formally charged with anything. They had taken him in for questioning in the murder of Olga Saavedra. They were also looking into a charge of possessing enemy propaganda. Portal didn't think the murder case would go anywhere. As for the other case . . .

"If they make a case for a political crime, you are guilty. That's it. If they arrest José for the political crime, he have a trial in two or three weeks. It is very hard to find a lawyer, very hard—no because the lawyer is afraid. The reason is, why to take a case if you know you lose?" Portal reached over and squeezed Yolanda's hand. "I don' give her bad news. She know already. This man is a lawyer of skill. Maybe he get less years for José. If the prosecutor say for ten years, maybe the lawyer get eight years."

Gail's lips moved soundlessly. *My God.*

"They can do what they want," Yolanda said calmly. "If José is in prison, I will do his work, and if they want me to stop, they'll have to put me in prison, too."

A murmuring went through the group gathered around her, and one of the men nodded. "They will have to take all of us."

"Can he be released on bail?" Anthony asked. *"Una fianza?"*

"I don't think so, on the murder case, no," Portal said. "On the political case, it's possible. House arrest is possible."

"The lawyer could do that much, couldn't he?"

Portal let a shrug stand as his reply.

The others started talking again about what they would do if José was indicted. Gail could read Anthony's thoughts. Hire the goddamned attorney to arrange house arrest. Forget the effing trial. Put José and Yolanda and Mario on a boat and get them the hell out of here.

Ever since finding Olga Saavedra's body, a memory had gone in and out of Gail's consciousness. Whenever it had occurred to her that she should mention it, Anthony had not been there, and when he had been, other events had crowded it out. The memory came again with such force that Gail felt the impact in her stomach, a queasy sense of dread. For several minutes she stared into the stained glass over the window, hearing but understanding not a word of the Spanish flowing around her.

She put a hand on his coat sleeve. "Anthony." When he finally looked around, she whispered, "Come outside with me."

Anthony told Yolanda they would be back in a few minutes. He followed Gail out the door and down the front steps. He asked her what was wrong. Pedestrians walked around them, and next door a crowd waited in line to get into a dollar store. Gail went the other way, and when they reached a place where no one could hear them, she reached for his hand.

"I have to talk to you about Marta. This might mean nothing at all, but you should know." Holding onto his arm, she told him what she had seen two days ago from the back terrace of his sister's house. Marta answering the phone, leaving quickly, coming back with Cobo, who vanished into his garage apartment. Marta closing herself in her room, washing out her clothes in the sink, explaining that she had dropped a carton of yogurt at the market.

"Anthony, she went to the market and didn't bring anything back."

Through pursed lips he took some breaths to steady himself. "*Ay, Dios mío.*"

"What do you want to do?" she asked.

"Yolanda is with her friends. She's all right. I'll tell them we have to leave."

When they arrived home, Gail watched Anthony walk up the stairs to the second level, then turn left out of sight. She heard a knock, then his baritone voice asking if he could come in. The door opened. Closed.

Gail leaned against the curved railing and looked around the empty living room. She wondered if Marta had canceled delivery of the tables and chairs for the party. The street was quiet, and in the other direction, the mid-afternoon sun slanted through the trees. Someone had left the sliding doors open, and she could hear the birds. Ramiro had left early for his office, and his son had taken off even earlier. Everyone else was in their rooms, probably packing. Anthony had told his kids that they might be leaving a little earlier than planned.

What would become of this house? It would be confiscated, she assumed, along with the years' worth of things the Vegas had collected, from the Limoges china once used by Marta's great-grandmother, to the awards Giovany had won for his swim team.

"Gail?"

Irene had come out of her room, a small nook with a sofa bed and an old upright piano. Her baggy red sweatpants and an oversized T-shirt meant she'd been inside all day, probably putting her things back into her suitcases.

"Hi, Mom. Yolanda is still waiting to speak to the lawyer. She seems all right. We're not sure about José. Maybe he can get out on bail. Anthony wants to talk them into coming to Florida. After this, they might listen."

"I hope so." Irene's hands were at her heart. "Honey, I'm a little worried about Karen. I sent her to the bakery with Danny. That was over three hours ago, and they aren't back yet."

"Danny probably wanted to go somewhere else. You know how he is. They didn't call?"

"No. I would have heard it. The phone hasn't rung."

"Well, he wouldn't have just left her," Gail said.

"I'm sure he wouldn't."

Irene's head turned toward a noise from upstairs, a long wail, muffled by distance and the thickness of a bedroom door. The wail turned to sobbing. There were voices. Then silence.

"What in the world?"

Gail said, "Anthony had to talk to Marta about something."

"Is everything all right?" Irene laughed. "Well, obviously not. Gail, it's been crazy around here. Anthony was screaming at Danny this morning so loudly it woke me up, and after you and he left, Marta started. If it wasn't Marta, it was Janelle, and then Angela wanted to go look for Mario, and I said absolutely not. Karen wouldn't stop asking me what was going on, and you know I couldn't tell her anything. I sent her to the bakery with Danny just to get her out of my hair, if you want to know the truth, but if something happened to her, I will never forgive myself."

"Mother, she's fine."

"You think so?"

"They're probably just having a good time and forgot."

"That must be it," Irene said.

Gail couldn't imagine Danny wanting to hang around with Karen, or vice versa. Perhaps they had called a truce. She crossed to the front windows. "They have to be all right. He's sixteen, and he's not small. And you know Karen wouldn't go anywhere with a stranger." She turned around and saw that her mother's forehead was still creased.

Irene said, "This isn't like Karen. She was supposed to go to the bakery and come right back. She's always very good about that."

"If she's with Danny, I'm sure nothing happened to them. Kids don't go missing in Havana." Gail looked out the window again. "Where's Cobo? If it would make you feel better, we'll send him to look for them."

"I thought of that, but he doesn't answer his door. He must have taken Ramiro to work. I didn't dare knock on Marta's door."

"When Anthony comes down, I'll ask him for the car keys," Gail said.

Irene nodded, then noticed what she had on. "I should change clothes. Don't I look a mess, though?" She went back to her room, and Gail went to stand by the windows. After a few minutes of staring at an empty yard, she opened the door to stare out at the street.

She turned around when Anthony's footsteps sounded on the stairs. He looked at her from halfway down, glanced to see if anyone else was about, then came the rest of the way. Gail followed him through the dining room out onto the patio. The sun had gone behind the trees to send shadows across the yard.

"It was Cobo," Anthony said. "He went over to Olga's to talk to her, they argued, and he killed her."

Releasing a breath, Gail put her forehead on his shoulder. "It wasn't Marta. Thank God. What happened? Can you tell me?"

"He called her from Olga's on his cell phone in a panic. She said she'd call him back, and she jumped into the minivan. She told him what to do. To clean everything he touched. Fingerprints, footprints. Not to leave anything behind. She parked a few blocks away, and when he was finished, she picked him up and brought him here. He had some bloody towels with him in a bag. When he got in the car, one fell out and landed on her. That's what you heard outside her door, Marta washing the blood off of her clothes. She said she had to help him. If anybody had found out, it would have been bad for Ramiro. Not to mention Janelle's party on Saturday."

Laughing wearily, Anthony put his hands on top of his head and walked to the edge of the patio. "My sister."

Gail looked up at the windows of the master bedroom at the other end of the house. The louvers were closed. She said quietly, "How is she?"

"Marta? Covering up a murder was easy. It's leaving here that's making her crazy. I told her that Cobo is going down for this."

"She's an accessory after the fact," Gail said.

"Not if she and Ramiro are out of Cuban jurisdiction as of tomorrow night, a fact that Cobo doesn't know about."

"Well, how are you going to turn him in?" Gail asked. "We're not planning to stick around, are we?"

"Before we take off, I'll give this information to Yolanda's friend, Carlos Portal. I won't tell him about Marta, just Cobo. He can find a way to get the information to the police. Cobo doesn't impress me as the kind of guy who could stand up to an interrogation. I think he'll crack."

"Does that mean José would be released?"

"Probably. If José can shake this murder investigation, he has a chance of getting out on bail. I could have them out of Cuba that same night."

"I'll say a prayer." Gail took Anthony's arm. "Listen, I hate to bother you with this right now, but Danny and Karen left over three hours ago to walk to the bakery, and they aren't home yet."

"They probably got interested in something and forgot the time."

"That's what I told Mother. She's worried about them. Actually, so am I."

"Karen is safe with Danny."

Anthony swung around to look at the garage. Two stories high, its yellow paint was faded and cracked. A window faced the backyard. The curtains were closed. "Where is Cobo?"

"Mother says he drove Ramiro to the Ministry this morning."

"No, I saw Ramiro leave. He drove himself."

"Well, she knocked on his door, and he didn't answer."

Anthony frowned. "When did you last see him?"

She thought about it. "When Marta brought him home."

"Two days ago." He looked at the garage a moment longer, then said, "Stay here."

A path had been worn through the grass, and Anthony followed it to the portico between the house and the garage. The living room furniture had been moved out here to make room for the *quinceañera*. Tarpaulins covered the sofas and chairs and side tables. Anthony went around the stacked furniture and up the stairs leading to the garage apartment. Gail hesitated, then ran after him. There was a landing at the top. The daylight leaking in through the decorative concrete block permitted a clear view.

Anthony knocked. Waited. He tested the doorknob. It turned. He swung the door inward. A few seconds passed. He stepped inside. She saw his hand reach out to flip a light switch.

Gail ran up the steps and looked into a room no wider than the single-car garage below it. Twin bed, small refrigerator, a table—

The image hit her brain before she could turn away, and she choked on the smell. A man seemed to be floating against the wall on the other side. His head was tilted, and his face was all wrong—a thick tongue and slits for eyes. His hands had gone puffy and dark brown.

Anthony turned around. "I told you not to come up!"

"Too late now," she said.

Cobo had hanged himself on a door. The rope around his neck went over the top of the door and into the room beyond, probably a bathroom. Gail couldn't see what the other end of the rope was tied to. He had stepped off a wooden chair, which lay on its side. A yellow chair with a rung missing. Funny to notice such details, she thought.

The window air conditioner was running; even so, Gail needed to breathe. She backed up and stood on the landing, concentrating on the worn-out jute doormat. "How long do you think he's been dead?"

"I don't know. It's cool in here, but he's starting to get ripe."

"Oh, lord, Anthony."

"I'd say he did it the night after Marta brought him home."

"Nobody even asked about him," she said. "Nobody missed him at all?"

"There was a lot going on."

"What about José?"

"He's basically screwed, unless Marta comes forward. I wouldn't advise it." Anthony's footsteps moved around the room. "There's no suicide note."

Gail ventured another look. Anthony was sitting on his heels next to a green plastic bag. "What's that?"

"The bloody towels." He carefully tipped the bag to show her. The fabric was more brown than white. He shook the bag and said, "Two or three of them."

"DNA," Gail said. "Can't they match the blood to Olga Saavedra?"

"I was thinking of that." He stood up. "I was also thinking that Ramiro and I should have another talk. He didn't want to help José. This might change his mind. He wouldn't want a body found on his property."

"What do you mean? No, you can't call the police. If they come over here, Ramiro won't be able to get out of Cuba."

"There is that to consider." Motioning for Gail to move, he came out and closed the door. He took a handkerchief from his pocket and wiped the doorknob.

Gail said, "We can't just leave him there."

"What would you suggest we do?"

She shook her head.

"It's not an easy choice. José Leiva or Ramiro Vega?" He smiled, but there was no humor in it. "Come on. Let's go make some decisions. We don't have much time."

They went through the portico and opened the kitchen door. Danny was standing by the refrigerator cracking ice cubes out of the tray. He looked around when Gail said, "Oh, Danny. I'm so glad you're back. Where's Karen?"

Danny looked from her to his father, then said, "I don't know."

Anthony said, "What do you mean, you don't know? Where is she?"

"I don't know, Dad. I just got here."

"You walked to the bakery together," Gail said. "Isn't she with you?"

"She left. I figured she came back here. I mean, she had the cake and everything."

"Danny, please," Gail said. "Where did she go?"

Irene ran into the kitchen. "What's going on? Is Karen home?"

"No! She's missing."

Anthony said, "Gail, calm down. She's probably fine." He pulled the ice tray out of Danny's hand and threw it back into the freezer and slammed the door. "What happened, Danny?"

"We— We were at the bakery, and I forgot my juice, so I went back inside, and when I came out, she wasn't there. She had the bag with the cake and stuff in it, so I thought she'd gone home."

"You didn't look for her?"

"Yes! I did! I looked all over the place. Maybe she stopped somewhere else."

"Karen doesn't do that," Gail said. "Karen wouldn't just go off by herself."

"Danny, listen to me. Did you see anyone? Did she speak to anyone?"

"No! She was right outside!"

Gail put her hands to her cheeks. "Oh, God!"

Anthony put an arm around her. "It's all right, Gail. We'll find her. I'll go to the bakery and ask who might have seen her." He took his car keys from his pocket. "Do you want to come with me? Or stay here and wait for her?"

"I'll come with you." Gail was aware of a phone ringing.

Danny said, "It wasn't my fault! I told her not to leave."

They were at the front door when Marta called down the stairs. "Anthony! Anthony, *teléfono*." Gail could see her standing at the upstairs railing in a robe. She was barefoot. She raked her hair out of her eyes. *"Es el general García. Quiere hablar contigo."*

Gail needed no translation. Abdel García wanted to talk to him.

nthony told his sister he would take the telephone call in Ramiro's study, and to hang up when he came on the line. Gail followed him across the living room and into the narrow hall. He allowed her to enter the windowless study ahead of him, then pushed the door shut. The heavy wood made a deep thump against the frame, closing out the noises of the house.

"Why is Abdel García calling you? What did Marta say?"

"I don't know what he wants." Anthony's face could have been cut from granite. He crossed the room toward the telephone on Ramiro's desk. *"Habla Quintana."*

His gaze drifted, unfocussed, and for a time that seemed to drag on and on he said nothing. Finally he spoke, but Gail could make no sense of it. Then she heard her daughter's name and ran toward him. She had to press her hand to her mouth to keep from crying out.

At last Anthony dropped the handset back into place.

"Karen! It's about Karen, isn't it?"

He put his hands on Gail's shoulders. "She's all right. García has her, but she isn't hurt in any way."

"He has her? Why? Where is she?"

"He wants Ramiro's files. I assume he wants to know exactly what evidence Ramiro has against him."

"What? I don't understand?"

"He wants the files," Anthony repeated. "If I give him the files, Karen can go."

"But you don't have them. Do you? You said Ramiro had to finish making a disk—"

"No, I don't have them, but I told García I did. I said we

needed time to get everything together. An hour. He'll call me back then on my cell phone."

"Where is Ramiro? We have to talk to him."

Anthony raised his hands. "Wait, I need to think."

"*Think?* I want García's superior officer notified. That general you talked to. Prieto. He won't let him get away with this!"

"Gail, stop! I can't call Prieto. I can't call anyone. If I involve the military or the police in any way, García said he would have Ramiro arrested. He can do it. He has the power. I can't allow that to happen. We have to get Ramiro and the files out of Cuba."

"But if he's leaving, it doesn't matter what we give García."

"It matters." Anthony began to pace nervously about the room. "If we give García the files, even a copy of the files, he will have a chance to rebut what is in them."

Gail swivelled to follow his motion. "Call Ramiro. Tell him he has to help us."

"No. I can't do that. Ramiro has to remain completely un-aware. He would do something. I know him. Then García would have him arrested, and that cannot happen."

"What do you mean? That filthy son of a bitch has Karen!"

"Listen to me." Anthony stopped in front of her. "García found out that Ramiro has been collecting evidence against him, but he isn't sure what it is. It's proof that García has been stealing nuclear materials. García, not Fidel Castro, not the regime. If he has the information, he will twist it to save himself. Céspedes told the Americans that Castro is orchestrating everything. It's a lie, but some of them, like Bill Navarro, believe it. Others don't. They need Ramiro Vega, and they need his files. You understand?"

She felt the panic rising in her throat. "Ramiro can tell them the truth. He can tell them."

"Yes. He can. But if García has a chance to make it look as though Ramiro is lying, who will the Americans believe? Céspedes? What will they do then? Wait until terrorists place a dirty bomb across from the White House? No, they will act. It would be a disaster."

With mounting horror, Gail said, "You want me to sacrifice my daughter?"

"I didn't say that."

"Karen has been kidnapped. To hell with your goddamned politics. I want my daughter back!"

"You'll have her, but I have to think how to do it."

"Anthony, please. I would die if anything happened to her." Gail's head began to spin, and she sagged against his chest.

"Nothing will happen to her. Come. Sit down." He led her to a chair. He crouched before her and took both her hands. With perfect assurance, his eyes sought hers, shifting back and forth as though searching for any doubt. A curve of white showed beneath the dark irises. "Don't be afraid. She is your blood, and I love her as I love you. You know that, don't you?"

"Anthony—"

"You know I would never let her come to harm. Don't you?"

"Yes." Gail's heart beat erratically.

"I will find her." Anthony's voice was low and steady. "I will bring her back to you safely. Whatever has to be done, I will do it. I swear it on my life."

"I hope you kill him. He's a monster. I want him dead."

Anthony kissed her face and hands. "Come with me. Let's go upstairs." He helped her from the chair and took his handkerchief from his pocket. "Wipe your eyes. We mustn't let the children see us afraid."

"I'm fine." She cleaned some smudges of mascara from beneath her lower lashes and gave the handkerchief back. "All right?"

He gave her a smile of reassurance.

When they came into the living room, Anthony's children were sitting on the stairs with Irene. Janelle and Marta looked down from the railing above.

Gail said, "Karen's all right. Someone picked her up, but she's fine. We're going go get her in a little while."

Irene reached up to squeeze Gail's hand. The touch said she knew there was more to it.

Anthony said, "Angela, sweetheart, would you bring some water to our room?"

Danny stared straight ahead, but as they passed, he said, "I'm sorry."

His father leaned down and kissed the top of his head. "We may be leaving tomorrow. I want you to pack your things. Please stay inside the house. Will you do that?"

"Yes, sir."

A few minutes later, when Angela came to the door with a tray and two glasses, Gail was by the window looking out at the street. Anthony had told her to lie down, but that was impossible.

She heard Anthony tell his daughter not to worry. He would tell her more later on, after Karen came home.

Angela said, "Mario's supposed to come over tonight. That's okay, isn't it?"

"No, better not. Try to get a message to him. Just say it's not convenient. Don't explain."

"What if he doesn't get the message?"

"Then he doesn't. *Gracias, m'ija.*"

Gail turned and exchanged a smile with Angela before Anthony closed the door. He poured a glass of water, which Gail drank thirstily. The water soothed the ache in her throat. She watched Anthony tapping numbers into his cell phone. He put the phone to his ear.

"Who are you calling?"

His eyes shifted to meet hers. "Hector Mesa."

38

ario Cabrera used to sit on the wall beside the ship channel and play his flute for the fishermen. He would be paid in *aguardiente* and a few of the latest jokes. He liked these men, so he decided to give them the bags containing his clothes instead of leaving them on the street for just anyone to find. He had a bag in each hand as he walked up the street that bordered the channel.

Tomás walked with him. They had just put Nico on a train for Las Tunas, getting him out of the city before nightfall. He would be across Cuba by morning. Tomás would have helped carry the bags, but he was working on the communiqué. He wrote as he walked, looking up just often enough to keep from running into a light pole or another pedestrian. He asked Mario if this phrase or that one sounded all right, and whether they should mention Chachi's murder. Tomás wanted to keep the length down to one page. Mario said to write it however he wanted.

The communiqué would be e-mailed to CNN as soon as Vega was dead, and copies would be left at the university and in the lobbies of the biggest tourist hotels. Others would be scattered around the city.

"It is starting, Mario. None of the bastards will feel safe after this. The wall is about to come down. Future generations will read your name in history books."

Small boats were anchored close to shore, and La Fortaleza rose from the hill on the other side of the channel. The sidewalk was very wide and clean. Ahead of him, Mario could see the fishermen casting their lines.

Tomás put his notebook away. "Mario, I must talk to you. Stop for a minute. It's important."

Mario came to a halt and turned toward Tomás. He noticed again how pale he was. Tomás was a musician. Even worse, an intellectual. He lived in his books. His beard was sparse, and his Adam's apple moved when he talked. He had no color, except for his blue eyes, magnified by his glasses.

"Your father was arrested last night. Some of us are worried about your state of mind—specifically, your ability to carry out the mission. I told them we can count on you, but be completely honest. Do you feel any hesitation?"

"No, I don't. My father will never get out of prison. He has a weak heart. He won't live long. What they've done to him makes me more determined, not less. All right?"

Tomás looked at him carefully. "Raúl thinks you're too soft, that at the last moment you won't do it."

"Then let Raúl do it himself."

"It's too late. Everything is in place. Are you ready?"

"Yes."

"Excellent. At seven o'clock you enter the house, and at seven-fifteen you carry out the operation. Is that correct?"

Mario smiled. "Have you already forgotten?"

"No, no. Seven-fifteen. And then you go over the back fence and signal Raúl. I'll tell him the time. Seven-fifteen plus a few seconds for your escape."

"And he must leave if I'm not there within sixty seconds."

Tomás's eyes darted to make sure no one was nearby. "We're counting on you. Don't hesitate. The moment you see him, kill him. That's the key. Do it quickly, before he knows what's happening. Vega is a soldier, and he knows how to react to a gun. Don't give him a chance."

"Thank you for the advice. Don't worry about me." When he began to walk, Tomás held him back.

"One other thing. Mario, put those bags down and listen." Tomás came closer. The full light of afternoon made him squint. "After you finish the operation, they'll want to take you alive. They won't shoot you. They will capture you and do to you what they did to Chachi. No, even worse, and they will make you talk.

You can't let that happen." Tomás put his hand on Mario's shoulder. "Our lives don't matter. It's the Movement that has to survive. Do you understand? After you kill Vega, if anything goes wrong, or if you can't get to him, you have to make a sacrifice for the struggle. Are you ready to do that?"

"Yes."

"We're with you, my friend." Tomás embraced him. "Your courage will illuminate our darkness."

Mario was glad when Tomás left. He did not want to be reminded of the likely outcome, nor to hear his courage praised. The truth was, he didn't have much of it.

He picked up the bags and walked to the end of the sidewalk. The fishermen leaned on the seawall, and as one of them raised his arm to circle the weight over his head, he noticed Mario and called out, "Our young friend! Do you have your flute? Play us a tune."

"Not today. I have to go somewhere, but I brought you some clothes. If you weren't so fat you could wear them."

The line sailed out over the water and the weight made a splash when it hit. "I'll take a look. Thanks. I have a nephew your size."

Mario had put his flute between two folded pairs of pants. He took it out and quickly walked away. Past the channel, the waves rolled and broke on the rocks. He climbed up on the seawall, held the flute under one arm, and dug his identity booklet out of his back pocket. He ripped out the pages, then tore the cover in half and threw it into onto the rocks. The next wave took the pieces, and he tasted the salt spray on his lips.

Taking the flute by one end, Mario pulled his arm back. He stopped in mid-swing and took another look at it. The mouthpiece was bent, and the underside was dented. But it was still a good flute. There was no reason to throw it away. Using his T-shirt, he wiped off some smudges, and the metal gleamed. He left the flute on the seawall, hoping that someone with talent might find it there.

39

Abdel García had taken possession of his country house twenty-six years ago. It was nothing, a poured-concrete structure with a flat roof, potato fields on one side, a narrow, weed-tangled stream on the other. García had made no changes, except for the trees that now hid any view from the road. Its virtue was privacy. His uncle, Heriberto, had once lived on the property. Heriberto had wanted an exit visa to the United States, not caring about the damage this would do to his nephew's career. García had pushed him into the well. He'd been a drunkard, and the neighbors assumed he had fallen in. This was so ironic as to be amusing, because now it was García who felt empty air under his shoes.

He slid back a panel at eye level. A painting had been hung on the wall in the adjoining room. Minuscule figures in straw hats and wooden sandals made their way up the side of a mountain whose top was shrouded in mist. The scene was hand-painted on glass. In his unlighted chamber, García could look through the pine trees and bamboo to see clearly the girl sleeping on the chaise longue in his bedroom. She wore a pink T-shirt and denim shorts. He had put her dirty sneakers on the floor to prevent soiling of the gold satin fabric where she lay. García watched for the rise and fall of her chest. She had small breasts and long legs. Her feet in their thick white socks hung off the end of the chaise. The girl had been delivered in this condition, injected with enough morphine for a man. García had wanted to shoot the soldier responsible. If she died, there would be problems, and he had enough of them.

With a corner of his folded handkerchief he daubed at his mouth. In fifteen minutes he would make another telephone call to her stepfather. His insides twisted with anxiety. Had Quintana

followed instructions, or had he contacted Vega? Would he obedi-
ently bring the files, or would the next knock on the door be
agents from State Security?

Whatever occurred, García had done all he could. At this moment lead-lined boxes were on a fishing boat between Cuba and
Mexico. The boxes would be sent overboard. The men who had
collected their contents would go in after them. He had erased his
name from certain documents at the Ministry. He expected these
precautions to suffice. Ramiro Vega would be a posthumous traitor. If events turned the other way, García would slip out of Cuba.
He would not live as well as he had hoped, but he would live.

With a last look at the girl—she was still breathing—he slid the
panel shut. He left the closet and stepped into his office. He could
work here, connected by computer and telephone to the Ministry,
but he preferred to dig in his flower garden. This time of year, a little care would produce abundant blooms and colors so intense his
eyes would sting.

Where in hell was Sergeant Ruiz? He was supposed to call with
the time of the operation!

Walking stiffly from one side of the room to the other, García
pulled back the cuff of his uniform shirt to look at his watch. Just
past five. Vega was at his office—García had arranged that he go
into a meeting, which would reduce the chances of Quintana's getting through. Vega would be home around six o'clock. But at what
time would the young assassin arrive? What time? Seven, eight, ten
o'clock? García had to know *before* calling Quintana, so that he
could tell Quintana what time to arrive *here*. That depended on
the timing of Vega's death, and so far García had heard *nothing*,
and it was making him ill.

Quintana could not be at Ramiro Vega's house during the operation. He would intervene. The boy might be captured alive. He
would talk. When the boy fired a 9mm bullet from the Makarov
into Vega's skull, Quintana had to be *here*.

Crossing to the window, García noticed that the trees were
painting shadows on the side of the barn, or what used to be a
barn, now empty but for an old tractor and lengths of pipe and
lumber. Purple shadows bleeding slowly up the white wall.

What time, what time?

Quintana would arrive, he would hand over the files and take the girl, then be on his way. If the records contained nothing useful, it didn't really matter. The thing was to keep him away from Vega's house.

A small sedan drove past the window. Breathing quickly, García placed a hand flat on the glass and pressed his face close to see who got out. The car stopped beside the barn, barely within his view. A big black man in civilian clothing appeared. Was it Ruiz? Yes. He limped around to the other side. A moment later García heard a car door slam.

He pressed his handkerchief to his forehead, then to his lips, clearing away a last drop of moisture with his thumb.

He sat behind his desk and lit a cigarette.

Waited. Footsteps came closer. A heavy hand rapped on the wood.

"Enter."

The sergeant came in first, his shoulders blocking the entrance for a second before he moved aside and let his associate in. Tomás Fernández. García had never met him, had only seen photographs of a weak-looking, bookish man with short brown hair and glasses that sat halfway down his thin nose. He stepped inside, took a quick look at the bare floor and wooden chairs, the desk, and the man behind it. The newcomer seemed slightly confused. Perhaps, García thought, he had expected to see olive green and campaign ribbons instead of this plain cotton shirt. At his country house García tried to live simply.

Ruiz saluted. "General García, this is Tomás Fernández."

The man smiled, lifted a hand in an imitation of a salute, and bobbed his head. "I am honored, general."

Leaning back in his chair, García spoke to Ruiz. "I expected a phone call."

With a dark look at his companion, Ruiz said, "I'm sorry, sir. He wouldn't tell me. He said he wanted to deliver the report personally."

García blew out a stream of smoke. "Do you have something for me, Fernández?"

"Yes, general. I have the details of the operation." Fernández interlaced his thin white fingers at the level of his heart. He was beaming with self-importance. He was foiling an antisocialist plot. He said, "As you know, I was recruited by yourself, through Sergeant Raúl Ruiz, to infiltrate the Twenty-Eighth of January

Movement, a counterrevolutionary organization formed three years ago to carry out terrorist attacks against the government—"

"Enough!" García saw the man blink. "I know how you became involved, Mr. Fernández. Just tell me at what time the operation will be carried out. What time?"

"Mario Cabrera, a founder of the Movement and also, as you may know, the stepson of the dissident José Leiva—" His words came faster as García made a circular motion with one hand. "Cabrera will arrive at the home of General Ramiro Vega tonight at seven o'clock. He intends to carry out the operation at seven-fifteen precisely. Therefore, our comrades should be placed inside the house by six o'clock."

Standing at ease, hands clasped at the small of his back, Sergeant Ruiz stared over García's head as Fernández continued to babble about the make of Cabrera's automobile, his pistol, the people who would be at the house, the layout of the rooms—

García waved him quiet. "Ruiz, do you have the list of the co-conspirators?"

"I have it." Fernández fumbled in a pocket of his baggy brown trousers and withdrew a piece of paper, which he unfolded. "There are seventeen members in the Movement. Shall I read the names to you, general?"

"No. Put it on my desk." García drew the paper closer and scanned the handwritten list of names and addresses. He looked up at Fernández. "Your name is not here."

"Only the counterrevolutionaries are on the list, sir. The name of Raúl Ruiz is not there either, as you see." Fernández took a step forward, pointing at certain names. "Some of them are only marginally involved. Those of more importance to the Movement are underlined."

"I see. Very good." He touched his lip with his handkerchief.

"What will become of them?" Fernández asked. "I— I am curious. That is all."

"They will be arrested and put on trial for treason. You will receive a medal for your service to your country."

Behind his glasses, Fernández's eyes gleamed. "Thank you. Thank you, general. Will I be introduced to President Castro? Do you think that is possible?"

"Of course." García put his cigarette to his lips, pausing to say, "He will want to embrace you."

Fernández made a strange gurgle of delight, then ducked his head in apology. "I am overwhelmed. Forgive me. The enemies of Cuba are many, and we must all defend the Revolution. It has been my honor, my privilege, to serve you, for in serving you, I serve the Cuban people, who suffer under threats from both outside and within—"

As he continued to talk, García swiveled in his chair and pressed a button on his telephone. A moment later the door opened, and two men in olive-green fatigues entered. "Mr. Fernández? You will please go with these men."

Fernández looked around, an expression of bovine stupidity on his face. He asked Ruiz, "Aren't you taking me back to Havana?"

Ruiz moved aside. García motioned, and the men took Fernández's arms. He stammered, "Where are we going? Please, not so tightly. I can walk. May I ask . . . for what purpose . . . ?" Like an animal sensing the imminence of its own death, Fernández rolled his eyes. "I can't stay. I need to get back. My girlfriend is expecting me for dinner." When they took him through the door, he was saying, "Wait. Please wait. Raúl, what is going on? I don't understand this."

When they had gone, García got up to stretch his legs. "Talk to me for a moment. Close the door."

The knob disappeared inside one of Ruiz's immense hands.

García said, "They'll wait for you to do it. I've told them that you will."

"Sir?"

"Fernández. I want you to kill him."

The impassive black eyes flickered. "With all respect, general, I'd rather not. I know him."

"All the more reason." García tapped his cigarette over the ashtray. Waited.

Ruiz nodded. "I'll do it."

"You can make it quick. It doesn't have to be messy." García reached across the desk and spun the list to see it. "Fernández mentioned a girlfriend. Is she here?"

Ruiz studied the names. "No, I don't see her. But she doesn't know anything. She wasn't a part of it."

"Let's not leave any loose ends, all right? You take care of it for me."

"She has two kids."

"And?"

The eyes flickered again. Ruiz said, "It isn't necessary, general. She knows nothing."

"Have you lost your nerve?"

"No. I'll take care of it."

García extended the pack of cigarettes, and Ruiz took one, lighting it from the matches on the desk. "What do you think, Ruiz? Will Cabrera follow through?"

"Don't worry. He's pissed off about Leiva's arrest. He blames Vega."

García smiled through an exhalation of smoke. He had called MININT himself to insist that Leiva be taken into custody. "And did Cabrera believe that General Vega was behind Olga Saavedra's death?"

"Yes, he bought that story, too. Who did kill her? One of us?"

García shrugged. "Maybe it was Vega. It could have been. It doesn't matter. Soon this will be over, sergeant. We can relax. Go now. I have to make a telephone call."

Before reaching for the handset, García paused to consider the sergeant's reactions. He had handpicked Ruiz from the best of the best. A skillful, fearless man, loyal first to himself. Such men responded well to money and power, and García had supplied them. He trusted Ruiz, but he was bothered by Ruiz's hesitation. He weighed whether to get rid of him. It wouldn't be a bad idea. But not now. Ruiz was brutal and quick. He would be needed when Quintana arrived.

García went back to the closet, closed the door behind himself, and once again slid back the panel to peer into the bedroom. The girl had not moved. But wait. Her arm now lay across her stomach. She would probably not die after all. He felt his mood lift.

Returning to his office, García looked at his watch. Five-thirty.

He picked up the telephone and dialed Anthony Quintana's number.

40

"Impossible," Anthony said. "I can't meet you outside Havana. If you want the files, bring Karen back to the city. We'll make the exchange in a public place."

García again demanded that Anthony drive into the countryside, a place south of Rancho Boyeros, where a car would pick him up and bring him the rest of the way.

"I am telling you, I can't do that." With effort, he kept his voice level. Sweat made his hand slick on the telephone. "It's my wife. She would never let me do it. I can't control her much longer. She is on the verge of calling Fidel Castro himself. . . . You've kidnapped her only child. How do you expect her to react? Name a place in the city, and I'll be there. . . . What about outside the Karl Marx Theater? It's in Miramar. . . . No, I haven't called Ramiro. I haven't called anyone. . . . We just want Karen back. We don't care about anything else. Please hear what I'm saying. I will not go outside the city."

The ominous silence on the line went on for a time before the general said what Hector Mesa had predicted he would say: "Come to my apartment in Chinatown." There was a pause. García added, "Bring your wife."

"Why? You and I are making a simple trade."

"Bring her. She will keep your mind on what you have to do. I can easily leave Cuba right now. How would you find the girl? It could take a long time. I wonder how long she would survive without water."

Biting back his first response, Anthony closed his eyes and pounded a fist silently on Ramiro's desk. There was no alternative. He said he would bring Gail with him.

García told him to arrive at six-thirty. "If you are early or late, you will find no one there."

At a quarter till six they were driving past the Capitol. Dusk had robbed all color from the sky. Sea mist made the streetlights appear wrapped in white silk. Anthony glanced over at Gail in the passenger seat. Her earlier panic had chilled to a fine-edged anger.

Leaving so soon after his conversation with García cut the risk that they would be shadowed. Anthony had seen no one trailing them, but he could not be sure. He believed that his advantage lay in a peculiar trait he had noticed in men of power. The longer they held it, the more complacent they became. They grew to believe that their power was a law of nature, like gravity. They assumed that those under their control would do as they were told.

Gail broke the silence. "I'm so scared, Anthony. Scared for her."

"She'll be with us soon, sweetheart." He took her hand and kissed it, hoping he hadn't just lied to her. She loved him, but Karen was her life. "Gail, I want you to do this. When we reach the apartment, stay on the street. I'm sure that García will have one of his men downstairs. He can confirm that you came with me."

"That's not a good idea," she said. "I'd rather do what García wants. Don't think I'm going to stay behind when Karen is up there."

"Are you listening? Stay on the street. You would be in the way."

"No." Gail stared through the windshield.

"Jesus." Blowing out a breath, he turned left into Old Havana, away from Chinatown. "Karen is enough to deal with. I don't want to worry about getting both of you out of there."

She looked at him. "You think he's going to do something. He might try to kill us. Is that what you're saying?"

He took her hand again. "No, sweetheart. I will give him the disk, and he will give me Karen. If you're there, it would be a distraction. That's all."

"Anthony, did you really put the files on the disk?"

"Yes. Do you think I would gamble with a blank disk?"

"But how did you get them off Ramiro's computer? How did you find them? You went downstairs and you weren't gone for more than fifteen minutes—"

"It was luck. I found them and I made a copy. I think I have them all." The lie came easily, flowing out of his mouth as though it had happened exactly the way he spoke it. The truth—that he had nothing at all on the disk—would have unhinged her. "Remember this. García doesn't know what Ramiro has, so whatever I give him, how can he say they aren't the right files, or that I have withheld some of them?" Anthony pressed her hand to his lips. "*Todo va a salir bien*. I promise you. Within an hour we will be back at Ramiro's house. All of us."

Gail stared at him for a few seconds, then sank back into her seat, silent again.

After making a complete circuit of one of the residential blocks and seeing no headlights following, he found an apartment building with space at the curb. He maneuvered the Toyota into the spot and killed the engine. A bare-chested man with a beer in his hand watched from the small porch of the building. Anthony held up ten dollars and asked if he could leave the car there for a little while. With a nod, the man pocketed the money.

Taking Gail's arm, Anthony crossed the street a block south of the Capitol. She had no trouble keeping up in her running shoes and jeans. They turned north, and soon the Dragon Gate came into view. The neighborhood was alive with people, color, and noise. Paper lanterns swung from lines crisscrossing the street. Music blared through the open windows of a bar. Hand in hand, they pushed into the crowd. A slender woman in a silk tunic waved a menu as they walked under the awning of a restaurant. He heard a loud pop and the laughter of boys running away. Smoke drifted upward, swirled, and vanished.

A small man came alongside, his head barely clearing Anthony's shoulder. In English he said, "Candy? Señora, some candy for your child? Only twenty-five cents." He held up a basket. Anthony saw a brown hand and the sleeve of an embroidered silk tunic. He looked at the man's face. Not a *chino*. A *mulato* with curly gray hair and glasses with old plastic frames. Hector Mesa. He dropped a wrapped sweet into Gail's hand. As though bumped by someone behind him, he lurched forward, and Anthony heard him say, "Wait for me at the bar in Tien-Lu. Two blocks north." He and his basket vanished into the crowd.

"What did he say to you?" Gail asked.

Anthony looked around for the nearest cross street. They followed it between buildings that crowded the narrow sidewalk. He put his arm around her and his lips close to her ear. "We're meeting Hector at a bar."

"When are we going to get Karen?"

"Soon. It's going to be all right, *bonboncita*. Just do what I tell you and don't ask so many questions."

She frowned but said nothing more.

The Tien-Lu was a dive with few customers. He installed Gail on a bar stool and signaled the waitress. The time was five minutes until six. The waitress set down a bottled beer that Anthony didn't touch. Gail stirred the ice in her cola. Fifteen minutes later Hector slid onto the stool to Anthony's right. He had ditched the costume.

Gail leaned forward to see him. "Hello, Hector."

"Señora." He smiled at her and clasped his hands on the bar. They were too big for his narrow wrists. The knuckles were like walnuts, and his veins roped across the tendons. The curved reflections of a red lantern obscured his eyes. In Spanish he said, "I saw the Chinaman go upstairs. A black man was with him, carrying a rug in his arms. I think it was not a rug. He was careful, so I am sure that the girl is okay."

"Who else is with them?"

"Two men. I see one of them at the entrance. The other went up the stairs. There may be others. I don't know."

Gail leaned around to ask, "What did he say about Karen?"

"They took her upstairs. She's all right."

She breathed. "Thank God. What time is it?"

"It's not time yet," Anthony said. "I need to talk to Hector. Stay here." He put a hand on her shoulder as she began to object. "Please."

They walked into the gloom of a far corner, and Anthony kept an eye on the door while Hector told him what he wanted to do. Hector moved closer, and Anthony felt a weight settle into the pocket of his coat. Five minutes later, Hector went out the back entrance of the bar. Anthony found the men's room next to the kitchen, which smelled of cabbage and grease. He shut the thin door and put the wire hook through the eye bolt. The urine-stained toilet had no seat. With one foot on the rim, he lifted his pant leg and strapped Hector's little Beretta to his ankle.

At twenty-five past six Anthony put some money on the bar. He and Gail walked outside. He had his hand around her wrist, and her pulse slammed against his fingers. Otherwise, she looked like she might be heading for a showdown in court.

The apartment would be two streets over, four down. He knew he was close when he passed under the scaffolding. He looked up and saw the shutters four stories above. Slivers of light came through.

Gail's gaze followed his. "Is that his apartment?"

"Yes."

They went around to the front and stepped into the entryway with its single bulb on the wall. The man waiting there was one of the phony State Security thugs who had stopped him outside the Colón Cemetery two days ago. He ran his hands over Anthony's waist and patted his coat. If he found the Beretta, Anthony thought he would probably have to kill him. The man didn't search below his coat pockets. He pulled out the disk.

"Put it back," Anthony said.

The man told Gail to turn around. She understood the Spanish and turned, holding her arms away from her body.

Anthony gestured to the man's cell phone. "Call the general. Tell him we're here, but my wife is going to wait downstairs with you." That produced a blank stare, but the man stepped farther into the foyer to make the call.

He came back and jerked his head toward the stairs. "He says no. You're both coming up. Go on. If you try anything, I'll blow your brains out, starting with her."

Anthony held out an arm. In English he said to Gail, "Come on. It's all right."

The guard fell in behind them. Going up the stairs, Anthony slid his hand on the wrought-iron railing. The street noise muffled their footsteps. He wiped his forehead with the back of his wrist.

He was sweating, and his breaths were too shallow. He slowed down, took his time. The fluorescent tubes in the stairwell put a thin gray light on the filthy walls.

He put his arm around her shoulders. "We'll go in, give him the disk, and get Karen. And you do what I tell you. If I say move, you move. No questions. All right?"

"Yes, but I'm not leaving without Karen."

The barrel of a pistol jabbed into his spine. "*Cállense.*" Shut up.

They reached the fourth floor. There was another man standing in front of the door at the end of the corridor. Anthony could smell the incense from ten yards away. The guard opened the door far enough to speak through it, holding his hand up to keep the visitors out. Then he stepped out of the way. Anthony recognized him: the *trigueño* who had driven the car away from the cemetery.

He followed them in as the first man took his position in the hall. A third man waited inside, the same big black guy with the limp who had pushed him into the car. He carried a holstered Makarov on his belt, and he stood with his arms crossed beside Abdel García.

The general was perched on the arm of his red brocade sofa. Gail let out a cry. Karen lay across the cushions, still as death.

Gail ran across the room. "What have you done to her?"

"She is sleeping." García's legs were crossed, and the toe of his polished brown shoe drooped toward the floor. His tan cotton shirt was tucked neatly into his pants.

"You drugged her!" Gail knelt beside the girl and touched her face, smoothed her hair. "Karen. Baby. It's all right. We're taking you home."

The *trigueño* had moved around behind them. Anthony kept him in sight.

García laid his cigarette in the ashtray on a mahogany end table. The lamp was a porcelain woman in a Chinese robe. García's hand slid in and out of the light, and smoke curled up through the lamp shade. In heavily accented English, he said, "Sit with her, please, señora. And you, Mr. Quintana." He slid off the arm of the sofa. "Sit down. Sergeant Ruiz won't hurt you . . . unless you disobey my orders."

The black sergeant—Ruiz—made no reaction to this, but his eyes followed Anthony as he moved Karen's legs aside. Anthony sat on the edge, one foot in front of the other, afraid that the lift of his trouser cuff would reveal the pistol strapped to his ankle.

García smiled at Gail. The skin gathered over his jutting cheekbones like folds in a crooked curtain. "She is very pretty, your daughter."

"Just keep away from her." She shot García a look of icy disgust. On the sofa, she pulled Karen's head and shoulders onto her lap and wrapped her arms around her.

Standing over them, García switched to Spanish. "Where are the files, Quintana? I see that you have nothing with you."

Anthony reached into his pocket for the disk in its plastic case. "This is from Ramiro Vega. He made it last night."

"I want the files. Where are they?"

"On the disk. He destroyed the papers weeks ago. He didn't want them found."

García's jaw slid to one side as he tightened his mouth. "You're lying."

"It has what you want," Anthony said. "Do you think I would risk that girl's life?"

García considered, then smiled again. "No, but all the same, I want to check it out. Half an hour? Maybe a little longer." He turned toward the man at the door and told him to take the disk to his house and see what was on it, then call him with the verdict.

Anthony said, "Let them leave, my wife and the child. I'll stay behind."

"No one is leaving yet." García reached a hand out, and Gail jerked away. Anthony hadn't realized he was on his feet until he saw the sergeant's Makarov leveled at his chest. García, who had frozen as well, finished his movement—taking his cigarette from the ashtray. "The disk, Mr. Quintana?"

The guard motioned, and Anthony put it in his hand. García said, "Tell López to come in. Sit down, Quintana. We will be here for a little while. Put the gun away, sergeant."

Anthony followed the movements of the *trigueño*, who crossed the room, reached for the doorknob, turned it, opened the door. He stepped through, then jerked, coughed, and grabbed at the door frame, at his own throat, at air. He staggered back. His shirt was brilliant with blood.

The Beretta was already in Anthony's hand when the sergeant

got his Makarov back out of its holster. Anthony fired. The noise from the small-caliber pistol was no louder than strong handclaps. Ruiz went to his knees, and the gun slipped from his fingers.

García saw it and dove to pick it up. He swiped, and the Makarov spun away under the sofa. García crawled toward it.

Anthony yelled, "Gail, get down! On the floor! Now!"

She pulled Karen with her and rolled to cover her body.

He was taking aim at García when the *trigueño*, still staggering, collided into him, then lurched into the end table. The porcelain lamp went over. Shadows loomed across the ceiling. Hector Mesa put a foot on the guard's chest and leaned over him with his knife.

As Anthony recovered his balance, he saw García ripping Karen from Gail's arms, Gail screaming at him to stop, then going for him with her fists. Holding Karen close, one arm around her waist, García shoved Gail aside. Karen's legs swung out as García turned. Anthony couldn't get a clear shot. García slid through the door to his bedroom. The door slammed behind him.

"He's got Karen!" Gail shook the knob. "It's locked. Kick it down!"

Anthony threw himself forward, putting shoulder and hip against the door at the same time. The wood cracked but didn't give. He took a step back and hit it again. The door flew open, crashing into the wall.

Hector rushed past him with his knife. The blade shone red.

"Gail, get back," Anthony ordered. Gun in both hands, he swung it around the room with only the light from a fringed lamp to reveal what was there: bed with four carved dragons climbing up the posts, silk brocade coverlet, black armoire, a framed mirror.

García had disappeared.

"Karen!" Gail spun around, screaming her name. "Karen!" Cold air came from a wall air-conditioning unit. Wooden louvers covered the windows. The place was tight as a tomb. Hector dropped to look under the bed as Anthony noticed a small black button on the wall. Hinges. A door.

He pulled it open and found a small dark room. Empty. He stepped in and noticed a window. He saw the lamp in the bedroom and realized that García had installed two-way glass in the mirror. He moved his hands over the walls, feeling for a way out. He found it—a handle.

"Hector! In here."

The door swung into another room, completely empty but for a narrow bed, a chair, some clothes on a peg. None of this would have been visible except for the faint light that streamed through a narrow doorway. The sheet-metal door had been pushed open.

They rushed across the room, and as Anthony stepped onto the flat roof he smelled gunpowder from fireworks, heard loud music, shouts, laughter. The buildings nearby were of the same height or less, and except for the ambient light from the city, the darkness was complete.

Gail pointed. "He's over there!"

A silhouette moved along the opposite edge of the roof. García had put Karen on his shoulder, and he moved quickly toward a ladder whose handrails curved over the low parapet.

They ran toward him, their footsteps thudding on the roof. The general's voice rang out. "Stay back or I will break her neck and throw her to the street." The silhouette shifted its burden and turned toward the ladder. The dim light shone on Karen's pale arms dangling on his back.

Hector circled left to the edge of the roof and followed it, crouching low.

"I said stay back!" García leaned toward the street, and Karen's arms swung.

Gail cried out, and Hector came to a halt.

García's voice floated to them, mingling with the sounds from the street. He was calm now, as if he knew that whatever happened next was within his control. "You will wait there, please. Half an hour, no longer. I will leave the girl unharmed at a location that I will communicate to you by telephone. You have your telephone with you, Quintana? Very good. I will call you when it is safe."

There was a movement along the parapet to their right. García didn't see it. Someone was coming, staying low. He dragged a leg, and one arm seemed to hang uselessly at his side. Unsure what to do, Anthony raised the Beretta.

García saw the gun. "Don't be stupid. If you fire, you will hit the girl." He reached for the railing and swung a leg over the parapet. He did not notice the man closing in until it was too late. The man reached out with one arm, trying to drag him away from the ladder.

In an instant Anthony was across the roof, struggling to get Karen away from García. He caught her as she fell from García's back. Now he could see the other man clearly: Ruiz. The sergeant leaned to one side as if in pain from the bullet Anthony had put in him, and blood ran down his arm, shattered at the elbow.

García turned under him and got a shoulder in his stomach. The sergeant stumbled against the parapet, flailed for one long moment, and dropped, vanishing over the side of the building.

Hector Mesa came from behind García, grabbed his hair, reached around, and slid his knife across his throat. When García went to his knees, Hector put a foot in his back and shoved. The general lay facedown, the blood spreading out around him, black in the absence of light, flowing around the gravel and weeds toward a low place in the roof.

Gail huddled over Karen, rocking her. Anthony knelt to make sure they were all right. He kissed Gail quickly, then stood up and walked over to the ladder and looked down. The soldier lay on the roof of a colonnade three stories below.

Wiping his knife on a cloth, Hector came over to look. "You see that, Señor Anthony? He jumped his boss. I wonder for what."

"He didn't like red brocade furniture. I don't know. What do you suggest we do now?"

"We should leave." Hector suspended his knife over the body below them and let go. "Now give me the gun." Hector meant the Beretta, which Anthony had forgotten he still held. His cramped fingers didn't want to straighten. Hector wiped off the prints and took it over to García and pressed it into his hand, then kicked it away. He stared after it as though sorry to leave his best friend behind.

Anthony asked, "Should we try the ladder?"

"No, no, the stairs. The ladder is not so easy. And if they see us, we are cooked."

Anthony lifted Karen from Gail's lap. Shaking, Gail steadied herself on his arm and stood up. "I could scream. I really could." She cupped Karen's face in her palm. "Baby? Sweetie?"

Karen mumbled in her sleep. Her eyes came open, swam to fix on her mother's face, then closed again. Gail said, "After all that, she's still out."

"You should be grateful."

"I suppose so. She'll be all right, won't she?"

"She'll be fine. How about you?"

"Dandy. I just want to get the hell out of here."

They retraced their steps, taking only enough time to wipe their fingerprints from whatever they had touched. The metal door leading to the roof. The handle on the door in García's *voyeur* chamber. The doorknob of his bedroom, the wooden carvings on the arms of his sofa. With Karen on his shoulder, Anthony looked around the living room once again and spotted the CD and its case on the floor beside the dead guard. He told Gail to pick them up. She gingerly did so, stepping around the blood.

"Are you going to give this to Bookhouser?"

"No, it's blank. But don't leave it behind. My fingerprints are on it."

She snapped the CD into its case. "You really didn't have to lie to me."

He remembered what he had told her earlier. "I am sorry."

"Like hell."

Hector opened the apartment door and peered out before signaling for them to come ahead. Blood spattered the floor in the hall from the wound Hector had made in the guard's chest. He quickly wiped it away. It was possible that the bodies would not be discovered for days, unless someone from an adjacent building noticed the man on the colonnade roof. By then, the sight of four strangers coming down the stairs might have been forgotten.

On the second level they passed some teenagers, who glanced at them without interest. Coming out of the foyer, they were caught in a crowd of tourists and Cubans out for the night. Half a dozen men, singing loudly in German, stumbled off the sidewalk. A horn blared. Anthony pushed through the crowd. He and Gail walked east toward the Capitol.

Three floors above, the block captain from the CDR sat in her rocking chair and sipped a cup of coffee. As she gazed down from her window, scanning the crowd, she noticed a tourist couple and their daughter. Where were they from? The man looked Spanish or Italian. The woman was blond. They had been too long in Havana, she concluded. The wife pressed close to her husband, whose expression said that he would rather be anywhere else than here in this miserable city. He was forced to carry their daughter, who was too spoiled to walk on her own feet.

The woman noticed the little *mulato* just behind them, close as a shadow. She wondered if he planned to beg a few dollars. It was suspicious, all right, the way he kept looking around. She thought about phoning the police, but the man was poor and probably hungry. If he took money from rich tourists, what did it matter? Those people had more than they needed. Anyway, this cup of coffee would be the last until she got her new ration card, and she wanted to enjoy it.

41

The gate at the Vega house was open when Mario arrived. He drove through, and his headlights picked up the blue Lada in the driveway. He didn't see the general's minivan.

He glanced at his watch. One minute past seven. In less than fifteen minutes the operation would have to be completed, but the general wasn't here. With a curse Mario put in the clutch and jammed the gearshift into reverse. The Fiat's transmission clattered and finally caught. He glanced through the windshield and saw in the porch light the front door opening, and a girl in a pink pullover coming out. Angela Quintana. She stood there waiting for him.

She would know where the general was.

Mario parked and turned off the engine. The flute case lay on the passenger seat. He picked it up and got out of the car with it. As he walked toward the house, he put the strap over his shoulder. The case hung just below his right hip. He touched the latches to reassure himself that his fingers would find them.

She met him on the top step and put her arms around his neck. His first thought was to push her away, but he kept his hands by his sides. When she turned into the light, he saw tears on her face.

"I left a message to tell you not to come. I'm so glad you didn't get it. Somebody took Karen right off the street. It happened near the bakery! We don't know who, but she's all right. My father and Gail went to pick her up. They just called a minute ago. We were all going out of our minds with worry." Laughing, Angela wiped her cheeks with the heel of her hand. "I don't mean to do this. Karen's okay. She's fine, but can you believe it?"

It took Mario some time to turn his thoughts away from General

Vega and understand what Angela was talking about. He had to search for the correct response.

"That's terrible," he said.

"They might have wanted a ransom. The army found her. We think so because a general called here to speak to my father. The people responsible for this have probably been arrested already."

"Good. I'm glad. Where is General Vega?"

"I don't know. Maybe he helped rescue Karen. We'll find out more when everyone gets home."

"They'll be here soon, then?"

"I think they're on their way. Do you want to come inside?" She took his arm.

"Who else is here?"

"Besides us? Aunt Marta and Gail's mother and Janelle and Danny. You wouldn't be a bother."

"Let's stay outside. Is that all right?"

"It's fine," she said. "I'd prefer it, really. Do I look all right? My eyes are red, aren't they?"

"A little."

As he took the metal chair beside hers, Mario glanced at his watch. In ten minutes the communiqué would be delivered to CNN. The notices would be dropped off at the university and the hotels. Soon people would begin calling Vega's house. The police would come.

Mario watched the street. Angela's voice seemed to fade in and out. He saw headlights approach, then pass by. He wondered if the neighbors would be able to hear the gunshots from inside Vega's office. He had prepared himself to die after Vega, but to die on the street would be better. He imagined a circle of faces looking down at him. They would ask who he was. A great pity to die so young, they would say, but he died for a reason.

The door opened, and a girl came outside, a short, plump girl, her full breasts hidden by an oversized T-shirt. Angela's cousin. He couldn't remember her name.

The girl came over and hung on Angela's chair and looked at him. "Angela, did you tell Mario about Karen? Isn't that horrible?"

"We were just talking about it," Angela said.

"I see that you brought your flute," the girl said. "Last time you were here you promised to play for me."

"Not now," he said. "Go back inside. We're talking."

"That's very rude." She glanced at Angela, who gave her a sympathetic look. She went in, and the door slammed behind her.

Mario thought of standing up, walking across the yard, getting into the car. Then he thought of the communiqué. In minutes the Movement would be claiming a victory in Vega's death. But he had done nothing. They had failed.

"You're upset about your father, aren't you?" Angela said.

He looked at her. "I apologize for being rude to your cousin."

"Don't worry about it. She doesn't understand. How's your mom?"

"You can imagine," he said.

Angela took his hand. She was saying something about her father trying to help José Leiva.

He heard an engine. Headlights flickered through the bushes, then appeared on the street, coming closer. A minivan. The minivan turned into the driveway. Lights moved across the trees and shone on the green Fiat. The minivan parked in front of the portico. The door opened, and he could see the general's bald brown head and olive green uniform. He got out with a leather briefcase. He looked toward the front porch.

Mario stood up. He would do it here, now. He would take the general here on the steps, then run out the gate and around the corner. Raúl would be on the other street any moment. Angela would see it, but Mario had no alternative. He touched the latches on his flute case. When the pistol fell into his hand, it would be ready to fire. He had already pulled back the hammer. One shot. Too fast for the general to react. Another if necessary.

The general vanished under the portico.

Mario heard Angela ask if he was all right.

He walked to the front door, opened it. Went into the living room. Empty. He processed distances and angles. Angela behind him, asking him a question. He heard his own voice telling her nothing was wrong.

To the left, the stone wall with the framed portraits of Vega and Castro and his collaborators. To his right, a corridor leading to the general's office. He passed the stairs, a curve of metal and stone. Upstairs, the bedrooms. Straight ahead, a wall and a long opening. Still farther, the sliding glass doors, then darkness. As he walked, the dining table and chairs came into view. To the right, the door to the kitchen.

He pointed at the table. "Angela, wait there. Sit down, please."

"Why?"

"Go over there and sit down."

"You're acting so strangely. What is the matter with you?"

He tuned out her voice as he approached the open door to the kitchen. Complications. Vega's daughter was by the sink talking to the red-haired woman, Gail Connor's mother. Mario was aware of Angela Quintana staring at him, coming closer. He held up his left hand to stop her. He heard a door close. Saw the general come in. Kiss his daughter. Briefcase on the table. Beer from the refrigerator. Gail Connor's mother going over to him. Talking in English.

Mario heard the name Karen. Karen. Karen.

The general set down his beer, walked quickly across the kitchen.

Mario stepped back as the general came through the door. He clicked open the latches of his case, and the gun fell into his hand.

"General Vega."

When the general turned to see who was there, Mario pointed the pistol directly at his face. He saw his eyes and mouth opening.

Mario circled to the left. He heard Angela yelling at him. The girl came out with a glass. It smashed on the floor.

"Everyone, shut up!"

The general had turned as Mario moved around him. His hands were out to his sides, a blind man feeling his way. "What are you doing?"

"Papi! Papi!" The girl's voice scraped like rusted wires.

Mario told her to be quiet. He grabbed the back of the general's collar and held him at arm's length. The pistol was to the side where Vega could see it. "We're going to walk across the living room. Go on. Walk."

"Why?"

"Just do what I tell you."

"Are you going to shoot me?"

The women started screaming. Mario yelled at them to go to the dining table and sit down. None of them moved. They stood there in a semicircle and stared and cried like dumb animals.

A movement on the stairs. A woman's bare feet. Señora de Vega came into the living room. Angela's brother followed.

Her robe swirled around her as she ran. "Ramiro!"

"Marta, don't come any closer, my love. This boy has a pistol."

"Why? Who is this? Oh my God. Leiva's son. What do you want?"

"Shut up or I will shoot him right here!" Mario told everyone to stand back. "General, come with me."

They would go left of the stairs along the wall, then into the corridor, then to the office—

The general didn't move. "Young man— Mario. That's your name, isn't it? Why are you here, Mario? To rob us? We don't have much cash in the house."

"I don't want your money. You and I are going to talk. That's all. Nothing will happen."

"Is this about your father? You want me to get him out of jail? Is that it?"

"Walk to your office! Now!" Still gripping Vega's collar, he gave him a shove.

The general leaned toward the table. "Come. Sit down with me. Don't be unreasonable. Let's discuss it."

"Walk, or I will wet the floor with your blood."

Vega turned his head. "You want to kill me. Yes. I see it in your face. I know that look. I have seen it in war. This is a very foolish thing, Mario. You can't get away. You know you will be tracked down."

"I'm not afraid to kill you, and I'm not afraid to die for it."

The general's wife screamed and put her hands together, begging. "Please, please. Have mercy. Don't kill my husband. He's a good man. He has a family. Kill me instead."

"I said to shut up!" Mario extended the pistol toward her. The gun went off, and a bullet whined against the wall. The heavy, gold-framed mirror shattered, and the pieces fell onto a cart underneath it, through the glass shelves, sending everything crashing to the terrazzo floor.

The women screamed again, and the daughter ran to her mother. Señora de Vega fell to her knees. She put her head on the floor and cried. "Sainted virgin, mother of God, have mercy on us, in the name of your son, have mercy—"

"I didn't mean to do that . . . but I will do it again if you don't shut up!" Mario tried to pull the hammer back, but his thumb was shaking. He jammed the barrel into the back of the general's neck. "I will kill all of them if you don't walk into the living room. Now."

The general moved, shuffling sideways. His head gleamed with sweat. "What have I done? Will you tell me what crime I've committed?"

"You are an enemy of the Cuban people!"

"Do you know, Mario, that I am on my way to Miami? That I am leaving Cuba and taking my family with me? It's true, isn't it, Marta? My wife has spent all day packing our things."

"Oh, God. Oh, God, please spare him. If I have committed sins against you, please take me instead."

Vega said, "I'm getting out of Cuba. Going. Good-bye forever."

"You have been indicted, tried, and found guilty by the Twenty-Eighth of January Movement for the crimes of greed, oppression, and murder." Mario glanced left to make sure that no one was in the way. "At this moment our manifesto is being delivered to CNN."

"What oppression? What murder?"

"Everyone in the army is an oppressor. You, particularly, are responsible for the deaths of Camilo Menéndez and Olga Saavedra. Camilo was one of my brothers in the Movement, who was tortured and murdered on your orders—"

"I never heard this name in my life."

"Olga Saavedra was your mistress. You killed her. Admit it!"

"Murdered Olga? Are you crazy?"

"Your mistress?" Señora de Vega's face was blotchy red. "What does he mean? Ramiro? Were you sleeping with Olga Saavedra? Were you? Answer me!"

The general nodded. "I'm sorry. Yes. But I never loved her. I've never loved any woman but you."

She wiped her eyes on her robe. "You liar! Bastard! I gave you twenty-two years of my life and three children, and this is what you do to me?"

"Both of you shut up!" Mario shook Vega by the back of his collar. "Keep moving."

The general's wife wailed. "No. Please. Mario, he may have cheated on me, but he didn't kill her. You're wrong, wrong. Cobo killed her. Our driver. Yes. He did it, I swear on the life of my grandson."

The general stared at her. "Marta, what are you saying?"

"It's true," she sobbed. "Cobo confessed to me. I saw the blood on his clothes. I couldn't tell you. You'd have gone to the police. It would've ruined us. A murder in our family. No, I couldn't." Tears dripped off Señora de Vega's face. "Mario, please. My husband didn't do it. Cobo was in love with her, and she wouldn't have him. He committed suicide. Go look if you don't believe me." She pointed. "Go look. My brother found him today. He hanged himself in his apartment in the garage!"

"Be quiet!" Mario thought he would go crazy, as crazy as this woman. "I don't want to hear any more. *Walk,* you son of a bitch."

The general's laugh was more of a moan. He clapped his hands. "I know who sent you. Yes. I know, I know. What a joke. What a joke on me. Abdel García. Yes, yes, yes. Marta, what do you think of that? Abdel García. Mario, do you know who General García is? He's my commanding officer. He's been trying to get rid of me. Finally he has a weapon. A credulous boy. He sent you, didn't he?"

"Keep walking."

They were halfway through the living room. Mario could see through the stairs to the front windows, the dark street. The four women and the boy trailed behind the general as if they were being pulled by cords tied to his belt.

"Mario? Don't you know you're being used? There isn't a counterrevolutionary movement in Cuba that hasn't been infiltrated. Not one. Think! If you have gotten this far, it's because someone wants me dead, and he's using you to accomplish it. If State Security doesn't know, it's because he doesn't want them to know. Mario, think."

They were nearly to the corridor.

"Why did he send *you,* Mario? José Leiva wrote articles about Abdel García. Is this García's way of evening the score? Call CNN. See if they received your communiqué. I will stake my life they haven't received a damned thing. Nothing."

"Shut up."

"What a naïve bunch you must be. I'll tell you where your

friends are right now. Being rounded up, as you will be too. You can live, Mario. Don't do this. You were tricked. There's no shame in that. You can live."

"Don't make me kill you in front of your wife and children. I don't want to do that, but *I will if you don't shut up*!" Mario fired into the ceiling, then pressed the gun barrel into Vega's neck.

The general winced. "That's hot. I'm walking. I'm going. Mario, your father writes against violence. Doesn't he? What would he say about this?"

"My father is already dead. He will never get out of prison."

"I didn't put him there, Mario."

"You and the regime. It's no different. Walk left. We're going to your study."

His daughter started sobbing again.

Angela said in a soft voice, "Mario. Mario, please don't. Just put the gun down and leave here. Please. My father will help you."

"Angela, be quiet!"

Vega put his hands over his face. "Oh, God. Is this what we have created? Young men with such hatred and passion? Are we to blame for this?" The general turned his eyes toward Mario. Sweat ran along the lines in his forehead. He whispered, "I need to sit down." He grasped the stair railing and pulled. Mario's shoes skidded.

"Keep walking!"

"No, I need to sit here. You have frightened me, Mario." The general sat heavily on the second step and leaned on the railing. "I can't walk anymore."

"Get up!"

"I'm a coward. I have betrayed my wife, and I'm deserting my country. Are you my punishment? Are you justice, coming for me in this way?"

"Get up! I don't want to kill you in front of your family."

"You don't want my family to see me die. Good. You have a kind heart. It would be kinder if you didn't do it at all."

The general's wife was crawling across the floor, weeping. "Ramiro. Ramiro."

"Get away from him!"

"No. He's my husband. Kill me too. I will die with him."

The others gathered in a mindless group by the stairs. The girl was sobbing for him not to kill her father. Danny was hiding his face against the red-haired lady, who was saying a prayer.

The world was insane. Nothing was real, all a lie, a trick. He could see it now: He had been used. Olga had tried to warn him. Who was it? Raúl? Tomás? There was no way out. Ever.

He backed away and put the barrel under his chin.

Angela screamed, "Mario, no!" She ran straight at him. Eyes growing larger. He saw her pink shirt, the crucifix on her breast, her hands reaching out. "Don't! I love you! Stop!"

He turned and fired at the photographs on the wall. Glass splintered and exploded off the stone.

He ran for the front door and out onto the porch—

Then he was flying . . . the world spinning . . . earth over sky . . .

His face in the dirt, the grass. He couldn't breathe. He pushed up slowly. When his eyes focused, he was looking into the face of a small *mulato*. A pair of plastic glasses and curly gray hair. Then a fist came toward him.

42

Standing in the junk-strewn garage, Anthony watched his brother-in-law go out the side door and look up the stairs. He heard the thud of shoes on wood, then the squeak of hinges. Nothing for a second or two. Then more footsteps, Ramiro walking around Cobo's apartment, thinking what in hell to do next.

Hector Mesa sat on his heels on the concrete floor studying the young man stretched out between a stack of paint cans and a folded pool table. Mario lay on his side, hands behind him, the cord running to his feet, which were also bound. He had been out cold for nearly an hour, ever since Hector had slammed him in the back of the neck.

Hector said, "The Twenty-Eighth of January Movement. What is that?"

"José Martí's birthday."

"Yes, so it is. Fools. What are you going to do with him?"

"How soon can you have a boat ready?"

"As soon as I make a phone call," Hector said.

"Make it," Anthony said, "before Ramiro comes back."

It had taken a while to sort out exactly what had happened. An hour ago, walking across the front yard, they'd heard gunshots from the house. Hector had gone to see what it was, and a few seconds later, Mario had come running through the door with a pistol in his hand. If Hector's Beretta had not been left in Chinatown, Mario would have several bullet holes in him. They carried him inside, limp, and the explanations began.

Leaving that job to Anthony, Gail went upstairs with Karen, who had begun to come out of her stupor. Anthony made sure his kids were all right after the shock of nearly seeing their uncle shot to death. Then Giovany came home, saw the shattered glass on the floor, and had to be held back from calling the police. A neighbor called asking about the noise. Ramiro grabbed the phone from Marta and explained that the kids had set off some firecrackers. As soon as the house was quiet, Anthony took Ramiro into the study and told him about García. Ramiro's first question: "Is Karen all right?" Anthony told him yes, she was. Second question: "Did anyone see you?" Ramiro was concerned about his own neck, a useful thing to know. Anthony said that if anyone had seen them, the police would have arrived by now.

It was strange, how distant the events seemed as they were happening. Reality came with recollection. Firing the pistol at Ruiz, the bodyguard, Anthony hadn't felt the recoil or heard the shots, and he couldn't remember how many he had fired, but the image of the man's shattered arm was still hot in his memory. García's face was still with him, too, stripped to one bare emotion: fear. Anthony's own gut-quivering shakes hadn't started then, but he'd felt them in his legs coming down the four flights of stairs, then again driving back to Miramar, his hands jittering on the steering wheel. It helped to know that the shit-sucking bastard had deserved it. But it didn't help much.

Hector closed his cell phone and slid it back into his pocket. "They need about three hours' notice. You let me know."

Anthony didn't ask who or what. The boat would be fast, and the people on it reliable. He leaned over and felt the knot under Mario's left ear. "I hope you didn't do any permanent damage."

"He's okay," Hector said.

Anthony tossed him the car keys. "Bring the car as close as you can to the portico. You have a place to take him tonight?"

Hector replied with a quick nod as he headed for the side door of the garage.

For a while Anthony looked down at the young man on the floor. He reached into his trousers pocket for the envelope that he'd promised Mario to deliver to his mother on Sunday. It had been written before José's arrest. Anthony had an idea what the letter might say, and he didn't want Yolanda to see it. He tore off the end and withdrew a single sheet of paper. The handwriting was small and neat, no cross-outs, as if copied from a final draft.

Translating the flowery Spanish typical of such correspondence, Anthony read:

> Dear parents of my soul, this letter arrives to your gentle hands to comfort you in this heavy hour and to beg that you will try to understand the reasons for what I have done. You have taught me that liberty is of greater value to a man than his own life. Without doubt some will say that what I did was evil, but what is evil? Malefactors like General Ramiro Vega laugh as they condemn the hopes of a people to the cold dungeons of despair. Do not weep for me, my dear parents, for I perished in the sure knowledge that my blood will bring forth flowers in the soil of our beloved Cuba.

Anthony groaned softly. "Oh, Mario."

> My dear sweet mami, I will set sail into eternity on the great ocean of your love. You must not forget to smile, for I will be watching from heaven. José, the father of my heart, you have given me courage. Do not cry for my passing, for we shall meet again. Until then, may God protect and keep you. With embraces, your faithful son, Mario Cabrera.

Elbows on his knees, Anthony looked at the boy on the garage floor. "Now what will you do, eh? When will your life ever again be this certain, this pure?" He leaned over and stroked the boy's curly black hair. "May I confess something to you, Mario? I admire this dangerous passion. I used to be as reckless as you are. Yes, I know what it's like, this feeling. You're going to miss it."

The door at the top of the stairs closed. Hollow thuds grew louder. Folding the letter, Anthony stood up and returned it to his pocket. Ramiro appeared. He flexed his hands, cleared his throat. "Whose blood is that on the towels? Olga's?"

"I believe so. Cobo removed his footprints and wiped off the weapon."

"What was it?"

"A carved wooden statue."

"And you say she died quickly." Ramiro passed his hand over his eyes, then straightened the front of his uniform shirt. "I told Marta, when the police come, she doesn't know anything about it. I will tell them I found Cobo like that. And now. What to do about this young man." Ramiro moved his eyes to Mario Cabrera. "Abdel García sent a boy to kill me. Clever. What is your saying? A wolf in sheep's clothing?"

"Not much of a wolf. He couldn't pull the trigger."

"Even so."

"Ramiro, you'll have to be careful about the police. Don't let them talk to the family, especially Marta. She's close to the edge. You're leaving tomorrow, and she could inadvertently say something to jeopardize that."

"I'm not leaving," he said.

Anthony had to replay the words in his head to believe Ramiro had spoken them. "Why not? Because García is no longer a threat?"

"That's part of it. Thank you for solving my problem for me. I often considered doing it myself, but then I would sober up and forget about it. I will stay in Cuba because I ought to stay in Cuba. Give Mr. Bookhouser my regrets. I'm not going."

"What about the disk?"

"What disk?"

"The disk with your notes on the radioactive materials that García stole. You brought it home with you, I hope."

"The disk stays here. The files contain other sensitive information that your government doesn't need to see. I was never going to give them the disk. I would have destroyed it and relied on my memory."

A switch had flipped somewhere in Ramiro's head, possibly from the electrical surge that accompanied the terror of imagining his own brains splattered on the wall.

"Ramiro. If we don't have you, we need the files. Otherwise, what's to stop Navarro and his gang from believing Omar Céspedes's story? They will say, because they want to believe it, that Fidel Castro himself is peddling radioactive materials to Al-Qaeda. You and I know this is a plate of shit, but since when does the truth count in politics? They might want to start sending Tomahawk missiles through Fidel's bathroom window."

The electrical surge had apparently vaporized Ramiro's sense of humor too. He said, "You tell them. You know it went no higher than García."

"No, I do not know that, and frankly, my credibility with Bill Navarro isn't something you should count on."

Ramiro shrugged. "You're an intelligent man. You'll think of something." Hands on his hips, he walked over to the prone figure on the floor. "I am sorry for Mario. I am sorry that you are friends of his family. Sorry he became involved with that group."

"Don't tell me you're planning to turn him in."

"What should I do, dust him off and send him home?"

"Ramiro, if you turn him over to the police, he will be lucky to get off with a life sentence."

"He tried to kill me!"

"He was being manipulated by Abdel García. I'll get him out of Cuba. That should satisfy you. He and his father can both be gone within twenty-four hours. You'll need to talk to MININT to arrange Leiva's release."

"I told you, I do not work for the Ministry of the Interior!"

Anthony could feel the heat building in his neck. He took a breath and said, "Then call the police. You have Olga's killer. Ask for Detective Sánchez. Tell him about Cobo. Show him the towels. The blood can be matched to Olga Saavedra. Say Cobo killed her because he couldn't have her. Say an injustice has been done, and you want Leiva released. They're investigating him for political crimes as well, but I think they'll put him under house arrest if you ask them to. Do that, and I will have the family on a boat out of here."

Ramiro's eyes flamed with indignation. "Why should I help José Leiva?"

"Because he doesn't deserve to be in prison, and you know it. At heart, Ramiro, you're not such a prick."

"What do I say, that Ernesto Pedrosa's grandson asked me to do it?"

"I don't care what you tell them. You have the power. García is gone."

"Mother of God." Ramiro lifted his hands. "You want Leiva? Take him. But not this kid."

"Mario Cabrera was used. He's innocent of everything but stupidity."

"Innocent? Ha! Now you're the one making jokes. Who brought a gun into my house? *My house?* Who threatened my wife and my family? I nearly pissed myself. He will be punished for this!"

He meant it, and Anthony could see that neither a plea for mercy nor a rational argument was going to make any difference. His voice rose to match Ramiro's. "I think Céspedes was probably right. What if I tell them that? Navarro and the Intelligence Committee should know that you and García were working together, and you had orders from the top."

Slowly Ramiro shook his head. "You would not tell a lie that big. You know the consequences."

"Absolutely. Picture this: an Abrams tank parked on the Plaza of the Revolution, firing rounds into Che's face."

"I don't believe you," Ramiro said.

"This regime should have fallen at the Bay of Pigs."

"Oh? When the Americans come, they can liberate José Leiva, because I am not going to do it!"

Anthony looked at Ramiro for another few seconds, then pushed past him, went out the door, crossed under the portico. He heard Ramiro behind him screaming, "Where are you going?"

In the kitchen, the kids sat at the table with sandwiches. Irene turned around from the stove. Still speaking Spanish, Anthony said, "Danny, Angela. Go pack your suitcases. We are leaving. Irene, you too. Where is Gail, still upstairs?"

He could feel their eyes on him as he went out of the kitchen. Marta was cleaning up the pieces of glass in the dining room, tossing mirror shards into a bucket. She had put on slacks and a shirt, but her hair was still standing out as though she had been tearing it. Behind him, Ramiro shouted, "Marta! Forget what I said. We're staying in Cuba."

"You told me already," she said. "What is the matter with you?" She yelled at the kids to go back to the kitchen and finish their dinner.

"It's your brother who is leaving," Ramiro said. "What a fool I was, opening my house to him, year after year." On the stairs he shouted, "All right! You can have José Leiva."

Anthony said over his shoulder, "Mario goes with him."

"Mario Cabrera is an assassin!"

The bedroom door opened as Anthony lifted his hand to knock.

Gail glanced past him at Ramiro, then said, "What is all this?" Beyond her, on the bed, Karen looked over her knees. She was sitting against a pillow, playing games on her PDA.

Anthony pulled Gail out of the bedroom and shut the door. "We're going to a hotel tonight, and in the morning we're going back to Miami. I want you to start packing our things."

Ramiro cupped his hand and yelled down the stairs, *"Marta, ¡Se va tu hermano. Despídete de él!"* Telling Marta to say goodbye, because her brother was going now.

Anthony wanted to put his foot between Ramiro's shoulder blades and push.

Gail said, "Anthony, what happened?"

"He says he's going to turn Mario over to the police." Anthony walked to the stairs. "Ramiro, what do you want me to do? Beg on my knees? He's no threat to you. To anyone."

"No threat? You saw what he did!"

Marta was running up the steps, her open-back shoes slapping on the stone. "Why is everyone shouting?"

Gail moved around Anthony and took Ramiro's arm. "Come here. Please." He didn't move, and she lowered her voice. "You can't."

"Why not? He tried to kill me."

"He's Anthony's son. Mario is his *son*."

"What?" Anthony said.

Marta slowly came up the last step.

Gail closed her eyes. When she opened them, they were focused on Anthony. "I'm sorry. Yolanda told me. When I went to pick up your father. She and I talked and . . . she told me. Ramiro, you have to let Mario go."

Anthony put a hand out to steady himself on the wall.

The flush of dark red still colored Ramiro's cheeks. He said, "Is this true?"

Unable to think what to say, Anthony continued staring at Gail.

She touched his arm. "Oh, honey, I never meant to tell you, not like this. I promised Yolanda I wouldn't say anything. She wanted to choose the right time herself."

Ramiro said, *"Mentira."*

"I'm not lying to you. When Anthony first came back to Cuba twenty years ago—"

"*Ay, Dios.*" Anthony clutched his head.

Gail said, "Ramiro, please. You can't have Mario arrested. They'll put him in front of a wall and shoot him. He's part of your family. Your blood."

"Not *my* blood!"

"Your children's."

"I don't care!"

Marta laughed. "Oh, my God. This is so funny. My nephew." She put her hands over her face and slid down the wall laughing. "*¡Qué cómico!*"

Ramiro looked fiercely at Anthony. "All right. I give him to you. Get him out of my house. Get him out of my country! He is never coming back here. Never. *¿Comprendes?*"

"What about José Leiva?"

"Yes. Take him too. Take them all."

"When will you arrange it with the police?"

"*Ahora mismo.*" He continued speaking as he went down the stairs, and his words echoed on the hard surfaces below.

Marta fell over on the rug laughing. She muffled her laughter in her hands, and her shoulders shook.

Gail looked down at her, then asked Anthony what Ramiro had said.

"That he's going to call the police right now. He doesn't want to go to sleep tonight with Cobo's body hanging in the garage." Anthony knelt on one knee. "Marta."

She wiped her face on her sleeve, sighed, and looked up at him. Her brows were penciled the same bronze as her hair, and in the last few years, the delicate skin around her eyes had crinkled like tissue paper. He saw his own nearly-black irises in hers. She touched his face. "Anthony. It's true. That boy is yours. I thought of this myself already, but I never mentioned it. I didn't want to believe it, but I would see him and think . . . maybe." She held out an arm. "Help me get up."

Feeling more than a little off-balance, Anthony pulled his sister to her feet. He said quietly, "Gail, I'd prefer it if you told me you invented this story."

She shook her head.

"Why did Yolanda hide it from me?"

"It was easier. You were married. She wasn't permitted to leave

Cuba. Then she met José. There were reasons. Someday she'll talk to Mario. She wants it to be his decision, whether to contact you or not."

"That's how to handle it," Marta said. "It's the right thing." She took Gail's hands. "My sister." She embraced her, holding her tightly. "I have so much in my heart to tell you, and now it's too late. It will be a long time before I see you again. Maybe never, the way things are."

"Things will change," Gail said.

"*Si Dios quiere.*" Marta put her hands on Anthony's shoulders. "Let me look at you. Think of me often, and know that I am thinking of you. The children will grow up not knowing each other. We have to stay in touch for them, if not for us. I want you to call us every week. We can trade our pictures by the Internet, eh? If I don't hear from you, I will be very mad."

"Marta, you can come for a visit. It's not that hard. A little paperwork."

"I don't know. The wife of a general. Maybe." She laughed. "Tell *abuelo* not to die yet. Wouldn't that be a shock, to see *me* walk into their house?" She patted his cheek, turned, and went down the stairs, curving out of sight.

Anthony leaned against the wall. He felt that his legs might give way.

Gail came over and put her head on his shoulder. He brushed her hair back to kiss her cheek, and his lips remained there. "I am his father? My head is spinning from this. What should I do? Should I talk to Yolanda? It's not right to have withheld the truth. She should have told me. I was always fond of Mario. Now I think of the years we've missed."

"You should wait," Gail said. "Let things settle a bit, don't you think?"

"So I will do nothing. It's not something I do very well. I should talk to her, not now, but soon. You don't mind, do you?"

"I don't mind."

"If that's what she wants, then . . . I'll leave it up to Mario. He can contact me or not, as he wishes. He has a father already. I don't want to disrupt their relationship, but this isn't something that can remain hidden."

Gail pulled away and looked at him. Lines appeared between her brows. "Listen, if the police are coming soon, you need to move Mario out of here."

"I think he's already gone."

"Where?"

"I'm not sure. A safe house somewhere in Havana. Hector took him when Ramiro and I came inside."

"How do you know this?"

"I gave Hector the car keys."

"Knowing he would take Mario."

"Well. Hector's mind works in that way."

"Yes, and he knows you very well, too. Marta told me that Ramiro has decided not to leave. Which I'm sure he told you about." When Anthony nodded, Gail said, "Then we have a problem, don't we? What are you going to give to Bookhauser?"

"Ramiro put the files on a disk," Anthony said, "but he won't let me have it. There are too many things on it that would compromise Cuban security. He expects me to persuade the Intelligence Committee myself."

"Fat chance. Where's the disk now?"

"He brought it home, so it's probably still in his briefcase."

"You have to get it."

"Gail, if that disk disappears, Ramiro would have every orifice of our bodies searched before we boarded the flight out of here."

"Steal it. Give it to Hector and let him get it out of the country."

Anthony said, "They call the women's prison 'Manto Negro.' You would go there, sweetheart. They would send me to Combinado del Este."

"So . . . what are you going to do?"

"*No sé.* I am trying to think of something, *querida,* but at the moment, with all that is going on, I am running a little short of ideas."

Gail's eyes shifted to a point past his shoulders, then widened. Surprise gave way to something closer to anguish.

Anthony turned. His daughter had come up the stairs. She stood there in the hall staring at him, and for only a moment could he pretend that she didn't know. Accusation and disbelief in equal measure were written on her face.

"It is true?" Her lips seemed too numb to move. "Is Mario my brother? Is he?"

There would be no gain in lying to her. "Yes. It appears so."

"How could you?" Color spotted her cheeks, and tears glimmered.

"I was never told, Angela."

"You let me go out with him?"

"I didn't know!"

"I hate you."

Anger flared. "Go to your room. We will discuss this later."

She wept. Her hair whirled around her head as she turned and ran toward the stairs.

"*Ay, Dios.* Angela!" He went after her. She was halfway down already, and at the bottom, Danny was looking up at him. Rushing past, his sister bumped his shoulder, but he didn't seem to notice.

Coming down another step, Anthony said, "I didn't know, son."

Danny looked at him for another few seconds, then stuck his hands in his pockets, turned, and walked out of sight.

43

It was past midnight when Anthony and Gail reached the southern coast, following Hector's directions. They took a wrong turn and nearly despaired of finding the departure point in time. Finally they took the same narrow dirt road that they had already passed twice. The moon had set, and when Anthony cut the headlights, it was as though a black bag had dropped over their heads. A flashlight went on, then off.

When their eyes were accustomed to the darkness, they walked down a sandy path to the shore. The sea gurgled among the mangrove roots and slapped at the pilings of a ramshackle wooden dock. There was a long, low shape beside it, and the silhouettes of men in the stern.

Hector aimed his flashlight at the ground. He said, "They wanted to wait for you, but we need to go pretty quick."

Anthony heard the crunch of shoes on the shell path, and three figures materialized out of the darkness. Mindless of the uneven terrain, Gail rushed forward to embrace them.

José Leiva's glasses and white beard seemed to float above his dark clothing. He kissed Gail on both cheeks, then reached for Anthony's hand and held it.

"We were worried what had become of you. Maybe an accident. Yolanda wouldn't go until she said thank you. I say thank you as well. You didn't give us much time, did you? I forgot my toothbrush! Our friends are saving what's left of the library, and it will go on. Someone will keep it alive. Everything else, well, the devil can take it."

"Godspeed, José."

Anthony embraced Yolanda and Mario, an arm around each of

them, and he felt Yolanda's tears on his cheek. "Good-bye," she whispered. "Thank you for my son. For his life. You are in our hearts."

The whine of an electric motor preceded the deep rumble of a marine engine. First one, then another. Water splashed from the exhaust. Faint lights glowed from an instrument panel.

Hector said, "Come on. It's getting late." He directed his flashlight to the gunwale as Mario helped his mother board the boat.

José waved. "Good-bye, my friends."

Gail put her arm around Anthony's waist. He raised a hand in farewell, and they stood like this until the sound of the engines had faded away.

44

R amiro Vega's influence bumped six people off a sold-out Mexicana flight so that his American visitors could leave the next day. So far no one had reported the bodies in China-town, but a general's absence would not go unnoticed for long. Anthony wanted to be out of Havana before State Security came around asking questions.

They could have taken an early-morning flight, but Anthony said his children shouldn't leave without saying good-bye to their grandfather. Gail knew the truth: It was Anthony who needed to say good-bye. When would he see his father again?

Sitting with Luis in the retirement home on B Street, Anthony endured demands that they stay for Janelle's birthday party. It was rude to leave so soon. Luis didn't buy Anthony's excuse—an emergency back in Miami. No, you have to stay, Luis told him.

The *quinceañera* was still on, resurrected from certain death. Marta was frantically calling anyone she knew who could help her get the house ready in time, for Ramiro was no help at all. He had waded into the debris of his office, vowing not to come out until every piece of paper was restored to its place.

Anthony apologized to his father, but there was no choice. They had to leave. Whatever Luis said in response, Gail didn't understand it, but Angela lowered her lashes, and Danny hid a grin behind his hand. Luis felt his way to Danny's bicep and gave it a hard squeeze. "Very strong. You tough guy, eh?"

The legs of Anthony's chair scraped on the tile floor. "I'm going to see what happened to those sodas." Luis had ordered the attendant to bring his grandchildren something to drink, but that had been twenty minutes ago.

The television news ended, and a documentary about carnaval in Rio came on. Luis cleaned his ear with his forefinger. Danny watched the television. Gail was about to get up and look for Anthony, but Angela got out of her chair first and said she would be right back. She went out in the same direction her father had taken.

This was hopeful, Gail thought.

When the woman came with the sodas, Luis slapped her on the backside, his aim evidently the result of practice, not eyesight. She laughed and said to stop it or she would report him. Luis asked Danny if the woman was as beautiful as her voice.

How long, Gail wondered, would it take for Luis to forget Yolanda Cabrera? He hadn't asked for her. She wasn't sure if he even knew yet that she'd gone.

She looked at her watch and her stomach did a little flip. It was getting late. She told the others she'd be right back. Following the hall, she came to the big foyer with its double staircase. The front door was open. She looked out to see the row of men in their chairs. At the far end of the porch, she saw Anthony and his daughter, nearly out of sight behind an umbrella tree whose branches had spilled over the railing.

Angela tentatively touched his arm. Past the curtain of her shiny brown hair, her profile was turned up toward his face. It appeared that she was apologizing.

He put his arm around her.

Gail waited a minute longer before crossing the length of the porch. Anthony saw her. She said, "Hey, you two."

Angela's eyes were red. "Hi, Gail. Is *abuelo* asking where we went?"

"No, it's just that we should leave soon or we'll miss the flight."

"I'll go tell him." As Angela passed by, she gave Gail a little smile. *It's all right now.*

Gail stood beside Anthony at the railing. "Don't you want to come say good-bye to your father?"

"I've already told him."

"Anthony. Really."

"He's a *guajiro* with a limited vocabulary and a fair amount of rough charm that he could get by on, thirty years ago. His life has come down to his old cronies, a bottle of rum, and a medal for bravery that he keeps in a box. The rest of the world can go to hell as far as he's concerned."

"Still your father," Gail said.

"I'll be there in a minute." Anthony leaned against the stone column. "Let the kids have some more time with him."

It might have been this cool dismissal that released in Gail an emotion that she had intended to save for later. When they were alone. Or at home again. Preferably at a time when he might actually listen.

"I didn't want to get into this right now, but I really need to say something to you."

"I know," he said. "Danny. I'm angry, Gail. I should get over it. That's what you would tell me, no? What he did to José Leiva . . . he's young. Immature. But how do I forget about it? I don't know what to say to him. Right now, I don't even want to see him."

The direction of Gail's thoughts had been reversed entirely. This is not what she had expected to talk about. She said, "You'll have to talk to him. He needs to apologize, and you need to forgive him."

"We don't have so much luck, talking to each other." With a chuckle, Anthony said, "We have always had a distance between us, from the time he was a little boy."

"Maybe it's rivalry. Or maybe he needs you and doesn't want to admit it."

Anthony crossed his arms and stared at the street.

"You have to accept who he is, Anthony."

"What if I don't like who he is?"

"He's your son. You have to reach out to him. You're the adult here. I think." Gail shook her head. "Go see a counselor. Obviously nothing I say is of any use."

"Yes it is." He put his arm around her neck and pulled her close. "Yes. I will try. Of course you are right. I know that." He grimaced as though in pain. "I will try."

Looking at her watch again, she took a step away. "We really have to go."

"What now?" He didn't let go of her hand. "Are you mad at me for something?"

"Not really."

"That usually means I'm in the doghouse."

"It's really nothing."

"Are you sure? I'm getting some very funny little signals from you."

"Let's go in."

He looked at her, then nodded. "All right. Let's go in."

"I mean, we really don't have time to talk about it."

"About what?"

"The fact that you lied to me and seem to think nothing's wrong with it."

Puzzled, Anthony said, "You mean about the files that I didn't put on the disk?"

"No. Don't be so dense." With a glance to make sure that the old men in their rockers couldn't hear them, she came closer. "Yolanda. You lied from the moment you first mentioned her name to me. My friend Yolanda. Just a friend of the family, nothing between us, never was—"

"Gail." He reached for her hand, but she was too fast. "I'm sorry."

"And that's it? That's what I get until the next time? I'm sorry? Why do you do it? I could have handled the truth, but when you lie, it's so destructive."

"I didn't want to hurt you. No. The truth is, I didn't want you to judge me for something that happened so long ago."

"Excuses."

"Don't say that, Gail." His tone was sharp. "You want me to forgive Danny. All right. Now I ask for your forgiveness. That is what I need from you." Unblinking, his eyes fixed on her. "I will not lie to you again. Ever. All right? And now I would like for us to drop this discussion."

Gail had to laugh. "You see how you are?"

"Yes. I know what I can take and what I can't. Will you punish me forever? I can't live with that. It's too much. I'm not like your American husband. I have too much pride. You take me as I am."

For one dizzying, sickening moment, Gail thought of leaving him standing there with nothing but his tattered pride, but that moment passed. As her mother had once told her, *Sometimes a woman just has to close her eyes and go on.*

"All right. Only if you do the same for me."

His mouth twitched. He took a breath. "Of course. You're my wife. I love you."

She took his hand. "Everything will be all right, once we get home."

It required both cars to get them to the airport, since Gio and Janelle insisted on coming along. The crowds were intense, and they had to say their good-byes at the curb.

Two men in olive-green uniforms stood behind the check-out counter. As the suitcases inched forward in the line, Gail could feel her heart racing. She nudged Anthony and asked if this was normal, the army screening passengers at the airport. He said it wasn't, but not to worry about it. "I think we'll be all right."

"You *think?*"

He told her to go ahead, she was holding up the line.

When their group reached the counter, Anthony presented their passports and tickets. The agent ran them through the machine, but she didn't give them back. One of the men stepped forward and signaled to Anthony.

Danny said, "What's going on?"

Gail told him she supposed it was one of those random security checks, not to worry about it.

With only their carry-ons, they were taken down a hall and into an area with cubicles and tables. The women went in one direction, the men in another.

The door closed, and an English-speaking female soldier told them they would be searched. She told them to take off their shoes and stand with their arms out. Her two subordinates patted them down. Hands slid up and down their backs and legs.

Angela was told to put her bag on the table. Gail gave her a reassuring smile that she prayed didn't look as phony as it felt. She boiled with anger and impotence. They slid Angela's things down the table, and she loaded them into her bag.

Irene was next. The story of their trip flashed by as they moved things from Irene's bag and set them on the table. Bottles of tissue-wrapped perfume. Six cigars. Three rocks. A black santería doll with big red earrings and a white dress. They squeezed the doll and lifted her tiny scarf. They unfolded a map. Ruffled through the pages of a phrase book, a tourist guide to Havana, and the brochures from six museums and three art galleries. They turned the bag over and shook it, slid their hands into every crevice, and felt the handles.

Then they dropped the bag on the table and gestured to the pile, indicating that Irene could put everything back. They gave Gail's bag the same treatment. When they got to the stack of CDs in Karen's backpack, they examined each one carefully, picking at the labels to make sure they'd been affixed at the factory.

The officer told them to wait until their suitcases were searched.

Karen came to sit next to Gail. She opened her backpack for her PDA and turned it on to play Tetris. Gail heard the little beeps and chirps. Without looking around, Karen said, "Mom, what they are doing is totally *not* routine."

The flight went through Mexico City before they connected with a flight to Miami. The sun was setting as they reached the soft green islands of Florida Bay. Gail gazed out the window at the swirls of turquoise and blue water and the reflection of clouds turning pink. By the time they reached the Everglades, the colors were mottled gray and green. Then Krome Avenue came into view, the westernmost street. Lights were coming on, and she saw the grid of the city, the turnpike, the houses and tile roofs and swimming pools and low, flat warehouses and car dealerships. She had forgotten how bright it was, a shimmering quilt of lights.

She felt for Anthony's hand and curled her fingers through his.

Whether it was a Latin custom or gratitude, Gail had never been sure, but as the jet touched down, the passengers applauded.

Anthony leaned across her to look out the window. "We made it."

"Praise God and all his little angels," she heard Irene say from the seat behind her.

Arriving international passengers were funneled through a corridor with glass walls. When they reached the top, with its turquoise-carpeted lobby, Gail noticed a man in a gray suit who seemed to be watching them. He had a short crew cut and deep-set blue eyes. She had never seen him before, but she could guess.

Anthony asked the kids and Irene to sit down over there and wait.

Gail held out her hand. "Mr. Bookhouser."

"Mrs. Quintana. Good to meet you. Everything okay? You survived your adventures?"

"We're fine. Thanks."

He looked at Anthony. "Well?"

Anthony took Irene's digital camera out of his carry-on. He flipped open the bottom and withdrew the slender blue memory card.

Bookhouser lifted his brows.

"Put it in a card reader," Anthony said. "Your people can figure it out."

"Give me a hint."

"We connected a PDA to Ramiro's computer and copied the disk onto it."

"The files are on this thing?"

"All of them," Gail said.

Reading the numbers on the front, Bookhouser said, "One hundred and twenty-eight megs. Room enough for a book. I'll be damned." He tore a piece of paper from a small notebook and delicately wrapped the memory card inside. He dropped it into his breast pocket. "I'll make sure it gets there safely."

As she watched him go, Gail said, "I feel bad, not giving Karen the credit. She was the one who actually did the copying."

"But it was your idea," Anthony said.

In the huge hall for immigrations processing, they headed toward the line for American citizens. Anthony slowed to make sure his little flock was all accounted for. His daughter hugged his waist. "We're home. I'm so glad."

"You can use your cell phone now to call your friends," he said.

"No. I think I'd rather decompress for a couple of days." Angela walked alongside, rolling her carry-on. "Do you think it would be okay if I came over to your and Gail's place tonight? Would I be in the way?"

"You're never in the way."

"I'll make dinner. Sort of a thank-you for the trip. Okay?"

"If you want." As he leaned over to kiss the top of her head, his eyes met Gail's. "Is that all right with you?"

She smiled. "Heck, yes. You know what *my* cooking is like."

Anthony turned to find his son. "Danny, come have dinner with us tonight."

Danny, who had kept several paces behind, gave a shrug. "I'm kind of tired."

"Come on. We'll all be there."

"I guess. Okay."

Progress, Gail thought.

"Next!" The immigration officer was looking at them.

Anthony said, "Go on, Gail. You first."

The officer stamped her passport and smiled broadly. He spoke with a Haitian accent.

"Welcome home."

45

"**M**eatloaf with mashed potatoes and gravy. And a Samuel Adams beer."

Gail handed the menu back to the waitress. Detective Sánchez had said he wanted to try some American food. He had told them that at his brother's house in Hialeah, all they ate was Cuban. He had found his way to JohnMartin's, an Irish pub in Coral Gables near Anthony's law office. The walls were dark wood, lace curtains covered the windows, and the murmur of the lunchtime business crowd filled the dining area.

"But I will tell you this about my brother and his family," Sánchez continued. "They're just like the Cubans at home. Just as loud, and maybe twice as crazy. He wants me to stay, then try to get my wife out, but I couldn't keep up with the pace here. It's too much for me. My brother says he'll come back to Cuba someday, but it won't happen. He has the house, his kids, his job. He won't come back."

Sánchez moved his elbows off the table so the waitress could put down their drinks. He lifted his beer mug. "Cheers."

"*Salud, dinero, y amor.*" Anthony was having a shot of Jameson.

"Health, wealth, and love," Gail said. "And the time to enjoy them." With a court hearing later that afternoon, she toasted with iced tea.

Sánchez ran his tongue over his lips, considered, then nodded. "I like it."

He thanked Anthony for arranging yesterday's tour of the morgue, which was, he had to say, more enjoyable in its way than Sea World, where his family had taken him last weekend. "And this afternoon, the crime laboratory. I will give you my impressions, but I think it will be quite wonderful. With such facilities, how do you have any crime here at all?"

When the food arrived, Sánchez rubbed his hands together theatrically and tucked his napkin into his collar. He sampled the meatloaf and looked toward the ceiling before giving a little shrug.

Gail laughed and turned around to ask the waitress to bring some hot sauce.

Sánchez bit into a roll, then dusted his hands. "I have something to report to you, Quintana. It was on my e-mail this morning from my office, the inquiry into the death of Abdel García. Here are the official findings: The sergeant, whose name was Raúl Ruiz, killed the soldiers below with a knife. García shot him, then ran out onto the roof. Ruiz followed and cut García's throat . . . and then fell over the side."

Sipping his beer, Sánchez waited for a reaction. Anthony said, "Is that so?"

"Mmmn." Sánchez drew his napkin across his mouth. "And here is a curious thing. García was found with a Beretta, but he had no ammunition for such a weapon. Another thing. If García had the gun, how did Ruiz get close enough to kill him? There were four bullets left in the magazine. A bit of a mystery, no?"

"I should say it is."

"The CDR in that zone never looked too closely at what was going on in the apartment, considering García's rank and so forth, but now that he is dead, they come forward with all kinds of bizarre tales, which . . . I will not repeat here." He shrugged, then set down his mug. He asked if he might sample Anthony's tuna melt. Anthony cut off a corner.

"Ah," said Sánchez, closing his eyes. "Very good. I wonder if they would give me the recipe?" He shook his head at Gail's proffered spinach salad. "No, thank you, Gail, my body can't tolerate so many vitamins."

He dug into his mashed potatoes. "The case of Olga Saavedra has also been officially closed. At first we suspected the driver who worked for your brother-in-law. Teodoro Cobo. We suspected him based on his past relationship with the victim, and the fact that he had hanged himself, but nothing conclusive came of our investigation. And then we received a tip from an anonymous caller that General García was responsible. Blood-soaked towels were found in his apartment in Chinatown. The DTI ran some tests and confirmed that the blood was indeed that of Olga Saavedra."

Anthony glanced at Gail. "Well. This is interesting."

"Isn't it."

"And strange," said the detective. "I did not see the towels during my initial search of the apartment, and I am sure we searched thoroughly."

Anthony said, "Strange indeed."

"You have nothing to add? It's just my curiosity, you understand. The case is closed."

"My information is even less than yours," Anthony said.

"Well. Then we drink to closed cases."

They raised their glasses again.

When Sánchez got up to leave, his foot kicked something under the table. "How could I forget this?" He picked up a paper shopping bag from Books and Books, a store on the next street. It appeared to have some weight in it. "For my new granddaughter," he explained. "Her name is Patricia. She's only four months old, a little too young for all these books, but she'll learn."

Anthony stood up to shake his hand. "You will come back to see us, I hope."

"*Si Dios quiere.* And thank you for the delicious American lunch." Sánchez put a kiss on Gail's cheek and dropped a Florida Marlins ball cap onto his gray hair. He waved at the door, then was gone in the blazing light of midday.

Gail said, "Ramiro seems to be surviving all this very well, wouldn't you say?"

"He has always had that ability." Holding his tie in, Anthony sat back down. He pushed his plate to one side and turned his chair. As he settled back against the wall, which was decorated with old photographs and Irish beer advertisements, he took an envelope from inside his suit coat. "This arrived at my office today. They had my business card, otherwise it would have come to our apartment."

Gail turned the envelope faceup. The stamp was from Spain. The postmark said the letter had been mailed a week ago. *Sr. Anthony Quintana y Sra. Gail Connor de Quintana.*

"Why didn't you open it?" she said.

"You can," he said. "It's to both of us."

She smiled. "Open the damn letter."

He slit the envelope with a steak knife and removed a snapshot and a single sheet of paper, which he shook so that it would fall open. "Ah. It's from Mario. I'll translate. 'To my beloved friends.' He wishes us well. He says thank you from the depths of his soul . . . his mother is fine . . . José is still writing . . . they expect a new book of essays soon . . . and Mario hopes to start at the university in the fall—"

Anthony cleared his throat, unable to go on. His eyes lingered on the photograph for a moment before he showed it to Gail.

It had been taken by the sea under a sun so bright it had made them squint. José was a little heavier. Yolanda's mouth was open, as if she'd just started to say something. The camera had caught Mario laughing, his black hair whipped by the wind, his arms across his parents' shoulders, and the misty coast of Spain behind him.

AUTHOR'S NOTE

It is fortunate that José Leiva and Yolanda Cabrera left Cuba when they did.

In March 2003, the Cuban government arrested seventy-five members of various opposition movements, including independent librarians and journalists. Agents of State Security, who had infiltrated the groups, called them "mercenaries" of the U.S. government. They were prosecuted under a law that criminalizes dissent. The charges included: writing articles critical of Cuba; communicating with international human rights organizations; having contact with individuals viewed as hostile to Cuba's interests; possessing items such as radios, battery chargers, video equipment, or publications; and involvement in "counterrevolutionary" groups such as unofficial trade unions, doctors' and teachers' associations, press associations, and independent libraries.

The trials, none of which lasted more than a few days, were held in May 2003. Everyone arrested was found guilty, and most received sentences of twenty years or more. I was dismayed, but not surprised, to learn that two men whom I had met in Cuba were among those rounded up. Hector Palacios, a librarian and a member of the umbrella group *Todos Unidos*, received twenty-five years. Internationally known poet and journalist Raúl Rivero was sentenced to twenty years.

I had originally intended that José Leiva remain in Cuba, but as I wrote closer to the end of the book, I couldn't bear to see him suffer the same fate as Palacios and Rivero and the many others whose love for their country gave them the courage to speak out.

To write a novel set in a country not your own is a challenge, particularly when your government won't let you travel there freely. If Cuba seems real on these pages, credit goes to friends on both sides of the water.

The initial spark for this story came from Ramón Colás and Berta Mexidor, a married couple who founded *Bibliotecas Independientes de Cuba* (Independent Libraries of Cuba) in February 1998 in the city of Las Tunas. At a book fair in Havana, they had heard Fidel Castro say: "In Cuba there are no prohibited books, only those we do not have the money to buy." Taking him at his word, they created the Felix Varela Library in their home, and within nine months supervised the opening of a dozen other home libraries throughout Cuba. In 1999, Ramón and Berta were detained by State Security and warned to stop. They were evicted from their home. After suffering continued harassment, threats, and confiscation of their books and personal papers, Ramón and Berta, along with their children, sought political asylum in the United States and arrived in Miami in December 2001.

The Independent Libraries project was left in the hands of Gisela Delgado and her husband Hector Palacios, who operated the Dulce Maria Loynaz Library in a spare room of their Havana apartment. The number of independent libraries grew to more than one hundred. In late 2002 I traveled to Cuba (legally) and took a box of books for their library. Hector and Gisela, and her daughter Giselle, welcomed me into their hearts with the generous hospitality typical of the Cuban people. When Hector was arrested, police seized their books, computer, fax machine, and personal papers. Through donations, Gisela is now working to rebuild the library.

I am also grateful to many others in Havana who must remain anonymous: N. R., A. C., E. S., V. R., N. V., R. V., O. S., C. M., B. N., A. C., J. D., M., and J.

On this side of the water, my sincere thanks to Dr. Jaime Suchlicki, Institute for Cuban and Cuban-American Studies at the University of Miami, and to Juan Pérez, Magaly Ferradá, and Dinorah Pérez. For technical information that I couldn't have done without, many thanks to Fred Rea and Robert Cole.

For the jokes, *gracias* to "El Pible." And for making sure the *español* was correct, *un abrazo* for Ellie de la Bandera.

You can find information on the libraries at *www.bibliocuba* *.org.* (Click on the English version.) There is no shortage of information about Cuba in printed form or on the Internet. For a list of the books I relied on most and some links I found particularly useful, you can go to my website, *www.barbaraparker.com.*

ABOUT THE AUTHOR

Barbara Parker is the author of nine other mysteries, including *Suspicion of Innocence*, which was a finalist for the Edgar Allan Poe Award for Best First Novel by an American Author. A former prosecutor with the state attorney's office in Dade County, she lives in South Florida.